I0703812

JENNY POWELL

But for These Chains

Jenny Powell

Copyright © 2025 by Jenny Powell
Published by Take Me Away Books, an imprint of
Winged Publications

Editor: Cynthia Hickey
Book Design by Winged Publications

All rights reserved. No part of this publication may be
reproduced, stored in a retrieval system, or transmitted in any
form or by any means—electronic, mechanical,
photocopying, recording, or otherwise—without the prior
written permission of the publisher. The only exception is
brief quotations in printed reviews. Piracy is illegal. Thank
you for respecting the hard work of this author.

"But For These Chains" is a work of fiction. All
incidents, dialogue, and characters, with the exception of
some well-known historical figures, are products of the
author's imagination and are not to be construed as real.
Where real-life historical figures appear, the situations,
incidents, and dialogues concerning those persons are entirely
fictional and are not intended to depict actual events or to
change the entirely fictional nature of the work. In all other
respects, any resemblance to actual persons, living or dead,
events, or locales is entirely coincidental.

Holy Bible, New International Version. NIV.
Copyright 1973, 1978. Zondervan Publishing for all scripture
quotations.

Christian Fiction
Historical Biblical Fiction

ISBN: 978-1-965352-58-8

Endorsements

A beautiful rendering of Biblical fiction, *But for These Chains* strikes all the right notes as it takes readers through the tumultuous life of Saul of Tarsus. From Saul to Paul, murderer to missionary, and persecutor to proclaimer, Jenny Powell weaves a compelling look at his life, his legacy, and his glorious redemption.

~Tara Johnson, Carol and Christy nominee of *Engraved on the Heart*

Scholars have long realized that if one is going to understand early Christianity, one is going to have to reckon with our earliest sources about it, namely Paul's letters, and that in turn means reckoning with the apostle to the Gentiles himself. In a helpful way Dr. Powell builds a plausible case for understanding Paul's U Turn on Damascus road, and the impact that had on the rest of his life and ministry. This novel makes the story of Paul and his companions come to life in fresh ways, and it teases the mind into active thought-- as any work of historical fiction should do. Especially noteworthy is the way the novel rightly highlights Paul's endorsement of various women as leaders in the early Christian movement.

~Ben Witherington, III, Amos Professor of NT for Doctoral Studies, Asbury Theological Seminary

I enjoyed this touching, heartwarming story. I appreciate Doctor Jenny Powell using her gifts to support women in ministry.

~Martha Tennison, Evangelist, Ordained Minister

Assemblies of God, 2022 Recipient of the Evangelist of the Year award with the Assemblies of God

In her captivating debut novel, *But For These Chains*, Jenny Powell takes readers on a mesmerizing journey through Saul's transformative experience on the road to Damascus and beyond. With a masterful command of language and a keen eye for detail, Powell brings to life the emotional depth and sacrifices of both historical and fictional characters, making them leap off the page with authenticity. Saul's passion is palpable, and the gripping narrative of dedication and determination will keep you riveted until the very last page. A must-read for fans of historical fiction and anyone seeking a powerful story of faith and redemption.

~Kara R. Hunt, Golden Scrolls and Selah award-winning author of *Paper Dolls*/Habakkuk series

Dr. Powell takes us on the miraculous journeys of Saul of Tarsus—as perilous as in any thriller. The book is true to Scripture, but some additional fictional events and characters fill in the gaps. These show the humanity of Saul and his associates and help the reader understand the daily life of the times and the Greek, Roman, and Jewish cultures. A unique, inspiring, and educational read.

~Jane M. Orient MD, Executive Director, Association of American Physicians and Surgeons, and author of *Sapira's Art & Science of Bedside Diagnosis*, and *Your Doctor Is Not In: Healthy Skepticism About National Healthcare*

DEDICATION

To all the women who love Jesus and are called to lead others to follow Him. To the feminine shoulders we stand on, the great cloud of witnesses, who may forever remain nameless.

And to Virginia Nansen (1922–2019), the best mom God could have given me. Thanks for picking me.

List of Historical Characters, in order of appearance

Saul of Tarsus, *Roman name:* Paulus, *Greek:* Paulos, Pharisee, lawyer, and scribe

Stephen, one of the Seven Greek-speaking leaders of The Way

Nicolaus of Antioch, one of the Seven

Nicanor, one of the Seven

Timon, one of the Seven

Ananias of Damascus, a follower of The Way

Joseph of Cyprus, AKA "Barnabas", Uncle of John Mark and disciple of Jesus

Judas of Damascus, wealthy Jewish business man

Jamelah, younger daughter of King Aretas IV of Nabatea

Malichus, son of King Aretas IV and half-brother of Jamelah

King Aretas IV of Nabatea, father of Jamelah

John Mark, nephew of Joseph of Cyprus and author of the Gospel of Mark

Simon, son of Jonah, one of the original Twelve, nicknamed Peter by Jesus, *Aramaic:* Kepha, *Greek:* Cephas

James, the Brother of Our Lord, brother of Jesus of Nazareth

Bar-Jesus, AKA Elymas, of New Paphos

Sergius Paulus, proconsul of New Paphos

Niger, Lucius and Manaen, leaders of the church in Antioch of Syria

Silas, a Jewish believer from Jerusalem

Judas Barsabbas, a Jewish believer from Jerusalem

Timothy of Lystra, a son of a Jewish mother and Greek father

Euodia, nicknamed **Lydia**, of Philippi

Aquila, a Jewish tentmaker and leather worker

Priscilla, wife of Aquila

Persis, a woman of wealth in Corinth

Crispus, synagogue leader in Corinth, along with **Sosthenes** and **Phileas**

Demetrius of Ephesus, a silversmith

Gaius and Aristarchus of Ephesus, associates of Saul/Paulos

Luke/Lukas, a physician originally from Philippi, Macedonia

Philip of Caesarea, one of the Seven

Agabus, a believer from the area of Caesarea

Porcius Festus, Roman procurator of Judea

King Agrippa II, Marcus Julius Agrippa, king of Chalcis, later Tetrarch of Batanaea and Trachonitis, the great-grandson of Herod the Great, the last of the Herodian kings.

Berenice, sister of Agrippa II

Publius, largest landowner on the island of Malta

Linus, a Gentile follower of the Way in Rome

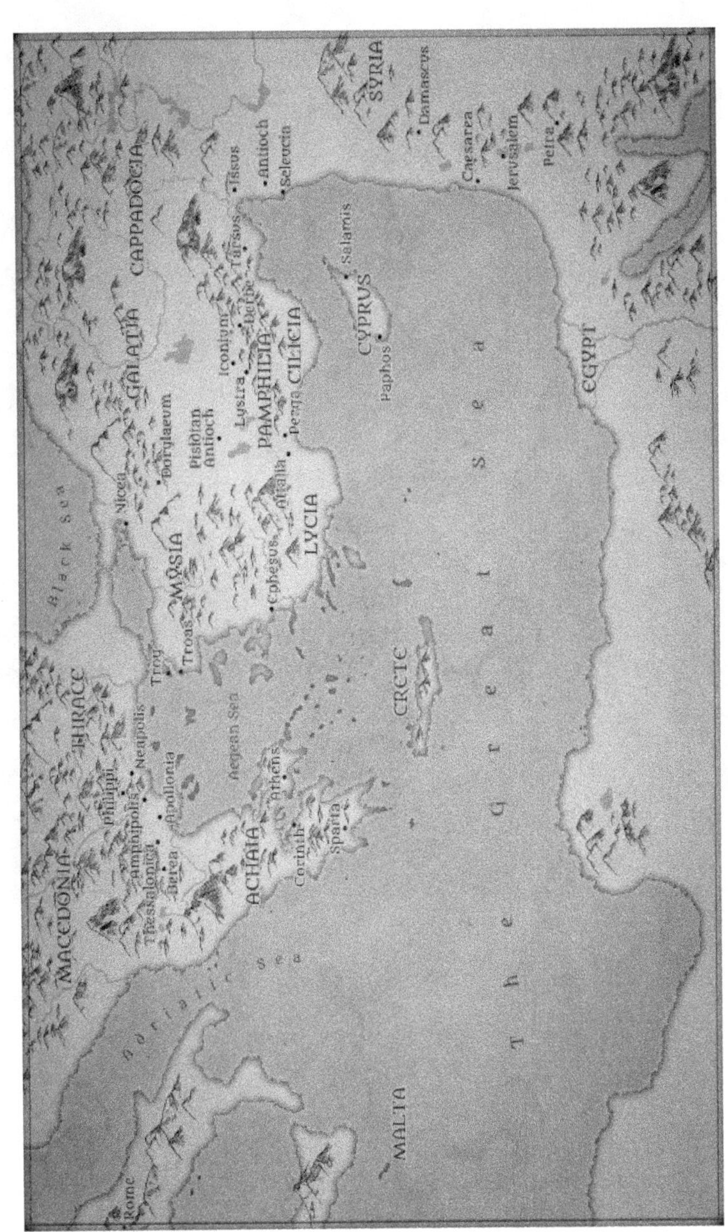

SYRIA
Damascus
Antioch
Seleucia
Tissus
Caesarea
Jerusalem
Petra
CAPPADOCIA
GALATIA
Tarsus
Derbe
Iconium
Lystra
CILICIA
PAMPHILIA
Perga
Attalia
CYPRUS
Salamis
Paphos
LYCIA
Pisidian Antioch
Dorylaeum
Nicea
MYSIA
Troas
Troy
Ephesus
EGYPT
Black Sea
THRACE
MACEDONIA
Neapolis
Philippi
Amphipolis
Apollonia
Thessalonica
Berea
ACHAIA
Athens
Corinth
Sparta
Aegean Sea
Adriatic Sea
Rome
CRETE
The great Sea
MALTA

Chapter One

**Jerusalem, Judea
31 A.D.**

The young Pharisee strode with purpose, his eyes focused on the narrow labyrinthine streets of the holy city he knew so well. Unlike Saul's boyhood home, Jerusalem was always crowded with people. Because the walls and cliffs of the city hindered sprawl, the inhabitants had either built up or stretched beyond the protection of the city walls. The masses of people lived on top of each other. It was nearly impossible for Saul to pass through her streets without having to touch someone.

The familiar morning cacophony of his city fell on his ears. The noise of merchants setting out their wares, morning preparations in homes, and animals wanting to be fed mingled as pleasant music, accented at the appropriate hours with horns calling the faithful to prayer.

Saul lifted his eyes to the Temple, the center of the city's life, towering lofty above him. Nothing in Jerusalem was higher or as massive. The inhabitants and all the objects were here because of the Temple, including him. On the Temple grounds, he sensed the very presence of God, and the thought made his chest swell, spurring him onward.

People already milled about, pressing against one another

about the stairs to the Temple. Saul sighed as he paused, waiting to be noticed. His white robe was still pristine, and the brilliant blue fringes of his prayer shawl were unsoiled. He fidgeted with the phylacteries, capsules containing sacred scriptures bound by black leather straps, one wrapped about his left hand and arm, the other adorning his forehead. The crowd parted upon glimpsing the important man in their midst. At this pace, Saul's perfect appearance—even the black of his beard and eyebrows contrasting with the white garments framing his face, creating a purer appearance—wouldn't help him reach the inner gates of the Temple before opening at the third hour.

As he passed through the crowd and neared the inner gate, he lost hope at an early arrival. The breezeway outside of the Court of the Gentiles, the outer portion of the Temple grounds, was where a particular crowd met daily. Saul's goal to arrive before they gathered was crushed as their incessant singing met his ears. Gritting his teeth, he strode onward. *How early do these dogs get here every day?* Any of those false-messiah people bothered him, but this group was the worst, their numbers growing daily. And unlike those on the streets, these people would not make way for him. No respect was shown for Saul's status.

Worse, in their fashion, the women were interspersed with the men. His brow furrowed. One must assume the women are unclean and, therefore, the men standing near them must be as well. Folding his arms under his robe to protect himself, he rushed forward. Bumping his way through, he found himself face-to-face with a man, forcing him to a halt.

"Good morning, good Pharisee." The words, spoken in a cool, succinct Greek, bit at him. "On your way to worship the Temple again?"

He glared at the man. "Let me pass."

"You know the Law. You revile the cult of the emperor and the cults of various city gods, but you are every bit as guilty, replacing the Temple itself for the one true God."

Under his robe, Saul's hands curled into fists. He shoved his shoulder into the man, but as he passed, the fringe of his shawl caught on the man's belt, yanking him backward. The man grinned at him as he reached out to pull himself free. The Pharisee's face flushed, and he finally burst from the crowd, thankful to have left the singing mob fading behind him. But not before, aghast, he acknowledged new words sung to the old song: the added phrase – 'Jesus the Christ.'

Nicolaus was late. After worship at the Temple, he had tarried, putting off the meeting with the other leaders. He slipped into the room where Stephen stood with his back to the door, praying before the other five men sitting cross-legged on the floor. Nicolaus would have been missed for the meeting. He leaned against the wall and bowed his head, ashamed and reminding himself what an honor it was to be one of those appointed as leaders of the fellow Greek speakers among them.

Not that the Aramaic speakers did not know any Greek. They did. The Greek speakers understood some Aramaic and Hebrew. However, the differing traditions of worship in the two groups were deep-seated. The Law and the Prophets had been translated centuries ago into Greek, and the assumption that Greek speakers would naturally assimilate with the Judeans and their mix of Aramaic and Hebrew in worship had been mere wishful thinking. The divide that instinctively occurred had affected the poorest and most vulnerable of the believers. Once the strife was brought to Simon Peter's attention, his remedy was to appoint seven leaders among them.

Stephen concluded his prayer and spoke in general to those gathered. "I have found that there is a general satisfaction with our work so far. What are you all hearing?"

Nicolaus admired Stephen's inborn gift. Appointing the man as chief among the leaders had been a logical choice. He had the compassion as well as the charisma required to inspire, not unlike Simon Peter himself.

"The people feel more connected with us as their representatives," Nicanor answered. "Since none of the Twelve are Greek speakers."

"The Jerusalem natives and Galileans are satisfied as well," added Timon. "They allow our people to go their own way."

"We all still gather at the Portico," Stephen reminded them.

"But now there's so many of us that we naturally separate,

even there. We may all be singing the same songs but in different languages."

"Nicolaus," Nicanor said, "come on in."

Stephen turned. "What is it, Nicolaus?" he asked. "Have you news from home in Antioch?"

Nicolaus shook his head. "No, it's nothing."

Stephen drew near to him. "Your soul is troubled, Nicolaus. Tell us what is on your mind."

Nicolaus shifted his stance to avoid the warmth of Stephen's eyes. He sensed the Spirit in Stephen, and it unnerved him. He knew the teachings of Jesus. He had been taught to turn the other cheek, to pray for his enemies. But there was anger simmering in his belly he wasn't quite ready to give up. Not yet.

"You had an encounter?" Stephen asked.

"Yes, this morning, at Solomon's Portico. Did you see that young Pharisee shove his way through us?"

Stephen shook his head. "No, I didn't. Did he say something to you?"

"Not until I barred his way through us."

"You confronted him? What did you do, Nicolaus?"

Nicolaus studied his feet. While emboldened by the encounter with the Pharisee at the time, he now avoided Stephen's gaze. "I greeted him and asked if he was there to worship the Temple again."

Stephen sighed. "Nicolaus."

"I know, I should allow only the Holy Spirit to guide my speech. But the opportunity was there. An open door. I couldn't resist the chance."

"You should only speak with boldness when the Spirit speaks for you, Nicolaus. We make disciples, not by bullying or confronting others, but through open discussion."

Nicolaus threw out his hands. "He was disgusted by us. The way he was careful not to touch what he believed was unclean!"

"I appreciate your passion, Nicolaus, I do. But you must be careful not to condemn others. It is not our job to judge." Stephen addressed the others present. "Watch for the Pharisee. Next time he approaches the Temple, we make way for him. This shall be our apology as one in the Spirit of Christ. I don't want to draw his anger. We want to convince them of the error of their ways, but gently, and only as the Spirit directs us." Stephen wrapped an arm around

Nicolaus. "Come, brother. Let's all sit and talk about the work at the synagogues."

A few days had passed. Saul stood in the shadows inside the synagogue as a small group of men surrounded one of the followers of the false messiah. After his confrontation with the group, Saul complained to Adlai the elder. To solve the problem of their harassment, Adlai advised Saul to track them. Catch them in blasphemy.

Daylight streamed through the open windows, casting beams of light on the men. The synagogue leader stood close to Saul's target as he questioned him. "I follow your argument, Stephen, of what the Psalms and prophets say about the Messiah. They do teach that he must suffer. But I find it difficult to follow that the Messiah would not be recognized by the high priest and the Great Sanhedrin."

"Jesus was a challenge to the power and standing of the high priest," Stephen responded.

"He said the Temple would be destroyed, yet still it stands!"

"We believe he was predicting his death and subsequent resurrection with that statement. You see." Stephen paused, glancing at the faces around him. He caught Saul's gaze and directed his next comments toward him. "Jesus the Christ knew that his role as the sacrificial lamb signified the ultimate sin offering for all of Israel. He came into the world not to destroy the law but to fulfill the law."

Saul's eyes narrowed, and he neared the periphery of the men.

"By fulfilling the law and atoning for our sins, those who proclaim his name need no longer offer any sacrifices, for our redeemer has paid the price."

In the hushed silence that ensued, bile rose in Saul's throat. "So, you do not offer sacrifices as required by the law?"

"There is no longer a need for us to do so. Christ Jesus died for my sin and was resurrected to reign forever."

Don't raise your voice. Not here. Not yet. The lawyer in Saul needed more. "Sacrifice is the sole purpose of the Temple."

"We continue to use the Temple to pray and to give offerings for the poor, the widows, and to the priests. But, no, we do not offer any blood sacrifices."

The leader of the synagogue spoke, shifting Stephen's focus. "The Temple is the earthly home of Adonai. His very presence resides in the Holy of Holies."

"Where did our God live before the Temple was built? Or after the first Temple, the one built by Solomon, was destroyed by the Babylonians? The Holy Presence is with us in the Temple *and* outside it. But it is through faith in Jesus that I stand justified. And that salvation is for all of us here, for all of Israel."

"So, you pick and choose what parts of the Law you feel need to be followed?" Saul asked.

Stephen was silent.

This man has sealed his fate. All Saul now needs is a larger audience and Temple guards to arrest him. He broke away from the small crowd and left the synagogue to secure authorization from Temple authorities.

Saul sat near the ledge of a rooftop patio overlooking the street, the door of the house opposite him in full view. He rubbed his wrist, naked without the phylactery, as he sat in the plain clothes he had had to purchase, sorely missing his prayer shawl with its blue tassels. It had been a couple of weeks since his encounter with Stephen in the synagogue, but he had failed to capture his slippery prey. Days before, Saul met with Joseph Caiaphas, the high priest. The urgency of the matter was too important to leave to Adlai. After disclosing what he had observed, Caiaphas assured him. The man would be found guilty if Saul delivered Stephen and presented the case against him before the Great Sanhedrin. The high priest remembered all too well the previous problems with the Nazarene and still suffered trouble from his followers. Therefore, he was quick to commission two temple guards for the purpose. They could not tolerate Jewish people in Jerusalem being encouraged to halt their burnt offerings at the Temple. There was too much at stake for their priesthood.

Saul brought the Temple guards to all Greek-speaking synagogues, but Stephen remained elusive. Saul was forced to devise a new strategy. Learning where the man resided in the holy city had not been difficult. The Greek-speaking leaders of their faction would leave soon to head for a synagogue on this Sabbath morning.

Faction. Saul refused to even think of the term "sect," as if that meager group of followers of the false messiah was equal to other sects of Judaism. *While we Pharisees and the Sadducees certainly have our differences, we both know God's Law is supreme.* "I hate double-minded men," he whispered, "but I love your law. You are my refuge and my shield. I hope in your word."

Rubbing his hands together, Saul leaned forward, his eyes never wavering from the doorway of the home. The very moment Stephen passed through, he would be on his feet to follow him.

How old had he been when he first made the journey to Jerusalem with his father, to offer a sacrifice? Five? Six, perhaps. His father had brought home a just-weaned male goat for Saul to raise. He grinned, remembering how much trouble that kid gave him. The kid would raise up and butt anything, including Saul, even when he fed him. The goat got loose often, and Saul would find the goat trotting after him.

Once the kid was a yearling, Saul and his father journeyed to Jerusalem, Saul in charge of his goat as they trudged along. With the commotion of noisy animals in the Temple, the constant sacrifices at the huge altar, and the many priests, Saul was forced to drag what had become his pet to the altar. He and his father pressed their hands on its head, and then the priest slit its throat. Blood was everywhere. The goat was cut into pieces before being burned as an offering to God.

Saul's heart was broken, but he did not dare cry. As they left the Temple that day, devastated, he asked his father how he was happy with the death of the goat. His father had dropped to his haunches to look his son in the eye. Saul still heard his father's solemn voice explain that what happened to the goat should have been him, his father! "I am the one who deserves punishment for my sins," he had said. "But the goat took my place. Do you understand?"

Saul had cried to his father, not understanding why it had to be his goat and not one purchased at the Temple. "Son," his father answered, "the sacrifice means so much more when you value something you raised for this purpose. The Lord doesn't want our leftovers. He only wants our best."

His throat tightened at the memory. He held many things against his father, and the loss of his pet was one of them. But the lesson had stuck with him. *This is why Temple sacrifice is so important. Am I still giving the Lord my best?*

Pushing away the wave of emotion that welled up inside him, Saul tore his gaze from the door opposite him to stand and survey the direction where the concealed guards awaited Saul's signal. The moment he resettled, the door swung open. Stephen passed through with two other men, one whom Saul recognized as the man who had accosted him that day at Solomon's Portico. He sprinted through the house and into the street.

By now, the streets were more crowded, allowing Saul to follow the men unobserved, with the Temple guards falling in step behind him. Saul spied the trio enter the Synagogue of the Freedmen, one of his favorites, attended largely by those whose parentage had once been Roman slaves. This group of freedmen, Greek-speaking foreigners though they were, were well-settled in Jerusalem and shared Saul's love for both the city and the Temple. Most of the service would be in Greek, their common language.

Saul stood as near the entry as possible yet still able to participate in the Sabbath morning service. Through the opening benedictions and the eulogies to the reading of the Law and its interpretation, he kept an eye on Stephen. He was waiting for the right time to signal the Temple guards. He desired as large a crowd as possible for what he had planned.

After the reading from the Prophets, Stephen pushed through the crowd of men. Saul tilted his head in wonder. Stephen was going to address the assembly. Saul's face wrinkled into a wicked smile. *Perhaps the fish will simply swim right into the net.*

As sunlight from the windows filtered onto Stephen, his voice steady and distinct, he started his talk with Abraham. Saul crossed his arms.

"The Scriptures tell us that our ancestor Abraham believed God, and it was reckoned to him as righteousness. Now, it was his belief, his faith, that earned him that righteousness, not his works. One earns wages for their labor. One is not reckoned their wages as if it were a gift. God gave Abraham the gift of righteousness."

Righteousness. We Pharisees are righteous because we follow the Law to the letter. Saul's father before him was a Pharisee, a perfect role model, making many treks to Jerusalem multiple times a year.

"So, we say that faith was reckoned to Abraham as righteousness," Stephen continued. "How was it reckoned to him? Was it before circumcision or after?"

"Before," Saul answered under his breath. Saul narrowed his eyes. *Where is he going with this?*

"It was before he was circumcised," Stephen said. "Was it before the Law was given or after?"

Saul drew in his breath as heat rose to his neck and up to his face.

"It was before the Law was given. God promised our ancestor Abraham that he would be the father of a great people, God's people. And the promise came not through the Law but through the righteousness that comes through faith. If it is only by obeying the Law that his descendants inherit the world, then the promise to Abraham is negated."

Saul's chest burned. Stephen was preaching against the Law and using the ancestral father of all of Israel as his tool. Propelling himself from the wall, his hands shaking, he forced his way toward Stephen. "You lie!"

The room erupted with the furious voices of men, drowning out the voice of Stephen. Saul took advantage of the ruckus and signaled the guards, who rushed forward. Saul held up his hands in an attempt to quiet the worshipers before turning to face Stephen.

"You have preached against the Law and against the Temple. I, Saul of Tarsus, have been given authority by the high priest, Caiaphas, to have you arrested and brought before the Great Sanhedrin for trial."

Saul turned, locking the eyes of the furious worshipers. "You are all witnesses of his blasphemy. Any of you may testify before the Council." He took a step back, allowing the Temple guards to seize the man. As the raging attendees parted to allow them through, Saul sought the face of Stephen's companion, the one he recognized from Solomon's Portico. Scowling, Saul strode toward him and leaned in. He snarled, "Watch yourself. You're next."

Once the Sanhedrin and high priest had gathered and the prisoner brought from the holding cell for trial, Saul flawlessly presented the evidence against him. Witnesses were not required as Stephen condemned himself, accusing the Great Sanhedrin and everyone in the Hall of Hewstone within the Temple of betraying and killing the Messiah and of opposing the Spirit of God. Then, before judgment was pronounced, he blasphemed, claiming to see the heavens opened, and amid shrieks of horror, he was grasped by the hair and dragged off the Temple grounds to this place.

A pile of robes covered Saul's feet as the crowd pelted the condemned man with rocks as large as the fists that clutched them. Saul's arms were crossed as stone after stone rained upon Stephen. Somehow, the man managed to lift his head to croak out some words.

"Lord," he cried, "don't hold them responsible."

Then, a stone hit him on the side of the head, and he lay still.

This. This is how that Yeshua of Nazareth should have been dealt with. Blasphemy like theirs deserves such punishment.

The stones stopped flying. The man appeared to be dead. So quickly. Too quickly. Someone stepped forward and peered at the broken body before dipping his head. It was done. One by one, those hands still gripping stones let them fall, shuffling to where Saul stood to gather their garments.

Saul glared at the body on the ground as he drew near. He stooped to grasp one of the stones. A surge of energy rose within him, his face burning, and the hand gripping the stone shook. Saul willed Stephen's body to quiver, anything that he might release the intensity coursing through his veins.

He startled as a hand landed on his shoulder. Saul spun, eye to eye with Adlai, the senior Sanhedrin member. "Well done, Saul."

Saul shook his head at him, wordless.

"He's dead," Adlai said. "It's over. Without their leader, those people will fall away fast."

"No." Saul stared at the corpse. "I don't believe that."

"They are sheep without a shepherd. You have taken care of

this trouble for us. Let someone else clean the streets." As he pulled Saul toward him, the stone fell from Saul's hand, and Saul was steered from the body.

After a couple of steps, Saul halted. "Adlai, there are six other leaders, and one of them is the man who taunted me. They will simply replace him with another. Mark my words. This group will be out in force again tomorrow, singing their psalms and blocking the entrance about the Temple."

Adlai cocked his head. "You killed their leader. Isn't that enough for you?"

"I didn't kill him. The Council killed him."

"Either way, he is dead. Isn't that enough?"

"No." A dull ache grew behind his right eye. "One is not sufficient. Have you learned nothing from that Yeshua business? What if they claim *this* one is raised from the dead as well?"

Adlai reached out his hand, but Saul pulled back.

"They must all be destroyed, or there will be no end. It is time for us to act. God's laws are being broken by people who claim to belong to Him." Saul took a breath, attempting to calm himself. "I said I would get the entirety of them, and that is precisely what I will do."

The news of what happened to Stephen devasted the community. Though all were filled with grief and concern for their safety, Zilpah had known, for the sake of the children, the importance of continuing with their routines.

A handful of days had passed since his death. After the men finished eating, Zilpah fed the children. Six boys and girls, ranging in age from a couple of years to ten, sat cross-legged on the floor with her. Zilpah pulled the youngest, a two-year-old girl, up on her lap. After washing their hands, they all dug into the common bowls of leftovers. There wasn't much chatter. Despite sufficient food, the children still seemed hungry much of the time. Caring for these orphaned children made her heart both soar and cry in regret. *Did her now-grown sons have children of their own?*

Zilpah dipped some bread in the pottage and handed it to the small girl on her lap. She had no daughters and hated that the little one had grown so quickly, already so independent. The child grabbed the bread and ate with both hands.

Zilpah thought back to those many months ago when she and her husband journeyed to Jerusalem for the festival, bringing their bread offering. Little did she know they would experience the Holy One in a brand new and overwhelming way. That day she and her husband heard Simon Peter and the other speaking in their native Greek. It astounded them knowing the men were Galileans, their native language Aramaic. But then they learned that Jesus, the Messiah, had come, and the two remained in Jerusalem. For two glorious months, they lived with the community of believers, and then, her husband grew ill and died, leaving her with nothing but their tent and their clothes. She had no family, no connections, and no money to return home. She did not have the means to leave but found she did not want to. The community of believers and Stephen had embraced her.

Stephen. She didn't want to think about what had happened. Instead, she focused on the memory of him placing his hand on her head, telling her how pleased they were that she was now part of their family. She vowed she would not leave the group of believers in Jerusalem until Jesus came back to gather them to himself.

Commotion from the front of the house caused her and the children to freeze. Men's angry voices lifted, tangling with grunts and the sound of fists meeting flesh. A young boy ran from the room toward the action.

"Lakobos!" Zilpah cried. She scrambled up, holding the little girl with one arm, and gathered the other children about her. Her instinct was to flee with them. But where was she to go? There was only one way out. Not a single window to scramble through.

A man appeared in the doorway whose uniform she recognized as belonging to the Temple guards. With his left hand, he held the young boy by the neck. His right hand held a dagger. "You will all come with me."

Sweating, Zilpah nodded at him, noting that the young boy battled against the guard's grip. "Lakobos." She kept her voice calm but firm. "Don't fight. Remember our Lord's words: those who live by the sword will die by the sword." The young boy stopped struggling but his face wore pained amazement. She directed her words to the guard. "Where are you taking us?"

He motioned with his dagger, and she, with the other children huddled at her side, made her way out of the house and into the street.

Timon, Parmenas, and the remaining men of the household stood shackled, with five other Temple guards making a display of having arrested them. Zilpah's eyes widened. Standing before all of them was the Pharisee, the same one who had arrested Stephen in the synagogue, the one who had condemned him to death. She no longer held in her tears as he turned, his heavy dark eyebrows drawn, and stormed up to them. *Not him. Anyone but him.*

"Leave the children," he demanded. "We do not arrest children. Only the men and women."

"No!" Zilpah protested, "They are orphans. There's no one else to care for them."

The Pharisee's dark eyes blazed, and his mouth set in a straight line. Zilpah had dared to speak. "That is none of my concern. It is not the children who have broken the Law, but you and your men."

She reached toward him. "But, sir, please. The children will starve."

Withdrawing from her, the man's eyes narrowed. "Perhaps you should have thought of that before you associated with a group of liars." He spun about, his arms outspread, addressing a crowd who had gathered to gawk. "Be warned." The Pharisee's voice boomed. "What happened to the leader of these traitors will happen also to them. You cannot disobey God's commandments and disrespect his Temple. If you, any of you, are associated with these people, I will find you, I will arrest you, and you shall feel God's wrath and justice." He raised both hands to the sky and shouted, "Hear, O Israel, the Lord your God is one."

The Temple guard at Zilpah's side threw the young boy onto the street and grabbed her by her neck, propelling her forward. She turned back to where the two-year-old was sitting in the dirt, crying and reaching out for her. As Zilpah pulled away to run back to her, a sharp, ripping pain sliced through her sides. With a scream, Zilpah collapsed, crumpling at the feet of the guard. She lifted her eyes toward the child and all turned black.

Chapter Two

**Damascus, Syria
32 A.D.**

S aul was uncharacteristically quiet. The group of Temple guards who traveled with him chatted nonstop along their journey, but he was in no mood to join in.

He hated to travel. He was disgusted by his rough, dirty travel clothes. He had left his phylacteries at home, although he intended to be seen at the synagogues in Damascus. He was forced to travel light, and there was so much he could not live without.

Saul disliked the clinging dust. He despised eating without a proper table and never found decent water to wash one's hands. The water they carried had to be reserved for drinking. The wine was strong and not mixed, leaving a bitter aftertaste that left him equally bitter. After tripping once early into their journey, drawing laughter from his companions, he surveyed the ground at all times. It infuriated him to be the source of any attention other than respect and envy. He sidestepped around wagon ruts, oxen dung, and stones on the path.

Worst of all was being away from Jerusalem, even for a day. He yearned to spend his day at the Temple, where he belonged. He missed the smells of the altar, the burning of sacrifices, burning oil, burning wood, the sounds of constant prayers and bleating animals, and the trumpet blasts that signaled all seven prayer times. He found it difficult to determine the prayer times in the wilderness, and it perturbed his companions each time he insisted on stopping and praying with him. To obey all the Laws, one had to be very disciplined. There was peace and satisfaction in the practices of the Pharisaic tradition. He often boasted of his blameless nature, and confidence and piety emanated from him when he was home in Jerusalem, in his beloved Temple. But out here? Without ritual, his life was chaotic, and a horrible anxiety chased after him.

Saul stopped and lifted his head. The mountain ranges had flanked them since reaching the Roman road near Agrippina, south of the Sea of Galilee. He had enjoyed reaching Caesarea Philippi in time for Sabbath, where they found a friendly synagogue leader who took them in. The ground sloped upward toward the pass near Mount Hermon, towering above them. He grumbled, believing mountains are to be admired but only from the comfort of a city resting in its valley or off in the distance, from the vista of the Temple on its high, flat plateau. His childhood home lay in the fertile land at the foot of the Taurus mountains, rolling toward the sea along a mountain spring-fed river. *I lift my eyes to the hills. From where does my help come?*

"Saul!" one of the guards shouted. "Come on. Let's get through the pass before it gets too hot."

He hurried to catch up with the others. The safest place for the one without a weapon was not at the rear of the pack.

As their way grew steeper, Saul busied his mind on the task at hand, and the order from the high priest rolled in his pack. Through those scrolls, Caiaphas gave Saul authority to enter the synagogues in Damascus and take captive any followers of "The Way," as they called themselves. Unfortunately, Temple representatives received respect in Syria only in the synagogues. But when his company finally arrives in Damascus, he and the Temple guards will receive their due respect. Greek and Roman influence was great in the city, but the Jews composed a tenth of the population. Consequently, Saul was able, as a Pharisee, to throw some of his authority around there. He was sure his Hebrew brothers would be happy to have their city and synagogues cleansed of the blasphemers.

Saul also looked forward to finding that insolent man he now knew was named Nicolaus. His spies believed he had gone to Damascus as well. Saul daydreamed of capturing the scoundrel and placing him in chains. He smiled to picture anguish on Nicolaus's face with fear in his eyes. He allowed his loathing for the man and his counterparts to flow through him. What a reputation Saul would earn the day he marched those blasphemers back into Jerusalem and handed them over for justice.

On the first day of the week, Ananias was up early, as was his custom. After morning prayers and a bite to eat, he made his way through the humble house to the attached woodshop. There, surrounded by his tools and many projects, he worked, thought, and prayed.

He didn't necessarily crave solitude. Ananias would make his way to the synagogue if time allowed. And he enjoyed the company of his young wife. In the quiet, surrounded by his handiwork, he communed with God and prepared his heart to be used however the Spirit pleased.

He wanted to reach for his pet project. The small bed was sized for a baby that would soon sleep in it. But he knew that the broken wagon wheel a Roman soldier brought before the Sabbath required his attention.

His rough hands, calloused by woodworking and repairs since he learned the trade at his father's side, reached for the large wheel. Certain that the soldier would come to fetch it today, he had best begin. The wheel had been designed to travel on solid Roman roads, but Ananias suspected the damage had been rendered when the wagon left the main path or by a large rock thrown by either horse hoof or another wheel on the wagon. Knowing how it broke helped guide him in the repair, strengthening the broken spokes to make it less likely to break again. He had built a reputation for repairing things in such a way that they were stronger than before they were broken.

As he leaned over, examining the wheel closer, the memory of the surprise visit right before the Sabbath came to mind. He found it interesting that the leaders of their movement would send messengers to Damascus from Jerusalem to warn him and his fellow followers of The Way that there was impending danger. Nicolaus must have done something very insulting that the persecutor would chase him all the way to Syria.

Ananias shuffled to his tool bench, remembering Nicolaus's face when Barnabas brought him the news. He had turned pale, fear in his eyes, and would not be comforted by Ananias's friend and their host, Elazar, even though he assured him Saul, the lawyer from the Temple, had no authority here in Damascus. Nicolaus's fear was replaced with determination at the suggestion he return home to Antioch and the believers there. At the suggestion that he should hide, Nicolaus offered to go out to meet Saul to sacrifice himself for the rest. He only relented when Barnabas shared that James, the brother of the Lord Jesus, desired him to go ahead to Antioch. He was to prepare a place for Lazarus and his household, as Jerusalem had become too dangerous for the four of them. Such devotion had Nicolaus for the Lord's mother that he readily acquiesced.

Ananias squinted at the broken spoke. A shadow dimmed the light, and he frowned at the interruption that darkened his doorway, laying aside his hammer.

"Bina told me I would find you here," the man-sized shadow said. "She's quite delightful, Ananias. How did you get such a sweet girl to say yes to you?"

"Ah, Barnabas, it's you." Ananias greeted his new friend. "The real question is why any father would allow his daughter to marry such a poor carpenter in the first place." He embraced the man. "Come in. I've got an urgent project to complete."

Barnabas followed him to the workbench. "A Roman wagon wheel? Solid material, quite impressive."

"Mm-hmm." He resumed his inspection of the wheel as Barnabas chattered like a child.

"I understand you are expecting your first child. I'm happy for you, though these are troublesome times, my friend, troublesome times."

Ananias paused from his inspections to study his companion. Crow's feet and a wrinkled forehead provided evidence of years of sun and grins. "And here I thought you were the Son of Encouragement."

The older man threw back his graying head in laughter, and

Ananias's eyes crinkled at his joke. "Chances are there are already so many Josephs among the believers that Cephas became frustrated and gave us all nicknames to tell us apart. The nickname Barnabus suits on most days."

Ananias smirked. The lack of originality in naming children led to the necessity of distinguishing titles. Though he did not know Cephas or the Twelve, he was sure they would call him 'Ananias of Damascus.'

Barnabas leaned against the tool bench as Ananias grasped his hammer and adze and returned to the wheel. Wood dust danced in the beams of sunlight pouring through the window of the workshop. Ananias broke the pause in the conversation.

"What do you know about this Saul of Tarsus that you warned us about?" he asked.

Barnabas sighed. "Saul." He crossed his arms. "Saul of Tarsus is a rich Pharisee who has lived in Jerusalem since he was a youth. I don't think he ever goes back to Tarsus, but he is sure to let everyone know he's from there. He likes to go to a synagogue and be asked to speak, but his favorite place to be seen is on his way to the Temple. He loves that the crowds part for him, in his fine clothes and showy phylacteries. He prefers to have to stop and pray in the midst of others, so they can all see how pious and righteous he is."

"Barnabas," Ananias interrupted. "Can you hold this right here for me for a moment?"

Barnabas obliged, while Ananias sought a different tool.

"Saul of Tarsus loves the Temple, that is obvious. But, oh, he loves the Law! No," Barnabas corrected himself, "he loves to *argue* the Law. He will take any opportunity he can, whether he is in the synagogue, or the Temple, or the marketplace, or the streets of Jerusalem. He is the 'go-to' if you have a question about the Law. Oh, and he loves to talk. Talk, talk, talk. I assume the man talks in his sleep. He never shuts up. Even at Stephen's trial, he was the main accuser. It killed him to stand and let Stephen talk in his own defense."

"Thank you." Sweat beaded Ananias's forehead, and he wiped his hands on his thighs, clammy with sweat and wood dust, before relieving Barnabas at the wheel.

"Saul was particularly peeved by what Stephen said that day," Barnabas continued. "That resulted in the persecution. Saul rounded up as many of our Greek-speaking believers as he was able. He knew them from the synagogues they attended because we believers are not shy to share the good news with our fellow worshipers."

Ananias eyed his handiwork. "You say he rounded up both men and women?"

"So it has been reported. The anointed leaders scattered after consulting the Twelve. A couple of them were promptly captured. We understand that they, too, have been stoned to death. Nicolaus is wise to leave. Saul has a vendetta against him and won't stop until he finds him."

Ananias straightened. He regarded Barnabas and said, "I don't think Saul will find many here in Damascus to welcome him. At this distance from the Temple, our Hebrew community is not as attached to it. We are pretty much left alone as long as we don't stir up trouble. Hand me that pot of oil, will you?"

There were a few minutes of silence between them as Ananias worked before raising his eyes to his visitor. "Why did you come to see me today, Barnabas?"

"Am I imposing on you?" he worried. "I'm sorry. I can leave if you prefer to work in solitude."

"No, no, brother, it's not that all. I get the sense that there's something you have come to ask or to tell me."

Barnabas relaxed and removed the concern from his face. "I was sent by the Twelve to Damascus to send the brothers here the warning of Saul's impending visit. But I'm here now at the insistence of the Spirit. 'Go visit brother Ananias,' I was urged. So, I really don't know why I'm here. To build our relationship? Maybe you can give me a tidbit of important information or guidance that will be useful someday? Or perhaps it is something else entirely. I may never know. But I have learned to follow the directives of the Spirit no matter the circumstances."

Ananias dipped his head. He knew well what Barnabas meant.

At that moment, another shadow darkened the doorway, the bulk and height much larger than that of Barnabas. "Are you done with the wheel?" the visitor asked.

"Just finishing," Ananias replied.

"I will wait out here."

"Give me a hand here, brother." Ananias and Barnabus lifted the heavy wheel from the worktable, and Ananias rolled it through the entrance of his workshop, where a massive man in Roman uniform waited. The soldier tossed a bag of coins at Ananias, who caught it with a single hand.

"Good as new!" exclaimed Barnabas as the soldier rolled the wheel away. "A man of few words, I take it."

With a shrug of his shoulders and a tilt of his head, Ananias returned to his shop, Barnabas at his heels. "Come, Barnabas, let's get something to eat. Then I can get back to work on the baby's bed."

The company had paused in the mountain pass, resting in the shadows of the rocks—a respite from the dry, gusty wind and hot, blinding sun. Saul stood apart from the others, reluctant to soil his clothes by sitting on dusty rocks or gritty soil.

He was so close. Once out of the mountain pass, the road will head downhill, and the city of Damascus will glimmer on the horizon like an oasis in the desert. Energy like fire filled his chest, and his legs ached for motion. His impending success was at hand.

Saul paced. A song rose up from within him and he opened his mouth, filling the air with learned praises. "O Lord, you have searched me and know me. You know when I sit down and when I rise up, you discern my thoughts from far away. You hem me in behind and before and lay your hand on me."

Eldad, the chief Temple guard, interrupted his song. "I wish the Lord was knowing you sitting right now instead of pacing and singing psalms."

Saul stopped, his entire face a frown.

"Aren't your legs sore from the clip we've been marching? I know mine are."

Saul continued pacing, his face uplifted, and he sang even louder. "Where can I go from your Spirit? Or where can I flee from your presence?"

"He's exhausting me." The guard took a drink from a leather pouch, some of the liquid running out of his mouth and trickling onto his dark beard.

"If I take up the wings of the morning and settle at the farthest limits of the sea, even there, your hand will lead me." The dust stirred about Saul's feet. Phinehas, the servant Saul brought with him, ducked his head, the corners of his mouth tugging upward. Phinehas had been with him long enough to know that Eldad's complaining led to louder singing and a faster gait. "If I say, surely the darkness shall cover me, and the light around me become night, even the darkness is not dark to you. The night is as bright as day." Saul spun. "Though the day shall soon be night with how many breaks you take. Finish quenching your thirst, and let's press on."

Eldad stretched the bag toward Saul. "I think you need a drink."

Saul stood, silent, glaring at him.

"We are all impressed with your endurance despite your lack of military training," Eldad said. "You don't have anything to prove. Worse, if your legs give out, you'll slow us considerably. It isn't laziness. It's practicality. Sit and rest, sir."

Saul flexed his hands, then released them. The man was impudent but correct. At the edge of the group, Saul spied a large rock, tall enough to be seated higher than any of them. Phinehas had already sorted through one of Saul's bags and hurried over to lay a thick, dark material over the rock. Saul sat upon it as Phinehas resumed his seat on the dirt floor of the mountain pass.

Eldad shook his head. "Those Yeshua followers have no idea what they're in for with you." He tossed Saul the bag.

Saul drank and then grimaced. "Your wine is too strong. You'd have us all drunk before we get to Damascus." He took a second swig before handing it back.

"Why do so many of our people find Yeshua of Nazareth fascinating enough to risk following him, even after he's dead? I don't understand." Eldad took another drink. "I don't see the attraction. You remember him, don't you, sir?"

"Yes, I remember very well. He was quite the enigmatic liar." Saul turned his eyes toward the mountain walls hedging them and then up at the intense blue sky. Not a single cloud. He stretched his legs in front of him. "I will never forget that Festival of Unleavened Bread, over two years ago now. As the week opened and worshipers from all over gathered, he and his rag-tag band of followers entered our holy city in a mock display of grandeur, poking fun at King Herod Antipas. I will never forget the commotion it caused. Everyone wanted to get a glimpse of the fake miracle worker of

Galilee." Saul shook his head. "Then he headed straight to the Temple."

Saul passed a hand over his face. His throat tightened at the unsavory memory, and he drew his brows together. "He marched into the Temple grounds as if he owned it. He had the nerve to upend the commerce tables and whip the vendors. Chaos in the holy place." A bad taste filled Saul's mouth. "Then he started preaching against us, the leaders of the Temple, strict followers of the Law. The Law! Right there in our midst. I stood dumbfounded at his words. 'Brood of vipers,' he called us."

"Caiaphas believed the words were directed at him."

"Yes, but it was directed at all of us. Scribes, Temple priests, the high priest, and his court, the Great Sanhedrin, Pharisees, and Sadducees alike. We knew he was talking about us, those of us who follow the Law, who do not twist and turn it to fit our agendas." His hands wrung an invisible rope to emphasize his words. "Brood of vipers!" Saul's words echoed off the bluffs about them.

"He paid for slandering all of you."

"Yes," said Saul, "indeed he did. But he played his part to the end: a lamb to the slaughter, without protest, without a word of defense. Fool. We were not misled by his performance, unlike his idiot followers. Then his body was stolen in the night, desecrating a grave, and on the Sabbath! Not one of them went through the purification ritual. Raised from the dead. Ha!" Saul jumped from the rock. "And now they continue the farce, drawing in the simple, the vulnerable, convincing them that the Law is no longer applicable." He beat his chest with a fist. "As if it were not the very heart of all of Israel. But I am bound to the Law and the Lord our God, and he has commissioned me to end this foolishness. What I began in Jerusalem was only the beginning." Saul scowled at his companions. "See if Yeshua can stop me now!"

He grabbed his pack, threw it over his shoulder, and stomped deeper into the mountain pass. Phinehas scrambled to his feet and packed the baggage, hurrying after him.

"Well, men." Eldad lumbered to his feet. "Break time is over."

Saul's fury spurred him forward. He knew his servant was running to try to catch up with him, but he didn't care. Picturing the humiliation re-lit the fire in his chest. "The Law!" He muttered under his breath. "The Law is eternal, the Law IS God, our God, the

God of Abraham and Isaac and Jacob. The Law, given to Moses, was the true salvation of his people, the Hebrew people, the tribes, rescued from slavery in Egypt."

As the mountain dissolved into the desert, an oasis lifted on the horizon, a tiny patch of green hope amid hot, arid nothingness.

"Damascus." Saul's heart warmed. There was his goal, so close he smelled it.

The warmth of the noonday sun bore down on his burdened shoulder, and the wind picked up. With his free hand, he pulled the cowl of his robe about his face. As he strode along singing to himself, he noted a light on the horizon, off to his right. It sparkled like a distant star in the midst of the desert sky. Odd. Sometimes one saw the moon in the daytime, but he couldn't remember ever seeing a star.

As Saul watched, the pinpoint of light grew closer. Saul slowed, squinting. The nearer the light came, the slower were Saul's heavy feet. Then he halted, the light so large and bright that he closed his eyes against it. His bag dropped to the desert floor as Saul covered his eyes with both hands.

The light fully engulfed him, and a cold, dark fear rose from within him. He was a frozen statue in the center of a brilliant, blinding warmth.

"Saul." A voice lifted from all around him.

The weight of his body overwhelmed his weak legs, and he fell to his knees. He was desperate to open his eyes, to see what was happening, but the light was so piercing he simply could not.

"Saul."

Fear struck him at his core. His mouth was dry, his lips parched. He attempted to speak but nothing would come out, not even a squeak.

"Why are you persecuting me?"

The words were spoken in his native Greek. Wildly, his thoughts churned. *Who was he persecuting? I must be hallucinating. Am I dreaming? Was the wine stronger than I thought?*

"Saul!"

In a hoarse whisper, Saul asked, "Who, who are you?"

"I am Jesus."

No, no, no.

"Jesus, whom you are persecuting."

This is a dream. I fell asleep in the mountain pass. A bad dream is all.

"I have chosen you, Saul. I will need you. You will stop your persecution."

"Jesus? Of Nazareth?"

"Get up." the voice commanded. "Get up and go to Damascus. You are to go on to the house of Judas as planned. You will receive further direction once you are there."

And then, the light was gone. Cold, trembling, Saul was plunged into a merciless darkness.

With no concept of the passage of time, Saul was certain his head was split open, cracking right between his eyes. He took short, shallow breaths as even the sound of his breath was amplified, like someone panting in his ear.

The pain was at least something familiar in this foreign place. Like an old, well-known enemy: the nausea, the vomiting, the splitting, horrendous pain, the sensitivity to sounds and light.

But he was not familiar with the total lack of light, this inky darkness.

And the blackness filled him, smothered him, consumed him. There was an iciness inside his chest, his empty belly. He lay on an unknown floor, alone and lost.

Every time Phinehas brought food or drink, Saul waved him away. Even the thought of swallowing anything, including his spittle, was out of the question. The waves of nausea formed drool he allowed to spill out of his mouth, onto his beard-covered chin. The stink of vomit and stale urine assaulted him, and something sticky and foul coated his cheek. He was too miserable to care.

He had refused the physician his host had called. *No,* he had whispered, clutching his head. *Leave me.* By now, though, the nausea had resolved. The pain was still there, but memories swirled around him. He remembered what happened. Now, he did not eat or drink for a different reason. Walking along, angry. Then, the bright light and the warmth, the peace. Saul clutched his forehead, remembering the stunning brightness, the memory causing a new wave of pain.

Surely, he dreamt it. That did not happen. He must have reached Damascus and had some bad food or drink. Or maybe the wine had been too strong. Perhaps he had had too much and passed out in the heat of the desert valley.

A psalm came to his mind, and he dared to whisper. "I have sought you with all my heart. Do not let me stray from your commands. I have hidden your word in my heart that I might not sin against you."

Saul covered his face with his hands in supplication, and he fingered his eyes. Tender growths smothered them, each touch sending lightning bolts of pain through his skull. If the blinding light had been a dream, how are the growths and the pain real?

Saul, Saul, the voice had said.

Why is this happening to me? I have kept God's precepts. I am blameless under the Law! Frustrated, unthinking, he smacked his hands against his forehead. *Why, Lord? What have I done to deserve your contempt?*

Silence swallowed Saul whole. A chilling darkness of sound. How dare God ignore him? Anger clawed at Saul's throat. *You! You did this to me. All I ever wanted was to please you, to follow your Law, to earn your favor.*

Frustrated, angry, cold, and in pain, Saul drew up his knees, curled himself into a ball, and wept.

Hours or perhaps entire days had passed. Saul lost track of time. He attempted to open his eyes before remembering the growths.

Saul, Saul.

He was on his back. The pain had subsided and settled into a persistent nagging ache. The stench wafted around him, and he sat up. Saul removed his tunic and crawled away from the sticky floor. His mouth was dry, and his lips were cracked. His empty stomach cramped. *Where is Phinehas? Where am I?*

Gingerly, he touched the rough growths covering his eyes. Swiftly, he lowered his hands. His stomach rolled in disgust.

The tile floor was cool on his near-naked body. It was a mystery to him how his body was hot on the outside when his soul, his very essence, was frozen cold.

Saul, Saul.

Who are you?

I am Yeshua.

No! He straightened. *It could not be.*

Saul hugged his knees. He had seen that man hanging on a cross. He knew he was dead. Dead, buried, his body stolen during the night. People don't come back from a death like that.

He pictured it. The man hanging there, arms outstretched in a vulnerable position, nails in his wrists. Someone had wrapped thorns into a makeshift crown and shoved it on his head. The clotted blood painted the man red all over, and his eyes were closed, head bowed. But to Saul's horror, the head raised, the eyes opened and fixed on him.

Saul, Saul.

Saul rocked forward and back, forward and back, until his skin chafed. But the voice would not go away. Would not be tamed.

Saul, Saul, why do you persecute me? Who are you? I am Yeshua.

Saul dropped his cold, clammy hands to the floor. His entire body shook as memories filled him. A stone nestled in his right hand. The eyes of another man met his. Instead of throwing the stone, though, its weight pulled on him as if it hung around his neck.

Stephen. The man was Stephen.

But he had blasphemed against the Temple, against the Law, against the Lord.

Saul, why do you persecute me?

Who are you?

"Look," Stephen had said, "I see heaven open up and the holy one standing at God's right side."

I am blameless. The man had blasphemed. Stephen had received the punishment he deserved, and yet . . . *Who are you, Lord?*

Ananias's heart was warmed by the morning sun streaming into his workshop. The morning was his best time: his mind was clear, and his energy level was at its highest. He relished the time to plunge into several projects he wanted to complete before the Sabbath began at nightfall.

He assumed Barnabas was still at Elazar's and hoped he would be there the coming evening, as they had an open invitation for Sabbath every week. Ananias thought back on the pleasant interruption of Barnabas's visit to him. How that man talked! And to think that Barnabas had visited only because the Spirit had urged him to come.

Ananias paused and straightened. As sunbeams danced with the dust of the shop, he breathed in the heavy scent of wood and oil and was satisfied. Satisfied with life, with the work of his hands and mind, with his little family. He closed his eyes and raised his arms to praise God.

Saul. The name came to him, and his smile faded as he lowered his arms. Ananias wondered if Saul and his company had arrived at Damascus.

Ananias shook his head at the audacity of rounding up fellow Jews at a time when there were so many problems with the ever-present, ever-dominating Romans in the world. Did Saul really come with the authority of the chief priests to go into the synagogues? The synagogue leaders knew very well which worshipers were followers of the Way. But he and his fellow believers didn't make trouble. Would the leaders turn them over to Saul? Should he and his wife even go to the synagogue tomorrow? Maybe he best stay home for a few weeks. If he were taken, what would happen to Bina and the baby without him?

I shall rely on the Holy Spirit to guide me in that regard. The Lord will let me know what he wants me to do.

The sunlight spilled into the workshop and bathed him with radiant light as a familiar warmth enveloped him. As he closed his eyes, Ananias was filled with a peace that he only experienced in the presence of the Spirit. After a moment of basking in the sensation, Ananias spoke. "Speak, Lord, your servant awaits."

Ananias.

Yes, Lord.

Go to the house of Judas on Straight Street. There, you will find a man from Tarsus by the name of Saul. He has had a vision of you coming to him to heal him.

Saul? Of Tarsus? Lord, this man has come with murderous intentions against your people.

I have chosen him to be my mouthpiece. He has been shown that he will suffer for my name. Go! Saul awaits.

Ananias hesitated but for a moment. "Yes, Lord," he answered. "I will go now."

Then the light was gone. Only the streams of the sun remained as before, though the warmth lingered inside him. Ananias abandoned his projects and left to tell Bina where he was going.

Chapter Three

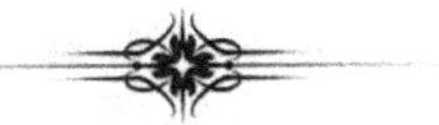

Saul was unaware of when or how the blanket had been wrapped around him. His lips were parched. He shivered. He tried his hoarse voice, and he sang.

"My soul faints with longing for your salvation, but I have put my hope in your word. My eyes fail, looking for your promise. I say, when will you comfort me?' Though I am like a wineskin in the smoke, I do not forget your decrees. How long must your servant wait?"

This was his punishment. Everything he had believed about Yeshua was false. Stephen was right. And he had led Stephen to his slaughter. He deserved no comfort from God.

He wrapped the blanket tighter.

A breeze floated toward him, carrying the scent of roses. The gentle warming wind and promise of a world where roses bloomed only served to remind him of his situation. His stomach growled, and a gnawing in his gut reminded him. *Is this hunger?* Though fasting once a week wasn't required by the Law, withholding gave him the opportunity to display his piety. But this consuming lack was more than a hunger for food. He was so alone.

"How long, O Lord," he continued to sing softly. "Will you forget me forever? How long will you hide your face from me?"

Saul, Saul.

A strange warmth trickled over him. He was still cold on the inside, but the warmth did not come from the blanket surrounding him nor the breeze hitting his face. It was oddly familiar.

Then, in his mind's eye, Saul saw him, saw the face, the eyes boring through him, searching his very soul as light and warmth radiated from the face. The face on the cross.

Saul, you will be visited by a man named Ananias. You will let him near you. You will let him touch you. You will let him heal you. I have chosen you, Saul. You will be my mouthpiece, my witness.

"I am not worthy of you. I have sinned against you."

You will suffer much for my sake, Saul. But you are mine. I claim you as my child, as my dependent. And you will not be alone. You will never be alone again.

Saul swallowed. His throat was as dry as his lips and his mouth. But he croaked out loud the words. "Your will be done."

Ananias stood patiently inside the expansive home. The servant who had answered his knock had left him in the anteroom, where a line of various footwear rested beside a wall, a bowl of water prepared for washing dusty feet. He was not at all surprised, not by the size of the home nor by the rudeness of the servants. Judas of Straight Street was well known not only as one of the wealthiest merchants in Damascus but also as one of the most arrogant synagogue leaders. Ananias regarded his dusty, still-sandaled feet.

He did not wait long. The servant reappeared but with the master of the house himself, whose personality alone filled the small space.

"What do you seek?" Judas demanded.

"My name is Ananias. I must visit a guest in your house, a man named Saul. He is expecting me."

Judas shook his head. "He is ill and not receiving any guests."

"Yes, I am aware. He is blind. That is why I am here. I have been sent to heal him."

Judas huffed in disbelief. "You? A carpenter? Are you going to heal the Pharisee from Jerusalem? He turned away the finest physician in Damascus."

Ananias brushed a hand over his tunic, speckled with wood dust, before he crossed his arms. "It is true that I am a carpenter. But, yes, that is why I am here and what he is expecting me to do."

Judas's eyes narrowed. "I know you from somewhere, but I cannot place it."

"Synagogue. I have seen you there. You are one of our leaders."

"Ah." Judas acknowledged, but Ananias knew he was lying. This man would never notice someone of Ananias's class in some place as important to his social life as the synagogue. "Well, Ananias, I'm afraid you will have to come back another day. He is not even receiving his servant."

"Ask him."

Judas tilted his head. "Excuse me?"

"Ask Saul. Ask him if he is expecting me."

"I won't—"

"Are you Ananias?"

Judas spun around at yet another servant standing in the doorway. "My Master Saul has been asking if Ananias has come," the servant added. "I thought him mad."

"Yes, I am he."

"Oh, sir! He's been waiting for you. He says you are coming to heal him. I am Phinehas."

Judas's mouth hung open as he moved his head from Phinehas to Ananias and back again.

Ananias addressed Saul's host. "May I go to him? Please?"

Judas blinked, and a muscle in his jaw tightened. Ananias held his breath. But Judas addressed his servant. "Sada, wash the man's feet, then take him to our guest."

Sada made quick work of Ananias's feet and led through the house and down a long hallway. Several Temple guards stood before a closed door but fell back as the four of them marched forward.

Laying his hand upon the door, Phinehas turned to Ananias. "Sir, you must understand. My master was not only struck blind, but he had a headache so painful it made him ill. He has not had any food or drink for three days now. I do not believe he has slept, and, as a result, he is very weak. Although I have cleansed him, his appearance may come as a shock."

"We sent for our physician," Judas blurted. "Saul refused him.

We offered food and drink."

"He refused all of it," Phinehas added. "We have been grateful for Master Judas's hospitality."

"Perhaps," Judas said, "you can convince him to eat and drink."

"I will try," Ananias said. "He will need to increase his strength if he is as bad off as you say."

Phinehas pushed open the door and addressed his master. "Sir, he's come. Ananias is here for you."

"Ananias?" Saul's voice was weak and hoarse. "You are here?"

Ananias eased into the room, the other men trailing him. Disheveled, Saul sat on the floor in a clean tunic, fresh bandages over his eyes. While Phinehas beckoned Ananias to approach Saul, a sour odor lingered about the room, holding the others near the door. Ananias crept toward the huddled bundle of flesh.

So, this is Saul. The memory of the fear on Nicolaus's face flashed in his mind. *Saul the persecutor, the man who arrested his fellow Jews and condemned them to death.* Ananias fought contempt bubbling up and allowed the Spirit to take over and behold the broken man before him as he was. *He does not appear so dangerous now.*

"Here he is, sir." Phinehas knelt beside the broken man, who reached out with shaking hands.

"You came."

Ananias took a deep breath and leaned in toward Saul. "Phinehas, remove the bandages."

As the servant did so, gasps filled the room. There were growths on the eyeballs themselves, pushing the lids apart. With only a moment's hesitation, Ananias placed his hands over Saul's eyes. "Brother Saul, the Lord Jesus, who appeared to you on your way here, has sent me that you might regain your sight and receive the Holy Spirit." Then he pressed his hands onto his thighs, waiting, watching.

The growths fell off in small pieces, flaking away until Saul's eyes were clear, dark, and burning, boring into Ananias's. Ananias fought the impulse to run, to flee from this man, this room, this house.

But then, grinning like a crazed man, Saul grasped Ananias's hands. "Thank you, thank you!"

Ananias stood. "Help him up."

Although Phinehas held Saul to help him stand, he sagged back to the floor.

Ananias turned toward the door. "May we get some food and drink for him?"

Judas gave a curt nod. "Sada, see to it." He glared at Ananias. "You are done here. You must leave."

"No!" Saul cried out. "Stay, please. Stay with me!" His eyes pleaded with Judas. "He must stay."

The guards had backed away into the hallway. Judas did not drop Saul's gaze as he finally spoke. "You came to my city to arrest people like this man, and now you want him to stay here, in *my* house?"

Saul was silent but did not break eye contact.

"The great orator has nothing to say?"

"Don't you understand what he has done for me?" Saul asked. "I was blind, but now I have my sight."

Judas's jaw clenched. "You may have some food and drink, but then you leave, both of you. Go, stay with him if you want. Just get out of my house."

The tiny home of Ananias was very dark. In a corner, Saul stood above the pallet Bina had prepared for him.

A few days prior, Ananias brought Saul and Phinehas home. After Saul had regained enough strength, he'd accompanied Ananias and Bina to the Sabbath meal at the home of their friend, Elazar. To say their host and his company were shocked at the identity of their guest was an understatement, and the man from Jerusalem, the one who answered to the nickname Barnabas, was extremely wary of him. However, by the end of Saul's miraculous story, they were convinced of his change in heart. Saul was strong, refreshed, and ready to take on the world.

Standing in the dark house now, he felt foolish among the snores and deep breathing in the house. Sleep. Saul knew he would not sleep, not tonight.

Maneuvering around a slumbering Phinehas, he crept toward the door. Closing it with caution behind him, he halted on the stoop and took in the starry sky. Touching the door frame, he recited the blessing and was out on the streets of Damascus. Aimless, he strolled the narrow streets, thinking.

The city was quiet. The only sounds now and then were a bark, soft lowing of oxen, a whinny of a horse.

"I am Jesus." Those words will forever be in my ears. How was I so blind? I know the words of the prophets as well as I know the Law. I know what the prophets had spoken about the messiah. I am such a fool! If I had only opened my ears and listened. Listened to Stephen, to Cephas. Saul shook his head. *If only I'd listened to Jesus himself.*

The face of the crucified was before Saul, the eyes boring into him, where all the pain, the burden, the humiliation were displayed. Isaiah had foretold it: *so marred was his appearance it was beyond human semblance.* Saul narrowed his eyes against the memory and recited under his breath, "He was despised and rejected by others. A man of suffering." Unimaginable suffering. Crucifixion was cruel and horrendously painful enough. But Jesus, Yeshua, had been tortured before he was crucified. Flogged until his skin ripped away, his muscles exposed, and then bleeding, bruised, swollen from a beating about his head and face, he managed to drag himself and his heavy crossbar through the streets of the holy city up to a hill where he was crucified.

Saul could not will away the memory of it. Yeshua had been the talk, not only of the entire Temple but of the entire city at the time. "He was wounded for our transgressions," Saul whispered, quoting the prophet. "Crushed for our iniquities." He picked up his pace as he walked the dark, silent streets. "He was oppressed, and he was afflicted, yet he did not open his mouth." Calm, like the many lambs Saul had observed at the Temple. The Temple, the place of atonement for the sins of the people.

"He was wounded for *our* transgressions," Saul repeated. He halted abruptly in the middle of the street, the short buildings hugging him. The city's walls closed in, and he had the impulse to run out of the city, back to that place on the road leading out of the mountain pass, where Saul had experienced Jesus. "Upon him was the punishment that made us whole. The Lord has laid on him the iniquity of us all." *My Lord and my God! My God, what have I done?*

As he stood, astonished and confused, a warm presence enveloped him. The furrow left his eyebrows, the corners of his mouth lifted, and the steel in his eyes warmed. "The Spirit of the Lord God is upon me," he whispered. "What would you have me do, Lord? How can I make it up to you?"

The Spirit of the Lord God is upon me because the Lord has anointed me: he has sent me to bring good news to the oppressed.

"Who are the oppressed?"

He peered about at the houses pressing on him. As he resumed, he wondered about the people housed within, sleeping or staring up at ceilings, lying awake with their burdens, sorrows, and pain. Servants and masters alike, rich as well as poor. Those in high standing. The Pharisee, the Sadducee, the Stoic. The orators in the city centers. The slave. The lame. The beggar.

He has sent me to bring good news to the oppressed, to bind up the brokenhearted, to proclaim liberty to the captives, and to release the prisoners.

One's position in life is meaningless. We have all sinned and fallen short, thus the need for atonement. The purpose of the Temple, the purpose of the Law. Until now.

"He was wounded for our transgression, crushed for our iniquities, upon him was the punishment that made us whole, and by his bruises, we are healed." Isaiah's words echoed in his ears.

Saul found himself at the door to Ananias's humble home, and a sudden exhaustion fell on him. Once inside, he removed his sandals, found the pallet on the floor, and collapsed upon it. He was asleep in moments.

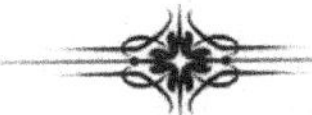

A handful of days later, Ananias and Barnabas had hurried Saul from the synagogue and were safely back in the confines of Elazar's home. Barnabas crossed his arms and sighed at Saul before him, his dark eyebrows drawn together. *Who knew the man would cause so much trouble so quickly?* "While your conviction is admirable, Saul, you're going to have to learn when to speak and when to be silent." Saul opened his mouth to respond, but Barnabas continued. "We've learned we must establish relationships outside of the synagogue. Engage the people where they are."

"But," Saul argued.

"You can't convince them without grace."

"I was about to get to where Isaiah—"

Ananias laid a hand on Saul's arm. "Saul, you must learn to yield to the Holy Spirit. Let Him do your talking for you. He will guide you. You have been called for a purpose. Sometimes, the purpose is to speak, to witness, to teach. But sometimes the purpose is to be silent and listen."

Barnabas wiped away the sweat beading his forehead. "I didn't think we were going to get you out of the synagogue unmolested. You put not only yourself at risk but all of us."

Saul held up his hands in defense. "It was not my intention—"

"Did you have the Spirit with you, Saul?" Ananias asked.

"Well, I." Saul pursed his lips. "When I realized Judas was there after you told me he is one of the synagogue leaders, I couldn't help myself. The look he gave me." Saul grimaced. "I took it as a challenge."

"Did you have the Spirit?" Ananias persisted.

Saul hung his head. "No, I did not."

Elazar entered the room. "I've made urgent preparations. There is a caravan from Petra—we did some business with them this week. They are leaving early in the morning to return home. I have acquaintances there, a good Jewish household who will take you in, Saul."

"Petra?" Saul echoed, stunned. "In Nabatea?"

"Your reputation will not be known there," Elazar explained. "Petra will be an ideal place for you to lay low. Only for a while."

"But I am not done here! I have to proclaim--"

Elazar held up a finger. "You are done here for now. In a single day, you have managed to destroy the tenuous relationships we have carefully built in that synagogue. We will all have to start afresh at a different one. You made some powerful enemies today. You are in danger, Saul, and your presence here endangers us all."

Saul lowered his head. "I forgot myself. This is not the Temple. This is not Jerusalem." He lifted his chin. "I would not have you imperiled as well. I will do as you say, Elazar."

Elazar's face relaxed. Barnabas blew out a breath.

Saul outstretched his hand to their host. "I will go to Petra, to all of Nabatea, if our Lord, Christ Jesus, wills it. I will simply have to proclaim him there."

Phinehas packed their few belongings the following morning and helped Bina pick up their pallets. Saul knew it was time to say farewell to his new friend, but he was reluctant. Ananias's warm eyes met his.

"You'll be back," Ananias said. "We will send for you when it is safe to return." He paused. "Saul." Ananias held out his arms to embrace him.

Saul did not know the man well, but Ananias had saved his life and had lifted him from the depths. Saul received the other man with stiff arms but whispered in his ear. "I am in your debt and can never hope to repay you."

Ananias pulled away and shook his head. "No, my brother. You owe me nothing. All to Christ Jesus."

Only Elazar and Barnabas accompanied him and Phinehas to find the head of the caravan. Elazar paid his fellow trader well to accommodate feeding and other travel expenses for the two of them. "I will repay you," Saul said.

"Take this letter," Elazar said. "When you get to the home of my friend, present it to him. Don't forget to send word from time to time. Let us know how you are doing. You will take up your father's trade?"

"Yes. I should be able to get my hands on some good Tarsian cloth and all the equipment I need."

"Then, farewell, Saul of Tarsus," Elazar said. "You will be in good hands."

Saul turned to Barnabas. "You will remain in Damascus?"

Barnabas shook his head. "No, I will return to Jerusalem. I left my nephew there, whom I am sure has been underfoot of Cephas and the twelve. I need to go back."

"Tell them my story, Barnabas. Tell them about the persecutor turned proclaimer."

"Of course." Barnabas lost his smile. "Be careful in Petra. Judaism itself is not overly popular in Nabatea. I don't know how you will be received. Don't talk too much!"

Saul and Phinehas climbed onto a wagon piled with delicate items, large jars, and fabrics. The two sat, legs crossed under them and hanging onto the sides of the wagon, jerking as the oxen pulled it away. Barnabas and Elazar stood in the street as the distance grew until the wagon turned a corner, and Saul saw them no more.

Chapter 4

Petra, Nabatea
34 A.D.

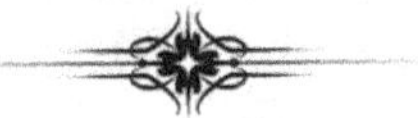

Saul's mother would be abhorred. He examined the callused hands in his lap by the dim light of a single oil lamp. He rubbed them together, amazed at how in only two years they had roughened, so unused as they were to manual labor.

As a child, his mother fretted whenever his father pulled him away from his studies to assist in mending a tent or fashioning a leather strap. Father always said a trade was essential for a man to learn because memorizing scrolls did not guarantee feeding a family. Reluctantly, Saul developed his leather-working skills until he left home to attend school in Jerusalem. He surveyed the neat stack of tools and supplies of his current trade, taking up enough space on the floor for a third person in the tiny room. Saul rubbed at his full belly, grateful his father had insisted.

Outside, a crash of thunder boomed, rocking the house. Next to him, Phinehas jumped in surprise.

"Late in the year for rains, wouldn't you say?" Phinehas asked.

Saul ginned. "The Lord is speaking." He opened his mouth and sang. "The voice of the Lord is over the waters. The God of glory thunders, the Lord thunders over the mighty waters." Torrents of rain hit the house, the thunder rumbling. "For once," he added, "I am glad for a windowless room to sleep in."

Phinehas agreed. "I wonder where Zafir moved what he had stored in this closet. It has become a real shelter from the storm!"

Saul shook his head at his one-time servant. In their former relationship, he had not known Phinehas shared his love for wordplay. Another boom of thunder shook the house. He sang, "The voice of the Lord shakes the wilderness, the Lord shakes the wilderness—"

"Of Kadesh!" Phinehas spoke the lyrics, finishing the line. "Do you suppose King David was talking about this area of Nabatea when he wrote that?"

"It's possible, though the thunder also shakes the wilderness of Judea. Remember how the rains would practically close down Jerusalem? The priests at the Temple struggled to manhandle the animals, already skittish from the storm." Saul closed his eyes, the familiar cacophony echoing in his ears, the scent of burnt flesh and grain wafting off the huge altar. The singing. The chanting. The mass of people, all there to praise God.

"You miss it, don't you?"

Saul opened his eyes. "Terribly," he replied.

Almost three years had passed since he strode out of his city with purpose, riding on a wave of success at the height of his career. He chuckled to himself, thinking back on his arrogance and misinformation. Thinking he had only a dozen or so believers to deal with, he had taken along but a small group of Temple guards. And Phinehas.

Phinehas was originally a servant at the house of Saul's sister and brother-in-law. After Saul left their household, having completed his studies as a grown man, he required a manservant, and Phinehas filled that role. "You must miss Jerusalem as well," Saul offered.

"It was my home all my life." He shrugged. "It was all I knew."

Saul examined his hands, willing away the feelings of loneliness and a longing for home that crowded the tiny room. *How long, O Lord? Will you forget me forever?*

Phinehas stood. "Let's say our prayers, Master Saul. We have to get some sleep."

"We'll have a mess to clean up at our booth at dawn."

"I turned the table so the rain wouldn't pool on it."

"You knew it was going to rain?"

"Yes, of course." The corners of Phinehas's mouth curled. "It's part of my job."

Saul straightened. "All right. Extinguish the lamp. We'll say our prayers, accompanied by God's voice lulling us to sleep."

Phinehas stepped the short distance from his pallet to the lamp, and it was dark.

The following morning, the two men arrived at the marketplace early enough to be among the first of the vendors. Thanks to the city's drainage system, there was little standing water. It was muddy in the open area across from them, but the sturdy walls of the row of booths afforded a much less messy setup.

There was no better way to advertise the craftsman of Tarsian talent than to use a hand-crafted tent for their booth, providing both shade and protection for the leather goods they had on display. Saul had crafted side panels and partitions in order to mend tents in the rear of the booth, while Phinehas manned the table selling leather belts, straps, collars, and bridles. The two were a perfect team.

Phinehas tied back the front panels of the tent and then laid out the display while Saul set to work, closed off from the world. He sat in the corner, most of his light coming in from one open panel, though the tent cloth merely filtered the morning sun. The sounds of the marketplace accompanied the dips of his needle and the pull of the thread. A man's tent was intended to last his lifetime. Any rip or hole in the fabric would extend without prompt, careful mending. Tent repairs were Saul's main occupation, and his reputation had grown in their short time in Petra. One might purchase good tent fabric almost anywhere, but a genuine tentmaker from Tarsus was a rarity in Nabatea.

About mid-morning, the crowding of the market peaked, and Phinehas stuck his head around the closed panel.

"Now would be a good time, Master Saul."

Saul laid aside his work. Moving to the front of the booth, he stood next to Phinehas, placing a hand on his shoulder. He took in the action in the market, full of both vendors and shoppers. He breathed in the scents, a mixture of spices, incense, perfumes, and animals. The last scent to hit him came from the leather goods lying on the table before him. *Not quite the scents of the Temple but this will do.* Grabbing his cloak, wrapping it around him, and over his shoulder, he left their booth.

Maneuvering through the crowd, he crossed the column-lined street. He chose the column directly across from their booth and stood upon its base. From there, he was able to observe Phinehas's expressions and better gauge the mood of his audience.

In his heart, Saul knew why he was sent to Petra. Coming of age and working in the middle of Temple politics, he knew the story of Herod Antipas, the king of the Jews, and his wives, the first of whom happened to be the eldest daughter of Nabataea's King Aretas. Herod had greatly angered Aretas when he divorced the King's daughter to marry his sister-in-law. Knowing the attitude of Nabatean royal loyalists toward Judeans gave Saul a unique perspective. Building on his Tarsian roots and looks, he played the part of a Hellenized Jew from Cilicia as opposed to a hated Judean.

Saul raised his right hand, left hand on his chest, and addressed the backs of the people gathered in the street. "Citizens of Petra, visitors to our great city, masters, servants, freedmen, and slaves. Allow me a few moments of your time."

After months of preaching six days a week, Saul knew most of the vendors and residents present would not cease their activities. But there was always hope. "Look about you at the industry here," he said. "As you walk around Petra's marketplace, you will find items from far reaches of the world. You'll find fresh foods grown here in Nabatea. Here, you will find almost anything you desire. All can be had for a price."

A small group gathered before him. And those who did not stop? They can never un-hear what he said. "Those of you who labor. Why is it you rise early to start your day of body-wracking work until you are sweating and your muscles aching, taking no rest until the end of the day as you fall exhausted on your beds, only to get up early the next morning to do it all over again? Why do you work so hard to create a perfect product, to make the sale, to run the household, to please your master? Is it to feed yourself, to provide for a family? To accumulate wealth? To avoid the lash? What is it all for?"

The crowd enlarged, adding to his satisfaction. Some of the

vendors paused, paying attention. Saul motioned to the hills surrounding the city. "There are large altars on those hilltops, where you sacrifice to your gods. Do you believe that if you diligently worship and offer sacrifices to them, these gods will smile on you, and your sales will be many, your produce will abound, your business flourish, and your wives and children will be fat and happy? Is that why you labor, is that where you have placed your hope?"

Saul's eyes flickered as the warm presence of the Spirit stirred inside him. *Ah, good.* Someone is present who needs to hear my message today. His attention was drawn to the rear of his audience. Then his eyes landed on her. Slight and delicate, veiled, wearing fine, colorful clothing, bejeweled, accompanied by a guard. All Saul observed of her otherwise was her eyes, but that was all he needed. Her soul was open and seeking.

Saul addressed her. "What are those gods of rock made by human hands? Do they have mouths to speak, eyes to see? Ears to hear, noses to smell? Hands to feel? Feet to walk? Did they create heaven and earth? Do they speak to your spirit, and do they provide you with a law to protect you and to set you apart?

"Oh, hear, oh Petra! The Lord our God, creator of heaven and earth, who is in heaven, the God of Abraham, God of Isaac, the God of Israel. The Lord our God is One! He is not an idol made by human hands. He is spirit, a spirit of love that does not desire sacrifice but desires mercy! And this mighty God, creator of the universe, loves you. He loves you so much."

Was that a tear rolling out of her eye? Saul had not broken his eye contact with her once he held it. "He loves you so much that he gave his only son for you, Jesus, the Messiah, who came into the world to redeem mankind of their sins. Jesus, who was rejected by his people and given over to Rome. Jesus, who died on a Roman cross, falsely accused of the crime of sedition. But on the third day, he rose from the dead."

Gasps came from the crowd. Saul broke eye contact with the woman and peered at the others gathered. Then, as always, one by one, his audience thinned. Saul was uncertain why resurrection from the dead was such an unbelievable idea for people, but this was where he tended to lose them. But she remained fixed, their eyes locked. "Yes, he rose from the dead," he continued, "and appeared to many people before he ascended to heaven. Believe in him, all you who are weary and heavy laden. His yoke is easy, and his burden light. Call now on his name and receive pardon and walk in his light!"

Her guard pulled her away, but she turned her head, holding Saul's gaze as she was hurried off. Saul followed her until she disappeared. As the crowd had dispersed, he lowered his arm, eased from the column base, and returned to his booth where Phinehas greeted him. "You really had their attention today," he said. "I like how you questioned the crowd. I haven't heard you do that before."

Saul shrugged as he removed his cloak, revealing his work tunic. Out of habit, Phinehas took his cloak from him. "The crowd was more diverse today," Saul answered. "And the Holy Spirit showed up." Saul contemplated the people milling about the market. "There was a woman."

Phinehas chortled. "There are always women who stop to watch you. You mean to tell me you only now have noticed?"

Saul shook his head. "There was one in particular. Wealthy, elaborately dressed."

"Beautiful?" Phinehas was smiling at him.

"The only thing I saw was her eyes," Saul replied.

Phinehas laid a hand on Saul's shoulder. "That's all you need. They can seduce you with just their eyes."

Brushing the hand away, Saul frowned. "I wasn't attracted to her."

"But you noticed her."

"The Spirit led me to her."

"Perhaps." Phinehas lowered his voice and spoke with tenderness. "Or, perhaps, Yeshua wants you to marry."

"Never!" Saul stormed away, back behind the partition, and resumed his work, fuming. *How can a young man keep his way pure? By living according to your word. Why does everyone always have to bring it back to baseness, to animal-like behavior? I have been called for a higher purpose.*

Phinehas' voice speaking with customers floated toward Saul and he took a deep breath. He willed his heart to slow its rapid beating. Sewing required a calm, steady hand. It did not lend itself well to relieving frustration. Leather work was far better for stress relief if going for a stroll was out of the question. Running or walking and praying. Those had always been his way of releasing aggression or anger or sexual desire, all feelings that may lead to irrationality. If there was one thing he loathed, it was to not be in full control of his actions, his words, and his behavior. Far better to go for a brisk walk.

When Saul knew the customers had left, he strode to the front of the booth. Laying a hand on Phinehas's arm, Saul said, "I'm sorry I lost my temper, but I am not attracted to that woman."

"I know."

"She must be someone important to God."

"The smell of food is making me hungry. Would you man the table for a while? I'll get us something to eat."

"Yes, of course." Saul waved a hand. "Go."

As Phinehas made his way through the crowd, Saul stood behind the table and waited.

Jameleh swept her long hair from her eyes. As soon as her guards returned her to the palace, she had gone straight to her room, peeling off layers of fabric and finally, once inside her sanctuary, she loosened her hair. Pushing away her servant girls, she sat on the upholstered bench at the only window in her large suite of a room and brushed her hair.

Cloistered. That's what Mother called it. Imprisoned is what she called it. It was all her sister's fault. Phasaelis had brought her shame home with her from Jerusalem to Father. It wasn't fair! It wasn't like either sister was in a position to make choices about their life. Father was the one who gave Phasaelis to Herod to marry in the first place. But her sister was unable to keep the man happy, to keep him from straying to his seductive sister-in-law.

Jameleh was seldom allowed to leave the palace. Today, she had begged Father to let her go to the marketplace. She wanted to check out the new fabrics and some of the finely crafted jewelry and perhaps find some pieces to replace some of her old ones. A breath of freedom in her sequestered life, hidden away until her father, King Aretas, found the right purpose for her, a strategic union good for Nabatea. Good for Father. Good for her brother, Malichus, who was next in line to become king of Nabatea.

Jameleh pulled back the sheer curtains at her window, basking in the sun. Sauntering elbow to elbow with all kinds of other people delighted her. She'd been thrilled to stop at the booths in the marketplace, touch the fabrics, and breathe in the delicious smells of food and perfumes. Being out overwhelmed her senses, leaving her heady and thrilled. And then, there he'd been.

She had been struck by his appearance. Greek dress on a manly frame, a neatly trimmed black beard, and an intriguing face. A face that made her think of exotic, far-off lands, dark eyes filled with passion.

It was his voice, though, that had stirred her. He spoke in clear, succinct Greek, with a touch of an unplaceable accent, running a surprising shiver of delight through her.

An unusual reaction. Men tended to repulse her with their smelly bodies and their unwanted touches. But this man, he was different. She had to be near him again. Had to hear that voice, have those piercing eyes bore into her, past her veil, past her flesh, deep inside her.

She didn't understand most of what he talked about, but she knew he spoke of love, and she wanted to hear more, to know him better, to have the love he spoke of. She wanted to possess him, have him all for herself. But how? Practically imprisoned in her home, she had to devise a plan.

Chapter Five

"Esther!" Jameleh exclaimed. "Why do we have to stand behind a screen?"

"Shhh!" Esther whispered. "Lower your voice, Princess. We are here to worship."

The tone the older woman exasperated Jameleh, but she said nothing. After managing several days of going to the marketplace where her man talked and noting him slip inside the tent maker's booth, she had dared to draw near to him one day. He had invited her to attend synagogue to learn more. Somehow, she'd managed to convince Esther, one of the household servants, to take her to the synagogue with her. She was in a place she had never been and surrounded by common people. For him.

Peering through the screen, Jameleh found him at once. She positioned herself where she hoped to observe him. He never turned toward the screen. How would she know she had come?

When the men started speaking, she whispered her next question. "What language is that? I can't understand a word of it!"

"It's Hebrew, Princess."

"You must tell me what they are saying."

"I will, Princess."

"Why can't they speak Greek?"

Esther sighed. "Many cities have synagogues where they solely worship in Greek. They use a Greek version of our holy writings. But this is the only synagogue in Petra, and it was not established by Greek speakers. So, most of the worship is in Hebrew. There will be some Aramaic. I will try to translate as we go along."

Jameleh attempted to ignore the other women around them, but they were packed rather tight behind the screen, and Jameleh was aware of their stares. She had worn her plainest clothes to blend in, but she stood out nonetheless. "What is he saying now?"

"We will recite the Shema," she answered. "Listen carefully to the Hebrew. I will translate for you." Then, with all the other women and the man on the other side of the partition, Esther sang:

Sh'ma Yisra'eil! Adonai Eloheinu, Adonai echad.

Esther leaned in closer to her. "Hear O Israel, the LORD our God is One."

She remembered. The tentmaker had said something similar. By the end of the worship, her patience had worn thin, as so had that of the women surrounding her, who kept glaring at her and Esther. Jameleh asked Esther what they were saying at each part of the worship, and Esther translated. As it concluded, Jameleh sought a way to the door, but Esther stopped her.

"No, Princess," she said, "we must go out this way." She indicated the side entrance they had used to enter.

Once in the street, Jameleh hurried around the corner of the building. Esther chased after her. "Princess, no!"

Jameleh halted but stood on her tiptoes. She spied him then, with three other men, heading away from them. She placed a foot in their direction.

"The palace is the other way!" Esther snatched her elbow.

Jameleh presented her servant with a dimpled expression and poured on the charm that never failed her. "Oh, Esther. I have learned so much today. I have to go for a walk, think about it all, let it sink in."

"It's not safe, Princess. I can't—"

Jameleh laid a firm hand on Esther's upper arm and squeezed it tight. "Go on to the palace, Esther. Be a good girl. I'll be right behind you."

"But—"

"Go. Now." Jameleh removed her hand, spun Esther around, and shoved her away. "Go!" She waited until Esther turned a corner and was out of sight. Then Jameleh hurried off in the direction of the men.

The crowd was gone at the end of the street, but she arrived in time to note the man who was always with her tentmaker enter a house off to her left. Jameleh noted the landmarks and location of the house before she turned and headed back to the palace.

As it neared sunset, ending the Sabbath, Zafir's wife and the household servants waited for the oil lamps to grow dim. They would refill the lamps after sundown, after the prayer praising God for the Sabbath, and then they would prepare a quick hot meal.

After the meal, Saul, Phinehas, Zafir, and his son-in-law lounged in the room Zafir used for entertaining guests. The refilled lamps burned bright, and the men cast long shadows across the room.

"Brother Saul," Zafir said. "In a few months, it will have been three years since you and Phinehas were my guests."

Saul raised his brows. "Do you need to raise our rent? Or do you require your storage room back?"

Zafir shook his head. "No, no, nothing like that. You know I don't like accepting rent from you. You pay me far more than that small room ever cost me. No, I ask because I wonder whether you and Phinehas will make Petra your home. You came to us as escapees from a hostile situation, but have you not found peace and prosperity here in Nabatea? Might you not decide to stay? You should both have no trouble finding a wife in our fair city."

Saul knew that, while Zafir denied wanting them out of his home, the storage room could be utilized for other purposes, especially as the grandchildren grew. Zafir was right. Petra was turning into a home. "You have been an excellent host, Zafir," Saul responded. "Phinehas and I have been blessed to be so well received. Petra is indeed an oasis in a desert land."

"I'm pleased you think it so."

"And if I were to choose a place to settle," Saul continued, "to marry, to raise a family, Petra would certainly be a perfect place to do so. You have everything a man might want. A fine house, a lovely wife and family, loyal house servants, an excellent trade, a thriving synagogue. Your country is at peace. What more can one ask for?"

Zafir's son-in-law stirred and murmured. "We have beautiful women here, too."

Saul sighed. "Yes, indeed you do, any of whom would make a wonderful wife. But"—Saul stood—"I know such a beautiful life is not for me. All my life, I have been aware that I was being prepared for something, something big for God. I threw myself, therefore, into my studies, assuming my destiny was to serve our God as a member of the Great Sanhedrin, perhaps." How to explain his restlessness? "I was so close. I had become one of the finest lawyers in all of Jerusalem. Ask me an infintesimal detail: what does the Law say about untying a donkey on the Sabbath? What sacrifice is a man required when he finds he overcharged a customer? Or if he is inadvertently touched by a woman who may be impure?" Saul pointed to his temple. "It's all up in here, and I can go to the correct scroll and point to it, show you where it can be found.

"Marry? Not unless I were in Jerusalem and had hopes of securing a position on the Great Sanhedrin. And now, we all know that will not happen. It can never happen. Zafir, you have been an excellent host, but I know I cannot stay. Christ Jesus will call me away, and where he leads me, I must go. I fear this"—Saul indicated with his arm about the room—"this is never to be for me. I wish it were, but I know in my heart it cannot."

Zafir stood next to him and clasped Saul's shoulder. "You are brave, my friend. I wish I had a portion of your passion. But as you have dedicated your life to God, you are right. You must be ready to go at a moment's notice, wherever he may lead you. And now," Zafir said, letting his arms drop to his side, "I am tired and believe I shall retire for the night." He addressed his son-in-law, reaching out a hand. "Come, let's leave these gentlemen."

His son-in-law scrambled up.

"We will see you two in the morning." Zafir followed the younger man out of the room.

Saul returned to his seat.

"I may stay," Phinehas said. "If you leave. When you leave. If I have your blessing, that is."

"Of course you do. What is her name? Did you meet her at the marketplace?"

As Phinehas was about to respond, one of Zafir's male servants appeared in the doorway. "Master Saul," he said, "sorry to disturb you, but a visitor insists upon speaking with you."

"At this hour?"

Then there she was, hovering in the doorway. Saul jumped up to his feet, and she ducked around the servant.

"Oh, Saul!" She dropped to the floor, kissing his feet.

Appalled, Saul pulled away. "Stop, stop! What are you doing? What are you doing here?"

She sobbed, her head bowed. "I'm so sorry to barge into your home. But I had to see you! I went to the synagogue, but I couldn't get to you, couldn't be near you. I—"

"Daughter," Saul said, his voice low and calm. "You shouldn't be in the synagogue for me. You should be there for God."

She lifted her head and her veil fell away from her face. Saul was shocked at how young she appeared.

"But," she countered, "you talked of love."

"God's love. Our God *is* love."

Jameleh's sobs intensified. "I don't want to live if you don't love me!"

Saul's eyes widened. "No, listen."

She stood and fell into his arms, crying. He held her at arm's length and winced. "Hear me. God's love. That is the kind of love worth dying for. It is everything that is good in the world."

When Jameleh again crumbled to the floor at his feet, Zafir and his son-in-law rushed back into the room. "What is going on here?" Zafir demanded. "Why is this woman in our house, and at this late hour?"

Her sobbing ceased as abruptly as it started, and Jameleh lifted her head. "Saul? This is not your house?"

"No, it is not," Zafir answered. He grasped her by the shoulder to help her stand. "It is my house, and these men are my guests. And my guests are not to be assaulted by—" Zafir stopped, and his eyes widened. "Wait, aren't you?"

Jameleh straightened and lifted her chin but did not answer. Zafir dropped his hand and slid away from her. "Saul!" he exclaimed. "Do you know who this is? You are the princess,

Jameleh, are you not?"

"Yes, I am."

Zafir's eyes flashed with anger. "This is not good. Do you know what danger she brings to my household? Do you?" He spun toward his son-in-law. "The princess must be accompanied back to the royal palace at once. I am sure the king is frantic, concerned that she is out alone, without proper escort." Then Zafir turned back to Jameleh. "It is dangerous for you to be out alone, Princess. We will see you returned safely home. Come," he said. "Come with me."

Jameleh's eyes filled with a sad longing before she shuffled toward the door. Zafir turned to Saul. His voice low, he hissed. "We will talk about this later." Then they were gone.

At Saul's side, Phineas shook his head. "I knew that girl was trouble."

"She's a mere child!" Saul replied.

"She knows exactly what she is doing. You are in danger now."

Saul shook his head. He did not sense any darkness about her. Misguided. That was all.

"Master Saul," Phinehas laid a hand on his arm. "Please, stay In Zafir's house tomorrow; work from here until all is forgotten. I can handle the booth myself. A few days, that is all. Indulge me. Please?"

Saul sighed. "You may be right. Perhaps she will not be tempted to visit the marketplace if I am not there for a few days. Though I don't think she is dangerous to me. I am sure her father has more pressing things to worry about than a poor tentmaker from Tarsus."

Phinehas shook his head. "I somehow doubt King Aretas will take this well. The only thing worse than a daughter spurned by a Jewish leader is to have a daughter spurned by a foreign Jewish lawyer, and one who preaches resurrection from the dead. No, I fear that if King Aretas learns of his daughter's affections, he will not take it well."

Saul lay on his pallet, eyes glued to the dark ceiling. Sleep escaped him. The scene of that night persisted to run like a loop, playing over and over in his head. He had tried not to let Phinehas note his concern, but Jameleh's words and her desperate eyes remained in his mind.

O Lord, he recited in his mind, *you have searched me, and you know me. You know when I sit and when I rise. You perceive my thoughts from afar.*

Had he led her on? Was there any glimmer of physical attraction in his soul that drew her to him? Had he touched her casually, had he made any gesture that would mislead her? Had she read something in his eyes that she misinterpreted? His worry was heavy on his chest. *What kind of punishment might she face at the palace?*

Search me, O God, and know my heart. Test me and know my anxious thoughts. See if there is any wicked way in me . . .

He prayed for her, for the child that she was.

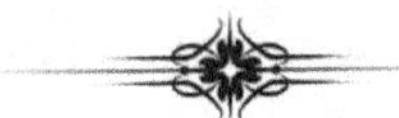

Phinehas arrived earlier than usual at their booth in the marketplace. Setting up with only one of them would take twice as long, but Phinehas had insisted Saul stay back at Zafir's house. He was uncertain how long it might be before Saul was safe to return. As Phinehas set up, he played through the previous night's scene. The princess throwing herself on the floor at Saul's feet. Saul's horrified reaction, Zafir's fearful anger, and the princess's anguish as she was exiled from the house. Phinehas shook his head. He had warned Saul. One should think that by now, Saul would have a better understanding of women. While he was always a faithful Pharisee and kept his distance from women, when at all possible, Saul had a mother and had lived with his older sister and her husband for several years before going out on his own. Surely, he knew women were attracted to him. He carried himself well, and confidence oozed out of him, quite enticing to potential wives.

Potential wives. Phinehas' chest warmed, thinking about the girl he left the booth to visit with daily. Earlier in the week, he had gained enough courage to speak to her. Though shy, she appeared pleased by his attention and had responded when he'd spoken to her.

Saul may not know women well, but he'd figured out why Phinehas wanted to stay in Petra. He grinned as he worked, thinking about her and her pretty smile.

Phinehas had not yet finished setting up the tent when footsteps thudded behind him. He turned as three men neared the booth. "Are you the tentmaker?" one of them asked.

Phinehas wet his lips. These were not the king's men. They did not wear the royal colors. *Perhaps they are fellow merchants.* Phinehas's eyes lowered to the weapons they bore. *Not merchants. Mercenaries.*

He could tell them the truth. He could tell them where they would find Saul. He knew what they wanted. Of course, the king would send mercenaries. No one would know the king had anything to do with it. *Perhaps buy Saul some time. Claim to be Saul. They will take him to the palace, the king will question him, and then, by the time they discovered he was not who they sought . . .*

"Yes, I am," Phinehas answered.

Two men grabbed his arms, one man on each side, and hauled him away from the booth and the open-air market, away from the marketplace and the center of the city. Phinehas assumed they were headed for the palace, but they passed out of the city itself. The sandstone hills and mountains surrounding Petra had, over time, formed a tunnel-like pathway through the mountain called the Siq. He stretched his neck up as they neared it, towering over them, and his chest filled with a cold dread.

"Where are we going?" he asked. "Are we not going to the palace?"

The men tightened their grip as their only answer. Phinehas's heart raced as sweat trickled down his face. They were going to kill him. Phinehas was going to die. If the king discovered they had killed the wrong man, Saul would be in grave danger. There was no time or way to warn him or Zafir's family.

"Stop, stop! What have I done?"

The third man grunted in response. Phinehas attempted to rip his arms free, but he was held tight as he was struck in the face. Numbness spread through his body as hot blood streamed from his nose. *I am going to die. This is how it ends. Oh, Lord! Come rescue me!*

When he closed his eyes and stopped resisting, a great warmth surrounded him, like a giant arm wrapping around his shoulders. A deep peace settled within him, and he knew it was going to be all right. He observed the scene from above with curiosity. The three men surrounded his body, two holding it upright while the third slipped behind and slit his throat. A sharp, piercing pain sliced through his body, and Phinehas was blinded by a bright light, which he moved into willingly.

Saul sat cross-legged on a cushion, working on another tent repair. He sat near a window in a room at the front of the house, where he would be out of the way of the servants as they went about their daily chores. After saying morning prayers and seeing Phinehas out for the marketplace, Saul had gone right to work.

His thoughts were no longer on Jameleh. Phinehas was heavy on his mind and heart. As Saul sat sewing, he wondered about the woman his friend had met. *What was it about her that had caught Phinehas's attention? Was she Jewish? Had she been attentive to any of Saul's street preaching? Was she a servant or a daughter of one of the merchants?* The corners of his mouth turned up. *If I know Phinehas, she is a beauty. When he returns later today, I will press him about it.*

Saul pondered on his mission. As Zafir brought up the previous evening, it had been nearly three years. Three years since he was stopped from hounding God's people. Three years since Christ Jesus came into his life and totally changed his course. Saul lifted his voice in song.

"I have done what is righteous and just. Do not leave me to my oppressors. Ensure your servant's well-being. Let not the arrogant oppress me."

He paused. He held the fabric up close to examine the fine stitches and gave a satisfied grunt. One would have to have foreknowledge that there was a repair done to the tent. Satisfied with his handiwork, Saul carefully folded the tent and laid it aside as Zafir rushed into the room. "Saul, grab your belongings, quick now."

Startled, Saul stood. "What? Why?"

Zafir neared him and grasped his arm. "You must leave. You

are in great danger. No time to explain right now. Gather whatever you can."

"But Phinehas. . ."

"Phinehas is dead."

"What? No." Saul peered at him in disbelief. "He can't be!"

"Some travelers found his body in the Siq this morning, his throat cut. A few of the vendors saw him leave with some men before the booth was open."

Zafir's son-in-law came into the room, carrying the tent for the booth and the leather goods Phinehas had taken with him. "I gathered these for you," he said. "Father, we have a wagon prepared to go to Damascus today. Should I--"

"Yes, place all of those on the wagon," Zafir interrupted. He indicated the folded tent on the floor. "Does this go, too?"

Saul shook his head. "No, it is ready to be picked up. You may keep the payment for it. I'll gather my tools and supplies. Zafir." Saul paused. "Are you sure it was Phinehas?"

"Yes, Saul. We identified his body ourselves. You must go. It will not take long for them to come for you. Our entire household will be at risk if they find you or evidence of you here."

Saul pursed his lips. "Yes, I see. So, I am going back to Damascus."

"Yes, Saul," Zafir answered. "And I am afraid that you must leave Petra the same way you entered it."

Jameleh flowed along the dim hallway, her well-practiced tread silent. Her eyes were no longer puffy. Two nights prior, she was escorted out of the house where her tentmaker was staying. The men who brought her from there told the guards she had been found in the street, alone. After she assured the king's guards that she had not been assaulted, she was brought to her father. Her brother, Malichus, tricked her that evening into giving her tentmaker away. Malichus easily discovered the man, as the entire marketplace knew of him. She had been punished that night, but not by Father. That was left to his heir apparent.

Malichus never struck her in the face or on the arms. His

bruising was always done on areas unnoticeable by any but her closest maidservants. However, the punishment that night had been the worst ever. He never touched her in an area that would one day be examined to assure her purity. But there were other ways.

After he left, her servants had eased her into a warm bath and had washed her, muttering sweet words as she sobbed, humiliated and in pain. They told her that she had to marry soon, to get out of the palace before Malichus hurt her any further. But Saul, her tentmaker, was the only husband she wanted.

She had learned that Father was holding a conference about her fate that evening, so she had left her room in silence to spy on them. Malichus's voice drifted into the hallway as she stood, flattened against the wall near the open door.

"No, the men I hired—"

"Were incompetent, it seems." That was Father. "But I am sure they were paid nonetheless."

"Yes, half before, the rest after they reported him dead."

"The man they killed. Are there any loose ends? Any way to trace—"

"No, Father. He had no one but the tentmaker."

"And where, then, is the tentmaker?"

"I have heard, Father, that he escaped to Damascus."

Damascus? Had he truly fled there?

"Then what are you waiting for, Malichus? Go to Damascus. Find him. Then bring him back here. Alive. No more mercenaries, no more dead bodies left for travelers to find. Understand?"

"I want him dead, Father. It will send a greater message."

"And I want him alive, Malichus. If I find he has violated any of our laws, then you may kill him. But I want him brought back to me alive. You may beat him, torture him, but don't kill him. Do you understand me?"

Jameleh hurried back to her chamber. Saul was in Damascus, and her brother was going to hurt him.

Once inside her room, she rushed to her wardrobe. Riding clothes. She had to go to Damascus, find Saul, and warn him. They could escape together. She would convince him to leave and take her with him.

She sent one of her maidservants to find a man's cloak, something dark. She swore the servant to secrecy before she hurried on silent feet to one of the servant entrances to the palace, the one closest to the stables.

Her horse knew her. She had to hurry, but she was not used to preparing it for a ride. The stable slaves always did it for her. She untied her horse and pulled him toward her.

"You there, where are you going?" She froze in place, the voice filling her with dread. *Malichus.*

"I said"—he grabbed her by the arm and spun her around—"where are you. . . Jameleh?"

They locked eyes. She wanted to spit on him, to beat him with a club. But she stood still, daggers in her eyes.

Malichus gave a short huff. "I know what you are doing," he said, his voice hushed. "You're going to run away, go back for your tentmaker, aren't you?" He closed in on her. "Are you sure it's not too painful to ride, my sister?"

"Guards!" she shouted. She knew they would be nearby. "Guards!" Before Malichus quieted her, several guards rushed into the stall. Malichus lowered his hand. "My brother has the need," she said, "of the King's fastest steeds."

Malichus turned to the group. "You there," he said to one of them. "Take the princess to the king. Report to him that I found her here, unaccompanied. We shall leave her in his custody to punish her as he sees fit."

The guard marched Jameleh back into the palace, her heart heavy and defeated. Once in the presence of her father, her brother Rabbal at his side, the guard gave his report as Malichus had commanded. Father was silent for a moment, taking her in. Finally, he shook his head and sighed. "Rabbal," he said, waving a hand. "Leave us."

Obedient, her brother rose and left the room, closing the doors behind him.

Jameleh scrutinized her father. When had he grown so old? Not only his temples but also his once-black beard were all shades of gray. Dark circles accented his eyes. Tears welled and escaped down Jameleh's cheeks. "Oh, Father." She sank to the floor at his feet, bowing her head. "It's all so horrible!"

"What is so horrible, my daughter? Do I not provide sufficient housing for you? Are you clothed in rags? Are you not fed well?"

"Oh, no, Father. You care for me so well."

"Then what can be so horrible that you would run away from me in the night?"

Should she tell him? What is the worst to happen? Malichus may kill her, as he had promised. But at this point, would that be so bad? "Malichus," she whispered, her eyes downcast.

"Malichus? Your brother? What about him?"

"He . . . he hurts me, Father."

"What? Hurts you?"

She lifted her head. How much should she tell him? She wiped away the tears on her face.

"How does he hurt you?"

"He does things to me, Father, things he says I should get used to, things a . . . a husband does to a wife."

Father was silent. Jameleh noted the redness develop on his neck and then rush to his face. His dark eyes flashed. "Get up," he commanded.

She stood but lowered her eyes and clasped her hands in front of her.

"Come here, Daughter."

She shuffled to him. He lifted her chin with his finger. "Has he?" Father took in a deep breath.

She shook her head. "No, Father. He has done many other things, but he won't do that. He says I have no value to him if I am impure."

Father dropped his hand to his side. He turned and took a few steps away. "How long has it been going on?"

Jameleh hesitated. *Father will be angry if I haven't told him sooner.* But it was time to tell him. "A long time, Father, even before I started my bleeding."

Her father hung his head. His voice was low. "Why didn't you tell me?"

"Malichus said he would kill me. I'm so sorry, Father! I believed him. I think he *will* kill me."

He turned and opened his arms to her. Jameleh ran to him, and he held her close. He let her cry for some time before he pulled her away from him. "I will not let him kill you. I have been priming him to take my throne. But Nabatea deserves better. I cannot hand my rule over to someone this cruel to their family. To treat my daughter like a mere slave! Tell me, Jameleh. Has Rabbal ever . . ."

She shook her head. "No, Father. Rabbal is a good brother to me."

He nodded. "Good. I will make him the next King Aretas, then. In the meantime, you are right. You must go from here. I cannot be everywhere to protect you. There is a good man, one who is kind and gentle. He does not want a wife. That is not his interest. But he would marry you and leave you alone. He would care for you and provide well for you. If you would go to him, Jameleh, if you would marry him, would you make a promise to me?"

"Yes, Father, anything."

"Have no children. Children will only bring you heartbreak."

Jameleh met her father's pained eyes. She thought of Saul, her tentmaker. If she could not have him, then . . .

"Yes, Father. I promise."

Chapter Six

**Damascus, Syria
34 A.D.**

Elazar shut the door behind him and glared at Saul. "You should not have come here," he said. "You place our entire household in danger."

Saul bowed his head. "Elazar, I am so sorry."

"It was my idea." Ananias spoke as he removed his cloak. "Saul surprised me at my workshop. If he had sent word—"

"My circumstances did not allow time to send you notice, and for that, I apologize." Saul grasped Elazar by the arm. "I would not bring trouble on your house, Brother Elazar. You have shown me such kindness. Zafir knew nowhere else to send me but back to Damascus." Saul met Elazar's eyes. Something new was there, something that was not there when he was hurried out of Damascus. "Back to you."

Elazar sighed. "Zafir didn't know that Damascus has not forgotten you. Three years is not enough time. However, you are here now. You might as well take off your sandals. Where is your servant? Phinehas, correct?"

Ananias bowed his head as Saul hesitated to answer. "Phinehas was killed in Petra."

"How terrible!" Elazar exclaimed.

"I should have left him here. He would still be alive."

"Phinehas is at peace," Ananias said.

Saul peered at Ananias. "You know this?"

"Yes, Saul."

"He was more than a servant to me. We were a team, Phinehas and me." Saul passed a hand over his eyes. He spoke into his palm. "I miss him."

"Are you hungry?" Elazar asked. "Have you eaten today?"

Saul blinked. "I don't recall."

Elazar shook his head. "Let us get you fed, and we can talk. You can fill us in on what has you fleeing from Petra."

As Saul drew his story to a close, Ananias shook his head. "The princess? Oh, Saul! If you had stayed a Pharisee, this would never have happened! You know better than to trust a Gentile woman!"

"Any woman," Elazar added.

Saul shook his head. "No, the Spirit guided me to her, was drawing me to her. I thought."

"You mean to tell me," Elazar interjected, "Saul of Tarsus, that you misinterpreted her sexual allure for the Holy Spirit?"

"It wasn't like that!" Saul attempted to stand, but Ananias pressed a hand on his shoulder.

"He means no insult," Ananias said. "But I do agree. She had you under a spell. I can't imagine any man being able to resist the charm of the princess Jameleh. I've heard she is a beauty."

Saul attempted to conjure her face, her neck. Her veil had fallen away as she groveled at his feet. He shook his head. "I cannot say."

"What? But you spied her several times, you say!"

"Yes," Saul admitted. "I suppose she is a beauty." Her eyes, so full of spirit and eagerness, how she seemed to hang on every word of his preaching. "But I didn't see that," he insisted. "What I saw was a soul open to Christ and his teachings."

Elazar chuckled. "I'm sorry, Saul. I think your strict efforts to withdraw yourself from women in your former life have addled your brain. Not see a woman's beauty? Not have any desire stir your heart?"

"I have always believed chastity is what was intended by the law of circumcision. It is good to be married if one can't control their desires for flesh. But even then, when the desire to satisfy one's sexual appetite is greater than the desire to possess God, that opens the door for evil."

Ananias shook his head. "No wonder Yeshua chose you."

Saul winced. "It wasn't until her veil fell from her face that I noted how young she is. Her behavior was that of a more mature woman."

"They learn it early in the royal household." Ananias laid his hand on Saul's arm. "Don't blame yourself."

Saul's eyebrows furrowed. He hadn't thought about what kind of childhood she had had, assuming she would have lacked for nothing. How might she have learned, at such a young age, the ways of men?

"The fact remains," said Elazar, "that you are threatened here, regardless of what may have happened in Petra. The church in Damascus has grown, but we are no longer welcome in the synagogue."

"No longer welcome?" Saul exclaimed. "How can that be? You are sons of Abraham!"

Ananias shrugged. "Judas has convinced the other leaders of the synagogue that the name of Yeshua is not to be proclaimed. And when he found you had fled Damascus, he filed charges. Upon your return to Damascus, you are to be arrested and brought before the magistrate."

"Under what charges?" Saul asked.

"For the spread of the good news of the Messiah. Your impromptu speech, while it caused the need to flee, brought many who were present to believe."

Saul brought his hands together. So, the Spirit *had* used him. He thought back on that day, the shame he had felt, sitting on the back of Zafir's wagon, fleeing Damascus like a runaway. Damascus was not Jerusalem. It was not even Tarsus. And Petra. Petra was another place altogether.

"You should go to Antioch," Elazar said. "Nicolaus sent word about the small group of believers there, and he is the only one who knows you."

His ears grew warm. Nicolaus. Would the man he had so fiercely pursued ever be able to welcome him? He replayed their first encounter at the Temple, how his heart had burned with anger and hatred for the man. He shook his head. "I don't think Nicolaus will want me there. There is no love lost between us."

Ananias laid a hand on his arm. "Nicolaus is filled with the Holy Spirit. Now he will consider you as a fellow disciple. The old Saul, the Persecutor, is gone. He died at the home of Judas."

Saul reflected on the way Ananias had entered his life and rescued him, healed his blindness, shared the love of God, baptized him, and prayed over him, all the while in grave danger for his life. "If you are sure of that, my friend," Saul replied, "and the Spirit says I should go to Antioch, then to Antioch I shall go."

Bina was quite pregnant with their second child, and she grunted every time she bent awkwardly to help pack another bit of travel gear for her husband. Saul noted her discomfort. "You don't have to accompany me, Ananias. You shouldn't leave your family here alone."

"Nonsense. It will take at least four days to get there, and the roads are not safe for one to travel alone."

Saul sat silent. He'd been self-sufficient since he left his sister's home, but now, he was relegated to the role of a child. "I would like to stay long enough to earn some money," he said. "Stay in your workshop, send Bina out with some worked leather—"

"Saul," Ananias interrupted. "You must learn to accept help. You don't have time to waste, and you insult me by refusing."

Bina lifted her eyes to Saul. He sighed. "You're right. I am being ungrateful. Thank you."

"That's better." Ananias rolled up a couple of extra cloaks and blankets. "We will borrow a donkey from Elazar. He can spare one."

At that, the door opened, and Elazar hurried inside. "Ananias! Saul!" he exclaimed, breathless. "You must go tonight."

"Elazar!" Bina hurried over to him. "Sit and rest."

"No, no," he panted, gesticulating with his arms. "It's worse than we thought."

Saul took Elazar's cloak from him, and Bina led him to a cushioned bench near the door. Ananias peered out at the street before closing the door.

"Malichus." Elazar said. "King Aretas's son and heir-apparent. He is in Damascus with a small force."

"Malichus?" Saul let this register. *Jameleh.*

"He is here from Petra to find you. They have placed guards at each of the city gates, searching everyone who attempts to leave or enter."

"The gates?" Ananias echoed. "How shall we get to Antioch but through the gates?"

"We'll have to hide him." Bina plunked onto the bench across from Saul. "How long before they tire of waiting for him to enter or leave?"

Elazar shook his head. "They are searching the city as well. They have split their force into small search parties and inspecting businesses and homes. They stormed through my warehouse, turning over tables and searching under blankets."

Ananias jerked his head toward Bina, without a word.

Saul paced. "This is all my fault. I should never have come here."

"Saul, no," Ananias neared him.

"I should give myself up to Aretas. Spare you all."

"Nonsense," said Ananias. "Now you're talking like Nicolaus did when you were hunting him."

"Arieh." Bina spoke under her breath. She raised her head. "Ananias, my uncle Arieh."

Ananias tilted his head. "Yes? What about your uncle?"

"Uncle Arieh's shop is adjacent to the city's south wall."

Her husband's face brightened. "Oh, that's right."

"His shop is on the street level," Bina explained to the others present, "but he has living space upstairs and, from there, steps that lead to the roof. My cousins and I played on the roof as children, throwing rocks over and climbing on the city wall."

"How is this helpful right now?" Elazar asked.

"The gates are not the only way out of the city. Brother Saul and Ananias can go over the wall."

In wonder, Saul considered Bina. She had been quiet and shy around him the few days he was a guest in their home before fleeing to Petra. She had been expecting then as well and was now a mother. He had not suspected her cleverness.

"You mean," Elazar interjected, "jump off the wall? They'll

break their necks!"

Bina giggled. "No. They can climb down with a rope. My cousins would do it sometimes, then climb back up. You can climb a rope, can't you, Brother Saul?"

Elazar squinted at Bina. "But you said the south side?"

"Yes, not far from here."

Ananias scratched his beard. "The guards at either gate will surely spot us if we go around to head north to cross the river. We'll have to go south."

Saul pictured a map of the area in his mind. Ananias was right. To go to Antioch, they would have to go south for some way and west before heading north toward Aleppo.

Elazar sprang to his feet. "We must go now to your uncle's house and pray he will help us."

"He will help us," Bina asserted. "I will get Elon up from his nap."

"Wait!" Ananias held up his hands. "We can't traipse through the streets with a fugitive. We must hide him. Elazar, go fetch a wagon and fill it with carpets" He eyed Saul. "I have an idea. Saul, come with me. We'll contrive a good way to hide you."

In the workshop, Ananias measured Saul's height and breadth. Then he measured a couple of longer boards and grunted. Saul assisted him as he bound the boards together in several places with wide pieces of leather. He attached three wooden hoops and pieces of wagon wheels to the backboard. By the time they were finished, Elazar had arrived with the wagon.

"This is a day," Ananias said to Saul, "that I am glad for your tendency to eat light."

Saul crawled onto the boards between the hoops and laid on his back. Ananias threw the rug over him. As Saul was lifted off the ground, he gripped the sides of the boards tight, certain he would fall. But then he heard a whisper: *watch your fingers.* He drew his hands back, understanding. A thud told him he must be on the wagon. The rug was stifling, making him glad for the cooler weather.

As the wagon lurched, Saul experienced every bump and rut in the road. What would have been a short walk took forever before the wagon came to a stop. Then, he was pulled off the wagon and carried again. Muffled voices floated back and forth, a door opening then closing, and he was lowered. The rug was pulled away, and he scrambled up. Breathless, he stood with Elazar, Ananias, Bina, and their son, Elon, as Bina introduced him to her uncle.

"You had best bring some of the other rugs inside," her uncle said. "It will appear less suspicious." Arieh then turned to Saul. "You need to get out of sight. Bina, lead him upstairs."

Saul followed her through the back room of the shop, part kitchen, and part workshop. The child, Elon, was already playing in the myriad of baskets of varied sizes, and a couple of women stood in the kitchen area.

"Aunt Danya, Raya," Bina said in greeting. A stairwell climbed the right wall, and Bina was already on the stairs. Saul followed her, where he found himself in living quarters, sleeping areas cordoned off with curtains. Bina pulled aside one of the curtains but stopped short and stooped, making an exclamation.

"Bina? Are you—" Saul's eyes grew wide at the pooling about Bina's feet. He did not know what was happening, but he was sure this was not normal.

"Oh, no!" Bina exclaimed. "Brother Saul, I'm so sorry! Fetch my aunt. She's in the kitchen. Tell her I've lost my water."

Saul flew down the stairs and stood panting before the men. Ananias, taking apart the backboard, turned with a question in his raised brows.

"Bina!" Saul gasped.

Before more was said, Ananias ran up the stairs past him. The older of the two women raised her head, and when her eyes met Saul's, she dropped the basket she was working on and flew after Ananias. As Arieh and Elazar came into the workroom, the younger woman hurried up the stairs as well.

"Saul? What is it?" Elazar asked.

"Bina, she's leaking."

"Bleeding, you say?"

"No, no. She's . . ." What were Bina's words? "She's lost her water."

"Ah," said Elazar, far too calmly. "She's having the baby."

"That's supposed to happen?" Saul was shocked. "Will she have it soon?"

Elazar shook his head. "No, this is a mere signal of the beginning."

Ananias appeared from the stairs.

"We need to move that wagon," Elazar said.

"I'll go with you." Ananias strode toward the door.

Saul's head bobbed from one man to the other, unbelieving. "You're going to leave your wife right now? She's about to give birth!"

"It will be a while, Saul. I have time to help Elazar with the wagon. You, however, need to get out of sight."

"But where do I go now?"

"Go upstairs."

"Are you insane? There's. She's . . ."

"All right then, stay here for now. But if Aretas's men come in, you had best make haste."

The two of them left Saul standing with his mouth agape. Arieh slipped into the shop, leaving Saul to pace the workroom, weaving around barrels and tables. Saul had only made a few turns of the room when the men returned. Ananias strode up the stairs while Elazar sat at a workbench.

Finally, Elazar spoke. "Brother Saul, I fear the Lord will call you to step out into unknown territory tonight. Do you sense that too?"

Saul ran a hand through his hair, digging beneath his concern for Bina and the families who were at risk because of him. What was there? "Trapped," Saul replied. "That's what I sense. I can't stay here. But I can't escape while it's still daylight, either. I am not sure what I am to do. Perhaps I should have stayed in Petra. But no, that was impossible. Oh, Elazar, what am I to do? Where am I to go?"

Elazar's face softened, and he tilted his head. "Where do you want to go, Saul?" he asked.

Saul leaned against a wall, his arms hanging at his sides. "Home," he replied. "I want to go home."

"Tarsus?"

Saul shook his head. Tarsus had not been home for a long time. "Jerusalem."

Elazar's eyes misted. "Oh, Saul, you don't think you should, do you?"

"I don't know. I don't know! Probably not, but my heart aches for it."

Ananias and Bina trundled down the steps. Bina had changed

her clothing. Saul was concerned for her, but observed that she was in no distress. Once off the stairs, she bowed her head. "Brother Saul, I apologize."

He shook his head but did not know what to say.

"It has been cleaned up. You must come upstairs now. I have an idea of how to hide you until it is dark enough to go over the wall and escape. I have discussed it with my husband. Please, follow us upstairs."

Saul eyed Ananias with an unspoken question, who dipped his head. He did not appear thrilled about it, whatever her plan, but was agreeable.

Upstairs the curtains were all pulled back. Three separate beds nestled together on one side. But one bed, piled with pillows and blankets, sat in the far corner. Upon entering the room, that bed would be the first thing someone would spy. The women were preparing the area as if for bathing. They'd spread a couple of large bowls of water and a knife and twine at the foot of the bed. A knife?

Saul jerked his head toward Bina. She reached for some dark clothing draped on a chair and brought it to him. "Brother Saul," she said, holding out the clothing. "You will need to wear this over your cloak. Aunt Danya and I can help you if needed."

"What are you doing, Bina?"

"We are disguising you, Saul. You will pose as a birth attendant."

Aghast, he shook his head. "No, no, Bina. I—"

"Brother Saul."

Then, the familiar warmth filled him, the peace deep inside him. The presence of the Spirit. Saul closed his eyes against it, but a breeze caressed his face, brushing the hair from his eyes.

As he stood, trance-like, Bina and Danya pulled a large black robe over his head and then veiled his head and face. Then they positioned him at the head of the bed, his back to the stairwell.

"I will be propped up on the bed," Bina said. "You will hold a wet compress to my head, my neck, my face. My aunt will be at the other end, and I will be pretending that the baby is coming. No matter what happens, do not speak or turn around. Do you follow?"

Wordless, Saul locked eyes with her.

"Good. Brother Saul," she added, "look at me. You can do this. It will work."

Ananias clamped a hand on Saul's shoulder. "We will make a lot of noise if they enter, so you will know to get into your positions. You can do this. You must do it. Remember, she's only pretending. Don't panic or faint on us." With that, Ananias descended the stairs, leaving Saul alone with the women.

During the next couple of agonizing hours, Saul was not sure what was worse: Bina's pacing, interspersed with times she would stop and grit her teeth, soft growling sounds coming from her while she held her belly before straightening up to resume her pacing, or her aunt's resentful glares. Saul did not need her to tell him that he did not belong there.

He sat cross-legged on the floor, miserable. Bina had adjusted the veil so only his eyes were exposed, and the thick dark cloth was stifling. How did women endure this? He dropped his eyes to his hands.

I will call with all my heart, O Lord, and I will obey your decrees. I call out to you. Save me, and I will keep your statutes.

"Shhh!" Bina had stopped pacing. She faced the stairwell and raised her hand. Men's voices raised. Stomping footsteps. At once, Bina grabbed a cloth, dipped it in the water, and handed it to him after wringing out most of the water. Then she was on the bed. She grabbed his hand and placed it on her forehead. "Like this," she whispered.

Saul was horrified as Bina hiked her garments to her waist, and Danya was between her legs, the other woman at her side with towels. He concentrated on the compress and Bina's forehead, averting his eyes from anything else as Bina wailed.

The noises from downstairs grew louder. Ananias shouted, warning the intruders away from the upper room, but then boots pounded up the stairs. Bina grabbed her legs and screamed as Saul held the compress to her with vigor, his other hand on her back. It was so real that he was certain the child was coming.

Male gasps came from behind Saul, followed by retreating footsteps on the stairs. Ananias again shouted with anger before all was quiet.

Danya promptly replaced Bina's clothing and jumped off the bed. Saul sat back, open-mouthed, at the bravest person he'd ever met.

Ananias rushed up the stairs and gathered his wife in his arms, laughing.

"They are gone. Oh, Bina, you should have seen them. They were so scared you were having the baby in front of them. They nearly fell down the stairs."

Embarrassed, Saul thrust to his feet, yanking off the veil. He hurried to the stairs, Danya's scowl following him.

They waited until well after full dark. Arieh led the men in prayers, and they shared a meal. The women remained upstairs, and Saul noted less and less time between Bina's pacing overhead. "Will it be soon?" he asked.

"I am not sure," Ananias replied. "Last time, it took forever. I don't know how women can stand it. When she stops pacing in between her pains, it will probably not be much longer."

Elazar stood. "It should be dark enough now," he said. "If you are going to place some time between you and Malichus, it is best to go now."

Saul turned to Ananias. "You can't go with me now. I will have to go alone."

"I am sorry, Saul," he replied. "You are right. I can't leave my family now."

"How do we get to the roof?" Saul asked.

With a long length of rope in his hand, Arieh led the way. The curtains had been pulled, but Bina was still pacing.

She stopped to offer him the dark robe he had worn as a disguise. "You must wear this," she said. "It will hide you in the darkness. And take the veil. It may come in handy." She leaned up and kissed him on the cheek.

Saul flushed. He draped the dark robe on over his cloak, and they ascended the stairs to the roof.

On top of the house, darkness shrouded the men. Elazar held a lamp as Arieh and Ananias wrapped the rope around Saul, discussing how they would handle the ropes while Saul repelled toward the ground. The top of the wall was low enough for him to sit upon with his back to the outside of the city. Elazar held the bag of food and water he had prepared for him.

Despite the cool night air, Saul dripped sweat. He attempted to focus on the directions Ananias and Arieh were giving him, but the pounding of his heart drowned their voices. As a small child, he fell off a high wall and hurt his leg. Since then, panic filled him whenever he was near such a place. He did not want to admit his terror to his companions. *I can do this*. But then Ananias was in his face, and the roaring in Saul's ears crashed into his vision. Ananias took Saul's face in his hands.

"Saul! Do you hear me?"

Saul was too weak to respond.

"What's wrong? Here, get up." Ananias pulled him to his feet. "Don't turn around," he said. "Keep your eyes on your feet. Okay, now lift one foot."

Saul shook his head violently. "No, no, no!" he cried. "I can't. I can't!"

"Saul, you must. You have to."

"I can't! I—" Saul dropped to his haunches, his head lowered. "I'm sorry. I cannot."

The men stood in silence. Then Elazar said, "If only we had something to lower him in."

"I have just the thing," Arieh said. "I'll be right back."

By the time he returned, Saul's heart beat a little slower, and the lightness in his head was gone. Arieh carried a large, sturdy basket. He and Ananias secured the two ends of the rope to the basket, running it through the weaves on each side before securing it tight.

"You'll still have to get into the basket from the wall," Ananias said, "but you won't have to stand on the wall. Do you think you can make it?"

Saul believed so. He sat on the wall facing them and took in a deep breath. "I owe you my life."

"We will visit you in Antioch, my friend," Elazar answered.

"Remember." Ananias gripped Saul's shoulders. "Go as far west as you dare before heading north toward Aleppo. It will take more time, but it will be safer. Travel south, that way," Ananias pointed behind Saul, "until you no longer spy any light from the city, then head west, to your right."

"Thank you, friend. I shall." They held the basket over the wall, and Saul spun about, placing his feet in the basket.

"Turn back toward the wall."

"Oh, Saul!" Elazar said, handing him the bag of supplies. "You will need this. Use it sparingly."

"Goodbye, friend," Saul said, looping the bag over his head.

"I'm sorry for the trouble I have brought to your houses." Then Saul gripped the sides of the basket.

The sensation of being suspended in the air was bizarre, and the lightheadedness returned. He was lowered in jerks, but after what seemed an eternity, the basket hit solid ground, and he let out a long breath. He climbed out of the basket onto uneven ground and grasped the rope, giving it a couple of tugs. In the dark, he made out a shadow of the basket rising into the air.

Saul took in the inky darkness of the moonless night. He held the bag close and took a confident step. His right ankle gave way, and he fell.

Chapter Seven

It had been a long night, but Bina delivered a baby girl. About an hour after sunrise, Ananias peered at them as they slept, longing to join them, but he knew sleep would not come. Arieh and his son-in-law would be open for business after a brief morning meal, and he wanted to fetch fresh clothing for Bina and more swaddling for the baby.

Damascus was wide awake as Ananias walked the short distance to his home, pondering names for his daughter. He was torn between family names and one that would well represent her. He knew he should have wanted another boy, but Ananias had hoped for a girl who would have Bina's beauty and intellect. The Lord had surely blessed him with Bina. Without her, he was sure Saul would have been captured and killed already.

He thought of Saul and how horrified he had been, having to pass as a woman, enduring a laboring Bina, and then his fear of heights. Ananias wondered where the other man was at that moment and how long it would take him to get to Antioch. He would hate to leave Bina and the children, but after he rested up, he would head that way himself. Perhaps Elazar would go along.

The huff of a horse made Ananias halt. A series of horses stood, stamping their henna-painted legs. Four parallel lines clipped from each horse's flank marked them as mounts for Aretas's royal guard. Were they at his house? He checked the street, but it was empty. Ananias took a deep breath. To run and hide would indicate guilt. He had to face these men. And Saul was gone, so there was no one to find, no danger. Straightening his shoulders and whispering a prayer for strength, Ananias strode to the door of his house. The muffled sound of men tossing and breaking possessions reached him. He did not own much, but what he had was his. He opened the door and shouted. "What do you think you're doing?"

In the shadows, a man oversaw the others destroy Bina's kitchen. He turned toward Ananias standing in the doorway and sneered. "I've been told," the man said, "that I might find the tentmaker here. You know him."

The man was dressed for battle, and over his uniform, he wore a crimson cloak wrapped around his left arm. On his head, he wore a laurel wreath. "You are Malichus," Ananias said.

"Very good," he replied. "And what did Judas's warehouse manager tell me your name is? Annie, something?"

Ananias said nothing. The guards headed straight to his marriage bed, tearing up the mattress, feathers flying. Bina's mother had made that for them, a present for their wedding.

Malichus followed Ananias's gaze. He scoffed. "That's enough," he said. "They didn't sew the man into their bed." Then he turned back to Ananias. "Where is he?"

Ananias studied Malichus. It would be easy to hate this man. Arrogant, rude, maleficent. But Ananias did not have it in him, even as the man destroyed his humble home. Ananias cocked his head at him. What horrible things must this young man have already experienced in his life? What kind of childhood must he have had? All Ananias held for Malichus was pity.

Malichus's eyes narrowed as if reading the carpenter's mind, and then he was on him, thrusting his right hand around his throat. "Are you deaf as well as dumb, man? I asked you a question. Where is the tentmaker?" Malichus pushed him away, and Ananias fell on the floor, coughing.

"There is a workshop attached to the house," one of the guards said.

"Go search it. If he's not here, this man knows where he is." Malichus turned back and kicked Ananias, the blow forcing Ananias on his back.

Oh God, come to my assistance! Oh, Lord, make haste to help me! Ananias closed his eyes, the warmth of the Presence surrounding him.

"Get up!" Malichus snarled. "Be a man!"

Ananias rolled onto his hands and knees. He was out of breath and bruised, but he was not weak. He stood, straightening, and met Malichus's dark stare. "I don't know where he is," Ananias said. *I know where he was but not where he is now.*

"I don't believe you," Malichus spat. "You know where he is, you and your people are hiding him. He did not dare to face me in Petra, so he ran back to his witless friends here. I know he is here somewhere, and when I find him, I'll kill him. Then I will kill you for hiding him."

The oddest sensation came upon Ananias. While Malichus stood in shadows, the sunlight of day filtered into the tiny house through the open doorway, bathing Ananias in bright sunlight. The two guards hurried back from the workshop, holding Saul's tools and a scrap of black tent cloth. Voices came as if from a distance. Emotionless, his eyes followed Malichus as he drew his dagger from its sheath and accused him. An instant sharp gasp of searing pain ripped through him, but his brain barely recognized it. He hovered above the scene as Malichus pulled out the dagger and stabbed him again. His body crumpled to the floor. Malichus withdrew his dagger. Ananias entered the blinding brightness and was absorbed within it, leaving his body behind.

The sharp pain in his ankle was subsiding, but Saul remained motionless in the same position he had fallen into.

He was a fool. He had forgotten the large rocks around the base of the city walls on the desert side of Damascus. He sat up, his back to the wall, and surveyed to his left where the torch at the south gate glimmered. Nothing but darkness to his right. Ananias had encouraged him to go straight south as far as he was able before turning west toward the mountains. He threw off the veil to help with his vision. Time to try to navigate his way over the rocks and head south.

He stood with care, trying the ankle, and gingerly placed one foot at a time, struggling through the stone yard, seeking smoother stones, avoiding sharp angles. His arms circled wildly as he attempted to keep his balance. Finally, his feet reached dirt, and he straightened his shoulders. Saul checked for the torch at the gate every few minutes, and once the light was not visible at all, he paused. He was in the Golan Desert now. The mountain range would be to his right.

As Saul turned back to where he knew the city stood, a wave of emotion hit him. Though it may cost his life, he fought the urge to run back. He was lost and alone. He was not made for solitude. He was most comfortable while surrounded by the noisiness of life. Here, it was dark, it was empty, and it was silent.

A yip from over his shoulder startled Saul and he spun around. Jackal? Hyena? Unarmed and alone, cold fear filled him. *What am I doing out here?* His heart raced, and he took a deep breath to try to still it.

I lift up my eyes to the hills, from where will my help come? The towering shadows of the mountains framed against the dark sky. Saul headed toward them. *My help comes from the Lord, the maker of heaven and earth.* Amidst his fear and loneliness, Saul knew he was not really alone. Each step he took was a little braver. *The Lord is my shepherd. I lack nothing. He guides me in proper paths for his namesake. Even though I walk in the darkest valley . . .*

He trudged on until the shadows cast by the mountain range covered him. Obedient to Ananias's instructions, he headed north. It would not be long before he reached the road to Damascus, and he needed as much distance as possible between himself and that city, and quickly.

The moment his feet touched the road, Saul knew it, sensed the familiarity. Saul paused and closed his eyes, bathing himself in the memory of his first encounter with Christ. It may have been in this very spot, he mused. The brilliant light blinded him even in the daylight, the warmth of His presence burning like the sun, the energy emanating from Him. Even now, the bright light bored through his closed lids and heat simmered around him. Saul wanted to tear off the hot, dark robe. He thought he heard Yeshua call his name.

Saul.

Tears of joy ran down his cheeks. It was a memory that would forever be with him.

Saul.

He opened his eyes. This was not a vivid memory. Bathed in brilliant light was Yeshua, standing before him. Saul sank to his knees before bowing low to the ground. "My Lord and my God!" he managed.

Saul, get up. Go through the mountain pass and head to Jerusalem.

Saul scrambled up. "Jerusalem? But I am to go—"

You must go to Kepha. He is expecting you, to instruct you. Once you are outside of the city, I will send Barnabas to meet you. Saul, you will suffer much for my name, but your work has not yet begun. Now, go.

Saul turned toward the dark and overwhelming mountain pass.

Then Yeshua was gone. His presence lingered near him, however, and that was encouraging. He held on to that, and his heart soared. He was going home.

In the dark shadow of the mountain pass, he strode up the incline, climbing until he came to a place where the pass widened and flattened out. He recognized it as the spot where he and his company had stopped for a break nearly three years before. He was not surprised when he spied a young man sitting on the rock. He appeared to be waiting for him. "Stop here and rest," the young man said. "Sleep for a while. I will keep watch over you."

Saul asked no questions. He removed the bag from his shoulder, then took out a skin and drank. Rolling up the veil to use as a pillow, he lay on the ground and fell right to sleep.

Saul's eyes flickered open. He was on his side, the hint of sunrise in the mountain pass, its early sunbeams hitting the path from the east. Something slithered near him, and he jumped to his feet as an asp wriggled by. He searched for the young man, but he was gone. Saul rubbed his eyes. Perhaps he had never really been there. It was either an angel or his imagination. No matter. Saul was refreshed and had slept unmolested by animal or man.

He opened the bag and pulled out a date and some flatbread. After following his meal with more of the water, he took off the robe, tied it and the veil about his waist, and headed toward Caesarea, toward Jerusalem.

While it took him most of the day to get to Caesarea Philippi, he did not tarry there long. He refilled his skins, paid a road tax with some money Elazar had placed in the bag, bought some fresh fruit, and rested his legs for a little while. Then he carried on, filled with an energy he had not experienced since before Phineas's death.

The road bypassed the lake and then traversed through a couple of small towns before reaching Bethsaida. The journey would take him all night. He knew the road would be dangerous for sleeping, but he also knew his energy would flag if he did not get at least an hour or so of sleep. As the sun was setting, footsteps sounded behind him. He had met several groups of travelers after leaving the city, but they would pass around him. This time, as he gravitated to the side of the road, the single traveler also stopped and waited for him. Saul had re-donned the robe for warmth in the cool evening, so he pulled back the hood to get a better study of his companion. He recognized the young man from the previous night. "Should I stop for some sleep?" Saul asked.

The young man answered. "If you do, I will stand watch."

Saul left the road and neared a copse of trees. He laid beneath one of them and slept in peace.

When he woke, the man was gone once again. Refreshed, Saul set out heartened. Once through Bethsaida, he followed the road around the Sea of Galilee, traveling through towns, and then he followed the Jordan River south. Every night, as Saul slept for a few hours before going on his way, the young man would appear as Saul considered stopping to rest. Every night that is, until Saul met up with a group of pilgrims from Decapolis on their way to Jerusalem, who invited Saul to join them. Happy for the company, Saul traveled with them through Jericho. As they neared Bethany, the great city on the hill was not yet in his vision, but he knew it was near. Jerusalem was so close he almost smelled it.

His fellow travelers wanted to tarry in Bethany, but Saul longed to travel on. He bid them farewell, thanking them for their company. Driven, he hurried through the town, not stopping until he reached its western edge. There he stood, shading the afternoon sun from his eyes. His chest tightened, and his breath caught in his throat. Jerusalem stood shimmering on the horizon, like a mirage, sparkling. *Home.*

He broke into a run. Ignoring the fatigue in his legs, oblivious to the heat of the sun, he no longer noticed his parched lips and dry eyes. The road was full of travelers at this point, but Saul paid them no attention as he ran through or around them until the walls of the city rose before him. Someone stood before him. Saul shifted to one side, but the man shifted with him. Saul attempted to go around him, but again, the man blocked him. Annoyed, he tore his gaze from the city walls and scowled at the man barring his path. He met familiar eyes.

Chapter Eight

**Jerusalem, Judea
34 A.D.**

Barnabas had no trouble identifying Saul despite the mass of travelers on the road. While every person appeared road-weary and dusty, Saul wore the appearance like a garment. And if that hadn't been enough, Barnabas knew those eyes at once. He was also not surprised that it had taken longer for Saul to recognize him. That man only had eyes for the holy city.

Barnabas pulled him out of the way of traffic, off the road, and kept his voice low. "Cephas told us you would be coming from this way and sent me out to wait for you. I brought you a robe."

"I have one."

"Put it on, pull up the hood. Follow close behind me, don't use my name, and meet no one in the eye."

"But -"

"No." Barnabas laid his hand briefly on Saul's arm. "The city has a long memory. You will be recognized." He waited as Saul pulled on the robe and lifted the hood over his head. "You appear exactly the same as you did when you left Damascus almost three years ago. Scrawny, but healthy." Barnabas gave him an approving nod. "I am glad. You are alone?"

"Yes," Saul replied. "It was . . . necessary."

"Good. You can tell me about it later. Follow me."

As they wound their way through the busy streets of Jerusalem, Saul's hood concealed much of his face. Saul knew the way. *But, of course,* Barnabas thought. *He knows these streets even better than I do.*

Once deep in the residential area, Barnabas halted, searching around for anyone who may have followed them. When he reasoned they were clear, Barnabas addressed his companion. "Are you ready?"

"Absolutely," Saul replied.

Barnabas led him up a flight of stone stairs to a second-story living area, and he pushed open the door. Barnabas entered the house, stooping to remove his sandals. As Saul closed the door behind them, Barnabas's nephew hurried toward them.

"You found him!" John Mark exclaimed.

"Marcus," Barnabas said, "this is Saul. Saul, my nephew."

Grasping the bowl of water near the door, John Mark stooped before him.

"I can do that," Saul said.

"No, sir," John Mark answered. "It is my privilege to serve you." Obediently, Saul removed his robe and sat. After his nephew untied the laces of Saul's leather shoes and laid them on the floor, Barnabas picked up one of them, curious. He turned the shoe over, examining it. "Interesting," he said, "whoever made this sewed a leather upper to an existing sandal." Then he stuck his hand inside and wiggled a finger through a hole in its sole. "You've managed some distance on this. I can fix this for you, should you like."

"Thanks," Saul replied, "but, given the correct tools, so can I."

"That's right," Barnabas said, placing the shoe back on the floor next to its twin. "I forgot. You're a leather worker also."

As John Mark had washed and was drying their feet, the doorway opposite them darkened with a familiar presence, and Barnabas stood. "Cephas."

Saul lunged to his feet, taking in the man opposite him.

"Saul." Simon Peter's arms were crossed.

"Kepha." Saul exhaled the man's name.

Barnabas held his breath. The hesitancy was maddening as neither man moved. Then Saul let out his breath, barely audible, and reached for the other man. Simon Peter's thick, muscular arms engulfed the slight, road-weary Saul of Tarsus. The embrace was swift, and then Simon Peter chuckled.

"Welcome to our home, Saul," he boomed. "You must be exhausted, thirsty, and hungry. Barnabas, Marcus, the table is ready. Let's eat!"

They followed him into the adjoining room, where the table was prepared with bowls of dried fruit and nuts and cups for the wine already on the table. All but Saul sat. He remained standing, waiting on his host.

"Sit here next to me," Simon Peter said. Saul hesitated, indicating his clothing and his hands. "It's all right. We will wash our hands at the table."

"I could use a bath," Saul replied. "I bathed in the river, but that was a couple of days ago."

Another deep, hearty laugh came from their host. "Saul," he said, "you worry too much. We've been expecting you. Yeshua told me you were coming from Damascus. We all knew you would want to wash up. But we've held the meal for you, and I'm starving. Let's eat first. Sit. Tell us your story since leaving Damascus for Petra. After all that, then you can wash off and get into some fresh clothes."

Saul sat. The entire room had turned a shade of pink from the setting sun. Simon Peter's daughter entered the room and lit the lamps. Her grandmother brought in a large bowl of stew and a stack of bread. Then she poured the wine into the cups before the two women sat at the opposite end of the table. Barnabas breathed it all in.

At that moment, the trumpet signifying sundown blared from the Temple. A low, guttural sound came from Saul's throat. The man stood and closed his eyes. He raised both his arms, palms up, tears streaming. He stood like that, as in a trance, and opened his mouth and sang.

Saul splashed water on his face, washing the sleep away. The morning sun lit the room with its warmth and Saul whispered a word of praise.

He had been a guest in Simon Peter's home for less than a

week. Though he felt less like a guest and more like a prisoner. Saul did not leave the house, and, other than when Cephas attended the meeting at the Temple, Saul's host was his constant companion. They spent all day and well into the night, Simon Peter telling him the stories of Yeshua, of their travels together, of Yeshua's teachings. The more Saul learned, the more questions he had, hungering for details.

Saul thought he knew Yeshua's teaching, as he had used some of his words against him. At one time, he believed that Yeshua hated the Temple and all of Jerusalem and that he had preached against the Law. But he realized that Yeshua had a far more complete understanding of the Law without the extensive education that Saul had received. Not only that, but Yeshua had also been drawn to the holy city and loved it as much, if not more, than Saul. The fact that the city Yeshua loved so much was the one to kill him filled Saul with shame and regret. Yet it was also the city of Yeshua's greatest triumph. Without his death, there would be no resurrection. And Saul now knew there most certainly was a resurrection. The stories of the many who experienced him, who saw him afterward, were the ones Saul most hungered for. Yeshua had once even appeared to over five hundred believers, all at the same time! How could Saul, the other scribes, members of the Sanhedrin, and the high priest himself scoff at those reports?

While Saul held rapt attention, he found the days exhausting. At night, when Simon Peter would finally yawn and stretch, Saul fell onto his pallet gladly and was asleep in a moment.

He reached for a clean tunic and pulled it over his head. As he smoothed his hair, he was again filled with wonder over being called. *Why did you choose me, Lord?*

Yeshua's choice of Kepha was understandable. A fellow Galilean with similar interests. But more than that, Saul found a good heart and soul in the former fisherman, a leader of the apostles, faithful, loyal, and devoted to Yeshua. *Not a sinner like me.*

The trumpet called out, time for morning prayer. Oh, how Saul wished to go with Cephas to the Temple. Seven times a day, his heart was pierced with the sound of the calls to prayer. But the horn blasts were also a blessing. Were it not for them, he might forget where he was.

Even greater than his desire to be on the Temple grounds, Saul ached to leave the house. He was discouraged from standing by the windows for fear of being spied from the street or a house across the way. Saul wanted to scoff at the idea. He had made it into the city without being recognized. He had trouble believing it would hurt to go for a short walk. All he did was eat, learn, and sleep. But he had a knack for placing his friends and hosts in danger. The last thing he wanted to do was stir up trouble for Cephas and Barnabas.

On the morning of the Sabbath, Simon Peter did not go to the Temple. Saul assumed they would all go to a synagogue and leave him alone in the house. But Simon Peter would not hear of it.

"If the rest of you want to go, then go," he said. "I will stay here with our guest."

Barnabas and John Mark also opted to stay. They praised God together. Saul quoted passages from both the Law and the Prophets. Barnabas gave a reflection on the words of the prophet, and Simon Peter led them in hymns of praise. It was not the same as being in synagogue, and the women in the house sat in the same room. Their presence during worship no longer made Saul nervous, and he had, in fact, begun to appreciate them. Being away from Jerusalem these last three years had eased him into relaxing some of his strict observances.

After worship, they all sat at the table. Simon Peter took the bread, broke it, and said, "On the night in which he gave himself up for us, he took the bread, broke it, gave thanks to God, and gave it to us. He said, take, eat, for this is my body, given for you and the sins of the world." Simon Peter handed half to Saul, and Saul's eyes filled with tears. He started to hand the entire piece to John Mark, but Simon Peter took it back, broke off a piece, and laid it in Saul's hand. "Brother Saul," he said, "his body was broken for you."

Saul shook his head. "I'm not worthy of his sacrifice. I have sinned."

"So have I. So have we all."

"No," Saul argued, "not like I have. I worked against him, plotted against him. There is blood on my hands!"

Simon Peter wrapped his right arm around Saul and took his hand, pressed the piece of bread into it, and closed his hand for him.

"Did I tell you about the time I denied even knowing him? While he was being tortured and mocked? Saul, there are no small sins or big sins. Sin is sin, and his blood has washed all of it away.

'Cleanse me with hyssop, and I shall be clean.' He has done more than that for you and for me. And he has chosen you to teach others. He chose sinful men for his purpose. Eat, and let me tell you about the last Passover meal we had together."

Saul took a bite. As he chewed, he thought of his encounters with Yeshua. He took a sip of his wine, and Simon Peter started his story.

"We entered this very room, about twenty-five or thirty of us, men and women. Lazarus's sister Mary had taken the bathing bowl." He indicated with a piece of bread he had dipped into the bowl of stew, dripping in front of Saul, "And young Marcus here, he had grabbed a towel. But Yeshua took the towel from him, wrapped it around himself, and then took the bowl from Mary. Well, when his intention was clear, I balked. 'Lord," I said, 'do you intend to wash my feet? I don't think so!'"

Simon Peter removed his arm from Saul as he ate the piece of dripping bread, drank from his cup, grabbed another piece, and continued. "Yeshua threw me a look, one that I received often, let me tell you. I believe I vexed him often. Anyway, he locked eyes with me and said, 'You cannot understand what I am doing now, but you will later.' I said, 'You will never wash my feet!' It was my place to wash *his* feet. But he said to me, 'Unless I wash you, you will have no part of me.'" Simon Peter clapped Saul on the shoulder, nearly causing him to choke on the food he was swallowing. "So, I said, 'Lord, not only my feet but then also my hands and head!'"

Saul covered his mouth with his hand. While the others at the table found humor in the story, Saul committed the story to memory. What would he have done in the same situation? Would he have allowed his Lord and Savior to play the role of a house servant? He regarded Cephas and wished he had been there with this man.

"What he then told us," Simon Peter continued, "was that he was setting an example for us. He said, 'If I, your Lord and Rabbi, have washed your feet, you ought to wash one another's feet. Whoever receives one whom I send receives me.'" He paused. "He sent you to me, Saul. I have been assigned the mission to teach all whom he has sent. But I learn from each and every one of you as well. Tell us again how Yeshua called you."

Saul was still pondering what Simon Peter had said about denying Yeshua during the peak of his suffering. It's not the same, he thought glumly. Anyone would have done the same thing. But then he remembered. He remembered how a handful of women and Lazarus stayed with Yeshua to the bitter end. He remembered hearing at the time with great satisfaction how all the other followers, and the disciples in particular, fell away like frightened sheep. "Strike the shepherd, that the sheep may be scattered," he quoted.

Simon Peter sobered and dipped his head.

"Zechariah. His prophecy. Of course, you all left him."

"I didn't leave him," Simon Peter said. "Not initially, that is. Not until I denied him, and three times, at that."

"It's not the same. You had to deny him. That fulfilled the prophecy."

"Stop defending me, lawyer. It is the same."

Saul drank it all in. Simon Peter possessed the qualities equipping him for his position. Outspoken. Loyal. Hardnosed. He may not have been the first to recognize Yeshua as the anointed one, but he was ideal as a spokesman and solid. Like his nickname.

Simon Peter pointed a hand holding a large bite of bread at Saul. "Brother Saul." The bread was dipped into the stew before Simon Peter tossed it into his mouth. Still chewing, he added, "It's your turn."

Saul raised his thick eyebrows. "Very well." He took another sip of wine and dabbed at his mouth with a towel. "Let me tell you a story." He eyed each person at the table, one by one, his eyebrows raised, the corners of his mouth tugging upward. "It's a long story." He leaned forward as if to tell a secret. "But it's a good one."

Saul had been with them for almost twelve days. Twelve days to convince them he would be fine alone in the house while they all headed to the Temple.

From the window, Saul waited until they were safely out of sight. Then he threw on the dark robe Bina had dressed him in back in Damascus, and, throwing up the hood, he eased the door open and hurried to the street. He knew the way.

Minutes later, he arrived at the house. He paused,

reconsidering for a moment. Then he rapped on the door. He waited a few moments and, hearing nothing inside, knocked again. He kept his back to the street. The door opened. The woman's face displayed confusion for a moment before his sister recognized him. She gasped, surveyed the street, and then grabbed his arm, pulled him inside, and slammed shut the door.

"Saul?" she breathed.

He pulled back the hood with a flourish. "Sarah."

She brought him in for an embrace and held him for longer than was comfortable before she pulled away from him. "You shouldn't be here. Everyone was searching for you. What did you do, Saul, that made them all so angry? Why can't you stay out of trouble? I've been so worried for you, not knowing if you were dead or alive."

Saul was delighted. Always his older sister, the mother hen. "What? No 'come in, Brother, have a seat, may I get you something to drink?'"

She frowned and crossed her arms. "Not a single word from you, only all the grumbling from my husband. The Temple is abuzz about Saul, the Traitor. Did you know there's a price on your head?"

"I hope it's high enough to make you a rich woman when you turn me in."

"Oh, stop it! Don't you know if any of the neighbors saw me let a strange man in my house while my husband is away—"

"Raz is not here?" She shook her head. "He and Lavi are at the Temple this morning, then they will go to the marketplace. It's only me and Chava here."

"No house servants? Did you dismiss them?"

She gave an exasperated sigh. "Of course, I have house servants, silly. They're working hard in the kitchen, preparing for Sabbath tonight. I happened to hear the door. And thank the Lord I did!" She glanced behind her as if expecting one of her servants to be standing there. "You can't stay, brother. I am serious about the price on your head. This city is a dangerous place for you. What are you doing here? What did you do to get yourself in so much trouble?"

"I had to come to the city for business. I couldn't be in Jerusalem and not see my sister."

"You haven't answered my question."

Saul took her by the arms. "I left Jerusalem in pursuit of the Nazarene's followers. On the way." He paused. "On the way, I encountered him."

Sarah's brows squeezed together and she gave a little of her head. "Him who?"

"Yeshua."

She shook her head. "I don't understand. He was crucified, correct? Charged with treason?"

"The same one."

"But how?"

"I am a follower of the Way now, myself," he replied.

Sarah's mouth dropped open. "I don't understand. The people you drove out of Jerusalem, you became one of them? Saul, that doesn't make sense."

Saul shrugged. "I know. But it's true. Sarah, Yeshua is the long-awaited Messiah."

"But he was killed, dead!"

"That trick of raising his friend, Lazarus? That was nothing. I know." Saul held up a hand. "It doesn't make sense. But all the prophets spoke of the Messiah, not only as the conquering king but also as the suffering servant. And He called me to teach others the good news of his saving grace. Sarah," he added, holding her gaze. "Believe me, I know it sounds crazy. But you, too, must believe. Please. Next time Raz goes to the Temple, go with him, take the children with you. Go to the gathering at the Beautiful Gate and seek out the one they call Kepha. Listen to what he has to say."

"Saul." Sarah shook her head. "You can't stay in Jerusalem. It is very dangerous for you. Do you have a plan of where to go?"

He studied her face. It was if she hadn't aged a bit. "I'm not sure where I am to go next."

"You need to go home."

"I am home."

"No," she said, "home, to Tarsus."

"There's nothing in Tarsus for me."

"Mother is there."

"And Father."

Sarah bowed her head. "No, Father is dead. Our uncles are going to take over the house and lands unless you show up to claim them."

Saul's eyebrows pulled together, crinkling his forehead. "What? They would put Mother out of the house?"

Sarah's head shot back up. "I did not know where you were to give you the news."

"Tarsus." Saul spat the word. He had not returned to his boyhood home since he came to Jerusalem to study. He had few fond memories there. Saul's sole desire had always been Jerusalem, to be here, to thrive here. But now . . .

"A price on my head, you say? Who's paying?"

Sarah shrugged. "I assume Caiaphas."

"The high priest himself?"

"I'm not sure, Saul. All I know is you're in a lot of trouble, and you can't stay in the city, and you shouldn't come back. Certainly not if you've joined the Yeshua group."

"But, Sarah. *Tarsus*?"

She pulled his hands into hers. "Mother needs you. Remember how she always supported you against Father and his wishes? I am worthless for her in this, except to offer her a home here with us if our uncles push her out. Saul, please!"

He took his sister into his arms and held her, wordless. They stood like that until a little girl's face peeked around at him. "You said you have a daughter?" he asked.

Sarah pulled away and turned, reaching for the girl. "Chava, this is your uncle, Saul."

The wide-eyed child stared at him for a moment before hiding in her mother's robe. Saul's face beamed. "Chava," he said. "She's lovely, like her mother."

"Saul," Sarah said, "you must go. You've been in here long enough for me to be the talk of the city by nightfall, and I'll be a ruined woman. If I'm to keep you a secret, you have to go, and you'll have to leave the city. Promise me you'll go home to Tarsus. Promise me you'll help Mother." She slipped the hood of his robe onto his head and kissed him. "I've missed you, Brother. But you must go. Promise?"

"I can't promise, Sarah. Only if the Lord sends me there. I have to do what he tells me to do."

"Then I will pray he sends you home." She opened the door and stood, blinking in the sunlight. "Keep the hood on, and don't speak to anyone in the street. Now, go!"

He turned back to memorize the moment, in case this was the last time they met. "Goodbye, Sarah."

"How many days have you been back in Jerusalem now, Saul? What does this make it?"

"Twelve days, Kepha," he replied.

Simon Peter seated himself and leaned in close to Saul. "Do you think it has been a productive twelve days? I know you are used to far superior schooling than what I can possibly offer, but I hope I have served you sufficiently."

Saul worried a loose thread on his tunic. Simon Peter had divulged firsthand stories that only he could tell and in such a detailed manner that Saul sensed the spray of the water or the hot sun burning down on him. "More than sufficient. Kepha, I must admit to you, I thought a day's worth of instruction was all I would require." He raised his head. "But I think it would take months, if not years, to learn all I need to know from you."

Simon Peter sat back, beaming. "Good," he said, "I was afraid I may have bored you."

"No one can ever accuse you of being boring."

"So, I have detailed Yeshua's teachings. I have told you stories of his healings and other works, as well as details of the week leading up to his crucifixion and death. I've told you about his time with us after. Correct?"

"Yes, Kepha, all of that."

"Before and after. I will forever mark time from that point. Not when I met him. Not his death. That was all before. Not when he was taken up from us. That was after. That first day of the week, after the worst Sabbath of my life. That was when time began for me."

Barnabas and John Mark entered the room and sat near them. "I wish I had been there," Saul said.

Simon Peter shook his head. "You were."

Saul dropped his head and heat flushed his face. "I wish I had been with you, adoring him, not opposing him."

"Yes, brother Saul," Simon Peter dropped his volume, "I know you do. But you are here with us now, and that's what matters. Have I answered your questions? What more can I tell you?"

"You've clarified my questions as we have gone along, Kepha. Is our time together drawing to a close?"

"I fear it is, Saul, and I'll tell you why. I have told no one about your presence here. The only people who know are the people in this house. But twelve days is a long time to keep someone like you a secret. To be with you as much as possible, I have let other responsibilities slip, and it has been noticed."

Saul's thoughts went to Phineas, and Safir, to Elazar and Ananias. He grew concerned. "Has my presence here brought danger to you and your household?"

Simon Peter shook his head. "No, no danger. But my absence has been questioned by James, the brother of the Lord. It was time to let him know. So, I invited him to our house today to learn for himself what has been more important than the other things competing for my time."

"James?" asked Barnabas.

"Here?" added John Mark. "Is he staying for the meal? Should I let—"

"Yes, please, let her know."

John Mark scrambled out of the room. Saul thought back, remembering something of James. He recalled the man as softspoken and unobtrusive. Why should this be someone he must meet? "He is not one of the Twelve, is he?"

Simon Peter shook his head. "No," he answered. "But he is a leader of us, nonetheless. Much like you, he was called by Yeshua after."

"His own brother?"

"He may tell you about it, but knowing James and his humility, he may not. He believes his refusal to take his brother seriously was as much a betrayal as was mine. He tells the story that at one point after their father was dead, none of the brothers wanted to take his mother into their homes. They tracked Jesus down. They wanted to remind him that she was his responsibility. But the crowd around him was so great they were unable to reach him. The brothers left her there to follow with the women in our group. But then Yeshua appeared to James after his resurrection, and it changed his life. Yeshua assigned him to the Temple to convince as many as possible there, to prepare the way for him to return."

"The Temple."

"James carries a great guilt," Simon Peter continued. "Like you and I, we've argued about which of us had the greater sin. He contends that his denial of accepting Yeshua all those years, not until he appeared to him, resurrected from the dead, is a much greater sin than my denying him three times."

"You should have been there." Barnabas interrupted. "Two grown men attempting to out-guilt the other."

Saul shook his head. "And then, along came Saul the Persecutor, the chief of sinners. I have you both beat in that arena. So, James has taken on the Temple as the focus of his work. And the Twelve?"

Simon Peter spread his hands. "Jerusalem, and the Dispersion."

The two men gauged each other. There was a reason Saul was sent here. Yeshua had first sent him not to Damascus but to Ananias. The second time, he was sent, not to Jerusalem, but to Simon Peter. The Dispersion, cities all over the world, where God's chosen people resided. Damascus, Antioch, Tiberius. *Tarsus.* "And where, do you suppose," Saul asked, "should be my focus?"

"I do not know," Simon Peter answered. "But I suspect he is preparing you for great work."

Saul sat back and lifted his eyes to the ceiling. "I've always had a home. First, Tarsus, a great city. But then I came to Jerusalem, and it has been a solid foundation in my life. High priests and Roman procurators come and go, yet Jerusalem is a constant. I know this city like it is a part of my body." He paused. "I have loved her like a wife. And Nicolaus was right. I adore the Temple. It has pierced my heart being here, what with the calls to prayer, to smell the Temple on all of you, knowing it is so close. I want to run to it, to have my feet touch its stones, to be surrounded by the praying, the talking, the bleating of sheep, the singing! But here I sit, like a babe waiting in the womb to be born, wondering if and when I shall ever be able to be a part of it again. As much experience as I have, knowing the ins and outs of the Temple as I do, every nook and cranny, why wouldn't Yeshua assign *me* to the Temple? Or you? You have been his right hand from the moment he called you. Why would he choose a brother who had rejected him, who didn't hear his teachings firsthand, who didn't suffer traveling with him, who didn't experience the arrest, the torture, and the death as you did?"

Saul sensed the presence in the doorway. There was John Mark with a man in a well-worn robe. Simon Peter jumped up. "James!" he exclaimed.

Saul stood, flushed. He searched James's face, wondering how long he had been standing there, how much had been overheard.

"James, come in, come in!" Simon Peter said, guiding him to have a seat with them. "Are you thirsty, may we get you—"

"Is this who I think it is?" James interrupted, his eyes boring unwaveringly on Saul.

Simon Peter's face displayed a plea for decorum. Saul did not hesitate to close in on James. "I've longed to meet you. I am Saul."

"I know who you are."

"James," Simon Peter said, "please, come in and sit with us. Let my guest tell you firsthand how he happens to be here."

"Shimon." James gave a slow and distinct reply. "Do you know how this man's presence threatens us all? Not only you or your household, but all of us? Do you know how hard I have worked to build relationships at the Temple?"

"Yes, we are all aware of your diligent work," Simon Peter answered. "And yes, I know the dangers. As does Saul. He has been careful to remain hidden here despite his strong desire to go to the Temple to visit old friends and family. Now, please? Greet our fellow brother in faith, who is here on the direction of Yeshua himself."

"Yeshua?" James asked, turning back to Saul. "Is that so?"

"Yes. I was on my way to Antioch from Damascus. He reappeared and sent me here to meet with Kepha to be instructed by him. I would not have come, knowing the dangers. But where he sends me, I have learned to go."

As the honored guest, James was seated before the others joined him. "Saul," James said, "the story of your change of heart was relayed to us from Barnabas here. That is quite the tale. Very dramatic."

"It was not an easy experience," Saul replied. "As Yeshua said to me, 'It's hard to kick against the goads.'" He spread his hands. "Ever see a stubborn ass kick against a goad as someone tries to prod it onward? Well, that is easier than changing the mind of this one."

Simon Peter and Barnabas chuckled, but Saul noted that James did not. It was clear it would take more than a joke for James to warm up to him.

"James." Saul took in a deep breath. "I was convinced that Yeshua was a blasphemer. And his followers? Worse than that. When Stephen declared in the synagogue that as Abraham was made righteous through his faith alone, those who called on the name of Yeshua were made righteous? I could not abide it! He claimed that Yeshua's sacrifice eliminated the need for burnt offerings, which I took as blasphemy against the Temple itself. I felt a deep obligation to stop him, to quench that fire before it became unmanageable. As a lawyer and scribe, I know the Law like few others, and as a Pharisee, I loved the Law more than my body. But destroying Stephen was not enough for me. I would not be satisfied until the heretics were all punished, and fleeing from Jerusalem only prompted me to run after them. I was on my way to Damascus to weed them out and throw them all on the fire!"

James's head was tilted, and he leaned in toward Saul. His hands relaxed in his lap. Saul continued. "My company paused for a rest right before exiting the mountain pass. I challenged Yeshua to try to stop me. And stop me, he did.

"But he did more than that. He broke me like a wild horse. Then, as I lay groveling on the floor amidst my disgrace, he lifted me and saved me. Me! I narrowly escaped capture in Damascus because of my zeal for him, and he saved me once again. Then, in Petra and again in Damascus, over and over, he rescued me. And then, believe it or not, he sent me here. Where I go from here, I do not know. All I know is this: he is training me to go where he leads and to rely on his judgment, not my own."

James ran a finger around the rim of his untouched cup. "I was skeptical when I heard that the persecutor was now preaching the good news. But the attitude of the Temple priests and the other scribes had convinced me that you had certainly done something that made you a traitor in their eyes. I fear for your safety here, Saul. The Temple and Jerusalem itself have become a hostile place for you. There may come a day, perhaps when there is a new chief priest and the Sanhedrin has turned over, that they will forget about you. But there were rumors that you had returned. That means someone must have seen you, or someone in this household has talked."

"None of us have said anything," Simon Peter replied. "I can assure you that."

Barnabas and John Mark chimed in, both swearing they had told no one.

"It may have been one of your women," James said.

"It does not matter who at this point," Saul interrupted. "The fact remains that they have a suspicion. I understand that there is a price on my head." As soon as the words were out of his mouth, Saul regretted them.

"Who told you that?" Simon Peter thundered.

Saul swallowed and hung his head. "I'm sorry, Kepha. It was irresistible. A few houses away from my only sibling and not check on her? So, this morning—"

"You left this house?" Simon Peter shouted. "Don't you know—"

"Of course, I know how dangerous it was. How long could you remain this close to your kin

and not see them?"

"For Yeshua, I gave up everything. And so should you!"

James held up his hands. "Shimon. Saul. Please, stop!"

The two men scowled at each other but were quiet. "That is better," James said. "Yes, Saul, your sister told you correctly. There is a price on your head. There remains little else for us to do now but to get you out of Jerusalem and soon."

"Kepha," Saul said, "I am so sorry." He reached out a hand and laid it on Simon Peter's. The man flinched but did not swipe it away. "I resisted the Temple as well as the synagogue. But I didn't know when or if I may ever see my sister again. I wasn't thinking. Rather, I thought only of myself and not of you or the others. I will find my way out of Jerusalem so as not to burden you further."

Simon Peter took his time before he answered, studying Saul. "You are not a burden, Saul. Just." He sighed. "A handful."

"Where will you go?" Barnabas asked.

Saul had not known for certain until the words came tumbling out of his mouth. "Home, to Tarsus. My father is dead, and my mother is about to lose the house and business. I am her only son, so I must go and claim my property."

"Then you must go," Barnabas said.

"How will you get there?" Simon Peter asked. "It's a long way on foot."

"My brother-in-law is a merchant. He has connections with ships that travel back and forth from Tarsus to Caesarea on a regular basis. You know that beautiful black Tarsian tent cloth in the marketplace? That's thanks to Raz. If we can send word to him that we have something, or someone, who needs to be hurried out of Jerusalem and on to Tarsus, I know he will accommodate us."

"He is not a follower of Yeshua, is he?" James asked.

Saul smirked. "Not yet. But he will be."

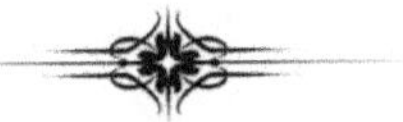

Saul stood on the deck of the ship, leaning against the starboard rail. Wind swept past him as it filled the center mast sail, and the waters of the sea lapped against the ship, sending fine spray on his face. He inhaled the aroma of it. The wood, the rope, and the sea itself mingled to remind him of the times he sailed with his father back and forth to Caesarea in Judea. It had been so many years, but the tangy odors brought those memories rushing to the forefront of his mind.

It had taken little convincing that the sole brother of his wife not only needed rescuing but should get to Tarsus urgently. The very next day, Saul had traveled to Caesarea with Raz. Getting out of Jerusalem had been as easy as getting in.

Loneliness descended as the port city receded from his sight. He gladly left Tarsus those many years ago, never intending to return. He also had ambiguous feelings about his father's death. Were it not for the support of his mother, Saul would not have become a scribe to the Sanhedrin but rather would have been stuck as a tent maker and leather worker in Tarsus.

He was more than ready to visit with his mother again. He owed her a great debt. If he had to leave Jerusalem anyway, it should be to claim his inheritance and allow her to stay in her home. It was his responsibility to both her household and Father's businesses.

Saul was almost glad to be away from the trumpet blast, seven times a day, calling him to prayer. Fifteen days in the house of Simon Peter, yet not able to go to the Temple itself was heartbreaking. Better to be away without the constant reminders.

Caesarea had disappeared on the horizon as the billowing sail distanced him and his old life. He turned away then and set his face north.

Chapter Nine

Tarsus, Cilicia
40 A.D.

It had been a hot, muggy summer. To escape it, Saul often rode up on the slopes of the mountains. He sat straight-backed on his horse, his view downhill toward the city of his birth.

His vision swept past the building, hugging the foothills, and followed the path of the river as it ran through the heart of Tarsus. The third largest city in the entire Roman empire, with all its history, the very meeting place of Cleopatra and Marc Antony, and its clash of cultures, where West meets East was his hometown. The menagerie of humanity huddled together on the banks of the crystal-clear River Cydnus before it emptied into the harbor and twisted to flow into the great sea. Long before Alexander the Great, they had drained the marshes and formed the harbor to provide a safe place from pirates. This made it an ideal port city, and despite the low, flat character of Tarsus, without a decent hill to build an acropolis, the city was full of everything else that made a Roman city great.

And yet.

Saul scanned beyond the city as if to see, shining in the distance, the center of Jewish existence. The connection between Jerusalem and the influential Hebrew presence in Tarsus was vibrant, and Saul had always been a part of it, raised in the affluent tribe of which his father had been prominent. He shifted his weight, and as he did, so his horse side-stepped only once. Upon his return to Tarsus six years prior, he had been surprised to learn how vast his father's business had become. Frustrated with delays in the process of obtaining quality cloth, his father had acquired flocks of the longhaired goats native to the area and then rehired the same goat herders to tend them. He bought out the weavers of the cloth and hired salesmen to sell all the cloth they produced above and beyond what his father required. Shortly before his death, his father hired the tanners to gain control of all the raw materials for his trade. The *cilice*, the tent cloth of Cilicia, was nearly synonymous with his father's name.

Saul sensed his mare's restlessness, and he leaned forward to pat her on the neck. He was reminded of the irony of her, his prized possession. Not long after arriving home, he learned of some Nabatean horses for sale in the livestock market. The mare had chosen him, her eyes following him as he drew near. He learned she was from the stables of none other than King Aretas in Petra, and Saul was determined to take her home. He named her Jameleh so that he may never forget. He required a constant reminder of how, in an instant, a person's life can be made or ruined, even by an innocent look, smile, or remark. He never wanted to forget that young girl and prayed for her every day, hoping she was safe and at peace. As a princess, a safe and happy life was very unlikely.

Saul directed the rein, and she turned toward the ridge. As a bank of dark clouds glided over and cast a shadow over them, a sense of unease arose inside him. For a few weeks now, a recurring dream plagued him. While the setting may differ and characters meld from those he knew to strangers, the theme was consistent. He would find himself alone at the center of an enraged crowd. As they shouted, fists raised in anger, he would trip, fall backward, or be thrown to the ground. It terrorized Saul as they raised stones and hurled them at him. Initially, the pain of the stones pounding against his body would wake him, but as the dreams recurred, the torment lasted longer and longer, and he would curl into a ball, throwing his hands over his head to try to shield himself. Eventually, the hail of stones would stop, and he would lower his hands, raising his head. Blood dripping into his eyes, he would make eye contact with one man, always one man. Sometimes the man morphed into Stephen, holding a stone and then tossing it up, catching it, never breaking eye contact. But recently, the man turned into the One on the cross, with sad, deep eyes and blood dripping down them in response.

Saul would wake up in a sweat, haunted by the images etched into his mind and with a restlessness deep in his soul. While never one to sit still for very long, this fitfulness was different. It left him with a sense of alarm, danger, loneliness, and fear.

Contemplating the dreams, he reasoned they were a reaction to his relative success in forming small communities of believers. In the neighboring cities of Mallos and Adana, where the citizenry was suspicious of anyone from Tarsus, he had preached and taught in the synagogues, convincing some that Jesus was the Christ, the anointed one for whom they had awaited. He had baptized them, organized them, and bred leaders among them. Saul visited as often as he dared, sensing disapproval from synagogue leaders. He had yet to be banished from their synagogues, unlike many of those in Tarsus where he was no longer welcome. Bad enough that he was one of the richest Hebrews in the city, but he was considered the upstart, wayward son of one of their most loyal and most philanthropic of their dearly departed.

Saul lifted his head to the sky, where the clouds gathered. The temperature had dropped, and he sensed impending precipitation. He reached behind and pulled out a cloak, throwing it around his shoulders. Thinking of his father tended to bring a chill as if the man was still imposing his oppressive will on his son. Saul followed the path over the ridge and into the short hollow at the foot of the mountain. He had come up to find the goatherds as an excuse to get away. Not that they required supervision. Raising and watching over the goats was something they knew far better than he. But checking in gave him a sense of purpose and importance. Every aspect of his father's operation was maintained by seasoned and capable managers, all who reported to the administrator, a man Saul respected and trusted. Saul was nearly useless.

He knew enough that if it was going to rain, the goats would make for a nearby cave, hating the rain as they do. He headed west, the Taurus mountains looming up at his right, where he assumed he would find them.

Between Antioch, Syria, and Tarsus

John Mark kicked at a rock on the road. It bounced off a paving stone before skittering off sideways. "If we're stopping at each town on the way," he muttered, "I don't know why we have to take along a tent and bedrolls."

"While I am prepared to exchange leather work for coin or a bed, we need to be prepared to face the elements, Marcus."

"But, Uncle, a caravan left the city not an hour before us! Why couldn't we ride along with them to Tarsus?"

"You know the answer to that. They would have charged us four times the road tax and still forced us to go by foot. Those folks don't like our kind. Best try to save what little money we have."

They left the city of Antioch behind, following the Roman road toward the Syrian Gates in the mountains. The ground already had a hint of an incline, and Barnabas's calves burned. He lifted his head to the mountain, disappointed that it still seemed so far away. The mountains appeared so close to the city you could touch them, but reaching on foot would take some time.

Barnabas's thoughts wandered to the send-off they had been given, each of the elders placing their hands on their heads, sparing a little bit of myrrh oil. They had blessed them before they set out and given them what little money they had left in their coffer. "Saul will replenish it," Nicolaus had said. "I have a feeling he's got it to spare."

"If he agrees to return with us to Antioch, are you hesitant to see him again?" Barnabas had asked.

"No," Nicolaus had responded, "the Spirit has given me peace. I only hope Saul has received peace as well."

Barnabas remembered how frightened Nicolaus had been in Damascus, afraid of the mean-hearted Saul of Tarsus, the lion of a man who had burned with zeal for the Law. He compared that image to the sober, humbled man Barnabas had met at the home of Ananias and then again in Jerusalem a few years ago, and he wondered how much Saul may have changed since they met.

"Surely we could have sold enough leather work to afford

passage on a ship," John Mark said, breaking his uncle's reverie.

"Marcus, we've been through this. The atmosphere in the city—"

"I'm tired already, lugging this tent on my back."

Barnabas sighed. He did not remember John Mark complaining on their journey from Jerusalem to Antioch. But then again, those were places they had traveled with Yeshua, and they had both bathed in the memories on the way. As they neared the shadows of the mountains, Barnabas addressed his nephew. "You may have been too young to remember, but there was a time that Yeshua gathered all us men and paired us up. Then he sent us out to the towns and villages to pave the way for him."

"Yes, Uncle." John Mark shifted the weight of the tent on his back. "I remember."

"Well, he sent us out, two of us per locale. We were not to take anything with us. No food, no water, no money, no wine, no bedrolls, no weapons. Not even extra clothing or sandals."

"How did he expect you to survive?"

At the time, Barnabas had wondered the same thing. There were thieves on the roads, and people were always suspicious of strangers. "We were to find one home in the place and rely on their hospitality. If no one would accept us, we were to leave and go elsewhere. He refused to go to a town that didn't take care of us."

They had picked up their pace, heading for the shadows of the mountains where they would be out of the direct sun, which was already warming them.

"And the place you went to, Uncle, the first place took you in?"

"Yes, Marcus, they did. And we were able to do many things there."

"Yeshua wanted you to learn to rely on the kindness of others."

Barnabas shook his head. "No, Marcus. If we entrust our lives to the kindness of others, we will starve to death or die from exposure. You can't depend on other people. That was the lesson for us."

John Mark stopped short. "I always thought the reason he sent you all out was to change the hearts of people, that by being kind to you, you were able to minister to them."

Barnabas shielded his eyes with his hand and tilted toward the bright sky, deep blue, with a few scattered, thin clouds. The brilliant sun reminded him of the brightness and warmth of the Presence. He sighed, lowered his hand, and met the expectant eyes of his nephew. "He sent us out 'like sheep among wolves,' as he said, for us to learn to depend on the Holy Spirit, on God alone. It could be interpreted as tempting God, going out without any provisions at all, to see if God would rescue us. But because Yeshua sent us out and his presence was with us, what had begun as doubt turned into joy. It was as if." Barnabas hesitated, searching for the words. "As if God himself prepared the way for us."

John Mark dropped his gaze to the stones they stood upon, and Barnabas did the same. Due to an abundance of traffic, little tended to grow amongst the paving stones on the road. But at their feet, a thin stalk grew, bearing several small, yellow flowers. Barnabas warmed at the sight of hope. "Let's go. I want to get through the Syrian Gates before it's too late to reach Pictanus before dark."

The two followed the Roman road through the foothills of the Amanos Mountains. The sun followed them, the shadows of the mountains always before them. Given the unusual warmth for this time of year, Barnabas eagerly anticipated the shade of the pass. Soon, he thought. Soon.

And then they were in the mountains, the road climbing through a widened pass. The road was designed to accommodate entire armies, their wagons full of weapons and provisions. Despite his opinions of Rome, Barnabas begrudgingly admired the ingenuity of their engineers. The two met several groups traveling in the opposite direction, yet there was room for them all to pass.

Barnabas paused after they made their way through the Syrian Gates, where the pass opened up to the view below on the other side. They both relieved themselves of their burdens and drank, wetting their lips, then took in the wide vista. Off to their right was a vast, low plain, green and lush, but before them was the Great Sea. Barnabas had missed the view, and the first glance always took his breath. There was Pictanus lying in the shadows at the base of the mountains. He closed his eyes, raised his arms, and prayed aloud.

The first night, in Pictanus, they had swapped some leather work for a couple of spots on the floor of an inn. The second night, they were allowed to sleep on the floor of the synagogue in Alexandria, provided they did not touch anything. The leader of the synagogue lived in a house next door, and though he had appeared suspicious of them, he nonetheless allowed his wife to feed them and gave them blankets.

But Mopsuestia was another story altogether. Even the Jews in the town would not receive them because the first thing the two of them were asked was whether they belonged to the Yeshua sect in Antioch. Word had got out, it seems. No one was interested in buying any leather products. No one had an open spot on their floor for them. No one would even sell them any food. They followed the river north right before sundown and set up the tent near the river's edge.

Which was a mistake. Barnabas and his nephew were nearly eaten alive by the mosquitoes while they slept. Lesson learned, Barnabas said as he would stop his work and scratch.

Once John Mark had the tent rolled up, tied, and secured to his back, Barnabas packed up his work and tools and bundled the bedrolls. "I suppose," he said, "we should get back on the road and head toward Adana. I'm hoping someone there will need some new sandals."

"Uncle," John Mark replied, "didn't you say Adana is one of the cities where Saul has organized a group of believers?"

"Yes, it is, Marcus. I had forgotten that."

John Mark helped his uncle strap his bundles to his back. "Maybe we should try to find them while we're there."

"Excellent idea! I knew there was a reason I brought you along."

"We should fill up the skins with water," John Mark said. "I should have thought of it before strapping on this tent." He untied his burden and took the two skins to the river's edge. As he stooped to fill them, a man on horseback galloped toward them.

"Uncle?"

Barnabas stood between his nephew and the horseman. They had had little company once out of the coastal town. Barnabas gauged the countenance of the man: eyebrows drawn, the mouth set in a line. And he wasn't sure that the man did not intend to run them over.

"Stop there!" the man shouted. "You are trespassing on this property. You must leave now!" The man laid his hand on the pommel of his sword.

"We are going on our way now, sir," Barnabas said.

John Mark did not rise. "I am only refilling our water skins."

"You will do no such thing!" the man declared as he pulled his sword. "You will rise, and the two of you will leave now."

John Mark remained squatting and locked eyes with the man.

"Marcus," Barnabas said, his voice soft but steady. "Get up and come with me. Now."

His nephew did not drop the gaze of the man as he rose in obedience. He reached to grab the tent as the man neared them. "I'm going to pick this up, and—"

"Leave it. Now, go!"

"But—"

"Leave it, I said."

Barnabas sidled between the two. "It's alright, Marcus. We won't need it where we are going."

"But—"

"We're going in search of a tent maker." Barnabas enunciated each word, then turned to the man. "It's yours. Do you need the bedrolls, too? Or a nice pair of sandals?"

The man's eyes flashed, but he lowered the sword. "No, just go."

The two of them turned back in the direction of Mopsuestia. "Not that way," the man shouted, and he pointed up the river. "Go back that way, where you came from."

Barnabas took John Mark by the arm and spun around, their backs to the man, and hurried upstream, away from Mopsuestia, away from the Roman road that would take them to Adana.

"And don't come back!" the man shouted after them. "I will remember you two!"

In all of Melcha's expansive home, the garden was her favorite place. Snuggled within the dwelling, accessible only from her bedchamber and the servant's hallway, she had developed the courtyard so that, no matter the season, she was able to sit in the beauty of her garden. The fall flowers were a blaze of color, interspersed with shades of green.

She sat, her legs tucked underneath her, her arms propping her up from behind. She closed her eyes and breathed in the out-of-doors. The comforting trickle of water ran through the courtyard before it flowed into the small pool in the corner. Her husband had created this extravagant artificial stream by diverting a small flow from the river flowing clear and strong through the city near their house. During drier weather, the garden had a continuous source of water. The late afternoon sun warmed her face and lit a blaze even through her closed eyelids. If she were younger, she could remain like this for some time. But Melcha found that her joints no longer liked being in one position for very long.

She drank in the moment. She was seldom alone as mistress of a busy household, so she basked in the luxury of rare isolation. While she missed her husband, she was never lonely. She did wish her daughter and family lived nearby, but the presence of her son filled her heart. She had never known as much joy six years prior when he returned unannounced to save both her home and her husband's businesses. Her sole surviving boy had always been her pride. Her first child, daughter Sarah, came early and easily in their marriage, but Melcha's disappointment grew as several pregnancies ended before birth. A handful of years passed, with great pressure from her husband to produce a son, an heir. Finally, she carried one to completion, and her boy was born. Sensing her child's greatness, she had begged her husband to name him after Israel's first king. The boy's Roman name could be whatever the father wished, but his Hebrew name, by which she always called him, was Saul.

She guaranteed he received the finest education. A fast learner, Saul mastered everything he set his mind to. He was obviously destined for one of the highest positions available to a Jewish man, and she was determined for him to become a member of the Great Sanhedrin in Jerusalem. She was proud of him, as he excelled in his studies in Jerusalem and made the necessary political connections as a scribe and counsel in the holy city.

Her shoulder grew heavy with an ache. Melcha sat up, stretching out her leg and bringing her hands into her lap. As she did so, footfalls sounded behind her, and she turned. One of her household servants stood in the open doorway to her bedchamber. "Yes?" she asked.

The girl cast her eyes to the ground. "Master Saul is here,

seeking your reception."

Melcha scrambled to her feet and smoothed her clothing. "Send him in." Moments later, her handsome son stood in the girl's place, swiping back the thick dark hair tumbling over his left eye. "Saul."

"I should have known to find you here, Mother." He reached out an embrace, and she kissed him.

"You were gone longer than expected," she murmured. "You were in Adana?"

"Yes, Mother. I wanted to spend the Sabbath with the fellowship there." His dark eyebrows drew together. "You've been sitting on the ground when I bought you benches for your garden?" He shook his head. "One day, you'll be on the ground and need help up."

"Oh, Saul! Don't be disrespectful!"

He steered her to a nearby bench, where she sat in obedience. He remained standing, his back to her, as he examined the garden. "I can't blame you for enjoying this space. It is a peaceful place in the heart of a busy city."

She admired him, memorizing the features of his body: his hands, strong and manly, his legs with their muscular calves. Between his money, his intellect, and his skills, Melcha had no understanding of why he did not have his choice of a great number of potential brides. "Don't you think it time," she suggested, "to find yourself a wife, my son? I'm not going to be around forever, and I will need a daughter-in-law to take over the household."

He stiffened. Though never so boldly, Melcha had broached this subject with him and sensed his resistance to discuss it. But it did not make sense. There was little for him to do. The businesses almost ran themselves, and the household was secure. "Have you thought about it at all?"

Her son turned toward her, and she was taken back by the sadness in his dark eyes. His hands hung at his sides as he measured his words. "Mother," he said.

"I'm sorry, my son." She regretted the pain her question had caused.

Saul gathered her hands in his and knelt before her. "No, Mother, *I* am sorry. I know what my marriage would mean to you. You deserve a household full of sons and daughters-in-law and their children and grandchildren for you to spoil and love." He paused and then indicated with his hand. "To have a garden of love and laughter, as beautiful as all your flowers here." As he met her eyes, it took her back in time to him as a small boy, when he manipulated almost anything he wanted from her with this look. She remembered it right before he left for Jerusalem as a youth and the way he had given her the same expression six years ago upon his return. The face had aged from the plump, rounded cheeks of the child to the smooth olive skin of the youth to the trim-bearded masculine face of her adult son. She fought the tears welling up, not wanting him to think her a silly, weepy woman.

He squeezed her hands as he spoke. "Mother, it is important that you understand. God has ordained me, destined me to be his instrument. I must be ready to do his work at a moment's notice. I cannot be burdened with the responsibility of a wife and a family, for what I am to do cannot be done with them. I must serve God. This is why you conceived me, bore me, and fought Father for my education and experience. Can you understand this?"

She hesitated to ask what was on her mind. Melcha knew that he held to the concept of sexual purity, as emphasized by the law of circumcision and the law of Moses, not to mention much of the philosophic thought to which he had been exposed. But his total avoidance of women had worried her. "Is it that you have no desire?" she asked. "For women?"

He tilted his head. "Don't let that concern you. Of course, my body has all kinds of hunger. But we are to be the masters of our bodies, and just as I have learned to ignore the pangs of hunger, I have learned to overlook the body's tendency toward lust. Otherwise, we are nothing but mere animals. Don't misunderstand. I know the importance of having children. It is a necessary means to that end, and I believe that men who are obsessed with lust are forgetting that we are created to be merely a little lower than the heavenly beings."

Melcha fell deeper into his eyes, and she fought the sense that she had already lost him to something. "Surely you can serve God here, in Tarsus. God would not ask you to desert the life you enjoy here!"

Saul sighed, dropped her hands, and perched beside her. They sat in the fading light of day, the only sounds the trickling of the water and the beating of her heart.

"What woman would want the life to which he calls me? I would never be home. I could die and her not know it. If I came home at all, I wouldn't know for how long and would have to leave at a moment's notice. She would live rejected by fellow Jews, unwelcome in the synagogues, and talked about by other women. She would grow to resent me." He breathed deeply. "And I don't know if I have room enough in my heart to love anyone outside of my love for God. I simply don't have time to devote to a wife, not as she would deserve." Then he held her hand. "And I have no desire to live for anyone but Christ Jesus."

They sat like that for a few sad moments. Melcha noted with surprise the thinned skin of her hand in his. "Do you love him more than me, Saul?"

He gave her his full attention. "Mother, you know I love you. You have always supported me, even against Father and his wishes. A son could not have more love and respect for his mother than I. But you are mortal. You will die one day, many years from now. 'Do not put your trust in princes, in mere mortal men who cannot save.' Yes, Mother, I love you, but I must love the living God more."

She leaned her head on his shoulder. Isn't this what she had prayed for her children? For them to be adults and fulfill all that God requires of them? She had sent him to school to learn God's law, and he fell in love with it. Now, he has fallen in love with God himself. "You will do great things for God, my son," she murmured.

Taking her by the shoulders, he kissed her on the forehead.

Saul's restlessness intensified after the talk with Mother. He sensed an impending change, its odor lingering in the air.

He sang the same song as always with his bedtime prayer: "I will lie down and sleep in peace, for you alone, O Lord, make me dwell in safety."

Peace. What is peace? *The closer I get to you, O Lord, the more I see how vile I am, and my guilt steals any chance at peace.* Saul believed his dreams stemmed from his guilt over the stoning of Stephen. How is evil like that, the murder of an innocent, ever forgiven? And even if God could forgive him, and Stephen could forgive him, can Saul ever forgive himself?

He took off his tunic and spread out on the bed, high off the floor. Mother had insisted he take the master bedchamber, a huge room with a large bed. Initially, he had balked at the thought of sleeping, not only in such luxury, but in the same bed in which his father had slept and died. He slept on the floor for the first two or three nights. But it was not long before he returned to his childhood ritual, enjoying a bath in their private bathhouse, rubbing on some oil, saying his prayers, and laying on the bed, his arms crossed behind his head.

As he lay there, eyes wide open in the dark room, the aroma of oil on his body surrounding him, he rationalized his anxious thoughts. He must fear sleep, concerned the dream will return. *Lord, take this dream from me. I give it up to you.*

However, visions of the city chased him whenever he closed his eyes. There were great extremes in Tarsus. Extreme riches and extreme poverty, extreme knowledge, as well as ignorance, freedom, and slavery. People starved to death while the very rich threw out food to rot. Parents killed their children rather than allow them to starve and die. Sin was ubiquitous: young women, old women, and young men gave themselves as prostitutes. Saul closed his eyes to the faces, the empty eyes that met his on the city streets, the helpless way he handed out what money he had on him or gave them food.

The worst was the children, their screaming, as girls and boys were dragged into buildings to be used and thrown away. Children, sold as slaves, torn from their siblings, crying, reaching out to the only family they had ever known. Lord God Almighty, how can I offer them the assurance of salvation when all they want is to be safe, to have their bellies filled, to sleep in peace, to stop the pain?

Fitfully, restlessly, Saul drifted off.

Saul is in the synagogue. Familiar. He stands before the people. He drops his eyes to the scroll, open to Isaiah. "The Spirit of the Lord is upon me," he reads. He raises his eyes and is surrounded by angry men, shouting, screaming, and tearing at their clothes; spittle lands on his face, in his eyes. He turns and meets familiar, blazing dark eyes. He knows this angry man in his face, screaming at him, who grabs him and hurls him. The crowd pounces on him and drags him into the street. The tops of his feet scrape along the rocky soil. His arms ache. The crowd grows until he is in the midst of a sea of humanity, all with murder in their mouths, their eyes, and their hearts. Outside the city gates, he lifts off the ground and sails above them. A huge group gathered below him, all the angrier that he was out of their reach. Higher and higher he goes, over mountains, over the sea. He has some apprehension, some sense that he must eventually return to earth, but he is finally alone.

Then there it is, the Temple shining in the distance. No, no! He tries to shout, but he has no voice. It is not safe for him to go there. He sails over the Temple and outside the city walls, where the crucifixions take place. He is too low to the ground and tries to will himself back in the air. He is grabbed by Roman soldiers and thrown to the ground. He screams silently at a piercing, a sharp stabbing at his right wrist. The pain is unbearable, and he fears it. His left arm is pulled away from him, and he watches in terror as the soldiers nail his wrists to the crossbar. The pain is intense, and his entire body shakes. Surely God will be good and wake him before it goes any further. Rough hands grab his legs, and the same sickening sound, the same sharp horrendous pain, the same attempts to cry out in silence. Then a horrible sensation as he is lifted, and the weight of his body pulls on his nailed wrists. This is unbearable! My God!

A face hovers before Saul. the sad, knowing eyes boring through him. Saul, Saul. Why do you persecute me?

My Lord and my God.

Saul. Follow me. Follow me.

Saul sat straight up in his bed, soaked in sweat, head spinning. He touched the bed, and his hand came back sticky and wet. He scrambled off and fell prostrate, sobbing, on the floor.

In the early light of morning, he awakened on the floor, remembering the entirety of his dream. He then stood above his bed and gasped. The sheets were stained with blood. He checked his wrists, remembering the sticky wetness. No wounds, no scars, no blood. No pain, no soreness.

I am crucified with Christ.

He sat, his back to the bed and placed his head in his hands.

As he sat on the floor of his father's bedchamber, one thought after another assaulted him. Overwhelmed and confused by the events of the night, he attempted to slow his thoughts, sort them in order. What did these dreams mean? They displayed his shame and his guilt, which was ever before him.

Against You, You only, have I sinned.

The lyrics of the song pushed to the forefront, giving him something to cling to. Under his breath, he sang.

"Have mercy on me, O God, according to your unfailing love, according to your great compassion, blot out my transgressions. Wash away all my iniquity and cleanse me from my sin."

His voice broke. King David wrote that song after his priest had pointed out his great sin against God. The agony in the lyrics, the penitence, struck a chord.

For I know my transgression and my sin is always before me. Against You, You only, have I sinned and done what is evil in Your sight.

He whispered the last few words, disgusted by himself. The eyes of Stephen, the face of Yeshua. There was no fleeing from the vision of them. "My God!" he cried aloud. "Forgive me!"

His eyes closed against his guilt. He sat for minutes before he smelled it. Spikenard. Anointing oil. Where? He filled his lungs as it emanated from and around him.

Saul, Saul.

He wet his lips. "Here I am, Lord," he whispered.

Why do you persecute yourself?

What? Myself?

The Pascal Lamb has been sacrificed for the forgiveness of your sins.

The song swelled back, filling him. "Cleanse me with hyssop," he sang, "and I will be clean. Wash me, and I will be whiter than snow. Let the bones you have crushed rejoice. Hide your face from my sins and blot out my iniquity. Create in me a pure heart."

Saul, you have not chosen me, but I have chosen you.

He stopped singing, the scent of the oil overwhelming him, and again closed his eyes. He swore a hand palmed his head, and oil soaked his hair, onto his scalp.

You will be my apostle to the Gentiles. You will go where I send you. You will teach what I instill in you. I give you the Spirit to dwell in you. What I have redeemed is purified.

A single drop of oil rolled onto his forehead.

Get up.

In his mind, Saul found himself in the city center of Tarsus. He knew the place, the open area where the orators stand. He leaned against a column while an orator gave a speech. I am to go into the city center, he thought.

A knock at the door interrupted his thoughts. "Master Saul?" A soft, feminine voice floated from the other side of the door.

Saul scrambled to his feet. He whirled about, searching for a tunic to cover himself. He reached for the one he had discarded the night before.

"Master Saul, are you awake?"

"Yes, a minute, please," he called out as he threw on the tunic.

"There is hot water in the bath, Master Saul."

How did she? Saul spun back to the bed. His mouth dropped open. The bed was clean. Slept in, but no blood. He shook his head before turning back toward the door. "Thank you," he answered. He raised a hand to his head, touching dry hair. Amazed, he headed toward the door.

He removed his clothing in the bathing room and entered the steaming water. He sighed as he lowered himself and threw his arms out, resting them on the edges of the bath.

"Oh Lord, our Lord, how majestic is your name in all the earth!"

He liked how singing in this room made his voice sound and hoped the sound pleased God. He thought back to his journey from Damascus to Jerusalem, dirty and dusty, how he had longed for the baths of the city. He knew how blessed he was to have a large house with a private bath. How blessed they were to have servants to help maintain it all. He thought of his mother's garden, the elaborate design Father had created solely to make her happy.

Father. Saul's arms slipped back into the water, and he lowered his head, immersing his face in the water. *Concentrate on your heavenly father. The one who loves you, the one who has blessed you.* Then he thought of his dreams. Each of them, him reliving the torture he had ordered or that came as a result of his actions. Stephen's stoning.

Saul threw his head up out of the water with a sudden realization. He wiped the water from his face, and his mouth fell open. Those dreams weren't memories of past events. He was not reliving Stephen's stoning in those dreams. They were glimpses of what would happen.

To him.

Saul closed his mouth. Yeshua had told him he would suffer much. And he certainly deserved it. But it would all be bearable, all because Yeshua had shown it to him. Saul knew what was coming. How much worse to not know, to worry in fear. This is how he would know that he was on the right track: The more he suffered, the more assured he would be.

And I shall be with you.

Saul's thoughts then turned to his vision of the orator platform, of himself in the crowd. *It's to remind me of the world of the Gentiles, isn't it? How can I possibly become an apostle to the Gentiles when I am immersed in my own little world? Here, in my father's house, sequestered away, living on the edges. I can never teach them from here.*

Get dressed and go.

Saul obeyed without hesitation.

Chapter Ten

Barnabas grasped John Mark's shoulder and led him away from the dangerous man on the horse. They followed the river for some time in silence. Out of the corner of his eye, Barnabas contemplated his nephew. No longer a youth, he had grown into a young man, his beard short and sparse. Barnabas's heart warmed. This young man was the son he had never had, and while Barnabas knew his nephew did not agree with their course of action, he was proud that Marcus had not argued and caused a scene. Instead, Marcus stepped carefully, perhaps wondering when they might head back, back toward Mopsuestia, back to the Roman road that would lead them to Tarsus.

"God has certainly sent his angels to guard over us." Barnabas broke the long silence between them. "Don't you agree, Nephew?"

"If God has indeed sent us on this journey, Uncle, then that man will be sorry he interfered with God's plan and with his people."

Amused, Barnabas asked, "You aren't praying for God to rain down fire on that man, are you?"

John Mark frowned. "Yes, Uncle, I am. Better yet, I'd like him to strike the man dead, like he did to that couple when they withheld some of their money from Cephas."

"Marcus!" Barnabas slowed to a stop along the river. The

water flowed past them, little eddies swirling around rocks, as stuck as his nephew. "What did Yeshua teach us concerning our enemies?"

John Mark sighed. "To love our enemies."

"And?"

"And to pray for those who persecute us."

"I don't think praying for that man's death is what Yeshua meant by that."

"But Uncle, that wasn't even our tent! It was expensive, and now we are out here on the prairie with no protection from rain or wind. He had no right."

"Perhaps we should consider that he needed it more than we did. Perhaps he had prayed for a tent, and God provided it for him."

John Mark appeared unconvinced. "If he needed it, Uncle, he could have asked for it, not forced it from us at sword-point!" "While that may be true, Nephew, rest assured that we don't need it. God did not lead us this far to allow us to die of exposure on the Cilician plain. What God has done is preserve us. We escaped that encounter unscathed. Before I met Yeshua years ago, I would have pulled out my dagger in response. But you and I are surrounded by angels. I know they are invisible to us, but I sensed them all the same. The Spirit of God leads me now. You must learn to trust Him. Come," he added, "let's pray for that man."

Incredulous, John Mark's mouth dropped open. Barnabas waited until he capitulated. "All right, Uncle. We can pray for him."

They stood, and both extended their palms upward in supplication, but neither spoke. "The prayer needs to come from you, Marcus," Barnabas said.

John Mark opened his mouth to protest but must have registered what his uncle's face expressed. Instead, he prayed. "Oh God, King of the Universe, thank you for seeing us safely thus far. Thank you for the food we've had to eat and for sending us your Spirit to guide us." He paused.

Barnabas waited.

"We thank you for the hospitality that has been shown to us in some places. We pray a blessing." John Mark sighed. "We pray a blessing on the man who took the tent and forced us away. Lord, I hope he needs the tent or the money he can get for it. May it only be used for good."

"That feels better now, doesn't it? To give up that anger and frustration?"

John Mark shrugged. "I suppose. But how will we get back on the road? How will we get to Adana now?"

"There must be another way to Adana, Marcus, some other road to take."

"But the other ways are not safe! At least that road is patrolled by Roman soldiers."

Barnabas shook his head. "It's not that, Marcus. I am out of money. I don't have any left for the Roman road tax."

"What? What are we going to do now?"

Barnabas shooed the question with his hand. "God will provide, Nephew. Let's keep heading this way, along the river. I sense we will find another way to get there, and we will find relief in Adana."

"All right, Uncle. I hope your senses are correct."

They startled frogs splashing into the river ahead of them. Barnabas was lost in thought. Tarsus was a large city. Was he crazy thinking he would find Saul in the midst of all that humanity? Of course, he knew to go to the Jewish quarters of Tarsus, but there was a large Jewish population in that locale. How long would it take to find one man?

The sun was high in the sky when John Mark suddenly halted. Without a word, he indicated ahead. Upriver, Barnabas could barely make out the figure of a person. Stalling for time, Barnabas took out his skin of water and drank. He sent out all his senses, urging the Spirit to guide them. Should they go forward, head back, or turn west away from the river?

John Mark whispered. "What do you think? Friend or foe?"

Barnabas was tugged, urged forward. Offering the water to his nephew and scanning upriver, he replied. "We keep going. This may well be an angel."

While they were still too far away to spy any facial features, Barnabas was able to judge body language. A man stood on the riverbank fishing with a pole, aware of their presence. Barnabas assumed by the way he turned toward them that the man was assessing whether they meant any harm. To reassure the man, he called out in Greek. "Hello! How is the fishing today?" The man did not respond. Barnabas slowed his pace so as not to frighten. He stopped a few paces away, respecting the man's space, John Mark directly behind. "I am Joseph, originally of Cyprus. This is my nephew, Marcus. We travel from Antioch to Syria."

The man's eyes met his, still clouded with doubt. Barnabas opened his arms. "We mean no harm. We were forced to travel upriver, away from Mopsuestia, away from the Roman road."

The man snorted and laid his pole on the ground. After securing it with a large stone, he hobbled toward them. "They are none too friendly to outsiders there," the man replied. He wiped off his hand on his clothing before offering it to Barnabas. "I am called Hyam. I live upriver, but this is my favorite fishing spot. I don't always catch much, but it's peaceful here, and I never have much company." Hyam squinted up at the bright sky. "These days, it is best that way."

"Is there another way to Adana?" John Mark asked. "We don't know the area, and there's no sense going back where we came from only to get chased off again."

Hyam grinned "Yes, there is another way to Adana. Let me pack up, and I will show you."

As he bent to grasp his fishing pole, John Mark further questioned him. "Is it safe? The only thing of value we had, a man on horseback took from us."

"What did you lose to him?" Hyam asked.

"Our tent."

The man whistled. "That's an expensive thing to have stolen from you. Bad luck too."

"And it wasn't even ours. We borrowed it!"

Barnabas laid a hand on John Mark's arm, wishing back his nephew's usual shyness. "We don't want to trouble you," Barnabas added. "Perhaps you can show us the direction to find—"

"I have to go partway on that road anyway," Hyam interrupted. "It is no bother." He gathered his belongings and was already turning away. "Follow me."

Barnabas noted the man's pronounced limp and checked out Hyam's feet. One stuck inward at an awkward angle. His gait caused Barnabas pain. He hurried next to him. "Here, may I carry something for you?" Barnabas offered.

"I've been carrying all this for many years," Hyam replied, "all by myself."

"Please, let me."

The man stopped short. "Does the foot bother you? Because it doesn't bother me. It's how I am. Everyone has always told me it's from something my father did, some sin he committed." He paused. "Do you believe that?"

The man's eyes held resignation, pain, and loneliness. But they also displayed a soul open and willing. "Hyam," Barnabas asked, "do you believe you can be healed? Because the God who formed you in your mother's womb is able to make you whole."

"Are you telling me to travel all the way to Jerusalem, to offer a burnt offering at the Temple, and I can be healed?" Hyam shook his head. "I've already been given that advice. My parents tried that multiple times." He indicated the awkward foot. "And here I am."

The Spirit took over Barnabas's body, his thoughts, his words. It was as if he stood from afar, observing himself and Hyam as he asked Hyam to lay aside his belongings and sit on the ground, as he knelt on the ground before Hyam, lifting his hands in prayer, then as he laid his hands on Hyam's ankle, the painful movement of bone and sinew snapping and cracking, Hyam's screams, then, silence. The occasional chirping of birds as they flew past them. The roar of the river behind them was accented by Hyam's laughter.

Hyam jumped up and danced, full of glee. Barnabas stood, grinning at him, waiting with John Mark. When Hyam finally stopped, tears flowing, he turned to Barnabas and rushed to him, kissed him, and hugged him. "Brother Joseph," he exclaimed, "you are miraculous!"

Barnabas shook his head. "No, not me. It wasn't me who healed you, Hyam. It was the Spirit of God."

"The name you used," he asked, "to heal me. What was it? I do not know of it."

"Jesus of Nazareth. It is through the power of the name that you are healed."

Hyam regathered his belongings. "Come, I will show you how to get to Adana, and you will tell me about this Jesus."

The uncle and nephew traveled the road from Adana to Tarsus

the following morning. The sun appeared brighter to him as Barnabas squinted at the blue sky. His nephew's mood had also lifted after the experience in Adana.

Hyam accompanied them into Adana itself, sometimes skipping on the way. He had received the good news of salvation and, hungry to learn as much as possible, led them to the house of the one that was rumored to belong to a new group, those who called themselves the followers of the Way. The men and women of that close-knit group had begged for the story of Hyam's healing and welcomed the strangers in as brothers.

They'd left Adana richer in heart and possessions. His nephew shifted the weight of the tent he carried on his back. They were well out of the city, and both the foot traffic and the oxen-led wagons and donkeys weighed down with packs had decreased in number. The din created by assorted feet and wheels muted enough for them to discuss the previous day's events. "I wish we had stayed longer," John Mark said. "We haven't received such a warm welcome, such a sense of brotherhood since Jerusalem. Of course, it's a much smaller group, but they make up for what they lack in numbers in hospitality."

Barnabas agreed. "I know what you mean. They wanted us to stay awhile with them, especially since Saul had not shown for Sabbath."

It was strange, that. The small congregation had told them that Saul tended to spend every other Sabbath with the small community of believers in Adana. They were concerned about Saul's absence, and their worry was contagious. "I hope nothing has happened to him," John Mark added.

"That is the main reason I wanted to leave today. If it is his custom to keep the Sabbath with his people in Adana, and he did not show nor send word to them, I do not wish to imagine what has happened. So, yes," Barnabas concluded, "I will travel on the Sabbath because Yeshua is Lord of the Sabbath, and he would have us find the one sheep out of the ninety-nine."

They settled into a pace behind a team of oxen pulling a wagon, keeping an eye on the road. It was not long before John Mark voiced his glee. "Wasn't it wonderful, Uncle, how Hyam was received by the believers in Adana? He reveled in their requests to tell his story, over and over!"

Barnabas agreed. "It was surprising that he chose to go all the way into Adana with us and spend Sabbath evening there. I think our host may have taken on more than he expected when he opened his door to us."

It was a good thing it was a large enough dwelling for that group, as both men and women had stayed through the night and re-gathered in the morning for prayer and worship in the house. Barnabas was told that they were no longer welcome at the synagogue if Saul was with them.

"If our rabbi is not welcome there," he was told, "then neither are we."

"It's all right," one woman had assured him. "I prefer to worship without a screen in my face anyway."

Barnabas had never thought about the screens from a woman's perspective. That was the way it had always been: the women separated from the men. But it was Saul who had established the new tradition, assuring the little congregation that in Christ, there was no distinction in class, country of origin, or sex.

"We owe Levi quite a lot for his hospitality." John Mark interrupted his uncle's musings. "Not only did he let us in and serve us Sabbath meal, he loaded us up for the road. Food and this tent." He indicated with a thumb the burden on his back.

"Oh, yes, of course. I emphasized that as we returned on our way home to Antioch with Saul, we would return it."

"It appears to be new. Or unused, anyway."

"Marcus, I told you God would provide for us."

"How do you think our people in Antioch will fare with Saul? He seems like such a large man in a small package."

"Saul is precisely what Antioch needs, Nephew. It doesn't matter what they think of him. He is what God wants for Antioch."

"I hope all is well with him," John Mark replied. "That his not coming to Adana is more because he is busy with another group of followers or his business."

Barnabas was confident that Saul was alive and well. "I don't know what may have delayed him, but the sooner we get to Tarsus and find Brother Saul, the better."

When Barnabas and John Mark entered Tarsus the following day, they headed straight to the marketplace. There they found several purveyors of the black goat-hair cloth for which Tarsus was famous. Surely, thought Barnabas, a vendor of the cloth used in tent making and repair would know of the particular tent maker he sought.

"There are many men named after the King of Israel. Can you be more specific?" the man asked.

"He's from Tarsus," Barnabas offered.

Incredulous, the man replied, "That doesn't narrow it down. Who are his people? What is his trade?"

"He is a tentmaker."

The man made a face and grunted. "Ah. That Saul."

Barnabas brightened. "So, you know him?"

"Know *of* him, yes. You should steer clear of that Saul. Bad news. If it's mending of a tent you need, I recommend a friend of mine."

"No, it's Saul, the tentmaker, that I need to find."

"I can't help you. And I don't associate with anyone who stays acquainted with the man." He turned his back.

"Perhaps," his nephew said as they hurried from the man and his booth, "we should try one of the synagogues?"

"Good idea," Barnabas agreed. "That's a likely place to find him. Or someone who knows him."

"That fellow seemed to know him," John Mark said. "Or rather, of him, as he said."

"Isn't that how it is with Saul? One either loves him or hates him."

They found a synagogue with ease, and pausing at the door to give a blessing, they entered. Inside, three men stood, talking with each other, and turned at the sound of the newcomers' entry. One broke from the group. "Greetings, travelers," he said. "We have no bread here if it is food you seek."

Barnabas greeted him. "We have no need for food but for a certain man named Saul. A tentmaker from this city."

The man scowled, and his companions' features hardened. The air grew cold.

"I know the man of whom you speak. He is not welcome in this or any other synagogue in Tarsus. He speaks non-stop about a false messiah and has led many of our people astray." He glared at them. "And if you seek him by name, you must be an acquaintance of his. No friend of his is welcome here, either." He jutted his chin toward the door, indicating that they should leave.

John Mark was out the door, but Barnabas paused. "Would you tell me where—"

"No, I will not help. Now, leave!"

Out on the street once more, the two travelers hurried out of the Jewish neighborhood and back into the center of the city. Barnabas had no idea where they were going.

"Where to next, Uncle?"

Barnabas shook his head. "Let's get a better sense of this place before we get thrown out of the entire city."

They passed a temple in honor of the city's prominent goddess. There was a heavy Greek influence in the architecture in Tarsus, but it retained a flavor of the native people. Tarsus had long been a seat of learning and was considered an important cultural center in both the Greek and now Roman world. The city was intimidating and Barnabas had little hope of finding Saul in a timely manner.

They reached a raised courtyard, surrounded on three sides by a pillared portico. They climbed the few steps where a crowd of men congregated, some half-sitting on ornamental planters, most standing, while a man stood on a marble platform, giving a speech.

John Mark was enthralled by what the orator was saying. Barnabas, less interested, scanned the crowd. Men stood in clusters of two or three. One would turn and utter something to his companions. Others nodded in appreciation or agreement. He was drawn to one jeering man leaning, cross-armed, against a pillar.

"The very best, then, we can do in this life," the orator said, "is to pursue our own happiness."

"What if one is hungry?" the leaning man shouted out. "How does one pursue happiness with their stomach in knots of hunger?"

The orator stopped and eyed his heckler. "Even the poor can—"

"They can? Hungry and in rags, unable to feed themselves,

much less their family?"

Barnabas recognized the voice and closed in to scrutinize the face.

"That is not—" the orator started.

"And how can I possibly pursue my happiness," the heckler continued, "when there are others—"

"Saul!" Barnabas cried.

He turned at his name, irritated at the interruption until his eyes flickered with recognition. His face lit up with joy. "Barnabas? Is it you?"

Barnabas pulled him away, and they rushed down the steps to greet each other, John Mark at their heels.

"Have you been in Tarsus long? Come with me," said Saul, not waiting for an answer. "Come to my house. You have much to tell me." Then Saul turned his eyes on John Mark. "Welcome to Tarsus. Your first time here, yes? I hope it has been pleasant thus far." John Mark ducked his head. Saul waved them on. "Come, rest your weary feet."

After ushering them into the extensive home, Saul summoned servants. "Have you eaten recently?" Saul inquired.

"Not since before we broke camp early this morning," replied Barnabas.

Saul tilted his head at John Mark. "Famished," came his reply.

"Perfect," Saul replied. "After you've washed and in some clean clothes, we'll get you fed. Barnabas, you bring me news from Jerusalem, I take it."

Barnabas shook his head. "No, not from Jerusalem. John Mark and I have been in Antioch for a while now. It is from Antioch we bring news. There is quite a growing group of followers there. When the Greek speakers were driven out of Jerusalem . . ." He paused.

"By my efforts," Saul interjected.

"Yes," Barnabas answered. "During that campaign, several settled in Antioch and preached there, mainly to the Greek-speaking Jews of the city. When the apostles in Jerusalem learned of it, they sent us to check on their growing community. The believers there have a problem unique to the city."

Saul stood silent, his face masked. "And how is that community? Is the Spirit with them?"

Barnabas wondered. Did he suspect, did he know, who had led

the believers to find Yeshua? "Yes, Saul. They were baptized by one of the seven." Barnabas noted the realization on Saul's face.

"Nicolaus. Of course," Saul acknowledged. "If this group was started by those I persecuted, then I owe them a great debt. Barnabas." Saul grasped him by the arm. "Can I ever make it up to them? Is there something I can do to help?"

A grin spread across Barnabas's face.

Barnabas's neck warmed from the morning sun as he rode on one of Saul's horses. Though his sloppy seat could hardly be called riding. He checked over his shoulder at his similarly inexperienced nephew. John Mark held the reins in a fierce grip as they made their way out of the city, back toward Adana. Saul was at home on his mount. Barnabas originally objected to traveling on horseback, but Saul argued that Adana was merely a day's ride. So, he had agreed without complaint.

They brought plenty of supplies along, including a nice tent to replace the original stolen one. Saul had also insisted on bringing a supply of tent material to be used in trade if needed.

After eating a morning meal, they left in a hurry, all having been prepared in advance. Barnabas would not have been as hasty to leave that beautiful home, were it his. He had suspected Saul came from money, but he had had no notion of the extent of the comfort with which he lived. He smiled to think of the well-dressed, proud Pharisee who had once glided through the crowded streets of Jerusalem. Saul's dress was still of high quality but far simpler and more comfortable. He sat tall on his elegant horse, and his eyes burned bright with earnestness. Not the cold arrogance Barnabas remembered from before Damascus.

There was a maturity Saul had acquired, a few lines around his eyes and on his forehead. Caring for his household and the businesses must have tamed him some.

"You're quiet over there, brother." Saul's voice startled him. "What are you thinking about?"

Barnabas shrugged. "It's been a few years since we last met."

"Ah, yes, so you're admiring my manly features. Have I aged

that much?”

"A little wiser, perhaps.”

"Stately.”

"Not so impetuous.”

Saul scoffed. "Impetuous? Me? Well, I suppose I may have learned to conserve my energy a bit. Use it more wisely.”

"Your work in Adana is impressive, Saul. I found the community there just as you described in your letter.”

"The desire for redemption draws the Spirit, and the desire, the need, for redemption is strong there. And I am merely a vessel. I let the Spirit work through me.” He turned back to John Mark. "Are you doing all right back there, Marcus? Do you need me to take the reins for you?”

Barnabas turned. His nephew blushed as he held the reins high. Saul threw back his head in his amusement.

Saul neared John Mark. "Relax, Marcus. Your horse senses your fear and will feed off anxiety. Relax your arms. There, that's good. Breathe. You're doing fine. Concentrate on a warm bed awaiting you at the end of the day, and all this will be worth it.”

Barnabas sensed something rare between them, something precious. Something only Yeshua brought. The sweetness swirled around them, wrapped about them, in the warmth of the sun and in the lightness of his heart. There was hope.

Saul resumed his place next to Barnabas.

"Are you going to miss Tarsus, brother Saul?” Barnabas asked.

Saul surveyed the road ahead. "Miss Tarsus? Not especially. I will miss Mother, but I know she is well and in good hands. Father's businesses will do well far into the future, and they don't need me there. I will miss the communities in Adana and Malos, but they have good leaders who will nurture them.” He reached forward and patted his horse on her neck. "I will miss Jameleh here when I have to leave her in Adana. Yes, we'll go the rest of the way on foot and send the animals home. I don't want to risk losing them to conscription in the city. The news you brought me of turmoil and violence is not anything that the tribes have not faced in other cities run by the Romans.” He shook his head. "No, I don't suppose I will miss it, Barnabas. I'm looking forward to whatever God has planned for me in Antioch.”

Chapter Eleven

**Salamis, Cyprus
49 A.D.**

"I sn't it beautiful, Saul?" Barnabas stood next to Saul along the rail as the ship neared the port city of Salamis. Sea birds flew close to the ship and covered the jetties nearby.

Though they'd been gone many years, Barnabus's love for his hometown was evident in the grin on his face.

The two of them had come a long way since the day Barnabas had found him in Tarsus. Nine years since they journeyed into Antioch together. Nine years of working side by side, either fashioning items to sell in the marketplace, earning money to benefit the city's poor or sending to the fellowship in Jerusalem suffering from the drought, or spreading the good news of Yeshua to the Greek-speaking Jews of Antioch. They ate side by side, slept side by side, worshiped and prayed side by side. They had not merely existed next to each other. They had flourished.

Barnabas was the brother Saul had never had.

And Saul had believed that it was to Antioch, side by side with Barnabas, he had been called. While he remembered well the words of Yeshua, that he would be the 'apostle to the Gentiles,' he had never questioned the work they were doing and had accomplished in Syria among their fellow Jews. Not until a few weeks ago, when he received visions of him and Barnabas on Cyprus, and the Holy Spirit came upon them and the elders in Antioch.

Set apart Barnabas and Saul to go where I send them.

And here they were, along with John Mark, though Saul made the point to his friend that the Spirit had not said, "set apart Barnabas, Saul, and Marcus." Nonetheless, the three of them set sail from the port city of Selucia, near Antioch.

Saul turned from his friend, back toward Salamis. If he concentrated only on the jetties or the stairs leading up from the pier or to the short, squat dwellings in the residential areas, he could appreciate Barnabas and Marcus's hometown. However, the large Roman temple that loomed before them filled him with disgust. While Tarsus had pagan temples, they had been native city goddess temples that the Greeks had converted. This towering edifice on a hill was of Roman design, perhaps a temple of Zeus, and a stamp of evil idolatry on this otherwise fair-appearing city.

"I did not realize you came from such a pagan city, my friend," he said, indicating with his head the Roman sacrilege.

"That's new," Barnabas replied. "While the island has been under Roman rule for some time, they focused on the western port, closest to Rome."

Saul wondered how the faithful Jews of Salamis felt about the new temple. "Well, other than that," Saul began. He stopped when he spied farther to his right as they closed in on the city. There were other public buildings, Roman in nature, and while they were indistinguishable to him, he knew that Salamis had been fully infiltrated and commanded by evil forces.

Once again, Saul was stepping out from the warm light of familiarity toward the shadows of unchartered waters.

A few short weeks later, John Mark shuffled his feet as he trailed them away from Salamis. Barnabas sensed his nephew's frustration.

"It's good that we are leaving," said Saul. "It was time to move on."

"We barely got to know the people there," his nephew

muttered. "There was much more to accomplish."

Barnabas stopped and turned to him. "Marcus, we must remember to follow what the Spirit says. We go when he directs us, as well as where." He motioned a summons. "Keep up with us, my boy. You're an important help to us in our efforts. We don't want to leave you in the dust."

John Mark muttered something indiscernible but picked up his pace to match his uncle's and keep up with Saul.

As they traveled the dusty road to Kitron, the trio had barely left Salamis behind. The way was the only major road on the island, dotted with villages along the southern border, leading to Paphos, the destination the Spirit had given to Saul. The sun was bright and hot, and Barnabas didn't know how long he would be able to keep the pace before having to stop and rest. Uncle Hyam had been generous with drink and food for their trip, enough to get them the several-day walk to Paphos in case they met with opposition in the towns along the way.

Despite sending word to his uncle ahead of their visit and the warm welcome all three of them received, they had not made many friends with their fellow Jews in Barnabas's old hometown. The friction this had caused in Uncle Hyam's home resulted in an eagerness to help them pack.

His cousins had not helped. They had gathered with their families at Uncle Hyam's home for the Sabbath meal. Barnabas had introduced Saul, forgetting how his Greek-speaking cousins, prone to teasing, might jump on the opportunity to provoke his friend.

"So, this is Saulus," Cousin Yefe had said as he sashayed flirtatiously, imitating the strut of a prostitute. "Let me see you walk again there, Saulus."

The uproarious laughter only grew louder as a deep color of red rose from Saul's neck to his ears. As his hands formed fists, he replied.

"My name." He enunciated each word. "My Hebrew name is Saul, named after the first king of Israel. But my Roman name is Paulus." After glaring at them for a moment, he added. "You may call me Paulos."

Barnabas had pulled his friend away, into the kitchen.

"Saulus?" Saul hissed. "You know what that means in Greek!"

"I'm sorry—"

"No! Don't refer to me with my Hebrew name again, not around Greek speakers. The last thing I will permit is the bastardization of that great name. Every time they are around me now, they'll be prancing around like a prostitute, poking their fun. I had to tolerate that as a child from my Greek schoolmates. I won't tolerate it as an adult!"

"All right, all right." Barnabas splayed out his hands. "Trust me, they like you. My cousins only torment people they like."

"I don't care if they like me or not!"

"Shhh, I know nobody else here in Salamis, so we must stay here. Try to calm down and at least pretend they don't bother you. For my sake? For the sake of the mission?"

For the sake of the mission. Which went nowhere in his family's hometown, as that was only the beginning.

Barnabas drew his attention to the road he remembered well. As a young child, he and his sister Mary would travel with their parents to visit their mother's family in Kitron. While much had changed in Salamis since then, the wide, dusty, well-traveled road was familiar. At this pace, they should arrive in Kitron well before the sun hung low ahead of them.

Barnabas thought back to the ship from Selucia that brought them close enough to make out the city of Salamis on the island's eastern shore. It was so unlike Jerusalem, but it shone nonetheless as he stood along the ship rail beside Saul, brimming with sentimental pride. He was born and raised there. In Salamis, he had learned the Law and the Prophets, had attended synagogue with his family, and had grown into a young man, learning his father's trade. It was expensive to travel to Jerusalem in order to fulfill their vows and make their offerings, but the few times they did, his return home always warmed him. He had had a sense of belonging in Salamis and of homecoming that he had never experienced elsewhere. After being gone so long, he was surprised to experience it again as he stood along the ship's rail next to his friend and brother in Christ.

But without his parents or his sister, Salamis was not the same. The town seemed smaller to him than he remembered. It had been good to reunite with his uncle and aunt, his cousins, and their families, and it was even better to stay with them. Barnabas knew that his nephew had sorely missed family and understood his hesitancy to leave. But things were simply not the same. Uncle

Hyam had not interrupted as he and Saul had talked about Yeshua and as Saul taught how Yeshua fulfilled the Prophets and the Law. He had not argued or thrown them out of his house. But he had remained unconvinced and had not been baptized. He had not received the Spirit, and that had saddened Barnabas, disappointed Marcus, and confounded Saul. When Saul announced the Spirit said it was time to go, Barnabas had sensed an urgency in Uncle Hyam, packing them up and seeing them out the door.

The journey from one side of Cyprus to the other was not difficult, as Saul and his companions stopped daily in each place along the way. They did not enter any synagogues or preach the good news outside of Salamis. The Spirit held them back. Saul told Barnabas he suspected that, while news of their efforts in Salamis may run before them, the big stage lay ahead in Paphos.

The cities of Old and New Paphos were notorious, even in Judea, for their grotesque worship of the Greek goddess Aphrodite. The area even claimed to be her birthplace. It didn't matter to him whether the legends were Asian, Egyptian, Greek, or Roman. The idols of the various cultures still filled him with disgust. Outside of Jerusalem, it was impossible to travel and not be bombarded by the false god cultures. Even hiding in the Jewish quarters of towns and cities could not spare them from the onslaught of the practices.

The trio had taken very few breaks after leaving Kourion that morning, and they made good time until traffic came to a near stop where the road crept toward the shoreline. The waves pounded on the shore. They inched around a gentle curve, and there before them were the beautiful rock formations.

"That may be what is slowing us," Barnabas pointed to the rocks jutting up out of the sea. "Aphrodite's supposed birthplace."

The famed area, said to be one of the most beautiful in all the Great Sea, had slowed traffic as the people stopped to drink it in. As the trio of men crept closer, the huge formations that appeared to have been hurled into the sea from the cliffs beyond the shore towered above them. The aroma of the sea air hit Saul, and he noted the glorious color of the water as it caressed the large rocks: emerald green and a pure deep blue. John Mark ran into the sea to let the water lick around his legs, cooling his road-worn feet. Barnabas leaned into Saul. "Beautiful, isn't it, Paulos?"

"It's lovely."

"It's magical," Barnabas added. "Can't you feel it in the air?"

John Mark came splashing up to them, excited. "Uncle," he exclaimed. "I'm told we need to experience the sunset here, that it is the most beautiful sunset anywhere!"

Saul frowned. "No. We've more than a couple more hours to go. It won't do for us to be—"

"We can stay here." John Mark pointed to the crowds. "There are others who are already setting up camp. Please, we can stay with them. We'll be safe from robbers. Safety in numbers!"

"Marcus, no." Saul laid a hand on his shoulder. "We can't risk it, not with this crowd."

John Mark shrugged off Saul's hand. "You never want us to have any fun, do you? I'm surprised you aren't standing on the road, yelling at me to get out of the water, like you're my mother!"

Barnabas did not have to say a word, not with the expression he gave his nephew. John Mark sighed, then lowered his voice. "Sorry. Okay, let's go." He stopped to pick up his pack. "But it's true," he muttered.

"Oh, to be young again," Barnabas said. "Come on, let's go before he changes his mind."

Chapter Twelve

**Old Paphos, Cyprus
49 A.D.**

They reached Old Paphos well before the sunset, and they headed straightway to the Jewish quarters of the city. It was not difficult to find the *proxinoi* for the neighborhood, whose job was to direct them to potential lodging, but the only shelter available at that hour was the lesche, a roofed public place with little protection from the elements or from would-be thieves. While it was far from what Saul had hoped, at least they would not be in the street.

"Are you sure you haven't somewhere with walls?" Barnabas had leaned in toward the proxinoi, an irritated, grumpy man who suspected their arrival on the opening night of a pagan festival was not coincidental.

"I assure you, sir," Saul added, "we are not here to participate in the idol worship. We are traveling from Salamis to New Paphos, and need accommodations for the night. Tomorrow we will be on our way."

"I've already heard this from a number of travelers preceding you," the man answered. "I'm afraid the lesche is the best I can do. Perhaps you should have chosen another time to visit."

Defeated, the trio investigated the simple lean-to, resigned to the fact that they were to sleep in the evening air. The sun had slipped behind the western hills and a few strangers were already bedding down, claiming their spots.

"I'm hungry," complained John Mark.

"So am I, Marcus," Barnabas replied. "Paulos? What say you?"

Saul, too, felt empty. "Yes, we can go to the marketplace. Perhaps someone is still open."

"We should claim a spot and leave our bags, don't you think?" John Mark was eying a space in the back corner of the lean-to.

Saul scoffed. "Unless you are willing to give up all our possessions, we had best take them with us. Come, let's hurry, or we'll find ourselves both hungry *and* left to sleep in the open."

They rushed in the light of dusk toward the Jewish marketplace. All but one booth was abandoned, with no one else in sight. The two men packing up their goods noticed the trio and straightened. "We're sorry," said the elder of the two. "We're closed up."

"Ah, well," said Barnabas. "We should have arrived in the city earlier."

John Mark, dejected, hung his head. "It's all my fault. If we hadn't delayed at the rock—"

"Don't blame yourself, Marcus," Saul added. "We will find something else." He turned to the men. "Might you direct us to some place to eat at this hour?"

"No," John Mark said. "It *is* my fault. If we'd been here sooner, maybe we would have found someplace decent to sleep as well as have had something to eat. As it is, we're likely to find ourselves hungry and sleeping under the stars."

"Where do you travel from, friends?" The older man left the rest of the packing to the younger.

"We come from Salamis, most recently," Barnabas answered. "But we sailed from Selucia. We are from Antioch, in Syria."

The man eyed them from under bushy eyebrows. "You are here for the festival?"

Saul answered. "No. Apparently, we picked a bad time to come to Paphos."

The man's entire face spread into a grin. "If you lived in Salamis, you would have known to wait until after the festival to visit. My name is Abreus. This is my brother, Dromeus."

"I am Joseph, this is my nephew, Marcus, and this is Paulos."

"Welcome to Old Paphos."

"You are Greek?" Saul asked.

"Our father was Greek. He gave us good Greek names."

"Your mother is Hebrew."

"Correct," Abreus answered. "She was. They are both deceased. Listen, where are you staying tonight?"

"In the lesche," John Mark answered.

"That will never do. We have some room in our house. It's Dromeus here, my wife, Chara, and me. I'm sure she would not mind. How long are you here?"

"We are actually on our way to New Paphos," Saul answered, "so we only plan to stay overnight. We don't want to impose."

"I would not have offered if I did not want you to stay with us. We have food and room in our house for you to sleep. It is no imposition."

"We can pay you for food and shelter," Barnabas assured.

For the first time, Dromeus spoke. "We will not hear of you paying." He eyed John Mark. "It will be a relief to be around someone my age, for once. And someone I don't have to take orders from."

"You complain too much, little brother." Abreus turned to Barnabas. "And he is right. We wouldn't hear of expecting any pay. Help us haul some of these boxes back home. We don't dare leave any here with all the revelers in town."

The trio followed the brothers toward the residential area of the neighborhood, passing the proxinoi's spot, which was now empty as well. Abreus assured Saul. "You can let him know tomorrow that you found housing with a resident."

Chara was surprised but not unhappy to have visitors, albeit total strangers. She appeared pleased that Dromeus and John Mark made fast friends and that Dromeus had someone to talk to. After offering them water to wash their feet and hearing the story of John Mark's dash into the sea, she showed them to a room where they could leave their belongings. "I'll make up pallets for you," she said, "but not until after you've had something to eat and drink."

The home was larger than Hyam's in Salamis. And unlike the lesche, it had walls. Saul said a silent prayer of thanks. He knew it was no coincidence that they had met Abreus and Dromeus at the marketplace. Even if they had had to sleep in the lean-to, he knew there would have been a purpose to it. He had been enveloped by the warmth of the Spirit from the moment they entered the city.

As they ate, Dromeus and John Mark had their heads together. Saul and Barnabas enjoyed a conversation with Abreus while Chara disappeared from the house. Dromeus had asked his sister-in-law if John Mark could share his room with him. Saul could understand their fast friendship. The two were both burdened by constant companionship with men older than themselves.

As Barnabas talked with Abreus about his childhood and early life in Salamis, Saul's thoughts drifted back, back to Tarsus, to Mother. He had returned to visit her after relocating to Antioch, but not often enough. The journey was not an easy one on foot. Watching Marcus and Dromeus, he wondered what it would have been like to have a brother or a best friend with which to grow up, to be close to, with whom to share stories. He thought of Phineas and took in a deep breath.

Not long after settling in Antioch, he was visited by Bina, the wife of Ananias of Damascus. She told him of the death of Ananias and her escape to Antioch. Bina had conveyed how she believed that saving him, Saul, had been Ananias's calling, his entire purpose in life. She had not returned to Damascus and begged him to avoid it as well. Bina and what was left of her kin became part of Saul's extended family in Antioch, but Saul could not shake off the sorrow each time he met with her and their children.

As soon as the meal was over, as one, Dromeus and John Mark stood. "We're going out," Dromeus announced.

Abreus's eyebrows shot up. "Out?" he echoed. "I don't think that's wise tonight."

Dromeus shook his head. "We'll avoid the crowds and the festival. Because the moon is full, I want to take him to the prominence, to see the view of the sea from there." He turned to Barnabas and Saul. "It's the most beautiful spot in all of Old Paphos and best seen at night. On a night like tonight, it will be at its most splendid." Dromeus turned back to his older brother. "I'll be careful. He may never have this chance again."

Abreus gave his assent. "Don't be out too late. Marcus is probably exhausted from his journey."

Delighted, the two scurried from the older men. Barnabas

watched as they closed the door behind them. "Are you sure they will be all right?" he asked.

"They will be fine," Abreus assured him. "Dromeus has lived his entire life here. He knows how crazy the city gets. Don't worry. They're grown men."

"That's what worries me."

"So," Abreus said, "tell me more about the purpose of your journey. Why, after living this long away from the island, do you return?"

Opening the opportunity to discuss their favorite topic, Barnabas and Saul launched in.

John Mark and Dromeus sat on the ground near the cliff edge, overlooking the Great Sea. The moon, in its rising, seemed to ascend out of the dark waves. Full and orange, it was huge, and its light reflected on the water, making the sea shimmer. The two of them sat without a word for what seemed like hours, though John Mark knew it had only been a few minutes. He let out a sigh, and Dromeus chuckled. "Aren't you glad you didn't miss this?"

John Mark had no words to express his wonder and awe.

"Speechless!" Dromeus said. "Good. I'll take that to mean you like it."

The words came to him. "Great are the works of your hand, O Lord!"

"Amen to that," Dromeus said.

The moon had risen in no time. It was a clear, starlit night, and the moon was bright enough that John Mark read the contentment on Dromeus's face. "It is absolutely splendid," John Mark said. "It's too bad the festival is going on. I can hear it from here."

"That's just the pre-festival celebration. The festival doesn't commence until tomorrow, with the parade to the temple in the morning. The temple is directly below us, to your left."

John Mark leaned forward. Over the prominence, he could barely make out the dark outlines of the huge temple, the light of torches illuminating the far-left side of the edifice. Music, laughter, and voices all blended, competing with the crash of the sea breaking against the rocky shore below. "There are a lot of people down there."

"Yes, there are. Marcus, there is safety in numbers. It's safer to be there with that huge crowd than up here by ourselves."

"Then I suppose we should go back to your house now." John Mark scrambled to his feet. Dromeus remained seated for a few moments longer, scanning the moonlit sea. "I'm glad you were able to experience this," he said, groaning to his feet. "The only thing more lovely than all the statues of Aphrodite."

They turned away. As they neared the path leading to the city, the light of the moon bathed their steps.

"The most stirring of all her statues is near the back of the temple. It is so life-like, you would swear it was a real woman." Dromeus paused. "She is fully naked, standing in all her natural beauty. Quite gorgeous."

"Really? She is at least thinly draped in all the statues I've ever seen of her and Venus."

"Not this one. She is the perfection of the female form. Men fall in love with this statue. Marcus?"

"Yes?"

"When were you last with a woman?"

John Mark stopped near the path winding into the darkness. A copse of trees hid Dromeus so that he seemed like a bodiless voice, but John Mark, who stood unmoving in the moonlight, knew his facial expression in response was visible.

"Ah, I see," Dromeus remarked.

John Mark shook his head. "It's not what you think. I've decided to remain pure until—"

"So, you've never—"

John Mark shook his head. "I have, well, the desire, of course, and there are times that I, well, you know."

Dromeus chuckled. "Yes, I know. Marcus, it's not good for a man to refuse the urges of his body. It can make you ill."

"Chastity is what was intended by circumcision, Dromeus. And until, if I marry—"

"That's your pious uncle whispering in your ear, Marcus. Listen, let's go check out the statue. Once you see it—"

"No!" John Mark exclaimed. "I can't go into a pagan temple."

"There is a backway inside," Dromeus whispered. "I have

gone there a couple of times solely to admire her. Marcus, it will give you something to think about when you're all alone."

"I don't think—"

"Come with me. We'll sneak a peek at the statue, and then, I promise, we'll go home. It won't hurt to step inside."

John Mark did not want his new friend to be angry with him. "It's just inside?" he asked. "We wouldn't have to go in where they perform the rituals and sacrifices?"

Dromeus stepped closer, back into the moonlight. "No, we will be far from the action. Everyone will be near the front of the temple, in the courtyard. If we cut through the gardens, no one will even be aware of us."

John Mark met his new friend's eyes, filled with sincerity and eagerness. "And then we leave and go back to your house?"

"Yes, of course. I promise. Come on, this way. I know it by heart."

"By heart?" John Mark said, amused. "But you've only been there once or twice?"

"Maybe three or four."

John Mark allowed Dromeus to draw him toward the temple. The sounds grew louder as they closed in, and the torchlight was so bright it lit up that entire part of the city. As they neared the crowd, Dromeus cut off to the right and headed toward the elaborate gardens filled with large trees. As they crept along on soft ground, Dromeus leaned in toward him. "Watch your step. There will be people out here, in the dark of the trees."

It was not long before John Mark understood. People were not visible, but even with the background noise of the music, singing, and glee, he could hear them. John Mark recognized the sounds and blushed in the dark. It embarrassed him but, nonetheless, stirred desire within him. This was all new to him and he wanted to hurry through this darkened place to escape it. He and Dromeus made their way through the garden, heading toward the rear of the temple.

John Mark stopped as they entered the shadow of the back portico of the temple. "Are you sure there's no one else here? Won't they have sentries?"

"Trust me," Dromeus whispered, "all the activity is elsewhere. Tomorrow it will be different. These entrances will be guarded once the parade reaches the temple. Until then, it's like any other night."

"You mean to tell me that that stuff goes on all the time?" John Mark indicated behind them, toward the gardens.

Dromeus shrugged. "They've been enjoying the wine and the oysters and are heady with the aromas and anticipation. Come on. This entrance is dark. Even in the moonlight, anyone who spies us won't care. They're either too drunk or too busy." Dromeus dissolved into the deeper shadows of the portico and led John Mark near a shadowed entryway. John Mark laid his hand on Dromeus's shoulder as it was very dark out of the moonlight. Without a sound, they made their way along a hallway. His eyes grew accustomed to the dim light. A soft glow shimmered ahead of them.

Incense and oils mixed with a smoky scent swirled around him, enticing. He now understood how people lost total control of their actions without any vision of the statue.

The two crept closer to the dimly lit part of the hallway, and then, to their right, was an open doorway, the source of the lamplight and the aromas. John Mark released Dromeus and was pulled into the room, as in a dream.

There, in the center, was the most beautiful woman he had ever laid eyes on. Life-size, she stood on a short pedestal, without so much as a drape over her shoulder, her breasts perfectly symmetric and full, pointing right at him, one hand whose fingers lingered over the opposing breast. Her other hand was splayed over her genitals. Her hair was long, cascading over her shoulder. The hollow of her neck was inviting. Her head was turned slightly and her eyes downcast while her mouth, her perfect mouth, was set in a slight smile as if she had a secret to share.

John Mark was so overwhelmed when they entered the room that he hadn't heard the soft murmurs and the grunting. By the time he did, it was too late for retreat. There was someone else in the room. Without thinking, he gasped.

Dromeus grabbed his arm and whispered. "Let's go." They turned to run. Shadows closed in on them.

Five grown men entered the light surrounding them, and they appeared displeased. A sixth man came from behind the statue, adjusting his clothing. "I've got her all warmed up, gentlemen. Who's next?" He stopped short. "What have we here?"

"Trespassers."

A large grin spread across the man's face. "It looks like we're in for a full night of fun, now, doesn't it? Hope you two didn't have other plans."

Saul stooped next to his sleeping friend, deciding that, under the circumstances, it was best to awaken him as gently as possible. "Barnabas, it's Paulos, wake up. The sun has risen."

Barnabas's eyes fluttered before they opened. Saul hovered over him. "That's it, wake up now."

"Sun up?" he croaked, then sat erect. "The sun is up. Oh, I. I'm sorry. I was dreaming. Saul." Barnabas frowned. "It was not a very pleasant dream."

"Get dressed and come on out. We're waiting for you." Saul hurried out the door, joining Abreus and Chara.

"You told him?" Abreus asked.

Saul shook his head. "Not exactly. He's coming."

At that moment, Barnabas appeared, still disheveled. "Where are they? Marcus and Dromeus." His voice cracked. "What's happened?"

Abreus shook his head. "They haven't returned. Dromeus's bed has not been slept in."

Barnabas cupped his forehead. "What happened? Where can they be?" He took a deep breath. "What do we do?"

"We go search for them," Abreus answered. "There's only so many places, but with all the visitors." Abreus's jaw tightened. "I don't know where to start."

Saul took a deep breath. Someone had to think calmly and clearly. Logically. "Perhaps we should start with wherever it was Dromeus was going to take Marcus. What did he say he was going to show him, the moon?"

"The prominence, overlooking the sea. It's a beautiful sight at any time, but with that big full moon—"

"Well, let's go!" said Barnabas. "Maybe they slipped and fell. Perhaps they've both been injured!"

"What is there between here and there, Abreus?" Saul asked. "Might they have run into trouble before even getting there?"

"It's always possible, but most of the Gentile crowds would

have been around the temple, preparing for the festival." Abreus paused and lowered his voice, turning his back on his wife. "Pre-festival festivities, as it were," he added.

"Oh, stop pretending I don't know what goes on," Chara exclaimed. "You don't have to protect me from anything. I'm so worried!"

"Abreus," Saul said, "The fact that both are missing leads me to believe that they are still together. If they were separated, at least one of them would have returned here, if at all possible, to get help."

"Paulos," Barnabas said. "Do you sense anything about them? Does the Spirit give you any indication—"

"The two have encountered danger," Saul said, choosing his words with care. "But I cannot distinguish whether it is physical or spiritual. Perhaps we should split up, go to different areas of the city, then return to a centralized location to report to each other."

"First," Abreus said, "we need to let the proxinoi know where you three are staying, as well as that Dromeus and Marcus are missing. Who knows? He may have heard something."

"That sounds like a good place to start. Then we can spread out based on what we learn there."

"It's decided then. Do you have any weapons?"

"I do," Barnabas replied. "Do you think we will need it?"

"Just in case," Abreus answered. "Be sure you have it on you, and I'll carry mine, too. Let's go."

As Abreus strapped his dagger to his side, they heard a caterwauling approaching the house. The singing, top-of-the-lung wailing was interspersed with drunken laughter. Then the door swung open, and in came Dromeus, half carrying, half dragging John Mark through the doorway. They were filthy. Their garments were soiled with mud, soaked in sweat, and stained with wine. Marcus's hair was matted and stuck to his head, hanging into Dromeus's chest. When Dromeus spied them all standing, staring at him, he paused his singing, and a huge grin spread across his face. "Brother!" he slurred. "You're all here. How wonderful!"

Chara hurried over to them. "Where have you been?" she shouted. "We've been worried sick. Look at you. You're a mess!"

"Chara, you're so *sweeeet*." He stumbled, holding on to John Mark.

Saul stood speechless next to Barnabas, the heat rising in his neck and then in his face. He and Barnabas had assumed they were dead or dying in an alleyway somewhere. As drunk as they were, there was no telling what sins they had committed in the night. Saul didn't trust what he would say if he opened his mouth, so he kept it shut.

"Maybe," Barnabas ventured, "you should both go sleep this off."

"Sleep?" slurred Dromeus. "I can't sleep. I'm not even." He crumbled, and Abreus lunged forward to catch them both.

"No, brother. Barnabas is right," Abreus said, holding Dromeus up. "Let's get you two into bed."

Chara positioned herself on the other side, and the four shuffled off to Dromeus's room. After the door to the room opened and the muffled voices of vague protestations tapered off, Saul dared to address Barnabas. "I'm so sorry, my friend," he said, speaking in low tones. "I should not have let him go."

Barnabas shook his head though he continued to peer toward where his nephew had been carried. "No, he's still my responsibility, Paulos, no matter how old he may be."

Saul took in a deep breath through his nose, attempting to calm his anger. Here they were, on a mission to spread the good news of Christ to the world, and John Mark had been gallivanting about the city on the eve of a vulgar pagan festival. There would be no hope of making disciples in this city, and now their journey to New Paphos would be delayed one more day. The fires of urgency burned within him.

Abreus and Chara reappeared, red-faced, and hurried up to them. "Friends," Abreus said, "I am so sorry. Dromeus is unable to tell us what happened to them, but I think it is obvious. I—" He shook his head. "I apologize. This behavior is unlike him."

"We have been careless hosts," Chara added. "We are in your debt."

Saul waved away their apologies. "They are both grown men who should be able to control their actions. They are not boys. And their selfishness has delayed us yet another day." He paused. "I'm afraid we find ourselves once again in your debt, Abreus. Chara," he turned to her. "Your food smells delicious. Oddly, I'm hungry."

John Mark lay on Dromeus's bed, his face buried in the mattress. He strained to hear as footsteps padded away. He was grateful the curtains were drawn across the window, blocking out the bright sun. He lay in silence, as his heart beat out of his chest. After some time, John Mark whispered. "Dromeus?"

An intake of breath floated from the floor next to the bed. "Yes."

"Do you think they believed us?"

"Mmm. Yes, I do. They were all properly horrified."

Every muscle ached, and John Mark was sore in places he did not know could hurt. The stench of his body assaulted him. "I'm afraid I'm ruining your bed."

"Marcus," Dromeus said.

"I'm disgusting. I reek. The wine can't cover up the smell."

"Please, be quiet. They will hear us."

Once they had been released, left to the elements or thieves or for other twisted revelers to stumble upon and further assault, a pact was made between the two of them. The problem remained how to return home without the truth revealing itself. It was Dromeus who had thought up the ruse.

"Have you ever been around anyone stumbling drunk?" he had asked him. John Mark assured him he had. "Then let's find some wine. Everyone will think we've been drinking all night. Marcus, do you think you can stand and walk?" He had tried, but he had received more attention from their abusers than did Dromeus once they had discovered John Mark was circumcised. Dromeus had dragged him to a row of tall hedges and did his best to hide him before going out in search of wine. The sun was up by the time he returned. He poured some of the wine on himself and then onto John Mark. "Sit up," Dromeus had said. "There you go. Drink."

"Straight wine?" John Mark had protested.

"Yes. It will help kill some of the pain. Its smell must also be on our breath. Marcus." He had held John Mark's neck with one hand while holding the wineskin up to his lips. "We have to be very convincing. My brother is no idiot. We need to be at least halfway drunk for real to be credible."

Which explained why the room was spinning. "Dromeus," Marcus whispered, "make the room stop, please."

But the only answer he received was a loud snore. John Mark closed his eyes, waiting for the sensation to pass, but fell asleep before it did.

They slept much of the day. John Mark's head was pounding, and in the late afternoon, when Chara brought in towels and buckets of warm water, she banged about as much as possible, muttering. John Mark moaned, holding his head, but Chara was all the louder. "Not only worried us near death," she growled, "sure we would have to bury you both, but missing out on income from the market and tomorrow, the Sabbath."

"Chara, sister," Dromeus said, "I am so sorry."

"Hmm, that's right. You are a sorry excuse for a responsible business partner."

She left them, and the two made eye contact.

"Don't worry," said Dromeus, "she won't stay mad for long. If she didn't love me so much, she wouldn't care."

John Mark did not find him very reassuring. He thought Dromeus should be more remorseful. None of this would have happened if they had only stayed at the house.

Despite the horrors they had been through together, John Mark found himself modest before Dromeus. John Mark lowered his eyes to the floor, concentrating on cleaning himself off. As he leaned over to pick up his towel, Dromeus gasped. John Mark spun around, holding the towel up in front of him. "What?" he asked.

"You're bruised!" Dromeus said. "I mean, all over."

John Mark was only aware of the bruises forming on his arms and the front of his legs. He forgot much of what happened, but the sight of the bruises was too much, and stomach acid burned in his throat. He ran to the window, threw back the curtain, and plunged half his body out of it, vomiting whatever was left in his stomach. Once fully emptied, he withdrew and, leaning naked against the window, concentrated on the floor, uncertain if he could ever make eye contact with Dromeus again.

The two appeared for the evening meal, but there was little conversation. The men sat in silence until Chara took away the platters and bowls. Abreus cleared his throat. "We are all accompanying Barnabas and Paulos to the capital city tomorrow. We will seek out Chara's kinsmen there. If they do not have room for all of us, they will be able to lead us to further accommodations."

Dromeus turned sharply to his brother. "Tomorrow?" he asked. "Sabbath starts tomorrow night. We always have our best sales those days."

Abreus glared at his younger brother, quieting him. "Now you are concerned about potential sales? You were not so concerned when you showed up mid-morning. You're responsible for the loss of additional days of income, Brother."

John Mark had kept his head bowed throughout the meal. He did not want to provoke any further scolding himself.

"We will spend this Sabbath with Barnabas and Paulos," Abreus added. "I don't know how long we will stay, so be prepared to stay for a few days or a few weeks. We will support their mission here on Cyprus."

"When should we be ready to leave, Abreus?" Barnabas asked.

"If we can leave at sunrise, we will make it to New Paphos by mid-afternoon," he answered.

"We'll be ready when you are," Saul said. "All three of us."

That night John Mark requested to sleep in the same room as Barnabas, "so we can be ready at the same time," he had explained. He made up his pallet next to his uncle in silence.

"Marcus," Barnabas said, "you understand that we were all very worried about you two, don't you? We were prepared to find your bodies." Silent, John Mark continued to smooth out the fabric that would be his mattress that night. "Marcus."

He lifted his head to his uncle, the only real father he had ever had. The debt he owed him was immeasurable. "Yes, Uncle. I know, and I am so sorry. It—" He shook his head. "It won't happen again."

Barnabas sat on his haunches. "It's that our mission is its early stages, and we, Paulos and I both, need to be able to trust you."

John Mark stood up with sudden anger. "I said I was sorry," he shouted. "What more do you want from me?"

"We want you to represent Christ, like us." These were the first words Saul had said to him since the previous evening. "In everything you think, in everything you say, in everything you do."

"I knew him far better than you!" As soon as the words were out of his mouth, he regretted them. Saul's dark eyes burned, and John Mark again dropped his head. "I'm sorry. I didn't mean that."

"Marcus!" Barnabas protested.

"I'm sorry. I'm sorry, Paulos." John Mark shook his head. "I let my guard down with Dromeus. I let him gain my confidence, my friendship, and then he led me—"

"Marcus, stop." It was Saul who interrupted him. "No one else is in control of your actions. Did he hold a knife to your throat? Did he pour the wine in your mouth?"

Well, in truth, yes. But John Mark was done talking. Dromeus had told some story that evening about how they ended up drunk and John Mark had muttered that he didn't remember much, not wanting to punch any holes into Dromeus's story. If he said anything further, the full truth would be sniffed out, especially by Saul, who John Mark suspected had his doubts but did not voice them. John Mark knew that Saul would not disrespect Abreus by questioning his brother's tale. He met Saul's eyes. "You are right, Paulos. It was my fault. It was my responsibility to follow my instincts, that leaving this house was a mistake. I disrespected both my uncle and you, and I am genuinely sorry."

Saul was silent as he regarded John Mark, then, satisfied, Saul gave a brief nod. "Good. Don't let it happen again."

Chapter Thirteen

New Paphos, Cyprus
49 A.D.

The last week had been exhausting but thrilling. It was no wonder to Saul that the Holy Spirit urged them to New Paphos. Many souls there were in need of the good news. The harvest was plentiful and ready for reaping.

All week, apart from the Sabbath, there was a line outside the home of Chara's kin where they were lodging. John Mark, Dromeus, and Abreus took on the roles of ushers as friends, families, and neighbors of the ill lined up for healing by Barnabas. Just like Abreus, Chara's family would not accept pay for their housing, though with the influx of six more mouths to feed, they did allow Saul and Barnabas to help pay for food. At their first attendance at the synagogue, Saul was asked to speak. Since then, he had been busy teaching and arguing. Meanwhile, after the initial healing the week before, the crowds had grown. Word of their presence in the city spread quickly.

Sweat beaded on Saul's brow and ran down his forehead, stinging his eyes. It was too hot to be standing for long in the mid-morning sun, but he was surrounded by several men, deep in discussion. Today there were more there to argue after his latest talk in the synagogue. When one spoke about forgiveness of sin, something only God could do, feathers tended to get ruffled.

"Did you or did you not claim that the Christ can forgive sin where the law of Moses condemns?"

The man's breath nearly knocked Saul over. "Let me ask you this," he replied. "Do those without the Law sin?"

"Of course!"

"And do those with the Law sin?"

"Well, yes, but—"

"All who sin without the Law will perish without the Law, and all who sin under the Law will be judged by it."

"Answer the question!" another man interjected.

"I am. Follow me for a moment. So, if someone without the Law nonetheless follows it, what then? Where is the condemnation?"

"We have several people who come to our synagogue who are Gentile believers. They learn the Law from us and only lack the one thing."

"Do you then hold them to a higher standard than yourselves?"

"We have the Law! And we are sons of Abraham."

"But because you have the Law, when you break it, is it not worse for you? What excuse do you have? But if they, who do not have the Law, follow it, their circumcision is not of the body, but of the heart. So, you see, Christ came to redeem Israel. For Israel's condemnation is great, since they have the Law and have no excuse. We are all under the power of sin, Greek and Jew alike. This is why Christ came, that both Jew and Greek might be justified."

"We are justified by the offerings we make."

"Difficult to give offerings every time you sin," Saul countered, "no? Do you take off for Jerusalem every week, every day?"

"But the Law—"

"Christ Jesus was the sacrifice. His blood was the atonement for all our sins. Is the Lord the God of only the Jews, or is he the God of Gentiles also?"

"You're a madman!" another interjected.

Saul pointed toward the house. "By what name are these neighbors of yours being healed?" The man bowed his head. "What is easier for you to believe? But look: the lame are made to walk and the blind to see. Physically, I was whole, and under the Law, I was blameless. It was my soul that was lame and my mind that was blind.

Praise be to God, I was healed!"

A sense of warning hit Saul. Darkness drew near. Saul looked about at the crowd of men surrounding him.

"Paulos," yet another said, "can you tell us some stories of Christ Jesus from his ministry? Some of the things he did and said?"

Saul was asked this often. He pointed to the doorway of the house. "Do you note that young man there? His name is Marcus. He and his uncle, whom we lovingly call 'Barnabas,' followed Jesus during his ministry. Marcus is the expert. He loves to tell those stories. Unfortunately, all I knew of Christ Jesus firsthand before his resurrection was at his trial. And I prefer to try to forget that." The man and a few of his companions hurried toward the house to engage John Mark's attention.

The sense of spiritual darkness again came over him. Saul surveyed the area to identify the source of the foreboding. A handful of Roman guards marched near, and the weasel of a man from the synagogue was with them. Saul did not know the man's story, but he was not surprised by the company he kept.

The men surrounding Saul fell back as the guards advanced. Whispers of "Elymas" swirled around him. Magician? That must be the reason he sensed the evil around the man. The magician pointed his finger at Saul and exclaimed, "That's one of them." The Romans closed in on him.

"Where are your friends, the two who were with you at the synagogue?" the little man demanded.

Saul looked intently at the man. It was not demon possession. A healing of that manner would not save him. Staring into the man's deceitful eyes made discomfort curdle Saul's stomach, so Saul turned instead to the Roman guard before him. "What do you want from us?"

"You are summoned by the proconsul, Sergius Paulus," came the reply. "You and your friends are to come with us."

"Go get them," Elymas said to him. "You don't want to keep the proconsul waiting."

Guards escorted Barnabas, John Mark, and Saul to the governmental complex sitting on a hill overlooking the great sea. They continued through several courtyards and porticoes before they halted at the heavy doors of an interior hall. The senior of the guards disappeared through the doors before returning to usher them in.

Seated at a table, the proconsul raised his head as the group neared. "Lucius, are you sure these are the miracle workers I've heard about? They appear so common."

"These are the men Bar-Jesus pointed out to us, Proconsul."

"Don't be deceived by their beggarly appearance," Elymas added. "They are wily and disruptive. One can barely navigate the street past the house where they are staying for the crowds."

Saul contemplated the proconsul. He had received no bad reports, but he was all too aware of the precarious relationship Romans had with the Jews, even outside of Jerusalem. Large gatherings of Hebrew people tended to result in a closer Roman eye, all for the sake of maintaining the "Roman peace."

Sergius Paulus rose and maneuvered around to lean on the front of the table. He waved the guards back, who retreated close to the door. Crossing his arms, he eyed Saul, Barnabas, John Mark, and Elymas standing before him. "Word is, you are preaching about another new savior for your people. You are not the first to bring Paphos news of this one. Bar-Jesus." He turned to Elymas. "What was the name again?"

"Jesus of Nazareth."

"That's right. Of course, another Judean. So, your topic is not a new one. But you bring us something that is new, different." The proconsul paused. "Eyewitnesses."

Saul dipped his head

"Tell me about him. What makes this one so different from the others that word of him would spread across Judea and onto Cyprus? And, if he is dead, why does his cult continue to grow? This makes no sense to me."

"He is not dead," Barnabas answered.

"But he was crucified, correct? In Jerusalem?"

"Yes, he was."

"So, he is quite dead."

"He rose from the dead." John Mark exclaimed. "We experienced him ourselves. We observed him taken down from the cross and buried, and then we saw him alive, the nail prints on his wrists!"

Sergius Paulus paused. He uncrossed his arms. "Is this true? How can it be?"

"It's a lie, Proconsul," Elymas hissed. "That is impossible!"

The proconsul held up his hand. "Let them speak, Bar-Jesus. I want to know what they've been saying. Now, back up. What did he do that had him crucified? What treason did he commit?"

"He raised a man from the dead who had been in the tomb for several days," Saul answered. "He traveled for a few years all over Judea, healing, teaching, and performing miracles. That was enough to get the attention of the high priest in Jerusalem. But when he was in their backyard, closer than Old Paphos is from here, he performed that greatest of all miracles. The crowds! The rallying of the people!" Saul shook his head. "And it was right before the Passover. Jews from all over the world journeyed to Jerusalem."

"An uprising," Sergius Paulus said, understanding.

"Exactly how it appeared. From that point on, for fear of Roman authority in the city, the high priest and the Sanhedrin, the Temple judges, so to speak, sought to end it. There was a price on the head of Jesus, as well as for the man whom he raised from the dead."

"To keep the peace."

"To keep the peace," Saul echoed. "We brought as many paid false witnesses forward to build a case of blasphemy against him. Blasphemy is punishable by death. It was best to silence him altogether."

"*We*?" asked Sergius Paulus, pointing at all three of them. "You were part of the court that tried him?"

"Not them," Saul answered. "Me. I was a lawyer and a counsel for the Sanhedrin. These two were Jesus's faithful followers. But me?" He shook his head. "I was his enemy. I helped condemn him and convinced the Sanhedrin that they had to take his case to Rome. We said that the people declared Jesus their king."

"Thus, crucifixion."

"Precisely. After his resurrection, as his following grew, I personally persecuted his people."

"How did you come to be with these, his followers?"

"I was traveling to Damascus, in Syria, to round up his believers there. As I approached the city, I was struck blind by a brilliant light, and I heard his voice. Jesus appeared in the light. He commissioned me. He blinded me. He then sent someone to heal me, then he sent me out to tell others about him, about his saving grace."

"You don't actually believe this story, Proconsul. It's a pack of lies!" Elymas blurted.

The Spirit urged Saul to turn his attention from the proconsul to Elymas. Fear engulfed Elymas's eyes and the darkness blurred and dimmed around the man.

"The magic they are doing," Elymas said, "the healings, it is nothing more than a suggestion, accomplishable by any good magician. Resurrection of the dead is impossible. I say these men are here to stir up dissension in the city, to start riots. You need to arrest them!"

"You son of the devil," Saul accused, "enemy of goodness, full of deceit and evil, when will you stop making crooked the straight paths of the Lord?"

Elymas's eyes widened.

"Now, listen: the hand of the Lord is against you! You will be blind for a while, even to the sun."

Elymas fell to his knees and, clutching his face, cried out. He slapped his hands on the floor and threw back his head, exposing the growths over his eyes. Exactly as Saul had experienced in Damascus. "Get someone to help him," Saul said to the proconsul. "He will need someone to guide him."

Sergius Paulus signaled at the guards, and one hurried over to help the man stand. Before they left with him, Saul laid a hand on Elymas's arm. "Brother Bar-Jesus," he said, "give heed to him when he comes to you. You have been blinded just as was I, solely so you might come to his light."

The proconsul cleared the room of all but Saul, Barnabas, and John Mark, and he scrutinized the trio through drawn eyebrows. "The stories you have told me do sound outlandish. But I find no sign of deceit from any of you. I am amazed at these revelations and have much to think about. While I should like to learn more, I fear for what Bar-Jesus warned. If you have not met opposition yet for drawing the crowds, you soon will. How long do you plan to stay in Paphos?"

"We stay until the Spirit tells us to leave," Saul replied.

The proconsul spread a hand toward them. "Stay and dine with me tonight, then you may return. If there's any rumbling against you, I will arrange for your way off the island."

"Dine with you?" John Mark asked. "You are aware that there

are things we may not eat."

Sergius Paulus scoffed. "I don't know what they prepare for me. I just eat. I want you to tell me more about Jesus of Nazareth, so eat if you want or don't. It's up to you."

A mere week passed before they received notice that the proconsul had secured passage for them to get safely off the island. John Mark was relieved. Word spread all across Cyprus of the miracle workers in the capital city. As the crowds grew in size, cluttering the streets of the Jewish neighborhood, the opposition grew louder. The day after they dined with the proconsul, the local synagogue leaders showed up and forbade them to return. Eating with Gentiles, especially the Roman proconsul, was more than they could abide.

John Mark remembered the meal, the three of them eating very little, unsure of how it had been prepared but eating enough so as not to be impolite. He warmed at the memory of how Paulos and then his uncle Joseph had torn off pieces of the bread before handing it on to him, exchanging knowing expressions.

When the synagogue closed to the three of them, it signaled that their time in Paphos was at an end. John Mark had trouble understanding why all this delighted his uncle and Paulos. The more opposition, they said, the stronger the work of the Spirit. Whatever that meant.

That morning, they'd packed their few belongings and boarded the vessel. Hours later in the dark, John Mark lay on a narrow wooden berth, his hand gripping the side, afraid the rough seas would toss him onto the floor below. He had no idea how anyone slept like this, especially considering he was on the top berth. Paulos was to have the bottom, but his seasickness prevented sleep. On the middle berth, his uncle Joseph snored, exhausted from the work of healing, teaching, and baptizing hundreds of people, and excited at the prospect of what Pamphylia, across the sea from Cyprus, had in store for them.

John Mark was much less enthusiastic. That Abreus and Chara, and then Dromeus and Chara's kin, had all believed in Christ

Jesus and were baptized, made him quite happy. He was glad for Dromeus, who, while he would never betray the pact of secrecy between them, confessed to leading them both into evil and was relieved of that heavy burden. The new group of believers had received the Holy Spirit and the Spirit's gifts. His uncle was relieved that among them came the gift of healing so that the work continued in his absence. Abreus and Chara learned many of the stories of Yeshua, and of course, they all knew the story of Paulos's encounter with the risen Christ. Paulos had made sure of that.

Below John Mark, Paulos moaned softly. The stink of the cabin clung thick like clothing, a combination of moldy wood, grease, and the poorest grade lamp oil, the smoke lingering in the air. The buckets of body waste added to the other odors made the cabin unlivable during the hot daytime. At night, it was only a bit less miserable. Twice already, Paulos had retched into one of the buckets. He said a silent prayer, thankful that he did not suffer from the same. He knew he shouldn't, but for him, it was a flaw in Paulos's otherwise strong disposition. That, and the headaches. His uncle did not have the problem, nor did Cephas, who was as much at home standing in a small vessel on Lake Gennesaret, rocking with the waves, as he was on land. But Paulos had not been raised to hard labor like most people in the world. Maybe this motion sickness was his recompense for a softer, less physical life. It was difficult for John Mark to be sympathetic.

Many had asked why Uncle Joseph was the only healer. Didn't the Spirit empower all of them to heal? John Mark knew that Paulos sometimes healed people, but Paulos would assert that the gifts of prophecy and discernment were strongest for him and that Uncle's inborn compassion for people is what made him an excellent healer. While it had always been understood in Antioch that Joseph was the leader of the mission, Paulos was assuming more of the lead. It was Paulos's organizational skills that had solidified the small group of believers, and it was Paulos who had left Abreus and Chara as the leaders of the fledgling church there. Never mind that Abreus, Chara, and Dromeus lived five hours away. They were expected to stay in New Paphos and re-establish their livelihood there. But if that was what Christ Jesus required, then that was what one did.

Did not he and his mother leave their home in Salamis? Didn't Uncle Joseph and Cephas and the Twelve all do the same? Even

Paulos left everything he had known, so what is five hours of travel time away? Where wouldn't he, John Mark, go if Yeshua bid it?

He sighed, longing to roll onto his side without falling from his berth. Thinking about the Holy Spirit these days depressed him. He was depleted of the Presence since that night in Old Paphos, which only led to more self-loathing. John Mark no longer blamed Dromeus or even their attackers. He had brought this on himself with his lack of self-control, to lust, to the great temptation, all things only he was able to control himself. He had failed, and miserably. He did not know how to atone for his failures or if the Spirit would ever again find him worthy. Every miraculous healing, every baptism, every work of the Spirit evident in the new believers served to make his failure and his loneliness all the more glaring. He did not dare talk to his uncle or, heaven forbid, Paulos about it. He wished to talk with Cephas. Cephas would understand without him having to tell the whole dark tale. He longed for the Temple, to take a vow, present himself and his offerings to the Temple priests, and find redemption and wholeness.

Another groan came from Paulos, followed by sounds of him lunging for the buckets and more retching. John Mark was glad that they would only have to spend that one sleepless night on this vessel together.

Chapter Fourteen

**Perga, Pamphylia
49 A.D.**

They made it to the port of Attalia so late at night that the crew had opted to stay aboard in the harbor overnight, waiting until morning to unload some of its cargo, the remainder bound for Perga to supply the proconsul and his garrison. Barnabas, Saul, and John Mark disembarked early afternoon and headed toward the city, which sat on the flat shore, the mountains jutting into the sky above them.

Entering the town, they found an inn near the marketplace and secured a room for the night. John Mark found the small Jewish community with its equally small synagogue. He talked with excitement about a group of young men his age he had found praying together. They were preparing for a pilgrimage to Jerusalem for the Day of Atonement.

The next morning, John Mark, wringing his hand in his robes, told his uncle of his plans to journey with the group and asked for his blessing.

"But, Marcus, why now? In the middle of our mission? We've only now reached Pamphylia."

Barnabas, bewildered, searched the face of his nephew.

"I know how it must seem to you, Uncle Joseph," John Mark

replied. "But I must go."

"It has not been a pleasant experience the last several days," Barnabas added. It was miserable enough on the ship. Since landing, however, it did no good to try to bathe, as the sweat poured from them with any exertion, and the mosquitoes assaulted them day and night, coating the netting over their rough beds.

"It's not that."

"If it's because of what happened in Paphos," Barnabas stopped at the pained expression on his nephew's face.

"Uncle." John Mark's voice broke.

"Did something happen, Marcus? Something you haven't told us about?"

Barnabas sensed Saul close in, his heavy eyebrows drawn together, concern showing itself on his face.

"I must go, Uncle Joseph." John Mark's voice was hoarse with his reply. "I must present myself to the Temple priests, bring a sin offering."

"No, Marcus," Saul injected. "No, you don't. You know your sin is covered—"

"I know that!" John Mark snapped at him. "You think I don't know, didn't experience the sacrifice of Jesus?"

"Then why?"

"Because, Paulos." John Mark's voice had raised. "Because I'm so distant from him!" He turned away from Saul. "Uncle, I observe the Spirit work through you. It amazes me over and over. And I watch the Spirit work in Paulos, filling both of you with miraculous power. And I? I am alone. The Spirit of God has abandoned me."

"Or have you abandoned him?" Saul's voice was low and gentle but with the edge of knowing.

John Mark shook his head. "All I know is this: I have sinned against God and against you, both of you, and I feel called to seek him in his Temple while I can. What better time than the Day of Atonement? I need my feet standing in her gates. I need to pass through Solomon's portico, to be with my people."

There was a moment of silence before Barnabas broke it. "But we are your people, Marcus."

John Mark set his mouth in a firm line. "We depart in the morning," he said, with finality. "I will need some money to secure my passage and for food until we reach Jerusalem. Then I will find Cephas and James, and the Jerusalem church."

Saul reached amongst his belongings and grabbed a bag of coins. He poured the contents into his hand, assessed it, and then refilled the bag. He returned to John Mark and held it out to him. "Take it," he said. "Don't let them cheat you out of all of it."

John Mark grasped the bag, and Saul covered his hand with his own. "Give our regards to the church in Jerusalem. Give them any of these coins that may remain. Tell them about our work here and what you have seen and heard."

Barnabas embraced his nephew, holding back tears. "Give Cephas our regards." He squeezed his eyes shut and whispered in John Mark's ear. "I don't know when we shall meet again, Marcus. God be with you."

John Mark pulled back, grabbed his belongings with one hand, and strode away.

The moment John Mark left to find his fellow pilgrims, wavy lines appeared in Saul's vision, the harbinger of impending misery. The pattern was always the same. It started small, in the center of his vision, and would gradually expand, disturbing his eyesight to the point that reading or writing was impossible. It might last hours or a few minutes. Sometimes no headache followed. This time, however, Saul did not need the gift of prophecy to understand his headache sickness was about to hit him. Within an hour, he lay on his bed in the gloom, glad for a room without a window. It was sticky, unbearably hot, and in the center of a loud public inn. But at least it was dark.

He lay on his side, his hands covering his ears, a wet cloth covering his eyes. Every sound was amplified, and waves of nausea still undulated through him. His eyes hurt to move them, even under closed lids.

It had been years since his last episode and even longer since he had had one this severe. Perhaps it was the heat. He wanted to figure it out, but it hurt too much to think. If he slept, maybe it would go away.

He was aware, off and on, of Barnabas coming and going. But even his soft footfalls on the floor pounded loudly in Saul's ears. At one point, Barnabas asked about a physician. Barely audible, Saul whispered, "No, just let me sleep."

Saul did sleep, waking on occasion. By the next morning, the headache was better but far from over. At least Barnabas's voice didn't clang like a cymbal when he brought him something to eat, which Saul refused. "I'm more thirsty than hungry," he said, slumping on the bed's side.

Barnabas handed him a cup of beer. "If you don't eat something, Paulos, you will get too weak. Try to eat something."

"Marcus?" Saul asked.

"They departed early this morning."

Saul laid back, closing his eyes. Even in the dim lamplight, the pain behind his eyes still stabbed. The heat of the day was rising, and his clothes were already sticky and damp. The sickness and head pains began as a youth. What was it that Mother would do to help him? Some herbs, perhaps?

"Paulos," Barnabas's voice still soft and low, "we need to get you help. Word is, there are healing pools, up north, in the mountains."

Mountains. Yes, sometimes going up in the Taurus Mountains would help, when he was young. "Yes," he whispered. "We should go."

"Do you think you can travel?"

"We need guides, with mules." Saul swallowed. He would never make it on foot. Even if he were in good health, it would take too long. The very concept of riding through mountain passes was foreboding. But maybe the healing pools would help. "Go, find some Gauls willing to pack us. Where are the pools?"

"Antioch, near Pisidia."

"Take some of the money. Pay half of what they want. Find out how soon we can leave. I'll rest while you find them. And Barnabas: douse the light when you leave, please."

The following morning, they met up with Acco and his

brother, Camulos, their guides through the mountains. Saul did well while it was dark enough that he even helped pack the mules. However, the bright daylight by mid-morning had him begging to stop, that Barnabas might help him tie some scraps of black cloth over his eyes and guide his mule. Barnabas watched over him, worried that, off and on, when Saul fell asleep, he was in danger of falling. The last thing they needed would be physical injury added to his friend's illness.

In the years he had known Saul, there were a few times he had had a bad headache, but those tended to improve after he slept. Never had Barnabas experienced anyone ill like this, and the sweating and weakness caused him to worry about the bad air disease. He hoped that the healing pools of Antioch by Pisidia helped if that were the case. It was difficult enough to continue the mission without his nephew. It would be impossible without his friend and brother in Christ.

Lonesome thoughts of his nephew swarmed him. Barnabas hoped John Mark met with smooth seas. His companions seemed to be good men, but that did not prevent him from worrying over and missing his nephew. The hope was they would reunite in a couple of months, as the plan had been to return to Syria before winter set in. Nobody wanted to risk the Great Sea in the wintertime if it could be helped. The church at Antioch had not sent them with enough money for an extended journey, in any case. If they were to have enough left for their return passage, they must rely on the hospitality of strangers from here on out.

Barnabas worried about spending much on guides, but Saul had insisted. Local guides would be the best protection from the dangerous mountain roads as well as the fastest way to get where neither of them had been before. And there were no better guards than Gauls. Even the Romans were wary of them and would hire them as mercenaries. Acco and Camulos were professional guides, and their reputation in Perga assured Barnabas that a safe arrival was guaranteed. They would also not want to tarry, as they were paid a flat fee. The duo needed to get to the destination as soon as possible so that they may be available for hire elsewhere.

Barnabas studied Acco, the largest of the two brothers, who had tied the reins of Saul's mule to his. He was a tall, rugged man and appeared very strong. His hair was a curly light brown that fell to his shoulders, and he sported a trimmed beard. Barnabas was fascinated by the greenish-blue color of his eyes. His hands were massive, and Barnabas suspected those hands contained the strength to crush another man's neck. What Barnabas noticed at once, however, was that, despite his foreboding appearance, Acco had a delightful laugh.

It was the brother, Camulos, who made Barnabas uncomfortable. Camulos spoke little and always wore a frown. He had an air of suspicion for everyone and sensed potential danger behind every rock. While the two brothers spoke excellent Greek to Barnabas and Saul, they used a language Barnabas did not recognize when they spoke to each other. Camulos would say something under his breath, and Acco would chuckle in response. The unknown communication only added to their intimidation.

Whenever night threatened, they would set up camp. One brother slept while the other kept guard. Barnabas never observed both of them asleep at the same time. After setting up camp every day, they all ate a little and drank some wine. Because it had become their habit no matter where they were, Saul blessed the food, speaking the prayer aloud. The Gauls said nothing.

One night, Camulos and Saul slept against a solid rock wall while Acco kept watch. He sat apart on top of the short outcropping, his back to them. The man's broad back was straight and rigid. Barnabas assumed he held his weapon ready.

Barnabas neared Acco. "May I join you?" he asked.

"Are you armed?" Acco answered.

"No, but I can be."

"That would make more sense."

Barnabas returned carrying his dagger. Spying it, Acco grunted his approval. As the night darkened around them, the buzzing of mosquitoes and chirping of crickets accented the initial silence. It was warm, but the absence of the hot sun was a relief, and it was not as muggy as in Perga. "Acco," Barnabas asked, "are you or Camulos married?"

Acco scoffed. "Are you?"

"No. Neither is Paulos."

"Why not?"

"Our time is dedicated to our God. It is no life for a wife and children."

"About the same as the life of a packer."

Acco never stopped scanning their surroundings, and they spoke in soft tones, keeping an ear out for the slightest sound of a footstep on gravel.

"Have you done his long?" Barnabas asked.

"You ask a lot of questions."

"We're going to be spending several days together. I thought it would be nice to know each other some."

"I thought you Jews didn't associate with others. You're the first one I've met who has attempted any conversation past business transactions."

"I think you will find that when he is more himself, Paulos and I are quite unlike what you are used to."

"You already are."

"We set sail to Cyprus several weeks ago, sent by our church in Antioch of Syria, to proclaim the Christ."

"The only thing I know about your religion is that you refuse to worship the gods."

Acco paused as his head snapped to the right, attentive and alert. Barnabas strained at whatever it was that had alarmed him, but only the nighttime sounds of the mountains reached his ears. The singing of the insects and the scampering of rodents. Barnabas wondered about any great cats that might be on the prowl, but he knew Acco was more concerned about other men. He had assured Barnabas that he and his brother knew the way well and that, while some of the passes offered shelter, others made them more vulnerable to attack.

Acco gave a slight turn of his head. "I think it best to have no more conversation tonight. Even slight sounds may represent danger. Try to sleep."

Barnabas agreed and left him to lie down near Paulos.

The Spirit urged him to speak again the following day. They had paused in the heat of the midday, tucked into the shadow of a mountain peak. The trees grew tall there and offered some shade as well. Barnabas still had some bread, and he tore off a piece and handed it to Saul. He was improving, and though the bright sun bothered him still, Saul regarded the brothers and held the bread out to them. Acco's mouth fell open in surprise, but Camulos grabbed the bread, tore the remainder in half, and then handed it to his brother.

"Wait," Saul said, stopping Camulos before he placed it in his mouth. "Let us tell you what this means to us first."

"It's bread," Camulos replied.

"Brother," Acco scolded. "Wait."

The two held their bread as Barnabas explained. "When you need to atone for something you have done, what do you do?"

"I never have to atone for anything," Camulos snapped.

"Your people, then," Barnabus said. "What do your people do?"

Acco shrugged. "We make offerings, hoping that the gods won't punish us."

"You go to a temple and offer up a sacrifice," Barnabas said. "Same for our people. But there is only one temple for us, in Jerusalem. As God's people migrated throughout the world, imagine the difficulty of giving a genuine offering!"

"Why not build more temples?"

Barnabas gestured with open hands. "Why not make only one sacrifice that will cover all sins? If everyone else is right, and multiple gods use people as playthings, and we have no free will, then it's not really us who sin. But if we are right, and there is the one true God who gives us free will, then there is sin. And if there is sin, and we are brought to recognize it, then we must offer penitence."

Acco pondered the words. "If it is as you say." He paused. His eyes bounced back and forth between Saul and Barnabas. "Then who can be saved?"

"Eat your bread, Acco," said Saul. "And let us tell you our story."

They paused too long in the shade, and, his eyebrows bunched together, Camulos complained. "We'll not make it to our next camping spot until well after nightfall now. Hopefully, the moon will be bright enough tonight that we can make out the trail."

"The sun is still agony for me," said Saul. "If there's enough moonlight to see by, why don't we travel at night and rest in the heat of the day? Don't the thieves do the same?"

"That's a good point," replied Acco. "Let's try to sleep here some now, and then as the sun goes behind the mountains, we will head back out."

Camulos frowned, not thrilled by the idea. But he said he was willing to give it a try. "Say," Camulos said to Barnabas, "if you healed all those people in Paphos, on Cyprus, why don't you heal him?" He pointed to Saul.

"It's not I who is the healer," Barnabas answered, "but the Spirit of God. I am merely the tool he uses."

"Okay, then, why doesn't the Spirit use you to heal him?"

Barnabas shook his head. "I don't know. Maybe this sickness serves a purpose."

Camulos opened his mouth, incredulous. "Still sounds to me like the gods are playing with you. Your stories sound amazing, but if you healed him in front of me using that power, I might be more likely to believe what you say is true."

"You are right, Barnabas," Saul said. "If I had not grown ill in Perga, would we still be there? But the Spirit is spurring me on, to get to Pisidia. Might the healing pools be where we need to be? Might something happen there that will be vital to our mission?"

Acco gave a short huff. "You think too much, Paulos. That's what makes your head hurt."

Late afternoon shadows indicated that it was time to continue on and they did so, reaching Lake Aksehir early morning. Several groups of people congregated in areas near the lake, and for the first time, Camulos relaxed. Barnabas wondered if they were near their home base. He had not learned any specifics about their previous lives or their families. Everyone grew up somewhere, and these two knew every rock, every outcropping, and every turn in the road.

Acco assured them that they were now within a couple of days from Antioch. Since their food supply was growing sparse, Camulos offered to go to the small town on the southern aspect of the lake and purchase more. Barnabas gladly provided him with more coins for that purpose, anticipating something fresh to eat, and then helped set up an awning near the shore where they might rest.

Chapter Fifteen

**Antioch near Pisidia, Galatia
49 A.D.**

I think they are very strange, and I am glad to be done with them," Camulos answered his brother once he entered their room at the inn, throwing their belongings on the floor. "Why would you give those Jews another thought?"

"But what if they are right?" Acco persisted. "About the one god and the man who was raised from the dead! What about that?"

"Brother, have you gone mad? Our gods were sufficient for our ancestors. When things go wrong for us, we take offerings to the god or goddess that we angered and maybe they stop being angry with us. When things go well, it's because the gods and goddesses are pleased with us."

Acco shook his head. "Just because that's what our ancestors and our people believe doesn't necessarily make it so. Have you never questioned that belief?"

"No, I haven't."

"But that means our lives have no real meaning. It means we have no free will, that we are simply playthings of the gods!"

"Believe what you want," Camulos said, gesturing with his money bag, "but I believe I have been paid, and there's plenty to drink downstairs and some women I can buy for the night. Come, let's get drunk and have some fun."

Acco always had a great time when they had money to burn, and part of him wanted to leave with his brother. Another part of him, oddly, did not. "I think I will go check on them," Acco said as casually as possible. "Make sure they are settled."

Camulos shrugged his shoulders and left their room. "Suit yourself, Brother."

Acco rapped on the door where they had left the travelers. Peeking out at him, Barnabas's eyebrows shot up. "Did we not pay you what you had asked?"

"Oh, no. I mean, yes, you did. That's not why I'm here. My brother," Acco indicated with his thumb, "he has already left, and I—"

"Your brother left you?"

"No, he, well, yes, but—"

"Come in and sit," Saul said.

"We were going to do some more work," Barnabas explained. "Prepare more items to sell in the marketplace."

Acco sat on the floor with them as they worked, their hands nimble, their leather work practiced and professional. He admired craftsmen. Acco's only skills were his physical strength and endurance. "Are you feeling better already, Paulos?" he asked.

"Manageable," Saul answered.

"But you are still going to the healing pools, yes? It's amazing how water can be so powerful."

"We're not going now," Saul replied. "We have to preserve our cash for our return passage. I'm afraid we can't afford it."

Acco frowned. He thought of his brother and what he was already spending his earnings on. "If you had not paid us, you would be going. I will take you to the pools tomorrow," Acco said. "I will pay for it. You must get well, to do what you came here for."

"You earned that money. I can't allow you—"

"I insist, Paulos. Let it be my donation to your mission."

"We do need for you to be at full strength, Paulos," Barnabas added. "I think it's a good idea."

Sighing, Saul conceded. "I can't fight you both. All right, we can go in the morning. But then we'll need to get to the marketplace and sell what we can."

"Do you still have the dagger scabbard," Acco asked. "The one with the matching belt?"

"Yes, we do," Barnabas answered.

"Could I see it again?"

Barnabas sorted through a bag. "This set? I have a few of them in here."

Acco smiled. "Yes, that's the one." He ran his hand over it, appreciating the quality of the leather and the expert finishing. Standing, he wrapped the belt around his waist and tied it. "Let me buy this from you. I need a new one, and this is perfect." He removed it and handed it out to Barnabas.

"Keep it," Barnabas said.

"I'll pay you tomorrow before we leave."

"Acco." Saul kept his eyes on his work. "Where is your brother?"

"My brother is currently enjoying the fruits of his labor."

"Why didn't you join him?"

Acco weighed his response as he resumed his seat. "I don't know. Normally, I would have."

"I thought I noted the innkeeper's eyes light up at the sight of you two." The corners of Saul's mouth were forming a little smile.

"We do have a bit of a reputation," he admitted.

"I find it curious that you choose to sit on the floor with two old men when you could be out with your brother."

"Me, too," Acco admitted. "I suppose there's something about you two." He paused. "Besides, I was able to get my hands on the scabbard before you sold it off."

Acco awoke at sunrise. There was no sign of Camulos, not that he had expected him. It might be a couple more days before his brother resurfaced, hungover, fully sated, and completely broke.

Outside the inn, Acco met Saul and Barnabas, all their belongings with them. "What is all this? You're taking everything you own to the pools?" He bent to pick them up. "Let me take these back to your room."

"We intended to spend only the one night here, Acco," Barnabas replied. "We'll have to find someone to stay with or sell some more leather goods."

"Nonsense! It may take all day at the pools." He scowled at the two of them. "Wait here."

Ignoring their protestations, he sought out the innkeeper. Obligated to assure their safety, the two would remain until he knew they had somewhere else secured. After he paid for another night for them, he returned and picked up their bags. "You won't need any of these at the pools," he said, marching them to their recently vacated room, Barnabas hurrying after him.

"Acco," he said, "what did you do?"

"You are staying at least one more night here. I insist."

Barnabas followed him into their room, still protesting. "Acco, we can't afford to stay another night! Paulos won't hear of it."

"It's too late. I've already paid for it." After replacing their belongings, he turned to Barnabas. "Come, let's take Paulos to the pools."

The first of the healing pools was a glorious tribute to Panacea, the goddess whose favor healed many illnesses. Acco was shocked when Paulos refused to enter.

"But Paulos, this is the best of all the healing pools," Acco argued. "Don't be concerned about the cost. They will all cost about the same."

"No, Acco," Saul frowned. "It's not the cost. I cannot enter a pool so dedicated." He indicated the massive statue of the goddess in the act of pouring out water from a jar.

"I don't understand."

"Is the pool dedicated to this goddess?"

"Well, yes."

"Are there any pools that do not require tribute to the goddess? Is there a common bathing pool, perhaps, that originates from the same spring?"

Acco's mouth dropped open, and his eyes squinted. "The pools are gifts from the goddess, as so are the healing powers within them."

"I thank you for the offer," Saul said, "but it is something I simply cannot do."

"We came all the way here to Antioch for this purpose! Then, when I insist on paying the tribute for you, you still won't enter the pools?" Acco shook his head. "I don't understand you. My brother was right, you are very strange, your religion peculiar." He indicated toward the pool with a hand. "These healing pools are the finest in all Galatia. You need healing, and I've brought you here. Get in the pool!"

Saul's face was unreadable. He may have insulted him, but Acco was frustrated with the little man and didn't understand Saul's refusal. "It's only a statue," Acco added.

"It's an idol. My God says, 'You shall have no other gods before me.' It is very clear cut for me, Acco." Saul's dark eyes bore into him.

Barnabas laid a hand on Acco's arm. "Perhaps this wasn't the true purpose of journeying here with you."

"Acco," Saul said, "the lake here. It has a river that feeds it?"

"Yes, of course."

"Is it nearby?"

"Yes."

"Might you take us there?"

"But these—"

Saul leaned into him. "Acco, the same God who created these pools created the rivers and the lake as well. If there is healing power in one body of his water, there surely is in others too."

Resigned, Acco sighed. "Okay, Jew. I'll take you to the river."

He led them on the long walk to the lake, then around to the mouth of the river that fed into it. They traveled upriver where it was shallow and calm, the riverbed smooth. Saul gravitated to a group of large rocks along the river edge and removed his clothing before entering the clear water, where he sat down in the middle of it. Acco found it amusing.

"I suppose he knew what he was seeking," Barnabas said, chuckling along with him.

Saul sat in the river, little eddies swirling about his chest, his eyes closed, holding out his arms as if to slow the river's progress.

Acco turned to Barnabas. "I still don't understand. If the pools and the lake come from the same source, why did we have to come all the way out here? A statue can't adulterate the water."

"To us, it can. Idol worship is one of the worst violations a God worshiper may commit, and it's so easy to get sucked in. Even if you paid the tribute for him, wouldn't others give the goddess the glory if he entered the pool and was healed? But here, if he is healed, the glory can only go to the One who created the river and wills his healing."

"And if he is not healed?"

"Then he knows it is not God's will, that it is something that the Mighty One wants him to carry, and then carry it he will."

"Explain to me again why you do not heal him yourself when you can heal so many others?"

"It is not I who does the healing, Acco. I am merely the vessel. The Holy Spirit does the healing."

"And this holy spirit does not heal him? Though Paulos dedicates his life to him? This is difficult to understand."

"Who can know the mind of God? Perhaps one day we will understand. But I suspect there is a purpose for not healing him, a reason for us to be here. And even this may not fully heal him. Take him in now, remembering how he was when you first met him." Barnabas tilted his head. "What do you think?"

Acco eyed the man in the river, immersing his entire body for several moments before he swung up, his peppered hair slick, sticking flat to his head, the water dripping from his face. "He looks much better to me." Acco paused briefly, studying Paulos. "There is a sort of peace about you, about both of you. I admire that."

Barnabas turned his full attention on him. "Acco, the good news is for you too. There is peace in knowing that all your sins are forgiven, and you can live at peace with God."

"That promise is for you and your people," Acco replied. "I know nothing of your laws or your ways."

"No. The promise is for you, too."

"For Greeks, too?"

"For Greeks, too."

Saul climbed out of the river, reaching for his clothes.

"Paulos appears as refreshed as others do leaving a healing pool."

"When the Jewish leaders refused to allow John the Baptizer to baptize in the purification pools in Jerusalem, he went to the river to baptize. He found it ideal for his purposes."

"Did he not get chased away from the river too?"

"He didn't stay in one place for very long. He made his way north, near the sea of Galilee, where he baptized Jesus." Acco squinted at Barnabas, scrunching his nose. "Why would Jesus need to be purified? You told me he was without sin."

Saul, fully dressed, joined their conversation. "That had surprised me as well. For him, it was symbolic. For us, it is like rebirth." Saul indicated toward the river. "The water in a mother's womb bathes the child before birth. When we leave the pool or the river after baptism, it is like we are being born into a new life."

"And this is for Greeks too?" Acco knew the Jews were racially exclusive. This baptism was closed off for him as well as were their other rituals.

"For Greeks, for Romans. Even for Gauls." Saul spread his hands. "It is for all who repent of their sins and accept the forgiveness through the grace of God, wrought through Christ Jesus."

Barnabas's eyes conveyed a warmth foreign to Acco. It was beyond his understanding, but he was filled with an overwhelming desire to be cleansed of his past and know the peace he sensed in these two. He turned back to Saul and blurted, "What must I do to be saved?"

Saul gazed at him intently as if peering into his soul. "Repent of your sins and be baptized in Christ Jesus.".

"Will I be different?" Acco swallowed. "I mean, will my life be changed?"

"Decidedly," Saul replied.

Barnabas led Acco into the river and baptized him with Saul supervising. In the years to come, whenever Acco was near any river, he would remember the day as the time he died and was reborn.

On Sabbath morning, Saul's eyes adjusted to the dim light as he and Barnabas stepped into the synagogue. Acco had assured Saul that this synagogue had a fair number of Gentile locals who worshiped the one true God, who observed the Sabbath and enjoyed worship in the synagogue on Sabbath morning. These God worshipers were not full converts, as that would require circumcision, a procedure considered objectionable at best. These Gentile faithful tended to be influential in the community and quite generous with their financial support of the synagogue.

Once inside, he and Barnabas were greeted politely and guided to their seats. Barnabas had spent the previous day in the marketplace, assuring that word of their presence in the city spread through the Jewish community so the synagogue leaders knew where they were from and that he was a well-educated student of the Law. Saul dressed accordingly.

Acco stood in the back with the other non-Jewish attendees. For the last day and a half, they had flooded their former packer with information, teaching him the history of the Hebrew people, summarizing the Law and the Prophets, and explaining many of the rituals he might experience. The three of them shared the Sabbath meal, Saul explaining how it might be encountered in a Jewish household, and Barnabas explaining how Jesus had asked his followers to remember him every time the bread was broken and every cup shared among fellow believers.

On the way to the synagogue, Saul had explained to Acco what was going to happen. Inviting visiting teachers and speakers to address those gathered regarding reading the Law and Prophets was customary. Saul knew he was going to be asked to speak, and he was ready. The Spirit would guide him, giving him the words and the boldness required.

Through the process, which, except for the Shema, was entirely in Greek, Saul sat next to a fidgety Barnabas. After the readings, they were approached by the *chazan* whose job it was to arrange for the readers and speakers. Bending close, he asked Saul if he would address those present. Saul gave a solemn dip of his chin and followed him to stand before those congregated. Saul scanned the crowd to the back of the room, where Acco stood amongst his people, then over to the screen the women stood behind. Saul placed his left hand on his chest.

"I am Paulos of Tarsus, of the tribe of Benjamin, a former scribe and expert of the Law in Jerusalem." Leaving the left hand in place, he lifted his right hand in his orator's stance.

"Men." He turned toward the screen that separated the women. "Fellow Israelites." Then he addressed Acco. "And all those who fear God, hear this. The God who created the world chose our ancestors as his people, the ones he set aside for greatness. He rescued them out of exile in Egypt, caring for them exclusively for forty years in the wilderness before he wiped out seven nations in Canaan and gave them their lands as theirs in a span of about four hundred and fifty years."

Saul swept his eyes across his fellow Jews seated before him, their heads bobbing in understanding.

"He then gave them judges to lead them, up to the time of the prophet Samuel, when the people demanded a king to rule over them. So, God gave them Saul, son of Kish, of the tribe of Benjamin, who reigned forty years until God removed him. He then made David, son of Jesse their king, commanding him, saying, 'I have found David to be a man of my own heart, who will listen to my voice.'"

Saul paused and shifted his attention to the men, including Barnabas, seated before him. "From David's descendants, God has brought a savior for Israel: Jesus, as he promised he would do. My brothers, to us this message of salvation has been sent because Jerusalem and her leaders did not recognize him or understand the words of the prophets. The same words are read every Sabbath. The leaders themselves fulfilled those words by condemning him. Though they found no cause, they convinced the procurator of Judea to have Jesus executed. When they had thus fulfilled what the prophets had foretold, they took him down from the cross and laid him in a tomb."

Those seated before Saul leaned in. "But God raised Jesus from the dead." Saul paused, waiting for the gasps to subside. "For many days, he appeared in the flesh to his followers from Galilee, who are now his witnesses to the people. And we bring you the good news that what God promised to our ancestors, he has fulfilled for us, his children, by raising Jesus."

Saul quoted several of the Psalms, those that explained the Messiah. The Jews present acknowledged their understanding. They knew the old Psalms. They knew the words of the prophets. Saul had the attention of those standing near Acco. This must be a new teaching to them.

"Let it be known, therefore, that through this man, Jesus, forgiveness of sins is proclaimed to you. By him, everyone who believes is set free from all that which one cannot be freed by the Law of Moses. Don't take this lightly! Beware that what the prophets say does not happen to you. 'Look, you scoffers! Be amazed and perish, for in your days, I am doing a great work, a work you will never believe, even if someone tells you.'"

Saul lowered his arms, and let them hang at his sides as he returned to his seat next to Barnabas. There would be an argument between them later as to what happened next. Barnabas always maintained that the synagogue immediately erupted in noise, men's voices expressing wonder and amazement. But all Saul remembered was the warmth of the peace inside him as he sat.

As soon as they stepped outside, they were surrounded. The chazan appeared and requested the two return the following week, to speak more to them. Whereupon they were pounded with questions about the Christ. Saul scanned the crowd, searching for Acco. He found him waiting outside the periphery of the crowd. They made eye contact, and Acco beamed. Saul turned his attention back to a well-dressed man who was asking him a question.

"I'm sorry," Saul said, "what did you ask?"

"I asked where you two are staying," the man replied. "If you have nowhere to go, you will honor me to stay at my house this week."

"We are staying at the inn."

"Oh, no, we can't have that. A great teacher like yourself!"

"I thank you for the offer, but . . . ." Saul stopped. How to tell him about Acco?

"One of our fellow brothers is staying with us," Barnabas interrupted. "Acco! Acco, come, please."

Acco made his way through the crowd and stood next to them.

"A Gaul!" the man exclaimed. "Of course, he is also welcome. Send him for your belongings and come; there is room for all of you."

"Paulos. Paulos, wake up!"

Saul sat up with a gasp. Acco and Barnabas stooped over him.

They sat in the dark of the room the three of them had shared in the quiet house of Agathon for the past week. Saul told them of his dream. "Your father?" Barnabas asked. "When was the last time you dreamed of him?"

Saul shook his head. "I don't know. Years, if at all."

"What do you make of it, Paulos?" Acco asked. "Do you think it was a vision?"

Saul sighed. He only ever shared his dreams with Barnabas, who had been his companion now for years, when he knew it was a vision from the Spirit. He did not want to discuss the dreams he had been plagued with in the years before he had moved to Antioch in Syria. "I don't think so. It was similar to dreams I've had in the past. No, I don't think it was a prophetic dream. I believe there is a message in it, however."

"It is believed that when the dead appear in a dream," Acco offered, "they are sending a directive to the living."

"What kind of message is it, Paulos?" Barnabas asked.

"Brother Barnabas," Saul answered with another question. "Which law calls for a father to stone his son?"

"I don't know. Some obscure passage in the law that no one knows but Pharisees like yourself, most likely."

"Wait," Acco interjected, "you have a law that allows fathers to kill their sons?"

"Does anyone even follow that law anymore?" Barnabas added.

"On rare occasions, yes. But the Torah is clear when it comes to a rebellious, stubborn son who doesn't honor both father and mother, who is an embarrassment to them and to the place they live. Both parents must file the complaint and bring him before the elders. They then take him to the city gates, where the men of the town stone him to death. Their purpose? To make him an example of what happens when the family structure is threatened. It has also been very helpful in taming the wild spirit of many young men, to have the threat of the law."

"You've had this dream before?"

"Not exactly. You know, the stoning of Stephen often creeps into my dreams. Sometimes it is Stephen. Sometimes it's as if I am Stephen, and sometimes it's only me, being stoned. But I've never had a dream of being stoned by my father."

"Were you often punished by your father, Paulos?"

"Not physically, Barnabas. I was not an overtly rebellious son. We simply didn't agree on what I should do for a living."

Saul sensed Barnabas peering at him in the dark. "Are you

being rebellious now? To what your father would have you do?"

"Most definitely. I sense our ministry is heading in a dangerous direction. We are walking in the way of Christ Jesus. Therefore, we will face similar opposition that he experienced. Some powers will want to silence us, to stop the momentum of the Spirit."

"And you are willing to take that chance?"

"Absolutely. Are you, Barnabas? Are you willing to go the way of Christ Jesus?"

"Yes," he answered. "Yes, I am. I have observed the enemy, lingering on the edges of the crowd. I have sensed the presence of evil, and I believe I am angering it as I do the Lord's work. But Paulos, the presence of the Spirit is even stronger. God is with us. I am not afraid, come what may."

Acco spoke. "It is my job to protect you two. Nothing will harm you. Do not worry yourself."

"I look forward to today," Saul said. "Acco, you are expecting a crowd this morning at the synagogue, yes?"

"Yes."

"You had best try to get more rest, then, Paulos," Barnabas said. "You're going to have to speak loud enough to be heard in the streets!"

Saul fell into a light sleep where dreams tumbled about, meaningless. Once he reawakened, all the pressure in his head was gone. He dressed in the same outfit he had worn the week before and reflected on what the Spirit was leading him to discuss. He anticipated that any large turnout of Gentiles at the synagogue, those not known to be God worshipers, might antagonize the synagogue leaders. But Saul was convinced that they needed to know that Christ came not to condemn the Gentiles nor the Jews but to save them both.

Jews of the Dispersion lived in a precarious position. Greatly outnumbered, they had learned how to get along with their non-Jewish neighbors without integrating with them. If they stuck together and did not interfere with the daily workings of the city, they might be left alone to practice their way of life. Saul suspected that what he and Barnabas were doing in Antioch would throw the city's delicate stasis off-kilter. It was quite possible they would be noticed and charged with disturbing that balance, if not by the

Jewish leadership, then certainly by the ruling Roman officials.

Their host joined them as they left the house and made their way to the synagogue. "The streets are oddly empty, don't you think?" Barnabas noted. "What do you make of it, Acco?"

"It is unusual," he answered. "Perhaps everyone's gone to the synagogue ahead of us."

They turned a corner, and all stopped short. The street was packed with a sea of people, filled with bodies, all chatting, the air static with excitement. "Paulos!" Acco exclaimed. "They all showed up. They're all here for you, to hear about Christ Jesus."

Saul turned to Acco. "Word spreads fast."

"How are we to get through the crowd?" Barnabas wondered aloud.

"Leave that to me, Brother Joseph," Acco replied, as he took Saul's arm and pushed through the humanity. "Make way. Make way!" Acco shouted. They neared the threshold of the synagogue, where the chazan and synagogue leader scowled, awaiting their arrival. Once Saul made eye contact, the chazan gave a curt jerk of his head, indicating that they should enter. Standing next to him was a well-armed man, who laid a hand on Acco's chest.

"You can wait out here." The man spat out his words. "With the rest of the dogs."

Saul spun on the man. "He is with us."

"So claim all these people." The man indicated with an arm at the crowd. "There's not enough room in the synagogue for all these Gentiles."

Saul, Barnabas, and Agathon's group were pulled inside, and it was soon obvious why people were standing in the street. The synagogue itself was at capacity, with people sitting shoulder to shoulder, and standing close together along the walls. Through the open windows, others craned inside.

He had not expected this kind of response, but Saul now understood his sense of foreboding.

The chazan positioned Saul and Barnabas in front of the room before the throng. "For many years," he proclaimed, "we have worshiped in this city and have managed to live largely undisturbed here in Antioch. We have never been visited by any Roman guard, and the leaders of this city have respected our presence." He turned on Saul. "How do you suppose they will respond to this?"

Saul was quick to respond. "These people are all present, hungry for the word of our God. His Spirit is doing great work among the inhabitants of Antioch. This is your chance to offer all the citizens of this city that for which they thirst."

"Do you see the number of Gentiles gathered here?" the chazan hissed.

"The Son of Man has come to draw all people to himself," Saul countered.

"No! The Son of Man is to come to redeem Israel, to restore the fortunes of Jacob, to free us from the dominion of Gentile rulers!"

"The Resurrected One—"

"The Promised One will belong to the tribes!" The chazan shouted in Saul's face. He swept his arm toward the crowded door, where Acco stood, peering in at him, concern coloring his face. "Unless each of these Gentiles fully converts, they can never claim to those promises."

Another man, seated in the row reserved for the speakers and dignitaries, stood. "I lived in Jerusalem for several years and know about your men. Word has it that the man's body was stolen so the followers might claim resurrection. If this Jesus was the Christ, surely the high priest would have recognized him. He would not have died a traitor's death!"

"I thought the same way as you at the time," Saul answered. "But when I encountered the resurrected Christ myself, then I was convinced."

"You liar!"

"Lies!"

Barnabas laid his hand on Saul's arm.

"I've heard enough!" the chazan shouted. "This is false teaching, and you will be punished. Send these people away, unless you want them to observe your punishment and learn how we deal with false prophets."

Acco filled the doorway, ready to force his way into the synagogue. Saul shook his head at him before he turned to the chazan. "I know the Law far better than anyone here. If it is your belief that we are leading the people in the wrong direction, sharing Shabbat with Gentiles, teaching them in the way of Christ Jesus, and if it is the consensus of the leaders of this synagogue, you must punish us."

"Paulos!" Barnabas exclaimed.

"But only punish me," Saul continued. "Leave Joseph and my companions out of it. I am the instigator. I am the one that won't be silent about what I know is the truth." He removed his cloak. "Examine me. Assure that I am physically able to take the forty, less one."

Barnabas leaned in and whispered in Aramaic. "Saul, what are you doing?"

Saul whispered back. "I'm daring them." Surely, with all the supporters here, they wouldn't go through with it. Saul gave his friend a gentle push.

As he stood before those congregated, Saul's tunic was torn to expose his chest and his back, and his eyes widened. The first lash hit his chest, and it took his breath. The blow was accompanied by the recital of admonition by the chazan and the cries of distress from those hanging in the windows and the doorway. Fourteen more lashes were received on Saul's chest, and the admonitions and cries accompanied every one of them.

Cephas had told him that the first several blows to a part of the body were the worst and that after a while, one became numb. But Saul experienced the sting with each lash, and the pain intensified as the blows came. Saul yearned to cry out, to express the pain, but instead, he forced himself to stifle the screams. He remembered: Yeshua received a far worse flogging. Saul wanted to picture Yeshua kneeling before him, but as he was pushed into a bowing position, all he made out were the feet of those sitting in the front row, calling out the recitals of his crime. The last twenty-six lashes were applied to Saul's back, and the freshness of the assault brought hot tears to his eyes. He tried to distract himself by counting each blow but didn't get far. The pain numbed his brain, and his thoughts were wild and disconnected. Once the thirty-ninth lash had been rendered, Barnabas dashed forward and threw his cloak over Saul's bloody body.

"Paulos," he said, "here, lean on me." But with great effort, Saul stood, laying a hand on Barnabas's shoulder as he whispered, "Praise be to God!"

Straightening as tall as manageable, Saul turned toward the synagogue leaders. "It was necessary," he said, hoarsely, gasping between every few words, "that the Word of God be spoken to you, but since you have thus rejected it"—Saul's eyes settled on the packed house—"you judge yourselves unworthy of eternal life."

Saul lifted his eyes back to Acco and noted the wild concern there. "Therefore, we now turn to the Gentiles."

The room erupted with angry shouts, mingling with joy from outside. "Let's go," Saul said to Barnabas.

As they shuffled toward the door, the chazan followed after them, shouting in anger. Saul, close to the door, slowly turned. "You have meted out your punishment. What more do you ask of us?"

"Do not return if you value your lives."

"Be amazed and perish." Saul repeated his words from the previous week, his voice rising above the din. "'For in your days, I am doing a work that you will never believe, even if someone tells you.'"

Then he and Barnabas reached Acco and stepped into the crowd outside, surrounded by Acco's people, neighbors, and believers.

Chapter Sixteen

Iconium, Galatia
49 A.D.

Absolutely not, Hodiah!" Uzziel did not turn toward his wife as she stood in the doorway of his bedchamber. He admonished the servant dressing him. "That's a little tight, there." He stood before a large mirror overseeing the servant's work, the sunlight from an open window filling the room. A robe was draped over his head, cascading over his broad shoulders. "You will wait until after I leave. I won't have you seen coming to the synagogue with me."

Uzziel finally turned to his wife. Hodiah was dressed and ready to go, except for her veil. Her lovely eyes were brimming with tears. For having borne him children, she still appeared young and lovely. Not like so many of the hags his friends called their wives.

She wrung her hands. "Uzi."

"No!" he shouted. The servant sank to his knees, his head bowed. Uzziel sneered down at him. "Go. I'm through with you."

The servant scurried toward the door, around Hodiah, and out of the room. Her eyes were moist. "They're all terrified of you."

"As they should be." He stooped to pick up his new pair of sandals. They had been specially handcrafted for him this last week and included his signature impression. He stroked the symbol of his business carved into the sole. He fancied others recognizing his personal footprint on the streets of Iconium.

Iconium had not always been his home. Born and raised in Tarsus, his father moved his family to join his brother, who had a more successful trade here. Now they were both gone, and, with the uncle without an heir to leave his portion, Uzziel had it all: the thriving business, the wealth, and the expansive home that the brothers had shared. And the servants.

Once sandaled, Uzziel again regarded himself. "If they are not in awe of me, Hodiah, they will conspire against me. Fear is a great motivator. Besides, when their people first came here, they thought to enslave the natives, as well as the descendants of Abraham. That did not work out quite like they had planned, now, did it?"

He noted Hodiah's blurry image in the mirror as she approached him.

"And the Iconium people?" He laughed. "They let the conquering Greeks in, let them change the name of their city, change the name of their town goddess, Cybel." He shook his head. "Oh, great Athena!" he mocked, raising his voice to a falsetto.

"Uzi." Hodiah was close enough to reach out to him. "Please, don't!"

He turned abruptly, meeting her eyes. Once so beautiful and sparkling with gaiety, they were clouded with tears most days now, since their son Kobi had left. "Are the girls ready?" he asked. He had four miniature Hodiahs, all as gay as their mother had once been.

"We've all been ready for a while now, eager to go with you." She laid a delicate hand on his arm.

Uzziel eyed her hand. "No." With a deep frown, he pulled away. "Kobi's shame follows all of us."

"Uzi?"

"You encouraged him."

"I did not!"

"He confided in you, and you did not tell me, talk to me, warn me! That"—he emphasized his words with a finger at her chest—"is the same as encouragement."

"We've been through this."

"And I do not change my mind." Uzziel pushed around her and started toward his bedchamber door before halting. Without turning, he added, "You will allow me to get there before you all leave."

Uzziel rushed from the bright of day into the vestibule of his hometown's synagogue and tread with purpose into familiar surroundings. He hurried across the cool stone floor toward the benches along the southern wall, where he sat as close to the bimah as possible in the front row. Bad enough to have fellow businessmen or the wealthy seated around him. The poor should stand at the back of the room with those impertinent Greeks.

Uzziel inhaled, his eyes fixed on the small table in front of him which would soon hold the scroll. The late morning sun filtered through the windows, flanking the vestibule, and angled toward the western wall where the chazan stood near the already-seated Rosh-ha-Keneseth. As Uzziel stared into the eternal lamp constantly burning before the small ark holding the scrolls of the Torah, he hoped the men had not yet selected readers for the service. He breathed deeply and closed his eyes. Here in the synagogue, he tended to forget his anger with God.

Others entered and settled behind him. Uzziel opened his eyes at the rustle of clothing as a man sat next to him. A round, smiling face was directed toward him.

"A fine day out there today, isn't it?" his unknown seatmate whispered.

Cheap lamp oil topped off the stink of a man's body. Uzziel jerked his chin in reply and turned away.

"Nice and cool in here," the man added.

In his peripheral vision, Uzziel observed that his verbose neighbor had a companion. Uzziel leaned forward and frowned at the severe face, a blend of Orient and Hebrew, but a nose that could be Greek. Or worse, Roman.

"Joseph, of Cyprus," said the talkative man, noting he had Uzziel's attention. "And this is Saul, of Tarsus."

Tarsus! Uzziel did not answer but turned both his attention and upper body away from them, toward the chazan.

"Is that the Rosh-ha-Keneseth standing there?" Joseph the Talker asked.

"No. The man seated is the Rosh-ha-Keneseth."

The man from Tarsus stood and made his way to the Rosh-ha-Keneseth, who motioned him to the chazan. He then spoke briefly with the chazan before returning to his seat. Open-mouthed, Uzziel was unable to tear his eyes away. The man gazed straight ahead. Joseph looked up at his companion, a question in his eyes, and Uzziel noted a brisk, short nod in response.

"Uzziel."

Someone stood before him. Uzziel shot to his feet. "Yes!"

It was the Rosh-ha-Keneseth. "You will read the Prophets."

"Yes, yes. Thank you!" He bobbed his head and joined other men receiving directions from the chazan. Uzziel let him know his job was reading the Prophets, then hurried back to his seat, believing every eye in the place was on him. Whatever job the stranger had would not be near as important as reading the Prophets. He paid no attention to his seatmates for some time.

"Shema Israel, Adonai eluhenu, Adonai achad." Hear O Israel, the Lord our God is one.

The Hebrew words rang out from every tongue. The only Hebrew most of the Gentile God worshipers in the room knew were these. "True it is," the Hebrew speakers alone continued, "that You are Jehovah our God." Both the strangers recited along. "A new song did they sing that were delivered to your name by the seashore . . ."

Thoughts of the riverbank filled Uzziel's mind: strolling along it with Kobi, his young son delighting at the frogs he chased into the water.

Kobi had been a high-spirited child, who found humor in everything. His only boy and the oldest of his children, Kobi was Uzziel's pride. His son would one day be a great salesman, a successful merchant like his father, and carry on the business. His son's laughter rang in Uzziel's memory. In his play, Kobi pretended common household items were people. A cup would speak to a spoon with a high falsetto, and the spoon would reply with a low rumble. Then they would dance off the table together, Kobi singing a tune of their new friendship.

Uzziel recited the eulogy responses by rote as Kobi's childhood face rose before him. Such a beautiful boy, with his long eyelashes and shiny black hair, Uzziel remembered with a residual flash of anger the day he found Kobi's sisters had dressed him in one of their robes and painted his cheeks a deep rosy red.

"But, Papa," the oldest had exclaimed, "he makes such a pretty girl!" It still stung Uzziel, the slap she had received from him. Pretty Kobi, who would never be a merchant.

Uzziel's heart turned black, his hands drew into fists, and bile rose in his throat. His seatmate nudged him, and Uzziel spun. Joseph the Talker cleared his throat and indicated toward the bimah.

Uzziel had missed the seven readings of the Law. It was his turn to read from the Prophets. He hurried behind the small table, the scroll already open to the spot. He surveyed the amused faces watching him. A woman's soft titter of laughter reached him. His face reddened with heat. He returned to the open scroll, bending over it, and found the starting point. He lifted his right hand and traced his index finger along the well-worn parchment where many fingers had traced the words of the prophet Jeremiah.

"The, the. . ." Uzziel licked his lips and started again. "The days are surely coming, says the Lord, when I will . . ." He narrowed his eyes. The lettering was almost blurred here. "I will raise up for David a righteous branch, and he shall reign as king, and deal wisely and shall execute justice and righteousness." A soft murmur reached him, a man's voice speaking with him. He peered up from the parchment over at the man from Tarsus, whose eyes were shut. "In the land. In his days Judah will be saved. And Israel will live in safety. And this is the name by which he will be called: the Lord is our righteousness."

Uzziel straightened, then took a step away as the man from Tarsus paced to the front of the congregation. Uzziel stiffened at the breeze created by the man's passing.

Saul of Tarsus stood before the bimah. He peered out at those gathered and gestured. "Brothers," he said, "what an appropriate reading of the prophet Jeremiah today."

Uzziel still stood, his mouth agape, mesmerized as the man's voice flooded him. Clear and succinct, he retold the story of the Hebrew people.

Joseph tugged on Uzziel's sleeve. Still standing, he spun about, his mouth hanging open. He plopped down on the bench.

This Saul of Tarsus was no ordinary man. He spoke with eloquence, pronouncing his words with care. He gestured with his hands as he spoke like a philosopher. The man would lock eyes with

Uzziel, holding his gaze as he spoke. Then he would look away to someone else as he traced Hebrew history and then at another as he spoke of the promised Messiah. Uzziel's heart neared to burst. His chest filled with warmth as the voice hypnotized him. Saul's eyes again fell on him. "God has then brought, of David's posterity, to Israel a Savior, Jesus, as he promised."

Uzziel frowned. Jesus? Who?

"Before his coming John had already proclaimed a baptism of repentance to all the people of Israel."

A buzzing, a ringing of sorts, started in Uzziel's ears.

"My brothers, you descendants of Abraham's family." Saul broke his gaze with Uzziel, directing his next words toward the Gentiles lined at the rear of the room. "And those of you who fear God, to us the message of this salvation has been sent."

Lightheaded, the ringing in Uzziel's ears grew louder.

"Because the residents of Jerusalem and their leaders did not recognize him or understand the words of the prophets," Saul waved his hand toward the open scroll. "The words read every Sabbath; they fulfilled those words by condemning him. They asked the Roman governor to have him killed. When they carried out all the prophecies written about him, they took him from the cross and laid him in a tomb."

Blinking, hot tears swam before Uzziel's eyes.

"But God," Saul's voice hit his loudest, "raised him from the dead!" There were gasps heard throughout the room. "And for many days he appeared to those who came up with him from Galilee, and they are now his witnesses to the people."

Uzziel closed his eyes. *Dear God, make him stop!* Like a low boil of water, the murmurs in the room served as background noise for the clear, piercing, unending voice.

The roar in Uzziel's ears deafened him. His head was swimming, and he feared he might vomit. The man's gaze was on him again, the dark eyes boring into him.

"Let it be known to you," the man from Tarsus exclaimed, "my brothers, that through this man forgiveness of sins is proclaimed to you, by this Jesus, every." He paused and then emphasized. "*Everyone* who believes is set free from all those sins." Saul raised his eyes toward heaven and again gestured with his hands. "Beware, then, that what the prophets said does not happen to you."

No. *No!*

Habakkuk was quoted as Uzziel leaped to his feet. "Look, you scoffers! Be amazed, and perish, for in your days I am doing a work—"

Uzziel was in the vestibule and out in the street before the end of the quote.

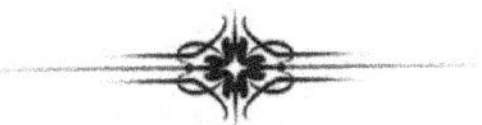

A few days had passed since Saul's first attendance in the Iconium synagogue. Unable to sleep, he slipped out for a walk. His stroll in the empty streets did nothing to ease his restlessness.

His teeth had been on edge since their arrival in this place. The city was not unlike Antioch. In fact, it was not unlike Tarsus. An ancient oriental city conquered and re-cultured first by the Greeks, then by the Romans. Public baths, temples, temple prostitutes, slavery of adults and children, arenas of torture. The usual sin-filled city of the Roman empire. Provide the people bread and entertainment, and they will sell their very souls for the privilege. What was different about Iconium?

Though he still said his prayers seven times a day, he had long stopped listening for the call to prayer during the watches of the night. But as he walked, he forced the prayer even while his mind wandered. Something was going to happen here, but he had no idea what.

Eventually, as the sun peeked over the horizon, Saul wandered back to the house where they were staying, bathed, and donned a new tunic and robe. It was time to do some teaching.

Saul sat at the rear of a large room in the house where they were staying, his back to an open window. He took in the men who crowded the room, some sitting, others standing with arms crossed. The man named Gallus, who followed him from Antioch, sat to Saul's left, and Barnabas was on his right, facing the rest of the room. Saul had been up for hours, but he felt no fatigue. The opportunity to teach was what he lived for.

After his talk in the synagogue earlier in the week, men had been coming to visit. Some came to learn more, to hear Barnabas's stories of Yeshua, or to bring their sick for healing. Some came to argue. Saul eyed those standing across the room from him, their arms crossed, waiting for him to utter some sort of blasphemy. Saul appreciated the irony. That had been him, not so very long ago.

Then he turned his attention to those sitting cross-legged before him, their eager faces yearning for the good news. Life was hard, and the concept of freedom sounded like a fantasy to many people. For him, the philosophical question of "what is truth" had been replaced with "what is freedom?"

"What is freedom?" Saul asked aloud.

His audience was quiet, assuming his question to be rhetorical. He raised his eyebrows and spread out his hands. "To you. What is freedom to you?" Saul was met with blank faces. "Let me ask you this: what have you been taught about the Messiah?"

"He will save our people," came a reply.

"And how will the Messiah save our people?" Saul asked.

"Destroy the Romans, give us back our lands." This came from one of the men standing in the back.

Another offered, "Rule the world with justice and judge the people with equity."

Saul's eyebrows again shot up. "Very good! What else?"

"He will be a great king, like David. The rest of the world will tremble under his rule."

"So, I ask you again. What is freedom?"

After another moment of silence, one man blurted out. "How would we know?" The man stood. "We have lived here, generation after generation, as long as my family can remember, always under the foot of some army, of some empire, some leader who tells us what to do and how to do it, and then punishes us if we do not. Freedom? Freedom to labor as we see fit, freedom to move about as we please, freedom from fear of punishment. Can there be such a thing in this world? Our daughters are stolen and sold for the use of their bodies. Our sons are drawn away from their faith by their desires. We are allowed to congregate as long as there are not too many of us, and we are obedient and peaceful. Our Temple in Jerusalem is constantly overseen by the Romans and our puppet king. We may travel there, on Roman roads built on our lands, paid for by our taxes. How long will it be before they try to force us to worship Caesar?"

"They already tried that, when Caligula was Caesar," someone else countered. "The fear of revolution is all that stopped it."

"If you were a prisoner and had lived in a prison cell for years," Saul asked, "what then would freedom mean to you?"

"Being out of prison." Gallus was prompt to answer. "Like an animal released from a trap."

"That is the sign of the Messiah, is it not?' Barnabas offered. "To set prisoners free?"

"Correct," Saul said. "Isaiah foretold it: 'The Spirit of the Lord God is upon me because the Lord has anointed me to bring good news to the poor. He has sent me to bind up the brokenhearted, to proclaim liberty to the captives and freedom to those in prison.'"

The room was still as Saul peered at them. A few heads bobbed, but most faces wore the frowns of confusion or ponderance.

"If Jesus is the Christ," one of them ventured, "why are there still those of us being held captive? Why are there those still in prison?"

Now they were getting somewhere. Saul grinned. "Excellent question. What was Isaiah's message to the people with that prophecy? It was a message of hope: hope that Israel itself would be redeemed, that it would be restored and be a shining example to the world of God's glory."

"Yet here we are," someone blurted out.

"Do you recall what happened," Saul continued, "when the captives returned from Babylon? That was a time of rejoicing and rebuilding of Jerusalem. But a couple of generations later, their freedom was gone once again. First Babylon, next Greece, then it was Rome. Physical freedom is short-lived until the next conquering power comes along. But Christ Jesus has proclaimed liberty to the captives and freedom to prisoners because there is a prison cell of our own choosing and making. It is our sin that builds the bars of our cages and each link of our chains. There is only one who can free us from our captivity. Christ Jesus frees us from our sins and therefore provides genuine freedom to us."

Turn to the window.

Saul frowned. What?

Turn to the window.

Saul turned. The window behind was filled with four or five veiled women, eyes wide and questioning. Saul's first reaction was to reprimand them, but he hesitated. The good news was for them as well. He had no idea how long they had been there or how much they understood. He fell deep into the eyes of the woman closest to him. The fires of a willing and open spirit burned within her, and he knew that he was to address her.

"Daughter of Abraham," Saul said to her. She flinched back. "No, don't go. The good news is for all of us. You included."

He stood and addressed the men. "Once you have heard this good news and accept it as yours, you belong to Christ. In Christ Jesus, there is no Jew," he indicated at his chest, "or Greek." He indicated toward Gallus. "Divisions no longer exist. Neither is there man and woman." He indicated toward the window. "Christ came to tear down the walls and screens that separate us. In him, we have freedom from sin and death and can know true wholeness."

Saul was compelled to draw near to the woman. He extended his hand and laid it on her veiled, bowed head. Once his palm touched her, he closed his eyes. An intense heat jumped from her head into his hand and up his arm. In his mind, a man was arguing with her, belittling her, striking her. He felt the sting on his face and absorbed her pain and humiliation. He opened his eyes, and the vision was gone. He removed his hand.

"The God of peace be with you, Daughter," he whispered before he turned back to the men, whose mouths hung open in surprise.

Hodiah huddled in the dark as close to the servant's entry to the kitchen as manageable. She had waved off the kitchen staff after the evening meal. Hodiah seldom had an interest in her husband's business meetings, but she knew this gathering was different.

Her first clue was the unexpected visit. She was not close to her male cousin from Antioch. But when he had arrived at her home earlier, flanked by a few companions, he failed to acknowledge her.

Dror was a handsome yet fierce-looking man, an influential businessman like her husband. But Hodiah did not recall a time her cousin had ever come to Iconium himself. His curt dismissal of her made her wonder if his visit had to do with Kobi.

She and the girls, forbidden to eat with the men, had taken their meal in the kitchen, raising her suspicions. If this were a business visit, she would have been expected to play her role as hostess, not relegated to the kitchen like a servant.

Uzziel had become more angry and hateful the last few weeks after he stormed out of the synagogue. Hodiah had been drawn to stand at the neighbor's window almost every day since the day Paulos had blessed her. The energy from his hand had filled her with a warmth and a deep peace she had never known before. She hungered to learn more about Jesus and his love. She knew Uzziel would be furious if he knew, but she made any excuse to linger at the window, to allow the words shore up her soul with hope.

She did not know how, since he never turned to face her, but she knew he was aware of her presence. He would talk about things that spoke straight to her, her life, her situation. As he taught, it was as if Jesus himself addressed her. Jesus knew the empty place in her heart left by the absence of her only son, and she was sure that, if she prayed enough, if her faith was strong enough, she would receive word from Kobi.

So it was that after their supper, hidden in the kitchen, the girls hurried off to entertain themselves, and Hodiah had helped her servants clear things away. Then, when the voices of the men drifted to her as they settled into talking, she shooed the servants out. "No, go," she had assured them. "I will take it from here." Then she lowered herself to the floor near the door where she ached for word of Kobi. The men's words were indistinct at first, but then Uzziel raised his voice.

"They *are* here," he said. "And up to the same tricks. There's a dirty Gaul who travels with them."

Hodiah frowned. Kobi was not traveling with a Gaul. Well, that she knew of.

"They stole many of our highest contributors amongst the Gentile God worshipers." Dror's voice was quieter, but he spat out the words. "Not to mention that the message they are teaching—"

"Blasphemy!" Uzziel boomed. "I couldn't bear to stay and listen to it, so I left."

Some question was raised, but the man's voice was too hushed for Hodiah's hearing.

"I started to," Uzziel answered, "the last two weeks, but when I saw them sitting there, I turned around and returned home."

Hodiah was seated, her arms wrapped around her knees, her

head bowed, her ears straining.

"They must be stopped, Uzziel," Dror said. "Before they ruin your synagogue, too."

At this, her head shot up. Synagogue? Were they discussing Paulos and Joseph?

"We'll drive them out of town!" Uzziel shouted. "Next Sabbath—"

"They will then go to the next town, and the next, leaving synagogue after synagogue reeling and split in two behind them. No," Dror said. "They must be stopped, permanently."

Hodiah gasped. She inched up on her feet, prepared to hurry away from the door, in case she was heard. But she did not dare leave. She needed to know more.

"You spoke correctly," Dror continued. "It is blasphemy. What is the punishment for blasphemy?"

She heard nothing in response though she strained to, laying her ear on the door.

"Lashes," Uzziel replied. Hodiah wanted to cry out at the thought of the lash hitting Paulos's back.

"We already tried that in Antioch. Flogging was clearly ineffective. No, Uzziel, the punishment for blasphemy against God is death, by stoning."

Hodiah's heart beat so hard she feared it be heard in the adjoining room. Ready to flee at any moment, she held her breath.

"I must return to Antioch," Dror said. "I am the chazan and have many responsibilities in the synagogue. I leave my friends here with you to be further witnesses. This Sabbath you must go to the synagogue. When he is accused in there, he cannot escape his fate." A pause. "Uzziel, you must be the accuser. See to it that this stops here in Iconium."

"Oh, I will see to it, all right," Uzziel thundered. "Justice will be served."

Hodiah tiptoed across the kitchen and slipped into the hallway. She headed straight for her bedchamber and closed the door behind her. Then she sank against the door. Paulos, stoned to death! *No, it cannot happen.* She had a little time. The plan was to accuse him Sabbath morning. She would go to him, warn him. They could hurry off before Uzziel even knew they were gone.

But what if Uzziel suspects she overheard the conversation if they leave before the Sabbath? Uzziel gave his word to Dror. He would be furious. Perhaps she should wait, perhaps it will all work out. *Oh, Lord! I do not know what to do!*

She closed her eyes and attempted to settle her breathing. She pictured Paulos's hand on her head, the warmth, the peace, the hope. *Jesus, please. What would you have me do?*

She didn't want to think about Paulos receiving the lashes. He had suffered through that, at the hand of her cousin and his people. Yet Paulos had still come to Iconium, knowing that he might face the same here. No, lashes would not silence him. Only stoning would. And she would not stand idly by and let that happen.

A plan formed in her mind. She would wait until the house was silent, deep in the night. Then she would go find him. She had to let him know.

"Paulos, wake up!"

Saul was deep in sleep amidst a clear and important dream that the words seemed to come from the dream itself. But his eyes flew open as he was shaken and the words repeated. Acco stood over him, holding a small hand lamp.

"Wake up, Paulos! There's a woman here for you."

He sat up on the pallet and shook his head to clear it.

Barnabas, now also awake, yawned. "What is it?"

"A woman. She refuses to go away until she speaks with Paulos."

Saul scrambled up, followed by Barnabas, and both threw on tunics and a robe. Saul ran a hand through his hair. "Now, a woman, you say?"

"Yes, Paulos. She is well-dressed and is familiar to me, though I can't quite place her."

"What does she want?"

"I do not know," Acco replied. "She will only speak with you."

"It's the middle of the night," Barnabas said. "What does she have to speak about that can't wait until morning?"

Saul moved for the door. "Let us find out."

They padded down the hallway. The moment Saul appeared in

the doorway, a tearful rushed to him, stopping shy of embracing him, and bowed her veiled head, her shoulders shaking. On instinct, Saul recoiled. *Jameleh.* He reached a hand toward Barnabas, who moved to calm the woman.

"There, now," Barnabas purred. "Calm down, so we can understand you." As he spoke, he took her hands in his and maneuvered between her and Saul.

Jameleh. He had not thought of her for some time. Saul studied the woman, her face still obscure. Her clothing was from the area. Her veil had slipped, and much of her hair was exposed, where silver strands coursed through the dark hair. Saul released his held breath. He lifted his eyes heavenward. *Thank you.*

"Here is Paulos," Barnabas said. "You need to speak with him?"

As she lifted her head, Saul recognized her face. The woman at the window. He remembered the vision that came when he blessed her. Saul frowned. "You are not hurt, are you, Daughter?"

She shook her head. "No, Paulos, I am not the one in danger!" Her words stuttered with emotion. She bowed her head and took some deep breaths before resuming. "I am sorry to disturb you. I know it is late. I would not have come if it were not so important."

"It is dangerous for you to be out alone this time of night," Barnabas chided.

"I am Hodiah, the wife of Uzziel. The first Sabbath you spoke at the synagogue, he read the Prophets."

Saul remembered the man. "Yes, go on."

"My cousin is Dror, from Antioch. He arrived at our home today with some companions. I overheard them speaking tonight after our supper." She dropped her head once again. "I know I should not have been eavesdropping, but I thought he was bringing news of our son, and I wanted to know what was said."

From Antioch. Saul's eyes questioned Acco, who shook his head as if to say the name was not familiar. Hodiah lifted her tear-filled eyes back to him. "Dror is the chazzan at a synagogue in Antioch. He said that they attempted to quiet you by flogging! Oh, Paulos, is that true?"

The chazan followed them here. A surreal sensation, a familiarity, draped over Saul. Not the flashback of Jameleh, but something else, something different. "Go on," Saul said.

"They did, didn't they?" Hodiah cried out. "He flogged you. My cousin?"

"It was the expected punishment. We left there because of the hardened hearts and came to Iconium."

"I am so sorry." Hodiah wiped her eyes with her hands. "Uzziel suggested they do the same here, but Dror said that you

would simply go on to another city and so on until you had spread—"

"He is right," said Saul. "We will go where the Spirit leads us. We are headed next to Lystra."

"Dror said you have to be stopped permanently. They plan to stone you . . . this Sabbath. Dror must return to Antioch, but he is leaving his friends to be witnesses against you. They will drag you out of the synagogue—"

"Paulos?" Barnabas interrupted. "What do you think?" Saul closed his eyes. The dream. The familiarity of this conversation, this setting. He had foreseen it. The Spirit had been warning him. He reopened his eyes and answered. "She speaks the truth. I dreamt this. I was dreaming of it when Acco awakened me tonight."

"Then the threat is real," Acco replied.

"Yes." Saul turned to Hodiah. "You were right to tell us, but this could have waited until morning. Why did you risk coming tonight?"

She dropped her head in silence.

"Look me in the eyes, Daughter." Saul peered at her. "Now. What was so urgent that you risked the dangers of the night to awaken us and the entire household? The Sabbath is not for a few more days."

"He will know that I told you." Her voice wavered. "If you do not go right away, Uzziel will figure it out."

Barnabas let out a soft breath. The weight of her message and what she had left unsaid filled the room with heaviness.

Saul reached out a hand and laid it on top of her head. "Hodiah, thank you for this gift. We would not have you suffer for us." Saul removed his hand and turned away from her. "Let us pack up now. We leave at first light."

Chapter Seventeen

Lystra, Laeconia
49 A.D.

Acco's hand gripped the hilt of his weapon immediately after the healing, moving swiftly between the crowd and his brothers in Christ. Their group had not been in Lystra but a few days, yet a miracle had just occurred. And, for the first time, from Acco's knowledge, it was Paulos who performed it.

Although the others were elated, praising God for the miraculous healing that had occurred, Acco understood the threat. These were simple people. Paulos's lofty words fell like stones at their feet. The only things that matter to them affected their hunger or pain. The Jews here had hardened hearts. None of them had opened their home, much less their ears to the message of Christ Jesus. How would they explain away this miracle? The simple folk of Lystra would realize that only God can heal someone crippled from birth.

No, he sighed, not God, but *a* god. They had no concept of the personal God of Abraham, Isaac, and Jacob.

The tension released in Acco's shoulders as the crowd carried the healed man toward the gates of the city. The immediate danger was past, at least for the moment. He spun, facing his brothers in Christ. "We must leave," he said, "while we have the opportunity."

Barnabas laughed at him. "Leave? Now?" He laid a hand on Acco's arm. "Paulos just found a way to get through to the people here. We cannot leave before we can give the credit to Christ Jesus!"

"He is correct, Acco," Saul said. "Let them celebrate for now. They will be back with their many questions."

"They will come back with their many ill and deformed friends and family, too," Barnabas added.

"Paulos, I have a bad feeling about this," Acco said, his voice lowered. "The news of this will spread quickly, and I fear it will bring the kind of attention we should avoid. I am only one man. I cannot defend you against an army."

"I appreciate your concern." Saul clasped Acco's shoulder. "But this is where we are supposed to be. Let us wait here for them to return."

"At least send a couple of us to follow that crowd," Acco begged, "to find out where they are going."

"We will go," Gallus offered, indicating his now constant companion, Yoni, who nodded his consent.

"All right," Saul said, "if it will give you peace of mind. We will be here when you return."

It was not long before Gallus and Yoni returned, running, out of breath. Acco's heart sank at the concern reflected on their faces. His question was not whether guards were on their way to arrest them, but rather whether they were Roman or local natives.

"What is it?" Saul asked.

Yoni shook his head as he slowed his breathing. Gallus, also breathless, stood at his side. "Oh, Paulos!" Yoni said. "It is bad. The crowd went to the temple of Zeus, outside the gates."

"Understandable," Barnabas said.

"The priest of Zeus is approaching. The people are thronged behind him. They have brought offerings!"

"Offerings?" Saul echoed.

Acco's stomach churned. Of course. Those were the Greek words amid the Laeconian speech that had tumbled from the mouths of the crowd. *Zeus and Hermes.* "They think you are gods," Acco said.

"Yes!" Gallus confirmed. "They have offerings of bulls, to sacrifice to you two!"

Saul and Barnabas both cried out and threw their hands to their tunics, tearing them at the throat. They ripped their clothing as they wailed unknown Hebrew words. Acco retracted in horror as Yoni joined them. Gallus's wide eyes met Acco's.

"This is terrible." Barnabas cried out. "Paulos, we must stop them!"

"Hurry!" Saul answered. "We must not allow them to do this horrible thing."

They rushed down the street, Acco at their heels. Protecting these two had suddenly become far more difficult.

With a gasp, Saul sat up straight, soaked through in a cold sweat. Disoriented, he only dared to move his eyes. He was damp and cold. He was sleeping on the ground. Above him stretched a black, starless sky. He was sleeping in the lesche. Around him lay the sleeping bodies of his companions, the sounds of their deep breathing and snoring reassuring him. He was still in Lystra.

The dream had awakened him before the knife cut his throat.

The dream had started as usual: he was surrounded by a large group of angry men who were cursing and shouting at him, the words garbled and foreign. He was then dragged by his hair, by his collar, through the streets. Sharp pain leaked through the dream onto his scalp and tore at his legs and feet as they scraped through the gravel. Then the thudding impact as they dumped him, the spinning as he stood panting with bleeding legs and torn clothing among a herd of oxen, horned, huge, and menacing. Caked with oxen waste, he was rank with their scent. Waves of nausea hit him, and he bent over while dry heaving. Spent, he leaned against a rough wall and squinted down a narrow corral. Ahead, men beat the cattle with goads. Saul feared the beasts would trample him, but the herd trudged forward. As the corral narrowed to single file, a man placed garlands about the necks of the bulls. Saul's turn. As he opened his mouth to protest, a garland was placed around his neck, and a sharp sting of the goad poked him on his back.

The herd was led to a high altar. Smoke rose, and the stench of burnt offerings stung his nose. But he was not Jerusalem. Pagan symbolism marred the walls and floor.

At the altar, charred thick with burned blood and flesh, Saul knelt at the feet of a priest, who held a bloody knife, the blood dripping down his arm, staining his once white robe and tunic. As the priest raised his knife with one hand, the other grasped Saul by the hair on his head, exposing his neck.

That's when he awoke. Saul's breath was still short as he relived the dream. He was certain it was brought on by the people of Lystra, who, days before, attempted to sacrifice to him and Barnabas. *Barnabas.* He turned to his right. Yes, there he was, still sleeping. Barnabas had been equally horrified, yet he slept soundly. Saul shook his head. To be so blessed with that gift.

Saul shifted, and the damp ground seeped through his thin pallet. The air was thick with a misty rain as if a laden cloud hovered above the ground. They had not been offered a dry house in Lystra, nor were they likely to. First, they had been ignored, then they had been adored. He and Barnabas narrowly prevented the people from sacrificing to them, proclaiming them to be gods. Yet, at the end of the day, their group returned to the lesche and slept, like the mere mortals they were.

After the healing, many came but were not interested in what he had to say. They only came for healing and to beg—beg for money, beg for food, beg for a job. While Saul spoke to them about Christ, his voice fell on closed ears. Maybe Acco was right. Perhaps they should travel on to Derbe.

But something held him back. The Spirit had urged them to come and stay without indication that they should leave. It was as if the Spirit was waiting for something. Or someone. Perhaps there is one person, a single soul, they had yet to encounter.

An awareness struck him, and Saul turned to his left. A couple of sleeping bodies between them, a wide-awake Acco crouched, gripping his dagger.

With a hushed voice, Saul's self-acclaimed bodyguard questioned him. "Are you alright?"

"Yes. Only a lively dream."

"You were moaning in your sleep. I almost awakened you but didn't want to disturb the others."

"A recurring dream. With a special Lystra twist."

"You dream often. Does God talk to you in these dreams?"

"Sometimes, but not tonight. Did I awaken you?"

"No. I cannot sleep. We are easy prey here, out in the open. Someone has to keep watch."

"Acco, try to sleep. I will keep watch. You need rest."

"No, Paulos. You would not fight to save yourself, though you might try to talk your way out of trouble to save the rest of us. I sense danger. I have since the healing. There is something evil in the air, and I believe it means to do you harm. I cannot sleep if I think you are at risk. We need to leave, at first light, head to the next town."

"Again, I appreciate your concern. But even if I agreed with you, I must allow the Spirit to be my guide. He leads me to understand that there is still something very important that we must do here before we leave for Derbe."

"I respect your ability to converse with the Holy Spirit, but what about the Word? If you die, the mission dies with you. All the work you have done will be for nothing. The good news will die here with you." Acco indicated with his empty hand. "Do you think brother Joseph can teach like you? What about Gallus or Yoni? You must take the threats seriously. We cannot do this without you."

Acco's voice had raised, and one of the men stirred. They waited in silence until the man returned to his snoring. Saul replied in a quiet whisper. "I do not believe our Lord has brought me all the way here to Laeconia only to die in the middle of our mission."

"Do you want to die?" Acco hissed. "Is that it?"

Saul shook his head. "It is not my goal to die. In fact, I must admit, I believe that is what my recurring dream is about. I may very well be killed at some point. In my dreams, I have nearly died in a great number of ways, and every time, I am terrified. I am afraid to die. Though I want to be with Christ Jesus, I cannot get over my fear of death."

"Well, Paulos," Acco sighed, "it is my job to make sure you do not die, and the fear of failing is what keeps *me* awake. You should go back to sleep. I hope the Spirit will come to you and tell us to leave this place, and soon."

Saul knew Acco was right. Regardless of what awaited him when the sun arose, he should sleep to prepare himself for it.

A stone wall enclosed a courtyard near the orator's stage in the marketplace. Saul ran his hand along the rough, damp stones as he passed. Barnabas strolled next to him with his perpetual contented smile. Behind him, Acco bristled with concerned energy.

The sky was overcast, as it had been for days, either raining or threatening it. When they reached the spot where they had gathered almost every day, Saul sat on the cool stairs, the dampness oozing through his clothing and into his skin. He shivered.

"We usually have folks waiting for us." Barnabas turned, frowning. "This is odd."

"Do you hear that?" Acco asked.

As the sounds of a distant crowd became more distinct, a cold darkness came over Saul. It was as if one of his dreams was becoming reality. He turned to Acco, who already held a weapon in each hand and had maneuvered himself before their group protectively. Beyond him, a mass of humanity swirled toward them. As they closed in, he noted the attire of those leading the way, recognizing them as sons of Abraham. *Come, Holy Spirit, come.*

Once the crowd was close enough to make out faces, Saul recognized a few. When they were within a couple of paces, the leaders of the group stopped, and the one in front held up a hand. The crowd grew quiet behind him.

Saul reached forward and laid a hand on Acco's shoulder. Leaning toward him, he said, "Stand down, Acco."

"They will have to go through me."

Saul slipped in front of him. "No, we will need you when we return to Antioch. We are outnumbered, and we will not tempt them to violence. Do you understand?"

Then Saul advanced on the menacing crowd. "Whom do you seek?" he shouted.

"Paulos, of Tarsus, and Joseph, of Cyprus," answered the man in front.

Saul recognized him. Hodiah's husband. Uzziel, she had called him. "I am Paulos of Tarsus," he replied. "And you are Uzziel of Iconium."

There was an initial sting of surprise on the man's face, but then his eyebrows furrowed. "And we also seek Joseph of Cyprus."

"Any business you have with us, you may conduct with me," Saul said with authority. The warmth of the Spirit blazed inside him, and he let it grow. He would wear it like armor if this were to be a fight for his life.

Uzziel's eyes burned with a dark intensity, and he clenched his jaw. But he turned to those behind him. "Bring him forward," he demanded.

The crowd parted, and the man Saul had healed stumbled forward. Uzziel indicated Saul with his head. "Is this the man?" he asked.

"Yes, that is the man who healed me."

"Admit it," Uzziel shouted, "who has the power to heal someone born crippled?"

"Only one of the gods, of course!" the man answered. "That is why we headed straightway to the priest of the temple. He has known me all my life and knew I was born that way. Therefore, we brought sacrifices to offer."

"I have heard enough!" Uzziel thundered. He stood before the other Jews gathered about him. "Are there any other witnesses to this man's blasphemy?" he asked.

Two strangers came forward. "We are both from Antioch, in Galatia. This man was flogged for his false teaching in our synagogue. He led many people there astray."

Saul frowned. They had come all the way from Antioch? He studied the stern, angry faces of his fellow Hebrews, but Uzziel was the only one he recognized. The smell of sulfur stung his nose and his lungs. It was as if a dark cloud churned around Uzziel, flowing through him and about his head.

Uzziel shared how Saul and his companions had escaped in the night rather than face his accusers in Iconium. "And now, here he is in Lystra, claiming to be a god! What is your charge, you descendants of Abraham?"

As if on signal, all of them tore their garments. Then they rushed at Saul, who did not resist. The warmth of the Spirit encompassed him and, while vaguely aware of the hands that grasped him, of the angry shouts, the insults, what he experienced was surreal, even more like a dream than his premonitions had been.

He was dragged to the same wall along which he had run his hand. Saul was positioned before the contorted faces of his accusers as stones were distributed. The crowd closed in. Above the angry din, the voices of Acco and Barnabas shouted. But the crowd swallowed their faces.

Uzziel grasped a stone larger than the palm of his hand, and Saul squared his shoulders, heeding the whispers of the Spirit.

Uzziel noted that the first three stones hit the man simultaneously. The impact spun him such that he faced the wall, on which he laid his hands to steady himself. The next one hit its target below the right shoulder blade, crushing ribs. The man gasped, breathless. Another landed on his mid-back, while yet another smashed into the back of a knee, knocking him to the ground. He struggled to raise himself before his arms fell, and he crumpled to the ground, fueling the shouts of the crowd.

"Blasphemer!"

"Liar!"

"You shall have no other gods—"

More stones flew at the body lying in a heap. One cut a long, jagged gash in the right upper arm, which was wrapped around his head. Blood soaked his garments.

"Stop. Stop!" one of the man's companions shouted. Uzziel raised a hand in command. The crowd quieted but pressed in closer.

Uzziel eased near the broken, bloody body. *Filthy.* His eyes narrowed, checking for movement in the chest. Struggling, but still breathing. Uzziel weighed the large stone in his hand. Tossed it. Caught it. Bulky but not too heavy. He stood over the broken body, the right arm angled away unnaturally. Uzziel leaned in close and whispered forcefully. "Where is your savior now?"

Incredibly, the man lifted his head, slowly, painfully, until their eyes met. Uzziel's throat choked off in disbelief. Who would not show fear or hopelessness at this point? But the man's eyes held none of that. Only a deep, pitiful sadness.

The parched, bloody lips quivered. Water? No, not water. Mercy? He leaned in closer, his lowered right hand still gripping the stone.

"Adonai," the man croaked. *Hebrew.* "Elu—"

No. Not that.

". . . Adonai achad."

The *Shema.*

Uzziel straightened abruptly and fell back. His right arm shot up, and he hurled the stone with all his strength. It impacted the man's forehead and right side of the face, caving in the skull above the eye and the upper and lower jaw. Teeth flew, the face split open like a fruit. The man's body tightened, straightening oddly, and then convulsed, flailing in huge spasms. Uzziel retreated into the crowd, waiting for the body to finally lie still.

Someone pushed through, hurrying past Uzziel to kneel next to the dead, broken body. When he turned toward Uzziel, glaring, he recognized him as the man's companion in the synagogue.

"You murdered him," the man shouted. "Without a trial, without defense. You killed him!"

Uzziel ignored the rant as he turned his back on the man, facing the crowd. "Take him out of the city," he ordered. Some Gentile men grabbed the body, kicking the companion out of the way, and dragged it toward the city gates. The crowd followed until they passed through and dumped the body along the Roman highway.

The man's companions, a handful in number, stood around the corpse, tears streaking their dusty faces. As the others drifted back inside the gates, Uzziel remained, disgusted with the wails and tears of the mourners. He scowled at them. "Go home. Go home, all of you, and do not come back."

Uzziel spun away, his robes billowing, and he strode through the city gates, which closed behind him.

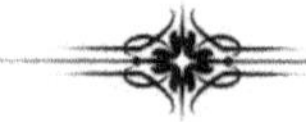

Defeated, Barnabas sat along the dusty roadside. He pulled the broken body of his friend onto his lap, bowing over it, sobbing. It had all happened so fast. Aware of the others standing over him, Barnabas raised his eyes. He was horrified as they looked to him for an answer, their faces asking the question that flooded his heart.

What do we do now?

Except Acco. Acco paced, beating his chest, sobbing, his words unintelligible, occasionally shouting out a curse.

"Please," Barnabas said. "Help me."

"It is too late to help." Acco's voice was hoarse with emotion. "And it is all my fault. Mine! My job was to protect him, and I failed. Why didn't he listen to me? If we had gone on to Derbe, none of this would have happened. Look at him!" His voice broke.

"Please," Barnabas pleaded. "Come, sit with me."

"And do what? Pray? You going to heal him, huh? I know you can heal crippled limbs and leprosy, but can you resurrect the dead?"

"Acco," Gallus said, holding up a hand to touch him. "That is enough." Acco backed away.

"I should have known," Yoni added. "I'm familiar with these people—the ones that came from Iconium. I should have known their purpose for coming here."

"All of you," Barnabas croaked, "please." He sniffed. "Sit with me."

Yoni and Gallus sat as close to Barnabas and the lifeless body of Saul as they were able. Gallus attempted to reposition the floppy, dislocated arm. Acco closed in and stood directly behind Barnabas, then fell to one knee, resting a hand on Barnabas's shoulder, wordless.

"I don't know what we are to do." Barnabas swallowed. "But I know what Paulos would have us do."

"Pray," Yoni said.

"Yes." Barnabas took in a deep breath through his nose, his eyes never leaving Saul's still body. "Pray until we sense the Spirit and then pray that the Spirit guide us. I cannot, will not, believe that our Lord would bring us all this way only to have us give up and leave. There must be some greater purpose in this." Acco's hand tightened its grip. "Now, please, let us seek His counsel."

Barnabas dug deep inside himself, pursuing the peace and warmth of the Spirit. Barnabas lifted a prayer from a pure, contrite heart in the shadows of the city gates. As he prayed, the overcast sky stirred with a warm breeze. The sun peeked from behind darkened clouds, the breeze picked up, and the wind swirled dust around the believers in a loud roar. The men proclaimed the glory of God in foreign tongues as tingling and heat boiled in Barnabas's chest, shooting down his arms and out through his hands.

Barnabas shouted over the clamor. "Place your hands on him!"

They knelt over him, each with a hand somewhere on Saul's still body, dust blowing about them. A burning heat radiated from Barnabas, and the body under his hands shook violently. Then, it lay still, and the wind abruptly ceased, leaving a stunned silence in its wake.

Barnabas pulled his hands away. The dust settled about them while the sun illuminated Saul's bruised face, dried blood caking his right eyelid. Barnabas gasped as Saul's eyelids fluttered. Startled, the others stumbled back. Saul's left eye opened wide as his lungs sucked in air. Then, he blinked. Saul took several deep breaths. He whispered, and Barnabas leaned closer. "What? What is it?"

"Paradise," Saul whispered hoarsely.

Saul struggled to sit with Barnabas's help, open-mouthed at the miracle before him. Saul rubbed his right arm, no longer limp or angled. Except for the bruising, the dried blood, and the filthy garments, Saul was in one piece, and all his limbs worked. He sat for a while, blinking, before he attempted to stand. Acco held out a steadying hand to pull him up and balance him as he swayed. Saul took a few tenuous steps as if trying to knock the rust off an old tool. He laughed at himself. Relieved, Barnabas jumped up and pulled him into a hug, holding him tight.

They all burst into questions, but Saul was silent. His watered eyes crinkled. Saul then turned toward the gates of the city. He sucked in a deep breath. "Lystra?" he asked, his voice still hoarse.

"Yes," Acco answered. "We are still in Lystra, though I wish it were not so."

Saul neared the closed gates. Barnabas called to his retreating back. "Where are you going?"

He turned. "To answer the question."

Barnabas, shaking his head, had to ask. "What question?"

"Where is your savior now?"

Chapter Eighteen

Antioch, Syria
50 A.D.

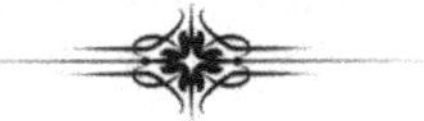

Nicolaus stood in the doorway. Saul was bent over his writing, his nose close to his work. It was the rainy month, and the natural light did not help much. The windows were covered to prevent rain from soaking the floor. Saul wrote by lamplight, slowly, meticulously.

Saul and Barnabas had not returned to Antioch alone from their travels. They had left as a trio and returned as a trio, but not the same three. Saul's ever-present bodyguard sat on the floor, sharpening a dagger. News of John Mark's abrupt appearance in Jerusalem while Saul and Barnabas were still on their mission had reached the Antioch church. John Mark himself then visited, accompanying Simon Peter as they traveled from church to church in the region, though not in the few weeks since Saul and Barnabas's return.

The two missionaries were not the same men they were when they left Antioch. Barnabas seemed distracted, longing to see his nephew. Nicolaus wondered if he had grown weary of Saul's company.

That Saul had changed was evident. The man had always been driven and methodical, but now he worked non-stop and with an intense urgency. If he was not teaching, writing, visiting, or organizing, he was mending tents, working leather, and scrounging money to distribute to the poor. He awakened early, spent hours in prayer, and received visitors.

He seldom ate, and when he did, it was only with the body of believers. Tireless, Saul seemed fueled solely by the Holy Spirit, who was always with him.

And he was fearless. Nicolaus knew that had nothing to do with his bodyguard, the Gentile Saul referred to as "Titus," who seldom left his side. As Saul painstakingly scratched the letters on the page, Nicolaus mused that it was not a bodyguard Saul needed as much as a scribe, someone to write for him as he dictated.

Saul's body was also no longer that of a fit man. He was broken. The way he stooped after sitting for any amount of time, stiff and painful, spoke to that. Barnabas told them stories of the punishments that had been meted out on him, but Saul would always change the subject of conversation to the groups of believers in Galatia and Laeconia and of the people there.

Titus lifted his eyes to Nicolaus and dipped his head in greeting before returning to his sharpening. Nicolaus cleared his throat. "Paulos? You wanted to speak with me?"

Saul paused, his reed pen raised in his left hand. "Nicolaus!" He laid down the pen and stood to embrace him. "Thank you for coming. Have a seat. I have something very pressing to ask you. Titus, would you kindly leave us? I have something to discuss with Brother Nicolaus."

"Yes, Paulos." He scrambled up, giving a nod to Nicolaus as he closed the door behind him.

"He seldom leaves your side, Paulos. Does he not trust us?"

"Titus does not trust easily. He blames himself for the punishments I received on our journey. Sit with me, please." Saul indicated a chair across from his writing table.

Nicolaus looked down at the papyrus before them. "You are always writing."

"I went too long without writing. I have to make up for lost time." Saul lowered his voice. "Nicolaus, I know we are not to talk about his whereabouts, but I have an urgent need to speak with Lazarus."

Nicolaus sat back and crossed his arms. He had not expected

this kind of unreasonable request.

Saul sighed. "I know he came to Antioch to flee the danger in Jerusalem. For now, this area is far safer for them. I know he treasures his privacy, and for good reason. I know he likely can never trust me, and there is little I can do or say to change that. I would not ask if it were not extremely important."

Only a handful knew of Lazarus's whereabouts, and they had all been sworn to secrecy. On occasion, one of them would check on how Lazarus and the women fared and bring any needed supplies. Nicolaus was unsure how a request for an audience would be received.

He again looked down at Saul's writing: even, careful lettering, the Greek characters expertly drawn. "I do not think he will agree to meet you."

"Nicolaus, I would not ask if it were not exceedingly important. We can meet someplace neutral, assuring we are not followed."

That was a possibility. It was more *her* safety Lazarus was concerned with than his own.

"Please. Ask him for me."

"May I ask, because I know he will want to know, what is so urgent you need to speak to him about?"

Saul shook his head. "You may ask, but I may only speak to him about it." He wet his lips. "Tell him that the Lord has forbidden me to speak to anyone else about it. He will understand."

Nicolaus sighed as he stood. "I cannot promise, Paulos. But I will try."

Acco distrusted the Judean visitors. He was no more thrilled with their presence than he had been of Paulos slipping out in the middle of the night to visit the man known as Lazarus. At least Lazarus did not want anyone else to know about the visit and was as paranoid about it as Acco. On the other hand, these Jewish men had arrived at Antioch unannounced and sought out Nicolaus at once. Niger, Lucius, and Manaen. They were dressed in elaborate robes and wore boxes on their heads. Acco thought they looked ridiculous.

Their appearance did not make them any less dangerous, however. They sat at the table with the leaders of the group of believers here to share the Sabbath with them, all the while regarding Paulos with haughty glares.

Acco sat between Barnabas and Paulos. Barnabas broke the bread and handed one half to him. There was a barely audible intake of breath from the visitors as he tore off a piece before handing it on to Paulos. Acco understood that these fancy-dressed men were followers of Jesus too, and that, being from Judea, they were stuck in their ways. He also knew that Paulos had been one of them at one time, although they had not greeted or addressed Paulos, only addressing the other leaders of the Antioch church. That was reason enough for Acco to be suspicious of them.

The quiet that followed the eating of the bread was broken by one of the guests who spoke in a language Acco did not know. Nicolaus answered him in the same language.

Acco leaned into Paulos. "What are they saying?" he whispered.

Paulos did not lower his voice in answer. "They are speaking in Aramaic, Titus, despite being served in a Greek-speaking household. Allow me to translate for you."

"It is not necessary to translate, brother," the Judean replied. "I was not aware that the Sabbath meal should be taken in a foreign language."

"You insult your hosts with your piety, Ira," Paulos retorted.

The man's brows furrowed, and then he uttered a string of words in what Acco now assumed was Aramaic.

Paulos responded to what must have been a question. "That is because Christ Jesus was born in Judea and preached through Judea. He has appointed these brothers to preach to Greek speakers. And if you have any condemnation of our Gentile brothers in Christ, you would do best to proclaim it in a language they will understand."

Acco trusted them even less as the visitors exchanged knowing looks. This had the stench of a setup. He wished that he and Paulos shared a language that no one else at the table knew. He wanted to warn him. Or at least get his own jab in.

The main speaker took a drink from his cup, swallowed, and then resumed, this time in Greek. "We appreciate that Christ Jesus came to proclaim good news to the entire world, even to the

Gentiles. We know that He seeks to bring all men to Him." All heads bobbed in agreement. "But the Christ came to the chosen people first, to the tribes of Israel. He has redeemed *His* people. You say this yourself when you preach and when you write: The Christ is the redeemer of *Israel*." The man paused as Paulos dipped some bread in the stew pot and took a bite, silent. "The only way the Gentiles can be one of us is to become one of us. They must be circumcised and keep the law of Moses."

Paulos took his cup. Before he drank, he held it aloft. He lowered it and took a drink. He set it back down on the table and turned his eyes on the visitor. "My brother, if you know who I once was, you will know I know the Law. I was once like you. I was born of the tribe of Benjamin and was circumcised on the eighth day of my life. I followed the Law to the letter. Is this to what I may credit for my salvation? Is it by circumcision and following the Law of Moses that has preserved my soul? No, my friends, I am justified by faith alone. Circumcision and the Law cannot accomplish this. Only the blood of our Lord Christ Jesus can do that."

The face of the main speaker had reddened. "You say there is no value in circumcision? It was a command of God. It was not a suggestion. The law was given to Moses, to the tribes of Israel. This was to set us apart. We are His chosen people!"

Acco sat back, amazed. Before, this argument would have riled Paulos. He would have sprung up from his seat and started pacing, gesticulating with his arms, raising his voice. But here he was, relaxed, his face open.

"My brother," Saul replied, "we know a man is justified, not by the works of the law, but through faith in Christ Jesus, yes?"

"Yes, but—"

"And we have come to believe in Christ Jesus, so that we may be justified by faith in Christ. Yes?"

"Yes."

"It is not by doing the works of the Law because no one will be justified by the works of the Law."

The man shook his head. "They are necessarily exclusive."

Paulos took in a deep breath. "The law was given because we are all sinners. Then, in the fullness of time, God sent His son, born under the law, to redeem those who are under the law. Through the law, I died to the law, that I might live for God."

Acco closed his eyes. He knew these words. Much of the time, when Paulos went on about the law, Acco had trouble following his logic. But in this light, before those to whom the law of Moses was the very foundation of their faith, Acco had an inkling of their perspective.

"I am crucified with Christ," Paulos said. "It is no longer I who lives, but it is Christ who lives in me. This is the grace of God. I do not nullify the grace of God, for if justification comes through the Law and through circumcision, then Christ died for nothing."

The man again shook his head and spoke again in Aramaic. He raised his voice as he pointed at Acco, then beat his fist against his own chest. This still failed to get a rise out of Paulos, who tilted his head and let him rant on but said nothing more.

The room echoed with the man's last word. There was a pause before Barnabas broke the silence. "Perhaps we should take this question before the church in Jerusalem, before James and Cephas, and all the leaders of the church there. I know we cannot solve this here, at this meal. We appreciate you bringing your concern to us, but we are the ones doing the Lord's work with the Gentiles. Let us present the arguments before them and have more discussion then."

Brother Joseph was forever the peacemaker. This appeared to pacify the visitors, and for the remainder of the meal, Barnabas related stories of their travels. One thing was for certain. As far as Acco was concerned, if Paulos was going to Jerusalem, Acco would be at his side.

Organizing the council in Jerusalem took longer than to travel there and back. However, the news of Paulos and Barnabas's return the night before had spread like fire.

Nicolaus sat with his elbows on his knees and his chin in his hands while Saul and Barnabas stood before the assembled believers in Antioch, who were eager for the news of the council. Nicolaus had attempted to catch Saul's enthusiasm about what happened at the council in Jerusalem and the subsequent letter, but a dark cloud hovered over him. Saul believed the matter settled, but Nicolaus had his doubts. Gentiles would not be accepted by the strong adherents of the Law unless they took on the full culture of the tribes of Abraham. Can the love of God provide the necessary glue to hold together multiple, often conflicting, cultures?

Nicolaus appreciated an animated Barnabas, who retold the story of what transpired during the council on the Mount of Olives, downplaying his important contribution. Instead, Barnabas recounted how Cephas so eloquently brought the actions and teachings of Yeshua to the forefront before the council. It was Cephas's argument supporting Saul and Barnabas and opposing obligatory circumcision that swayed the council in the end.

His eyes rested on John Mark, sitting before his uncle, sober but attentive. Nicolaus was still unsure what to think of him. John Mark was always polite and friendly, not only to him but to everyone in the faith, much like his uncle. But he was hard to get to know. Everyone in leadership in Antioch knew of his separation from his uncle and Paulos mid-journey. The story John Mark told was that he had grown homesick for Jerusalem. Nicolaus understood that. Though Antioch had always been home, Jerusalem had a way of tugging at one's heart, drawing the devoted to her gates. But upon arriving in Jerusalem, John Mark had attached himself to Cephas and followed him everywhere. Missing his uncle, some had said, shrugging it off, but even when word of Barnabas's return reached him, he did not leave Cephas. John Mark's eyes shifted away from his uncle, meeting Nicolaus's glance. And now, here he is, back in his role of the adoring nephew, ready to be at his uncle's side wherever he may go.

Barnabas finished telling his portion of the events in Jerusalem and gave the floor to Saul, who stood, letter in hand. As he related James's compromise, as Saul referred to it, there was a shift in the attitude of the assembled people. *After all this man has gone through for the faith. The scourging, the stoning, a war of words. It was not enough to win the trust of the church in Antioch. If *I* can forgive his past,* Nicolaus thought, *why can't they?*

Titus stood away from the group, leaning against the wall, scanning the crowd, arms crossed. Nicolaus did not know the man's given name. Saul had introduced him with the nickname and there was no other title by which he was referred. He was never far from Saul for very long, so devoted he was to him. If that man were as devoted to the Christ, Nicolaus thought, he would be as great an evangelist as Saul himself.

Before reading the letter to a quiet reception, Paulos introduced the two respected prophets sent with them from Jerusalem, Judas and Silas. Nicolaus warmed, remembering a conversation on the road returning from Jerusalem. "I am confused," Nicolaus had said. "James referred to you as Saul, yet Paulos calls you Silas. What is your name?"

With a wide grin, Silas explained. "Silvanus is my Roman name, Saul my Hebrew name. I believe Paulos refers to me by the shortened version, Silas, as he does not want us to be confused for one another."

"As if that could happen." Nicolaus smirked, knowing Saul as he did. "How do you manage to have a Roman name, Silas?"

"My father was a freedman, living in Tarsus, when I was born."

"Well, that explains a lot. Not only can there be just one Saul, there can only be *one* Saul of Tarsus!"

Silas had nodded. "Precisely."

It also explained why Silas had taken so quickly to Saul. Sharing a hometown had drawn them together. That, and the tight community of freedmen in any city meant shared connections and experiences. It would not surprise him if Silas chose not to return to Jerusalem with Judas Barsabbas and John Mark. And the Pharisees.

Nicolaus turned his attention to the small group of Pharisees huddled together, arms crossed, their hands inside their spacious robes. Titus also eyed them, his hand on the hilt of his dagger as Saul read the letter from the Jerusalem Council. Although these same Pharisees had been present at the council and had heard Cephas and James state their positions as well as the testimony of Barnabas and Saul, Nicolaus knew they remained unconvinced.

Saul concluded the letter. He rolled it up and held it out. Then he peered at the small group of Pharisees.

"Brothers," he said, "today, with this letter, the body of Christ is bound together with one purpose, one Lord, one resurrection. For in Christ Jesus, there is no Gentile or Jew. We are one in Christ."

When Saul rejoined the assembly, the Pharisees filed out. Nicolaus followed their receding backs and knew, with sadness, that they would never accept the Jerusalem compromise.

Several days passed. Judas Barsabbas and some of the others had returned to Jerusalem, though Silas remained. Barnabas was not surprised.

Yes, the Antioch gathering of believers appreciated Silas's gift of prophecy. But even more, since their return from the Jerusalem council, Silas was often with Saul, their heads bent together, discussing only the Spirit knew what. When Saul was not talking with Silas or teaching or meeting with Nicolaus and the other leaders of the Antioch church, Saul was writing. It was painstaking work. The beating he had taken had wrecked his body, and sitting bent over his writing made him worse. But he never complained, making a joke of it, if anything.

Oftentimes on the return journey, Barnabas questioned Saul about what had happened, trying to engage him. But about what he had experienced, Saul remained silent.

The way Saul had entered Jerusalem this time, so different than when Barnabas had disguised and snuck him in, had astounded him. Grinning, absorbing it all, relishing the crowds, spying old faces, and greeting them like it was a big, happy reunion. It warmed his heart as Saul showed off the city to Titus, for Barnabas remembered a time Saul mourned over the city like a lost loved one, sure he would never enter her gates again.

It had been good to be with Cephas again, though he, too, had changed. Highly respected, everyone gave patient regard to his many stories, though they had heard the tales repeatedly. His nephew, Marcus, adored Cephas, and Barnabas appreciated that Cephas had accepted him as his own. Marcus had accumulated some of Cephas's stories, writing them down "for posterity," as he would say.

Cephas had roared with mirth, throwing back his head, before reminding him that Yeshua would return soon. "Posterity," he said, "will all be with Yeshua!"

"Then I will leave them behind for the damned," Marcus replied.

Barnabas shook the memory away as Titus addressed him.

"Paulos asked me to summon you," he said, "if you're not busy."

Marcus, who had remained in Antioch rather than return to Jerusalem with Cephas, trailed along behind Barnabas. In Antioch, Marcus had no other identity than as the nephew of Barnabas. Always with Cephas or Barnabas. Marcus must attach himself to one of his pillars in order to stand.

When Barnabas entered, Saul was slouched over his writing desk, his face close to his work. He had problems with that eye, the one that the killing stone had injured. It was a wonder he saw anything at all.

Titus, Silas, and Nicolaus greeted him, and then Saul rose from his seat, grinning. "Brother!" he exclaimed.

Barnabas embraced him and greeted him with a kiss.

"Sit." Saul indicated the chair he had vacated. "Brother, I was so pleased with the results of the council in Jerusalem. It is good to have the blessing on our mission to bring the good news to the Gentiles, as God has appointed and commissioned us."

"Cephas was commissioned first to be the apostle to the Gentiles," Marcus quipped. Barnabas jerked his head at his nephew's interruption.

Saul did not appear perturbed. "Indeed, he was. His encounter with Cornelius is well-known and respected. But I must ask you, Marcus: how many new gatherings of Gentile believers have Cephas established?"

Barnabas willed Marcus not to reply, but a flash of anger showed on his nephew's face. "He doesn't need to start new gatherings. His job is to strengthen those already established, to fill in the blanks left by those who weren't one of Yeshua's chosen disciples."

The awkward silence that followed was deafening. Barnabas cringed for his nephew, preparing for the onslaught of rhetorical battle. The old Saul would have taken these words personally.

Saul reached out a hand and laid it on Marcus's shoulder. "There is no one better for that task, Marcus. I understand you are writing down some of Cephas's stories, so we might all share them with those who have not heard them in person."

Marcus's eyebrows shot up as his mouth opened in surprise. "Why, yes. Yes, I am."

"Good," Saul said. "Make copies for us as well. Sit, get

comfortable!" Saul let his hand fall and turned toward Barnabas. "Brother Barnabas, I am eager to share the good news from the Jerusalem council with our people in Galatia. They need the same strengthening from us as the Judean believers do from Cephas. I understand that their enemies continue to harass them." Saul waved a hand toward the writing table.

Multiple small scrolls were tumbled on the desk, rolled up and tied. Many of Saul's outgoing letters were in response to cries for help. For a moment, Barnabas was back in Iconium, back in Derbe, surrounded by angry, jealous men, desiring nothing more than Saul's death, to silence the uttering of the Name forever. Barnabas gazed up at Saul, whose dark, piercing eyes read his thoughts. Barnabas stood, joining him.

"You are right, Paulos," he said. "The churches of believers in Galatia will need this encouragement."

A grin spread across Saul's face. "Excellent!" he said, then he turned toward Nicolaus. "We will not need nearly as much financial backing this time. Don't worry. We will go by land, head toward Tarsus, and make our way to Galatia through Cilicia." Nicolaus nodded in response. "Barnabas, Titus, and I will not require much. We are well familiar with those roads by now."

"I will go with you, Uncle," Marcus said as he stood beside him.

Barnabas tilted his head, his mouth parting open. Marcus had hated the journey last time. "Are you sure?"

"No." A cloud passed over Saul's face. "No, that will not do. The churches there know the three of us. The message that we are not afraid to return must be clear to their enemies. To *our* enemies."

"Be that as it may," Barnabas replied, "there is safety in numbers. When we return, but with a larger group, it sends the message that we are stronger than ever before."

"We have an army of angels around us. No, it gives a far better impression of God's might with only the three of us, and the same three who left there not so long ago. We were not chased out, nor did we sneak out. We left them in the hands of capable leaders, and we must return as we left."

Barnabas crossed his arms. "Marcus was with us all through Cyprus."

"Not all the time, and certainly not in usefulness."

With a huff, Barnabas narrowed his eyes and tilted his head. "Was he such a burden?"

"I do not know what happened that night in Old Paphos," Saul asserted, "but I know, whatever it was, it was inappropriate for a disciple of Christ. We cannot afford to have a single speck of misbehavior. It will be like a scab. Those vultures will pick at it until we are powerless. Marcus is far more useful to the Spirit in his present course of action, with Cephas."

With an audible exhale, Barnabas uncrossed his arms and balled his hands into fists. A burst of energy shot through him as he shook his head as if to dismiss violent thoughts. "Is anyone ever good enough for you, Saul?" Barnabas spat out the words. He thought Saul had changed, had been touched by the very hand of God, but here was the old Saul of Tarsus, holier than anyone else, refusing to forgive one night of indiscretion. "You know where Acco came from! Marcus is far purer and has not had to be instructed in the ways of our people." Titus jumped to his feet. Barnabas had slipped, speaking his given name in front of the others.

"I am not implying—"

"Of course you are. Saul of Tarsus, blameless under the Law, forever the Pharisee under those rags! My nephew goes with us, or you go without me."

At once, a flicker of hurt showed in those dark, piercing eyes, and Barnabas regretted the ultimatum. For what seemed an eternity, the only sound in the small, close room was his heartbeat. He searched Saul's face, willing it to soften. He sought the relenting friend he had once known, squatting on a floor side by side, working leather, mending tents. His hope rose at the slight tilt of Saul's head.

"My brother." Sauls's brows pulled together, and his dark eyes mellowed. "I am sorry you feel that way. What kind of message will it send to our people?"

"These are our people, Paulos!" Barnabas swept his arm. "Here, in Antioch. There, in Jerusalem."

Saul shook his head.

Barnabas grabbed Marcus by the shoulder. "Come, Nephew," he said, heading for the door. Then he turned back to Saul. "You go on to Galatia. Give my regards to the people there. But do not go to Cyprus. You leave Cyprus to us."

Then he and Marcus left the room.

Chapter Nineteen

**Lystra, Laeconia
50 A.D.**

Acco was wary to re-enter Lystra, the city where the stoning had taken place, although Paulos had no such reservations. "They are afraid of us, Titus," Paulos had said. "They know we are protected by a mighty God and speak on his behalf."

On their way from Syria, they had visited the small gatherings of believers in the cities between there and Tarsus, meeting people Paulos had kept in communication with all the many years since he had been with them. When they stayed in Tarsus, Acco considered himself to be very much a spare, the only one of the trio without history and family there, although both Paulos and Silas's families warmly welcomed him.

He and Paulos had stayed with Paulos's mother, a graceful lady whose good health and mature beauty explained so much about Paulos's background and rearing. The grandeur of her home left nothing to the imagination of his upbringing. Paulos came from money. Not so with Silas. His family lived much more humbly yet were every bit as welcoming. Unlike Paulos, Silas had a huge family, and they all gathered to greet their son, brother, nephew, and cousin returned for a visit. Acco was introduced to so many names, several repeated a couple of times, that they all laughed in his dismay. Why would anyone want to leave that?

However, he had wondered the same thing, sleeping in the most comfortable bed of his life and bathing in the expansive and luxurious bath at Paulos's house. If you lived in such luxury, what would compel you to leave it all, to roam about the known world, to sleep on the hard, cold ground, to risk falling victim to robbers, murderers, and the elements? Or to walk boldly back, again, into a place that had stoned you? In Syrian Antioch, Acco was aware of the whispers, the stories of Saul of Tarsus, the zealous young Pharisee with murder in his heart. It had been difficult to find that man in the Paulos he had always known. This must be what he meant when Paulos spoke about how Christ changes a man: the old falls away, and God creates one anew. Yet Acco was the same old Acco. He believed all that Barnabas and Paulos had taught him, and he was fiercely loyal to Paulos, supported his work, throwing all he had into following him. Barnabas had the gift of healing and was full of the Spirit. Silas, like Paulos, had the gift of prophecy. In Antioch and Jerusalem, Acco had noted many signs of the Spirit in others. Wisdom, speaking other tongues, teaching, and encouragement. But him? He was little more than a tag-along.

After leaving Tarsus, they returned to Derbe, sharing the letter from the Jerusalem council with the believers there.

Acco shook his head. And now, here in Lystra once more, he sat again as Paulos taught. Young men and women sat at their teacher's feet, absorbing his every word. This evening, after everyone left for home, Silas would say something about how the Spirit's presence was strong, and Paulos would say how it would accomplish much here among the believers. And Acco would once more wonder what in the world they were talking about.

Upon their return to Lystra, Paulos sought out the two leaders, Ayelat and her daughter, Bracha, whom he had assigned to the believers here. These ladies opened their home for gatherings. The men in the Lystra group were no longer welcomed in the synagogues. But because they were women, Ayelat and Bracha continued to worship in the synagogue on Sabbath mornings and would bring back the teachings to share with the rest.

The ladies remembered Acco and graciously accepted Silas in place of Barnabas, though Acco sensed some disappointment. Although Acco barely remembered their son and grandson, Timothy had greeted him like a long-lost brother. And Acco liked him. Timothy was soft-spoken but observant, absorbing every word that Paulos spoke. He was younger than Barnabas's nephew, who Acco was relieved had not come along with them. If Paulos had an issue with Marcus accompanying them, that was good enough for Acco. And while Paulos may have missed his former partner, Acco was not aware that he ever let on.

"So, this good news of Christ Jesus that I re-emphasize to you all is this," Paulos was saying. "The divisions that once separated us from one another no longer exist. Trust me. I know the pride of these strict adherents of the Law. They are descendants of Abraham? So am I. I am of the tribe of Benjamin. I, too, was circumcised on the eighth day. I was raised to be a Pharisee like my father, and I studied the Law at the feet of the great teacher in Jerusalem. I was a scribe and consultant for the high court of the capital city. Do they know the Law? So do I. I lived it, breathed it, ate it. But what good is all that when faced with the perfection of Christ? Christ Jesus has, with his saving blood, paid the price and in so doing has broken down the walls, not only between Pharisee and the common folk but between Jew and Gentile, rich and poor, slave and master."

Acco sighed. *I wish I could have met Jesus while he walked this earth.* He envied Barnabas and his nephew for that.

A strange sensation at that thought rippled over him, a warmth like a blanket draping over his shoulders, and peace fluttered within. His wonder at the sensation gave way to acceptance, and all his angst and foreboding melted away. The peace in his heart was an assurance for him. His belief was a living thing, a deep and all-encompassing knowledge. Without warning, he neared Paulos and proclaimed the glory of God in a foreign tongue.

Paulos halted his speech. His face glowing, he motioned as Acco raised his arms, his face upturned. Then another voice rang out, and then another, all praising God for the glory the Spirit revealed to them. Paulos joined their praise in a loud voice, and the entire house was filled with the sound of adoration.

Afterward, Paulos pulled him into a hug. "I had wondered when the Spirit would come to you," he said. As they prepared for sleep, Silas asked Acco what he was prepared to do for the kingdom of God now that he had found his voice.

"What do you mean?"

"The Lord has chosen you, Titus. How far are you prepared to go for him? Do you know what this means for you?"

Acco paused. He thought of the beatings and opposition Paulos had endured and the wreck it had made on his body. He thought of Christ Jesus, who had suffered so much for him. "I have the best role models." He chose his words with caution. "I know that suffering awaits me. But what is any of that compared to the glory of God?"

"Indeed," Silas replied. "Well said."

Later, while on his back on his pallet, the voices still filled Acco's ears. His life was forever changed, and he longed for all to know what he now knew and to experience what he had experienced. Acco laid flat, staring upward, too worked up to sleep. *What now, Lord? You are equipping me for a life of service to you, but where will you bid me go? Must I leave Paulos? He has been my rock. I left everything for him.*

Acco took in the sounds of the sleeping men around him and of an unfamiliar house. As he was about to drift off, a thought came to him, strong and knowing, and he sat straight up. *Camulos, my brother. A lost soul.*

Saul.

His eyes flicked open, and he turned his head. As he did, his neck gave a sickening crunch. The floor was cool and the pallet thin, and a chill had crept into his joints overnight. Early morning light already filled the room where he and Silas slept. He had missed cock crow.

Saul missed Barnabas. He missed the rhythm of their day and the prayers through the night. It had become their habit, and with both Barnabas and now Acco gone, his sleep pattern had been thrown out of rhythm.

At their last visit, his mother complained of his weight loss when they stopped over in Tarsus. He had not told her that he had gained weight since the journey on foot through Galatia, having burned off what little he tended to eat. To her, he attributed it to poor cuisine. She remained unconvinced and accused him of fasting too much. "How are you going to serve God if you wither away to nothing?" she had asked. Mother had aged with grace and still reigned supreme in their household, despite the fact that technically and legally, it was Saul's household. He was thankful that the businesses were in excellent shape and could more than afford to add to the mission's coffer.

Silas stirred, and Saul sat up with effort, his back aching and stiff. Together, they said their morning prayers, sitting on their pallets. Silas reached out a hand, offering to help, but Saul brushed him away. He bid his legs to fold under him to rise, but his body did not want to cooperate. He rolled on his hands and knees but was halted by a sharp pain in the shoulder.

"Here, allow me," Silas insisted.

"No, I can do it. The joints are not moving well this morning."

"Paulos, please. The Lord sent me to help you. Let me help."

On his haunches now, Saul growled. "He sent you to help spread the good news, not to drag a wretch off the floor." He paused. "Are you laughing at me?"

"Yes. Yes, I am. Here." He came to his side. "Use my arm to pull yourself up."

As Saul stretched up with one hand for Silas's strong arm, Timothy appeared out of nowhere to help on the other, and they pulled him to his feet.

"You need a bed," Timothy said. "I'll give you mine tonight." "No, no," Saul argued, "I have slept on far worse. It's merely the dampness." He waved them away as he took some painful steps. "Let a man tend to his morning routine."

Timothy and Silas both turned away and waited until Saul reached for his clothing. "Mother and I are acquainted with an excellent physician in Troas and Philippi," Timothy stated. "He is a follower of the Way, too."

"I don't need a physician but thank you."

"He might be able to help you."

"Timothy," Saul's words were clipped. "I do not need a physician. What I do need is to stretch out these bones. I am going for a walk."

"Excellent idea, Paulos!" Timothy said. "May I come along?" "Of course, you may. Silas?"

"No, thanks. I'll wait for Ayelet's list of what she needs to be purchased for tonight's Sabbath meal, then head to the market for them."

"Use our resources to pay for whatever they need." Saul's joints were already looser as he and Timothy entered the street. He sensed a restlessness the longer they remained in Lystra, as he did if he lingered in any one place for a time. Perhaps his body remembered Lystra all too well. Though it took him out of his way, he purposefully avoided the location where the stoning took place. Their visit to Lystra was drawing to a close. It was time to go on to Iconium.

"Brother Titus left quietly." Timothy broke the silence between them.

"He has business near Pisidia," Saul replied. "The Spirit spurred him ahead of us. We are to meet up with him in Antioch."

"That is where you and Brother Barnabas met him, correct?"

"No, we met Titus and his brother in Perga. They were packers and guides for us through the mountain range."

"Oh yes. He told me that." Timothy was quiet for a few more paces. "You are leaving soon, too, are you not? You and Silas?"

"Yes." Saul was glad he had broached the subject. "And I need to ask something of you. You have been prominent in my dreams of late. I believe you are to go with us. What are your thoughts about that?"

"Me?" Timothy stopped.

Saul turned toward him. "Yes, you. Come, do not stop. I am not all stretched out yet." Once they were moving again, Saul resumed. "Do you sense the Spirit urging you on with us?"

"Yes, I do. I have had dreams, too. I am young and have much to learn, but I believe God is preparing me for work."

"It is a hard road, fraught with danger and rejection." Saul scrutinized Timothy out of the corner of his eyes as they strode down the street. They had made their way through the residential area and had reached the city center. Here he stopped. "Some days, food is scarce. You will often sleep under the stars, on the hard ground, subject to wild animals and thieves. You will suffer physically. You will be beaten and whipped and thrown in jail with criminals as your companions. You will be spat upon and called all kinds of vicious names. In other words." Saul placed a hand on Timothy's shoulder. "It will not be pleasant."

Timothy straightened, tall as he could manage. "But I will not be alone, for the Spirit of God will go with me. He is my strength and my shield."

Saul grinned and pulled the young man in for a hug. "Then you shall go with us." Releasing him, he glanced around. They were far too close to the wall where the stoning took place. Saul turned them both in the direction they had come from, to head back to Timothy's house. "We should go back and make a list of all you will need for the journey."

"There is something I need that we will not find in the market," Timothy said. "Something I sense I must do, and I need your guidance."

"The road is not a good place to fulfill a vow, my son."

"Not a vow, Paulos. You know my father was a Gentile."

"Yes, but you were raised in our tradition. Children are to follow their mother's religion."

"It is true," Timothy answered. "I was raised in the tradition of my maternal grandfather of the tribe of Benjamin and, until late, attended synagogue with my mother and grandmother. But I was not allowed to participate in the school or the readings."

"Because your father was a Gentile?"

"No, Paulos. Because my Gentile father would not allow my mother to have me circumcised. Paulos, my father is dead, and I honor his memory. But I want to represent Christ Jesus to our people. How do I do that uncircumcised? How can I be taken seriously in any synagogue? I want to be a full member of the faith of Christ Jesus and of you."

"You do not have to do this," Saul responded. "You can represent your father's race. They will give you heed."

"No. I am not accepted by them either because I was raised by my Hebrew mother, in a Hebrew tradition."

Saul sighed. "Timothy, did we not recently receive a great victory for the physically uncircumcised? Is it not our hearts that need to be made right with God, more so than our bodies?"

"Paulos." Timothy shook his head. "I know all that. But I have prayed about this, and I am strongly compelled. The right to be circumcised still exists, does it not? I know it doesn't mean that I am any more accepted by Christ Jesus either way. But if I am to turn my life over to him, I don't want to do it as 'half-Hebrew' or 'half-

Greek.' How can I expect to stand in any synagogue and teach unless I am considered Jewish?"

He made a valid point. Timothy had obviously thought this through, perhaps for years. Saul pursed his lips. If the Spirit was compelling him . . .

"Have I angered you, Paulos? That was not my intent. I thought you would understand and would help me."

Saul paused and folded his arms. "You have not angered me. Quite the contrary. I suppose we'll have to find a *mohel* around here willing to do it for you."

Chapter Twenty

**Philippi, Macedonia
50 A.D.**

The thick dampness of human degradation lined Silas's nostrils and coated his tongue. The floor of the cell was cold hewn stone, and a sharp edge dug into his bruised hip. With their feet in stocks and their wrists in chains, he and Saul were forced into impossible sitting positions with legs, buttocks, and backs that the Roman Philippians had been beaten raw. Everything hurt, and both men were held firmly in place. Each time Silas adjusted his body, a sharp pain shot through abused muscles. They were both exhausted, but neither could sleep.

They should have been miserable like the rest of the prisoners, whose anguish permeated the neighboring cells of their cave prison. Moans, cries of pain, and curses echoed and only intensified when Saul opened his mouth and sang.

Earlier in the day, they'd freed the girl of the demon that possessed her. The girl's owners had accused them of theft and loss of the income they'd been making off her demon-possessed prophecies. Saul and Silas had received no opportunity of a defense before the magistrate. Once the complaint against them was pronounced, they were beaten with rods in the owners' presence. Refusing to cry out, both of them received their punishment in silence. But as the two were dragged into their cell, Saul raised his voice, singing praises to God, and in Greek so that all might understand.

When they first arrived in Philippi, Saul appeared far less road-weary and exhausted than any of their company, despite Silas being a good decade younger than Saul. Timothy was even younger. The stay at Euodia's home had refreshed them all. Silas warmed to reflect on the sigh that escaped from Saul when he once again lay on a real bed, soft and downy. But even then, the man seemed to never sleep. The habit of many years of waking with the signal to pray in Jerusalem had so ingrained itself in Saul that it was not unusual, if one awakened in the night, to make out whispers of praise emanating from him. When Saul was finally sleeping, Silas knew he dreamed. Sometimes, Saul shared the dreams but often kept them to himself. How he had the energy to go, day after day, with catnapping and his habit of frequent fasting, Silas could only wonder. Saul seemed to run solely on the Spirit of God.

In the prison, Silas sang along with Saul, but his thoughts were with their companions nearby at the home of Euodia, nicknamed Lydia. She was an interesting member of their company and an unlikely one at that. The dream God had given Saul, the one that encouraged him to come to Macedonia in the first place, had featured a man, not a woman, begging him to come there to help. Not finding enough Jewish men in this city of retired Roman soldiers to necessitate a synagogue, Saul and Silas were directed to a Jewish gathering outside the city, on the river. When they arrived, they found but a small group of women. Saul had not hesitated, however, worshiping and praying with them. Then he taught them about the Christ. While all were attentive and interested in the teaching, it was Lydia, a God-worshiping Gentile woman, who was moved by the Spirit, and it was Lydia they baptized right there in the river.

She had a fine, large home in the city. Widowed at a young age, she had continued her husband's successful business, selling the fine cloth desired by wealthy Romans for which Philippi was strategically located for its export. Only those closest to her even remembered her husband. All her patrons cared about was access to the high-quality cloth she provided.

Silas shifted his weight again from one buttock to the other, but it did no good. He needed to ignore his body, something to learn from Saul, and concentrate on the Spirit. He sensed the prayers going up for them: Lydia, her entire household, Titus, Timothy, and the physician, Luke. Well-educated and wise beyond his years, Saul had appreciated Luke at once, recognizing the necessary humility in Luke's personality to receive the Spirit when they met him in Troas. It was while staying at Luke's residence in Troas that Saul had his dream about the Macedonian man, and it was at Luke's table that Saul shared it. Fortunately, Luke hailed from Philippi and was eager to show off his childhood home. But his people did not well receive his conversion to a religion revolving around the Jewish God in a city founded by retired officers of the Roman army. So, although Philippi had been home, Luke found himself following their small band about the city as they preached and taught.

Singing praises did not lessen the taste thick on his tongue, and he was thirsty. Saul's voice was hoarse from his constant singing. In the gloom of dim torchlight, Silas observed Saul's head bent over his chest and wondered if the man was singing in his sleep. He had started the long psalm Silas knew was one of Saul's favorites. It was so long that Silas had never bothered memorizing it. He tended to get the verses out of order.

"Remember your word to your servant,
In which you have made me hope.
This is my comfort in my distress,
That your promise gives me life."

Saul broke off, his head lifted, alert. "Do you feel that?" Paulos asked.

"Feel—" Silas began. The floor and walls of their cell trembled and then shook violently, dust falling about them. What if the cave walls tumbled in, crushing them?

As deafening sharp cracks surrounded them, Saul shouted in the din. "Silas! Do not be afraid!"

"What?"

"God has heard the prayers lifted for us!" Then Saul called out encouragement to the other prisoners above the clamor of shifting rock. "Do not be afraid. Have courage!"

When Silas thought the dank dust and rocks falling about them was merely the onset, the violent shaking stopped, and shrieks of iron squealed as the door to their cell swung inward.

Euodia had known that nothing good would come of it, but she had not anticipated things would escalate so quickly. When she learned that the fortuneteller had begun to follow the men as they left her house to preach, a sense of foreboding came over her. Paulos had attempted to reassure her.

"She is quite irritating," he had admitted, "but she is harmless."

"Good advertising," Silas had added, smiling. "You worry over much, Lydia." But she knew that Titus and the physician, Luke, agreed with her. Their eyes would meet hers and, better knowing the ways of the retired Roman officers who populated the city, they understood that what was tolerated in places far more remote from Rome would not be tolerated in Macedonia, and certainly not here in Little Rome, as Philippi was nicknamed.

How her life had changed the day Paulos and his friends happened upon their little gathering at the river! Euodia had long been fascinated by the stories of the God of her trusted employee and, for years, had joined her and the other Jewish women of the city, away from the spying eyes of neighbors and patrons, away from the docks, away from the authorities. They had so needed a leader to emerge, to help the women with their worship and their understanding of the Law and the Prophets. She had prayed for them to come, and then, there the leaders were, sitting with them, praying with them, singing with them. And then they shared Christ Jesus with them, and she was no longer the same.

She reflected on the light in Paulos's eyes whenever he spoke of someday going to Rome as if it were a paradise destination. While human beings can be cruel, the Romans used cruelty to control their world. She also lived daily knowing that at any moment, if her precious purple cloth displeased a Roman buyer, if there was even a tiny flaw, it would be the end of her business and her household and might very well be the end of her. Based on the behavior exhibited by the retired Roman officers, Philippi was as close to Rome as she ever cared to get.

And then her fears had solidified into reality. Paulos and Silas had been taken. She was not present when it happened, but when Timothy, in tears, reported the events and their powerlessness to stop the arrest and punishment, she called all the believers together. This time, she served no food. They fasted and prayed. Luke and Timothy had held back Titus during the beating. Rods were the favorite of the Roman authority, who were efficient in doling out punishment.

Local authorities had longed for an excuse to rid themselves of the traveling Jewish teacher stirring up the city. When Paulos cast the fortunetelling demon out of the slave girl, the authorities happily charged Paulos and Silas with the destruction of property.

Euodia prayed that Paulos and Silas would survive the night. Beating by rods was not fatal, but Paulos's body was already severely damaged, and Luke worried about broken ribs and problems breathing. And what about Lydia's little band of followers of Christ? Was the message of hope to end here? Were they who had to remain in Philippi to face similar punishments?

She had led them in prayer and then allowed the Spirit to do the rest. The prayers rose up in waves as they sat on her tiled floor. Euodia's eyes swept warmly over the gathering of believers. She need not worry about the future of their group. They all belonged to Christ Jesus. She was filled with the warmth and reassurance that their hope was not displaced.

Euodia closed her eyes and concentrated on Paulos. She let her soul fly to that prison. She sensed Paulos and Silas chained separately, their feet in common stocks in a central cell. She allowed her spirit to hover around Paulos, like a guardian spirit, and was not surprised to sense his head lift and his face light up. His lips formed her name. He knew she was there. She decided to stay with him, to bring his spirit comfort, though she knew it was unnecessary. The small cell was brimming with angels.

Then the house trembled. On the wall and on the floor, the rattling of furnishings echoed. Her eyes flew open to the equally concerned wrinkled brows of the others.

"Is that—"

"Lydia!"

"Earthquake!"

The others scrambled up and ran for the door. Earthquakes were commonplace, and the instinct was to hurry to an exit. But Euodia still sat, eyes wide with terror, knowing that Paulos and Silas were trapped inside a shallow cave. She pictured the ceiling of their narrow cell falling in, crushing them.

Oh, Lord Jesus! Preserve them!

The torchlight had been extinguished. Screams of men accented the sounds of falling rock and cracking metal. Saul's nostrils filled with dust, and he coughed. It took him a few moments to recognize the screaming was coming from his friend. On instinct, Saul reached out to calm him, forgetting the chains that bound him. But when his fingers touched Silas's arm, he drew back, surprised.

"Silas! Silas, we are all right. Everything is going to be fine."

In the inky blackness, Saul held his hands before his face. Despite their invisibility, he knew his hands were free. He searched around on the floor and found the cold metal that had once bound him lying helplessly. Saul expelled a short chuckle, resulting in yet more coughing.

Silas had stopped screaming. "Paulos?"

"The chains! The force of the earthquake. Stand up, brother," he commanded.

"I can't. The stocks—"

Silas scrambled up. As he did, Saul realized the stocks holding them had collapsed.

He should not have been as surprised as he was. "Help up a broken old man, please?" Saul reached out and found Silas's two strong hands and managed to pull himself up to stand. While the floor had stopped moving, dust still settled about them. Harsh coughs arose from neighboring cells. Kicking away the shattered stocks, Saul shuffled with caution in the direction of the doorway. He reached blindly for the door, which was swung inward. He grinned, touching the door with his right hand. Stopping at the threshold, he called out to the other prisoners. "Is everyone all right?

Is anyone hurt?"

Reassurances were shouted back to him. All were dusty, but none of the ceilings had caved in. "Stay where you are," he demanded. "The guard will be here soon, and escape will only add to your sentences."

Saul sensed the jailer hurrying to assess the damage. It would fare best for the man if the ceilings had all collapsed and all within had perished than for the cells to not properly hold the prisoners. The jailer's cry of dismay signaled Saul that the man was withdrawing his dagger.

"Stop!" Saul cried out. "Come and see! We are all here. Do not harm yourself!"

Later, Silas asked him why he did not encourage the other prisoners to flee to freedom. Saul explained that they all had broken the laws of the city and received their just punishments. "Even us, Silas. Well, even me. You were guilty by association."

"Are you saying, Paulos, that we earned our beating?"

"Laws are not always just. But we know the laws of Rome, and by entering the city of Philippi, we agreed with the laws there. You will always have more credence if you appear to follow the authority of men. Of course, it is often difficult or impossible to follow both the Law of God and the law of man."

The jailer hurried to them with a torch in each hand, checking the cells, his mouth agape. He hovered in the doorway, peering in at Saul and Silas, who stood waiting for him. Spying the broken chains and shattered stocks, his head shot up at Saul in amazement. Securing one of the torches on the wall, he turned toward them, holding the other up high.

"The other prisoners are still in chains," their jailer gasped, "but remain in their open cells. Here you two are—"

"We serve the Living God, the creator of the universe." Saul inched one foot forward and raised his hands. "The God of Abraham, Isaac, and Jacob."

The jailer licked his lips, his eyes still wide. "You are Jews."

The man's eyes filled up, threatening to spill over. The hand holding the torch started to fall, but Silas quickly caught it. He held the torch as the man fell to his knees before Saul. Despite the pain, Saul sank back onto the filthy floor with him. "Tell me your name."

The man sucked in a deep breath and then lifted his head. "I am called Accius Casca. I am from Rome. I served in the military, following the orders of my superiors and my emperor. We—" He stopped and eyed Silas. "Well, everyone but the Jews have many gods." Accius dropped his gaze. "My wife is Jewish," he continued. "She has taught me much about her faith. I . . . I am in a predicament and do not know what to do. In my frustration, I admit, I have been praying to her god." Accius met Saul's eyes. "Your god, I suppose."

Saul sat back and gave the man some time as he sobbed into his hands. The flames from the jailer's torch, clutched tight, illuminated Silas's face. When Accius recovered, the man again raised his eyes to Saul. "Sir," he said, "please—"

"What can I do for you, Accius?"

Accius held out his hands to him. "What must I do to be saved?"

Accius's home was near the cave entrance, and he led Saul and Silas the short distance. His entire household was awake, as the earthquake had made the house a mess. Accius's wife greeted them warily but brought water and herbs to cleanse and dress their wounds from the beating. As Accius and his wife worked, Saul and Silas explained the means of salvation.

"This Jesus was beaten, like you two?"

"He was scourged before his crucifixion."

Accius was appalled. "Crucifixion is usually reserved for political prisoners . . . treasonous men."

"The people had proclaimed him a king," Saul answered. "The Roman authority was convinced that to claim a kingdom was to proclaim yourself a king. Thus, treason."

The resurrection story fascinated Accius, and when he learned it was an earthquake that rolled away the great stone blocking Jesus's grave, he exclaimed, "Much as an earthquake gave me new life!"

Saul baptized Accius and his entire family that night. They broke bread together and chatted until sunrise threatened.

"You will be released this morning," Accius said. "But I suppose you should not be found in my house when the city officials send word of it.”

“No,” Saul agreed, “you are correct. Lead Silas and me back.”

Standing again in their cell, Silas cast his eyes on the floor, noting the dusty chains and the broken stocks. “I am ready to get back to Lydia’s,” he said. “The accommodations are much friendlier there.”

“We will go back after we are done here,” Saul replied. “To say our goodbyes and prepare to go on. Brother Luke will stay to help Lydia with the church. They will welcome Accius and his clan into their gatherings, and this little group of believers will do great things despite the hostile environment.” He paused as in thought. “Ah, the messengers from our gracious hosts have arrived! Silas, we wait but a little longer before taking our leave.”

Silas cocked his head at Saul, who stood, arms crossed, waiting.

Accius stood before their cell, and the door swung wide open. “Sirs, the city authorities have sent word that you are released. You may go.”

Saul shook his head. “No, my friend Accius, we shall not go. Not yet.”

“But Paulos!” Accius replied. “You are free! Go now, before you anger them and they persecute you, or me, any further.”

“Accius, please tell the messengers to go back to their superiors and tell them we demand justice. They doled out punishment upon and then imprisoned citizens of Rome, without a trial and without allowing ear for our defense.”

“Citizens of Rome?”

“Yes. If I report this—”

“I will tell them, Paulos,” Accius said as he turned away.

“Paulos,” Silas murmured. “I am not—”

“No, but I am,” Saul interrupted. “I demand an apology. Do you know what will happen to them if I report this incident?”

“An apology? Paulos, let’s leave while we have the chance! What are you thinking?”

“Silas, if we leave now, it will be because we have their permission. But they have no authority over us. And I want them to be aware of that fact.”

Silas kicked at the broken stocks. “Seems to me they had *some* authority over us.”

The doorway darkened with Accius and the magistrate himself. "What is the meaning of this?" he demanded. "Accius says you are Roman citizens?"

"That is correct," Saul replied. "And we were punished without trial."

The magistrate's hands shook as his face reddened. "Please." He gulped.

"I will not report you." Saul straightened as best he was able. "We merely require an apology."

"Please," the magistrate said, scanning the cell and eying the broken chains and stocks, "leave us. I . . . we had no idea." The man's lips quivered. "We want no more earthquakes from you or your god." His shaking hand clutched the front of his robe. "I am sorry," he said, his voice soft and quavering. "Please, just go."

Saul frowned and scowled at him. "We have people here. Perhaps we shall stay."

The man rushed forward, falling at Saul's feet, his robes stirring up the dust. "No! Please, sir, I beg you! Leave us, and don't come back."

Saul, arms crossed, cast his eyes down at him. He let out a breath through his nose. "Get up. We will go."

The magistrate scrambled up, dusting off his robe. "Thank you, thank you!"

Saul motioned Silas toward the doorway and limped after him. He laid his hand on the open metal door before turning toward the magistrate. "Our God has a message for you. 'Go and learn what this means: I desire mercy, not sacrifice.'" Then he turned back, patted the door frame, and was gone.

Chapter Twenty-One

**Corinth, Achaia
50 A.D.**

After Philippi, Acco and Paulos traveled to Thessalonica, where the experience had been horrific. While they made some great strides for Christ there, they also met with terrible opposition. Apparently, when a preaching of truth threatens to topple the major economy of a place, the city leaders get upset. They were chased out of Thessalonica quite unceremoniously. Beroea was much more accommodating, and the church established there was strong and growing. But when the oppressors from Thessalonica received word of it, he and Paulos had had to escape, once again.

And then there was Athens. Paulos had long desired to visit Athens, as he told Acco both on the way as they traveled from Beroea and when they stood within the city's walls. According to Paulos, his hometown of Tarsus was second only to Athens in its production of philosophers and philosophical thought. As he laid out straps, bridles, and some fine footwear to sell in the marketplace, Acco grinned, remembering how Paulos had gained the attention of the philosophers of Athens.

Acco had been to many cities, but Athens was by far the largest he had experienced. And it was so old. He imagined that the very first people on earth had established it, paved the roads, and built all the temples. But even there, the shadow of Rome loomed. Acco sensed the people of Athens tolerated the presence of Roman authority. He suspected that when the few philosophers swept him and Paulos up the hill to confer with their leadership, it was largely to escape the watchful eye of Roman guards. Revolutions always started with ideas.

The teachings of Christ Jesus had not yet reached the great agora of Athens, where Paulos chose to practice his oration skills among the professionals. His "new teaching" captured much attention—a philosophy that taught that grace and not works redeemed a person. Some seemed quite interested after they further questioned Paulos, but the majority laughed at the concept of the resurrected Christ.

"How could they not believe," Acco had asked, "when it is the truth?"

Paulos was silent for so long that Acco wondered if the words had even registered. Stroking his beard and staring at the ground, Paulos eventually answered.

"We do not control how the plants are harvested, nor do we concern ourselves with how the soil has been prepared. Our job is to sow the seeds."

They did not linger in Athens. Within days, the Spirit led them to Corinth to sow more seeds.

Acco set up the table in a corner he had found in the large agora. The marketplace in Corinth was a busy, raucous place and he had found that if he arrived too late, he would find no place to sell their products. Acco's closest neighbor was also there, setting up. He liked this spot because the neighbor sold cloth and some pre-made outer clothing items, partnering well with the leather items Paulos and his new business partner, Aquila, fashioned. There was not much call in this industrious seaport for tents and tent mending. Sailors and those who entertained them were the major customers in Corinth. And everything was for sale.

Acco avoided the area in the marketplace where they catered to every sexual desire and fetish imaginable. While he had known plenty of the pleasures available and he had the natural stirrings of desire, his talks with Paulos had strengthened him. Paulos was super-human in his ability to brush away sexual desire, but his had been a lifelong celibacy. Acco assumed resisting temptation was easier for someone who had never experienced the sensual possibilities available.

"That is the point of living spiritually rather than physically," Paulos would say. "Men live too attuned to their bodies, ignoring their souls, that which is made in the image of God. The body is no more than a building meant to house the soul. You must learn to focus your efforts on your relationship with Christ Jesus and use your body to honor him."

Easier said than done.

Fortunately, they both now had an excellent example of a God-centered marriage to observe firsthand. While a few of the Twelve had been or were married men, including Cephas at one time, Aquila and his wife displayed how they were stronger together than apart.

It was no accident that those two were the first people he and Paulos met in Corinth. Paulos was pulled by the Spirit to get here, though Acco knew that reason was secondary to the pursuit of those who hated and would silence him.

Unlike Philippi, Corinth had a decent-sized Jewish population, and after the overt idolatry in Athens, Paulos hungered for Jewish fellowship. Oddly, it was in the agora where they had met Aquila and his wife, Priscilla. "I knew you were coming to Corinth," Priscilla had said to Paulos.

"I knew I would meet you here," had been his reply.

Acco wondered if he would ever cease to be amazed by the Spirit and how He worked through people. And especially such unlikely people. Paulos, he understood. Paulos had spent his entire life studying God and his law. He had, like all the other devout Jews Acco had ever met, been waiting for the Messiah. That the savior of the world would choose to reveal Himself to Paulos and then commission him to tell the entire world was no wonder. But simple craftsmen like Cephas, James, and Barnabas, and leather workers and tentmakers like Aquila? Packers, like himself. And women like Lydia and Priscilla. That was indeed a wonder.

Women.

Even Timothy, who had the great examples of his mother and grandmother, had problems leaving the small group of believers in Philippi under the leadership of Lydia.

But Paulos had assured him. "Euodia has the confidence of the community. She is already in a position of leadership as a successful business owner. And she is also valuable to the Roman community. God put her right where he wants her and for his purposes. Who are you or I to question God's decisions?"

Timothy had softened then in his attitude toward the woman, who Acco concurred was the most capable of all the believers in Philippi to lead.

Paulos had warned her that as their group grew, the more they would suffer.

Lydia laid a hand on his arm and smiled. "What have you told me, repeatedly, dear Paulos? 'I can do all things through Christ?'"

That did not stop Paulos from worrying over her, however. He received letters from all over, but whenever he received word from Philippi, he would drop all else, read the letter, and write back promptly. It was a wonder he could get any leatherwork done at all. Yet he did. Although his body was broken, Paulos sat, bent over his work the same way he bent over his writing. He might require a hand up or assistance getting dressed, and Acco often glimpsed the scars on his back from the scourgings and the stoning. The man's bones popped and cracked as he straightened, but Paulos never uttered a word of complaint.

Acco would have gladly taken the punishments for him, but when he said as much, Paulos shook his head. "I deserve these stripes," he would answer. "I persecuted the Way, and this is my punishment."

"Surely," Acco had responded, "your work building up the body of believers has negated your earlier work against it."

"Nothing I suffer can begin to compare to the suffering Christ experienced for me, for us. Let us never forget that."

As Acco finished laying out their wares, the agora filled with both vendors and customers, and the noise level grew. He looked up at his neighbor and dipped his chin as their eyes met. She always arrived before him, no matter how early of a start he managed. He assumed her to be a Greek. The women of Achaia did not veil like those in the East. It had taken some getting used to. Acco was not accustomed to the display of a woman's full head of hair in public.

She appeared young and quite pretty, but she seemed to be unaware of it. Tugging the top of her tunic self-consciously, she had never spoken a word to him. But Acco caught her stealing glimpses often, and each time their eyes met, she offered a shy smile and looked away.

About midday, half of the goods he had laid out were gone. He squatted under the black canopy, leaning back on his haunches in the shadiest part of the booth. Even in the shade, he wiped the sweat away from his brow with his sleeve. The agora was filled with people, animals, and activity, and Acco was tiring of humanity. He stole a glance at his pretty neighbor, again catching her looking at him. At the moment, their corner of the market was sparse of customers. Despite time-worn mores, Acco decided to speak to her, perhaps learn her name.

"Have you had a good day so far?" he asked in her direction, not looking at her. Receiving no answer, Acco turned toward her.

She stared at him, her lovely mouth with its lips parted as if gazing at a wonder.

"I'm sorry," he said, standing. "I am being rude. My name is . . ." He hesitated. Should he use the Greek nickname Paulos had given him or his real name? He looked into her deep brown eyes and placed a hand on his chest. "I am Acco, from Galatia."

Her eyes blinked, and she stood still as if frozen in place.

"You have nothing to fear from me," Acco said. "I am simply—"

He was interrupted by a group of armed men. Acco's head shot up, alert, and his hand slipped to the dagger he always kept on his side. Three men accompanied a heavily jeweled, finely dressed woman, who impatiently pushed through them.

"Well?" she said. "Is this it?" She looked at Acco's table, which had only a few items scattered on it. The woman turned to the largest of the men. "You told me this was the finest leatherwork available in Corinth!"

"This is it, madam," the man replied. "It is late in the day." He directed his attention then to Acco. "You are the leatherworker?" With a quick shake of his head, Acco answered. "No, I only attend their booth. What are you seeking? We will have more items tomorrow."

The woman fingered a belt, admiring the designs that Priscilla had pressed into it. Her head was also bare and her face painted, like an Egyptian. Everything about her, from her guards to her clothing to her attitude, screamed money. Acco erased any expression from his face. He knew her type.

"I want a saddle." She spat out the words. "I want to meet with your leatherworker and tell him exactly what I want. Where will I find him?"

While Acco did not want to take armed men to the home of Aquila, it appeared that his day in the market had come to a close. The woman would insist on his accompanying them. Might as well offer. Acco packed up what little remained on the table as he responded. "I can take you to the leather workers if you so desire."

"I do," the woman snapped. "You can leave your table. I'm sure your little friend will watch over it for you."

Acco looked up at the woman. Her lips were curled into an evil smile as she eyed his pretty neighbor, whose name was still a mystery. He turned to the girl. "I shall leave the canopy," he said to her softly. "Please, feel free to use it." To the woman and her guards, he then turned. "Come, follow me."

Priscilla served a lighter meal midday. With a full belly, even the coolness of the tile floor would not have kept her eyes from closing, and her job was one of the most tedious: that of the fine handiwork on the pieces fashioned by her husband.

Aquila preferred to stand or sit at a table, cutting the pieces from tanned animal hides. Nicely, the market at Corinth had good quality hides from which to choose. They had to sell all his tanning equipment at their house in Rome to pay for passage and to purchase accommodations here. Many things were less expensive in Corinth than in Rome, and they had found a comfortable place to call home, at least temporarily.

Priscilla had known, in the way that she possessed, that Corinth was where they were to go when they and their fellow Jews were forced out of Rome by Emperor Claudius. She was glad her father had not lived to experience his people exiled from the place her family had long called home. Her Roman roots ran deep. However, the worship of the one true God had no place in the imperial capital, which had easily adopted emperor worship with its many equally impotent house gods. The truth of Adonai created a stark contrast against the lies of darkness.

The exile had not been pretty, and Priscilla did not want her thoughts to linger there. It was divine intervention that brought them to Corinth as well as caused Paulos and Titus to find themselves before the couple's booth in the marketplace.

She glanced over at their new business partner. He sat bent over his work, his face impassive, and she smiled, shook her head, and resumed her work. She had dreamed of him before they met, even if it was only his outline. But when he limped up, road-weary and dusty, she knew him in an instant and had had to restrain herself from rushing to greet and embrace him like a long-lost brother.

And what a brother Paulos had become to them both. Rumors had reached them even while still in Rome of the coming of the Messiah, and they both had so wanted to believe and had longed to learn more. Had her people not been praying for generations for the Messiah to come, to break the chains of slavery to the empire, and to save their people? To think that this broken little man would be the one to tell them of the Savior of all mankind and invite them to teach others!

In only a few weeks, they had already developed a strong bond, Christ the mortar that held them tightly together. They attended the synagogue together weekly, and the synagogue leaders were astounded by Paulos's teaching. Priscilla sensed, however, that Paulos was holding back, waiting for his other companions to arrive. Mentally, she did a quick tour of her modest home, wondering where she might put more people, and how they were to feed more mouths. Then, she better understood Paulos's current industry. Titus was bringing them their profits daily, and miserly as they were, they had accumulated significant savings, even after their expenses, the synagogue tithes, and offerings for the poor. Paulos said this movement would eventually need the funds in Corinth. So, they labored on.

Paulos started humming. He was not a great singer, but he knew all the psalms and sang them often, lustily. "What psalm is in your head this time?" Priscilla asked.

His head shot up. "It's not a psalm," he answered. "A little tune my mother would often hum and sing. 'Someone is coming to call,' so it goes."

"I hope," Aquila added, "she sang it better than you."

Paulos stretched and put aside his work, then struggled to stand, holding on to a nearby table. Priscilla made to help him but was stopped by Aquila's quick shake of his head.

"Where are you going, Paulos?" she asked. "May I fetch you something to drink?" She scrambled up, ready to assist him.

Paulos turned to her, his face warm with regard. "No, I have no needs. I thought we might greet our guests." He chuckled at the confusion that must have shown on her face. "The ones Titus is bringing with him."

She spun at the sound of footsteps.

"Titus!" Despite sleeping in the same room every night, Paulos greeted his friend as if he hadn't laid eyes on him in ages. "You bring visitors."

An armed man strode into the room. Instinctively, Priscilla slid close to her husband.

Titus, surveying the area, was followed closely by a rich Greek woman, who likely had the authority to have them all executed on the spot. Priscilla immediately disliked this woman—the way she held her head as she surveyed the room and looked all of them up and down, sneering.

"This is it?" she said to Titus. "This is where the finest leather work in all of Corinth is fashioned? Here?" She strode toward Aquila as Priscilla hid behind him. "What are you working on?" Aquila opened his mouth to answer, but she brushed him away. "I saw what little you had left in the market. You have a reputation, Jew. Can you do larger pieces? I want a custom-made saddle with fine details. Sisyphus!" She turned to a second guard, who stood wordless in the door frame. "My drawings." He handed her a leather pouch. She snatched it from him and pulled out papyrus, spreading it out on the table over the leather piece Aquila had been cutting. "See here. I want it to look like this. I have the dimensions, the curve, and so on. But here is the jewel work and design I want."

Aquila bent over the drawings. He studied them as he ran a hand through his hair. "The saddle itself is no problem. This is a standard design." The woman crossed her arms. "But the elaboration—"

"Can you do it or not?" she snapped. "I can send the plans to Athens or elsewhere if I must."

"No, no," Aquila added, "we can do it." He turned to Priscilla.

"However, my wife does all the fine designs on our pieces. Priscilla?" He indicated the papyrus. "What do you think?"

Priscilla edged around him to peer at the woman's design. The drawing showed a saddle with finely detailed imprinting studded with jewels. She ran her hand softly over it. She enjoyed this the most: a difficult piece but worth the time it would take her.

"Can you do it or not?" the woman hissed.

Priscilla took her in, forgetting for a moment that there were others present. As she looked into the woman's eyes, something simmered there that told her all the arrogance and rudeness hid a deep pain. "Yes," Priscilla answered, "given the jewels to inlay, of course."

The woman did not drop her gaze. She again signaled the man at the door, who presented two small bags to Priscilla. "One contains the jewels," she said curtly, "the other, half the payment for the project. How long will it take?"

Priscilla deferred to her husband. As they discussed the composition of different parts of the saddle and a timeline for completion, Priscilla scrutinized the other woman, knowing that the saddle was a means to an end for both of them, yet uncertain of what that end was to be. She tore her eyes away from the woman to Paulos, leaning against the wall, the slightest of a grin on his face. She tried not to let her growing enthusiasm show. There was so much here: a project that would allow for the purchase of a building itself, opening a doorway between their races and a hurting soul seeking peace.

Priscilla called out to the woman's receding back. "What is your name?"

The woman stopped and turned about. "You do not need my name," she spat out. "I will send for the saddle with the remainder of the payment." She spun back toward the door, nearly knocking Titus over in her rush, but she stopped before she reached the doorway. Without turning, she answered, "My name is Persis." And then she was gone, her guards along with her.

Saul stood with his back to the wall, leaning against it for support. More and more, he struggled to ignore the burning aches of his body whenever he was not in motion. Sitting on the floor sewing was difficult, as was writing at a table. But because those were productive, necessary activities, he forced himself to do them.

Saul focused on his companions and their company as he attempted to fade into the background. He fixed his face with his long-practiced emotionless facade as he followed the interaction between Priscilla and their new patron, the one soliciting the saddle. He covered his mouth with a hand, to hide his amusement at the palpable tension between the two women. One meek in her strength, the other fierce in her insecurity. He perceived this was the rocky start of a long-lasting relationship.

Next to Saul, Acco shifted, but Saul kept his eyes on Priscilla, willing her spirit to assess more intently the woman before her. Priscilla's faith, intelligence, and receptive spirit were strong though she was so new to Christ. From the moment he met her, he knew that future generations would learn from her example and that even he would be amazed at her leadership skills. Aquila's role would change to supporting his wife's shepherding in the same way as she now supported his living.

The faith of these Roman Jews was impressive. Perhaps the closer to the heat of persecution one found oneself, the more one's faith was refined. Suffering, in general, did not make a man a saint. But suffering for Christ? That was another matter.

Saul knew Timothy and Silas had received his summons and that they were on their way. The Spirit had revealed that Corinth would be more than merely another Thessalonica or Philippi. The city was a cesspool of sin, and the harvest was ripe and plentiful. So many lost souls. When Timothy and Silas arrived, he would fully throw himself into his task. It might take weeks, perhaps months, but if God saved even a handful before Christ returned, it would be worth it.

"Tell me about her."

Acco and Saul were alone. Priscilla and Aquila had left them in order to gather materials they would need for the saddle. Acco tilted his head in question, but Saul's face gave nothing away. "The girl, in the marketplace. Tell me about her."

"There's not much to tell. I don't even know her name."

"But you told her yours?" Saul asked. He had sensed a change in Acco each day he came back from the agora, the kind of difference that told Saul there must be someone special there.

Acco gave a short laugh and shook his head. "I'm a fool."

"No, you are far from a fool, Acco. She is clearly different from anyone else you have met. I sense it."

"She glides through the marketplace. Gracefully. And she is pretty but self-conscious. Her eyes." Acco stopped and met Saul's eyes. "I haven't—"

"I know. Please, go on. She sounds lovely. There must be something special about her. A worldly man like you does not get giddy over just anyone."

"Giddy?" Acco's eyebrows raised. "I'm giddy?"

Saul laughed. "You are smitten, and I want to know about her, meet her."

"She doesn't talk much." Acco nearly whispered it. "Only when she has spoken to customers, and then very little. The marketplace gets loud."

"And you have leaned in to try to drink in her voice."

"Yes."

Saul tilted his head at him. "Acco."

The young man shrugged. "It doesn't matter. We're going to move on in a few weeks."

"Don't be afraid to woo her, to pursue her. I believe we will be here quite a while. There is much work to be done."

"What kind of life would this be for a wife? No permanent home, no fixed income?"

Saul laid his hand on Acco's shoulder, clasping it tight. "You will not always be traveling with me, my son. Christ Jesus has a plan for you, and you will need a helpmate. I sense she will become very important to you."

Acco shook his head. "I can't figure you out. You preach sexual purity and discourage unmarried believers to remain single! Yet, here you are, encouraging me to—"

"Priscilla and Aquila have shown me what a sacred marriage can and should be." Saul dropped his arm. "There are times he calls people to come together. He has a purpose for you, and I sense part of that purpose is to find that same kind of companion as has Aquila." He paused. Acco was still a young man, strong and virile. He will make a good husband for the right woman, as the right woman will enhance his life. "One who will also warm your bed, no matter where it might be. Follow what the Spirit leads you to do, and you will never fail to do the will of God."

"It's not so much you he detests," Crispus explained to Saul, "it's the people you attract. Sailors. Sinners. The unclean."

"And that they come here, to the synagogue, without knowledge of our traditions or respect for his authority." Sosthenes laid a hand on Saul's arm.

Crispus and Sosthenes, two of the synagogue leaders, had summoned Saul to a meeting, at a time when they knew Phileas would be preoccupied elsewhere. The three gathered in a sunny alcove in the recesses of the synagogue.

Crispus leaned against a wall. "Phileas has it out for you and has determined to put an end to your influence here."

"Since the arrival of your helpers," Sosthenes said, "you have been much bolder with your message, all around Corinth, in the agora, at the port. Phileas claims you have even been spied in the drinking establishments."

Saul had developed a fondness for these two, who had broken bread with the believers at Aquila's for weeks now. He crossed his arms. With a smirk, Saul interjected. "Sosthenes, haven't you heard? Christ Jesus came to deliver the sinner."

"I'm not condemning you, please don't misunderstand. I only mean to warn you. I'm not sure how much longer Phileas will tolerate you and those of us who openly agree with your message."

Those of us. Saul warmed at the phrase. "He has told you two as much, hasn't he?"

Crispus straightened and shook his head. "Paulos, Phileas is a blind man. Though you come to us as a prophet of the Most High, he refuses to absorb your message. He claims to honor God in all he does, but he rejects the message of Messiah. Though you preach with the fire of the Holy Spirit, he only sees the dredge of society in his synagogue. He despises the message of the good news that you brought us, to the city of Corinth of all places, and when the fruits of your labor gather on Sabbath mornings, to give thanks to God for the blessings of salvation—"

Sosthenes interrupted, throwing up his hands. "Changed lives!"

Crispus pointed at Sosthenes, dipping his head. "Exactly! Lives changed because of the message of salvation you brought. But Phileas can't get past their outward appearance."

Saul raised his hands to halt the two. "My friends, I appreciate your urgency and need to warn me. But remember, it is not *my* message of salvation. It is the message of Christ Jesus, with whom I have died and with whom I rise to new life. If he saved a sinner like me, his blood can save anyone."

Saul studied Crispus. The young man had much passion for God and would be influential in the group of believers here. His wife was also a believer and a good support for him. He had little to lose by following the message of the Christ. Sosthenes, on the other hand. He was wary. He believed the Messiah had come, believed in Christ Jesus, but was not yet mature in the Spirit. He was settled in his faith, settled in his position in the synagogue, and settled in his lifestyle. Saul considered him sadly, as he sensed Sosthenes would have to suffer much before his faith developed the character required for this journey.

Sosthenes shook his head and sighed. "I am sure Phileas does not consider himself in need of salvation."

Saul indicated with his hand. "Exactly right. Pride and smugness are the very reasons so many of our fellow Jews are hard-hearted to the message of salvation. They also find it difficult to stomach that they have followed God's Law for generations upon generations, yet these Gentiles, new to the faith and ignorant of the Law, are welcomed in the same vein."

"After being thought of as God's chosen people since Abraham," Sosthenes concluded, "can you blame them?"

Saul let that thought hang in the air around them. He had been one of them. *Had been.* "Yes," he whispered. He stood, suppressing a groan as his stiffened joints creaked. "The Christ has come, bringing salvation, not only to the chosen people but the entire world, that whoever hears His word and believes in Him will have eternal life." Saul shuffled with tenuous footfalls to work out the stiffness in his hips. "They must get over themselves if they are to be saved."

"I believe he will act tomorrow morning, with all gathered for Sabbath," Crispus added.

"That's been my experience with disgruntled synagogue leaders." Saul passed a hand over his face as if to erase the angry faces from the past. "Phileas will likely have us all thrown out. I may even suffer another scourging. It wouldn't be the first time. Nor probably the last."

Sosthenes's mouth dropped open. "You welcome the violence against you?"

"You get used to it."

"But Paulos," Crispus said, "what will you do if you are not allowed in the synagogue? You won't leave us, leave Corinth?"

"No. There is still much work for us here to accomplish for Christ Jesus."

"Where will you go? What will you do?"

Saul noted the concern on Crispus's face. The wrinkled brow. The downturned mouth. The sadness in his eyes. Should he let them know? God always has a plan for his people. "The Lord your redeemer, the holy one of Israel says," Saul recited, "'for your sake, I have sent an army to Babylon—'"

"'And brought down all the bars,'" added Crispus, "'turning the Chaldeans' singing into a lament.'"

"'I am the Lord, your holy one, '" Saul continued, "'Israel's creator, your king!'"

Sosthenes joined them. "'The Lord says, who makes a way in the sea and a path in the mighty waters?'"

"'Who brings out chariot and horse,'" Crispus said, "'army and battalion. They will lie down together and will not rise. They will be extinguished.'"

"'Don't remember the prior things.'"

"'Don't ponder ancient history.'"

Saul's grin spread across his face. "'Look! I am doing a new thing: now it sprouts up. Don't you recognize it?'" He let the room absorb the words of the prophet Isaiah, the dust dancing through the windows, his soul warm and at peace. After a few moments of quiet, he added, "How well do either of you know Titius Justus?"

Crispus replied, "The man who lives next door here?" He pointed toward the window.

"Yes." Saul meandered to the window, gazing at the house. "That's an awfully big place for just one man," he mused. Then he turned back to his friends, unable to stop the spread of a grin across his face.

Surrounded by his companions, Saul made his way toward the synagogue. Compared to the deserts to the east, Achaia was full of lush vegetation, and as he breathed in the sea air, the earth embraced him. For a moment, he was free of his constant pain.

Then Saul entered the synagogue. Filled with dark shadows he attempted to ignore, the synagogue swirled with angry whispers. His companions grinned, happily oblivious. Sunlight attempted to pour through the windows, but a gathering of darkness simmered about the place. Everything within warned him to flee, but he knew he would not.

Saul's eyes widened in terror as the dark gathered into a familiar sight: the billows of an oncoming dust storm. "Cover your faces!" he opened his mouth to shout out to his companions, but his voice failed him. Then the wall of dust hit them with a roar, and dust filled his eyes, his nose, his mouth. He dared not breathe. Blind and struggling, he was grasped by strong hands. The dust-filled wind screamed about him as he was tugged along until he found himself outside, on his knees, coughing out the dust in bright sunlight.

His rescuer stood at his doorway, beckoning his group inside. Saul floated toward him, stopping before the front door. He turned back to the synagogue, the dust debris hanging about the open windows. Then the voice sounded in his ears.

"Do not be afraid but speak. Do not be silent, for I Am with you. No one will harm you."

Awakening abruptly, Saul sat upright on his pallet, his mouth dry but free of dust and dirt. It was Sabbath morning.

Saul's skin crawled with an eerie sense of reenactment of the dream as he and his companions neared the synagogue. Saul had not discussed the vision with any of the others, though he knew they sensed the heaviness he wore about him. The all-too-familiar scenario had become a theme of his ministry. Initially, he was well-received in the synagogue and respected as a teacher. Then, as he persisted in proclaiming the coming of the Messiah, the leaders' power receded, and they fought against him. Then, the ultimate insult to their authority and their very essence, their purpose of being, was Saul's proclamation that Messiah had come to save all people, not merely the chosen people, which would result in full rejection of the Gospel and of his message, and usually ended with personal and physical injury.

The physical punishments were not what Saul dreaded. It was the loss of the synagogue itself that injured him. To be rejected by his own people, the Jews of the Dispersion, who had names similar to their local neighbors but observed the Sabbath, who embraced the economies of each place where they landed but not the cultures. *His* culture, *his* people, the very people for whom the Torah was translated into Greek so that they might hear God's Law in their tongue, to better understand it, and follow it. *His* synagogue, with its familiar routines and rituals. Yet each step closer to the synagogue this morning was more difficult than the one previous. He almost expected the dust storm from his dream in a climate where the only dust came from the street.

He was compelled to bathe himself this morning, to wash away the dirt packed in his ears, eyes, and nose, though the dirt and grime from the dream were not manifested. He rinsed and spat several times, though his rational self knew it was unnecessary.

Saul had discussed his meeting with Crispus and Sosthenes with the others so they might be prepared for what would happen.

"I'm surprised you lasted this long," Silas had quipped. "Will you once again receive the forty, less one?"

"No," Saul had answered, "I'm afraid my punishment will not be physical this time. Something much more painful."

And though he had anticipated his expulsion, knew in his heart what was coming, he had not been prepared for it to be so swift. They had no more entered the vestibule of the synagogue, eyes adjusting to the relative dark before a group of men faced them. Sosthenes was not among them. "You will not be speaking today," he was told.

Saul surveyed the room at near capacity. He knew many faces; a fair portion belonged to believers. He turned toward the women's section, where Priscilla already stood. Several pairs of eyes met his, warm with recognition. Most of the women were properly veiled, but not all. Saul was not sure whether the shock of uncovered heads and thick braids adorned with flowers and ribbons in the synagogue would ever wear off of him.

He was about to turn away when he eyed the woman who had commissioned the saddle, Persis. Recognition registered in her eyes, and she dipped her head slightly at him. This caught him by surprise, and not much ever did. He noted that Priscilla eased up to Persis and leaned toward her. Saul wanted to throw back his head with joy but dared not. He was not supposed to even be aware of the women. What will it be like in the future, he wondered, when they meet outside the confines of the synagogue?

"Paulos." Silas motioned with his chin. Saul turned his attention forward, remembering the synagogue leaders.

Phileas spoke. "Are you deaf? You are not speaking today, nor ever again. You are poisoning our people with your blasphemous talk, bringing in all kinds of riffraff—"

"I speak only the truth."

"Lies!" Phileas spat out the word. The entire synagogue fell quiet.

"I speak the truth," Saul repeated. "And those who hunger and thirst for the truth are refreshed."

The man slapped Saul's face. The sting served as a reminder, and slowly, dramatically, Saul turned his chin, offering him the other side of his face. Phileas did not hesitate. He slapped him again.

"You reject the very Word of God," Saul said to him.

"You are no prophet, Paulos of Tarsus," Phileas replied. "You are a manipulative scoundrel who bastardizes our faith, taking the Septuagint, twisting its words, then bringing in the filth from the streets." Phileas indicated toward Persis and the other women standing around her.

Rage rose inside Saul, and instinctively, he shifted between them as if his small, broken body might defend the women against the younger, larger, stronger man facing him. "Christ Jesus came into the world to fulfill the Septuagint, the Law, and the Prophets, bringing salvation that is not limited to Israel and Judah. I came to this city to offer you and others the good news. By rejecting that good news and rejecting those who have gladly received it, you condemn yourself." Saul paused and took in the room full of people, all with their varied reasons for being present. Some eyes were filled with hope, but many were filled with despair, hatred, and envy. His soul ached for them.

Speak, do not be silent. Speak.

Saul turned back to Phileas and he took hold of his own garments and shook them. Dust flew from them, billowing around those closest to him. Dust, as if the dream dust storm had been as real as this moment. Dust scattered throughout the room, to murmurs of wonder. Saul leaned into his accuser. "Your fate is in your own hands," he said. "I have done what I was sent to do." Saul threw his arms out wide and again took in the crowded room. "From this day, I leave you and take with me the message of salvation through Christ Jesus. From now on, I will go to the Gentiles."

Saul then lowered his arms, eyed Phileas, and without another word, left the synagogue, trailed by a dozen or so. Saul and his companions traveled only as far as next door, to the home of Titius Justus, who stood waiting in the doorway.

Chapter Twenty-Two

**Antioch, Syria
52 A.D.**

Saul ached for a walk. They had arrived before sundown the day prior, after much harassment at the Antioch city gates. At one point during the interrogations and searches, Timothy was near tears. Fortunately, Silas had wisely advised that they leave their few personal weapons on the ship as gifts for their shipmates. Saul was glad he had also left his tools with Aquila in Ephesus. He didn't know what to expect upon arrival in Antioch, but he had sensed hostility as soon as they landed on the Syrian shore. Saul had had no delusions that things had changed after so much time away, but it was as if he tread on foreign land no different than when he had entered Athens.

Their welcome at the home of Nicolaus was slightly warmer than what they experienced at the city gate. Nicolaus had not yet received Saul's correspondence from Ephesus, so their arrival came as a surprise. Saul brushed off the lack of genuine warmth and embraced Nicolaus anyway. After a cold supper, the exhausted trio made up their pallets in a small room off of the kitchen, where the warmth from the coals crept toward them along the floor.

As the morning sun threatened, Saul's stiff joints needed a stretch. He did not want to awaken his still-sleeping companions, so he quietly rose and sat in the adjoining kitchen. The city was not friendly to Jews, even less so to the sect mockingly called "Christians." The nickname amused him. Meant to harass, their tormentors did not know of the honor to be labeled thus. While he knew that today was not the day he was to be taken, to be held prisoner, or to be killed, it would not do to tempt others into confrontation either. So, he sat, his legs stretched out before the fire.

Someone had already started the bread, and its smell brought memories rushing at him, from childhood to Jerusalem to the breaking of bread at the many places he had traveled in the last few years. He took in a deep breath, eyes closed. *I am the bread of life.* Yeshua's words. Though its form differed from place to place, bread was an important part of every culture. Every place, every community had its version. As essential as air, bread easily translated across tongues and land masses. Saul appreciated how Yeshua had utilized this staple, not only as a metaphor for himself but also taking its use in the Sabbath ritual and making it new. Symbolic of his bodily sacrifice, bread now bound the believers in remembrance in their communal practices.

Soft footsteps interrupted his reveries.

"Of course, you're up already." Nicolaus sat next to him, and Saul opened his eyes.

"Old habits are the hardest to break," Saul replied. "I ache to go for a walk, but I dare not."

"A wise choice. The neighborhood has become increasingly hostile, especially to our kind."

Saul studied him. A flash of a memory, a defiant young man, blocking his way. Nicolaus had not been timid then. Saul started to open his mouth to comment but hesitated. Different. This was quite different. "'For everything, there is a season,'" Saul quoted. "There is a couple I met when we first came to Corinth. They were exiled from Rome."

"Emperor Claudius."

"Yes. He, Aquila, is an excellent leather craftsman with high-quality work. His wife, Priscilla, helps him."

Nicolaus tilted his head. "You found a fellow laborer."

"In both meanings of the word. Aquila, in leather work. In Priscilla, a disciple, a leader of people, open to the Holy Spirit. And a writer."

Nicolaus's eyebrows raised. "A woman, a leader?"

"I have been blessed to meet several women that God has used in that capacity. Christ Jesus uses the soul and conviction of people. Sometimes, the physical body is more of a hindrance to the work of the Spirit than a help. But, Nicolaus," he said, changing the subject, "tell me how things have changed since we left. I am eager to hear."

"We outgrew our meeting place last year."

"What? Such a large place to gather?"

Nicolaus shook his head. "It wasn't safe with that many of us in one place, illegal as it is, but people were spilling into the streets. And, as you know, the streets belong—"

"To Rome, of course." Saul's eyebrows furrowed. He pictured it: a building so full that there was no room for any more to fit, people crowded around the only entrance and exit, the Roman peacemakers on horseback, the violence against the people. No, that would not do.

"So now we meet in smaller groups, in several different homes. We tend to move about, week to week. Those who have a home to open do so."

"I see. And the synagogues are still closed to you?"

"Most definitely," Nicolaus answered. "Do not misunderstand. The Romans hate them as much as they do us, but that's not sufficient to unite us. It seems to disgust our Jewish brothers that we are seen as a sect of Judaism."

"It's a rather universal understanding. What do you have that binds all the believers in Antioch together?" he asked. "Do you make any pilgrimages to Jerusalem together?"

"As dangerous as it is to gather as one here, it is worse to be on the road together. We are even less loved in the gates of Jerusalem than here in Antioch. The current high priest and Herod run more than the Temple, but the entire city of Jerusalem. Of course, we can go to the Temple, but not as one body. And you should not go there, not ever again. They have spies everywhere, and you will bring in a handsome ransom."

Saul pulled his face into a sideways smile. "Has the price gone up any?"

Nicolaus laughed. "Yes. As word of your travels and the trouble you brought to each city throughout the Roman Empire, the higher goes the price. I wouldn't be surprised if they don't send mercenaries to find you."

Satisfied, Saul crossed his arms and sat back. "I do tend to create enemies wherever I go."

Saul and Silas's first Sabbath morning since their return dawned without a cloud in the sky. It had been well over two years since they were in Antioch, and Saul itched to worship with the believers in what had been his home base for so long. Remembering Barnabas at his side all those years made him forlorn. He had learned of Barnabas's death in Cyprus third-hand, and that alone pierced his heart. John Mark could have written Saul directly. Instead, John Mark had run back to Cephas and attached himself to his old mentor. Thoughts of Barnabas tightened Saul's chest, so he brushed the memories away with a hand.

Tensions in the city meant it wasn't safe for believers to gather in larger groups. Therefore, instead of attending the synagogue, Saul, Silas, Timothy, and Nicolaus made their way through side streets to the expansive home of a Jewish believer currently housing honored guests. Simon Peter and John Mark had stopped over in the city to visit and invited Saul and his company to worship with them.

The previous night, Saul, Timothy, and Silas had broken bread in the home of a Gentile believer. Saul quickly noted that all the believers present were Gentiles. No Greek-speaking Jews, including the church leaders, ever joined them. Saul knew Simon Peter often visited Antioch but these Gentile believers had never heard his stories of Jesus first-hand. Worst of all, the meaning of the communion cup was lost on the Gentiles. How had these followers of the Way been so neglected?

Saul's heart broke for the Gentile believers. He took time to instruct them on the Lord's meal and how it should be done. Then, he encouraged those present to go to the others like them and ensure they understood the meaning behind the sacrament. He prayed that the other house meetings learned of God's truth accurately. The separations in Antioch were concerning. Without coming together as one body, even occasionally, how would they ever build a culture where all were welcome? Would the church of Antioch not fracture into meaningless cliques with little in common except for the label of "Christian"?

Perhaps he would learn more at the small Sabbath gathering. Upon arriving, the servants led Saul and his companions to a large room where several had already gathered. The lamps were still lit, and their aroma filled the room like a smoky incense. As usual, Simon Peter was at the center, telling a story, with John Mark at his right hand. Saul's throat tightened at the sight of Barnabas's nephew. He tore away his gaze at the others gathered about them. Saul vaguely remembered some, but there were also new faces, all appearing very Jewish in dress and facial hair.

When Simon Peter finished his story, he glimpsed Saul and slapped his hands on his lap. "Well, it appears as if we are all here now. We can get started."

The worship closely followed the components one would expect at a synagogue. They had no scrolls, but Saul was not the only one who knew the Law and the Prophets by heart. Simon Peter taught, beautifully connecting the teachings of Yeshua with the scriptures. The presence of the Spirit was with them, and Saul relaxed and worshipped, sang, and prayed. All went smoothly until the memory of the previous evening came to him. Saul waited until worship itself was concluded before broaching the topic of his concern.

"Cephas." Saul injected before Simon Peter launched into another story. "Silas, Timothy, and I were at the home of Orius last evening for the Sabbath meal with some of the believers. They are all pleased you are in the city for an extended stay and would love to hear your stories. I told them I was sure you would be happy to visit."

Simon Peter flushed, and his brows drew together.

"They believe you will not break bread with them because they are Gentiles. Surely, they misunderstand."

The big man clamped his mouth shut and took a deep breath through his nose. The heat emanating from Simon Peter's face spurred Saul on. "Cephas, was it not to you God gave the vision of the unclean food? Did He not command you to eat of it?"

John Mark clenched his fists. "That was God directing him to go to Cornelius in Caesarea."

"Oh, I see." Saul did not address John Mark. "That was a one-time occurrence, not a call to slough off your bigotry."

Simon Peter was spry for his age. He leaped to his feet, grabbed Saul by his collar, and yanked him from his seat on the floor. "You," he spat. "Come with me." The big man pushed Saul toward the door and down a hallway. Simon Peter threw open a door, releasing Saul, and strode to the center of the room, his hands in fists. Saul secured the door behind him and opened his mouth to speak. Simon Peter held up a shaking finger to silence him.

"What is this all about?" Simon Peter's words were low, clipped, and stinging.

Saul did not cower or drop the man's gaze as he weighed his response. *Fill my mouth with your grace, Lord.*

"Is the body of Christ to be divided, Cephas? Is this what the Lord asked us to do, to divide into Jews and Gentiles?" Saul spoke in hushed tones, but his voice was unwavering.

Simon Peter did not answer, but his body shook, and his eyes burned.

"If he comes back today, perhaps as we dine," Saul pressed, "which table will he appear to first?"

Simon Peter turned his head, but his clenched fists still hung at his sides.

"This division is not what he intended. You of all people know this."

Simon Peter covered his face. He took several deep breaths into his hands before removing them, meeting Saul's eyes. "James, the brother of our Lord, has taken a Nazarite vow. He cannot eat what the Gentiles eat. How can we ask them to break their vows? Surely, the Hellenists—"

"They are your brothers and sisters." Saul swept his gaze about the room. "And James is not here."

"Then the Gentiles will understand. They will take a vow, too, and avoid the unclean foods."

"The law has been fulfilled, Cephas. The vows are unnecessary. The food laws are meaningless. Did Yeshua not die to fulfill the Law?"

The fire returned to Simon Peter's eyes, and he spat out his words. "Do not preach to me. I know what His sacrifice means. I was there, and you were not. Don't lecture me, lawyer."

Silent, Saul did not wipe away the spray of spittle that fell on his face. Simon Peter dropped his gaze and sighed.

"You don't understand the pressure I'm under." Simon Peter's words had lost their bite. "James is under pressure, too. He must maintain his vow to stay in good graces at the Temple. He is convinced that the Messiah will return to Jerusalem and that all the Hebrew people, all the sons of Abraham, must accept the Messiah." His eyes again met Saul's, displaying sadness in them. "I fear James will perish in his attempts to accomplish that."

Simon Peter's shoulders sagged, and his hands hung limply at his sides. The red faded from the man's face and his eyes drooped. Saul allowed the man a few moments before he spoke. "In Christ, there is neither Jew nor Gentile."

Simon Peter gave a curt dip of his head. He shuffled past Saul toward the door but halted as he touched the handle and spoke over his shoulder. "I know you are convinced of that. But I believe that this division is temporary. Yeshua is coming back soon, and then vows will not matter. What happens in Antioch will not matter. Yeshua will come to neither table tonight, Saul. He will come to Jerusalem."

Simon Peter opened the door and ambled out.

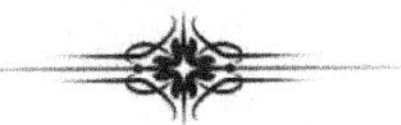

The stool creaked as Timothy sat. He tilted his head as he dipped the pen in the ink, the parchment spreading before him. He was appreciative that a writing desk had been furnished for Paulos. Writing was about the only thing the man was allowed to do these days. Timothy was also grateful for a bit roomier of a space to stay in Antioch. Not that Nicolaus had told them to leave. But after the confrontation with Cephas their first Sabbath back in the city, when one of the Gentile believers offered a room large enough for the three of them to sleep comfortably, the opportunity pleased everyone involved.

Paulos's eyesight had dimmed to the point that writing had become difficult. When he hunched over the desk for an extended period, it caused such pain and stiffness that even Timothy found it unbearable. So much so that he had offered to write for Paulos, who, saying that the writing slowed his thoughts down, appeared relieved.

Timothy had forgotten the typical length of Paulos's letters, which were already lengthy. Now that he was dictating and not doing the actual writing, the letters were even lengthier. But Timothy was faithful to his elder, his teacher. The man who was as a father to him now paced in the small room that consisted of the writing desk, a stool, a window, and two lamps, with enough floor space to accommodate their three-bed rolls. Tucked in the corner was some tent material for mending, shears, thread, and needles. Timothy and Silas had learned to thread needles after an exasperated Paulos thrust the needle and thread toward them one day. Apparently, clear vision was necessary for that task. Paulos often referred to himself as an old man, but the soul of the man was fierce. His shuffling back and forth in the sunlit room reminded Timothy of a lion, pacing in a small cage.

Exasperated, Paulos proclaimed. "Timothy, I cannot imagine how so many of the churches have been led astray. How could they misunderstand the simplicity of the Gospel?"

This letter was to be circulated among the churches in Galatia. Reports had reached them that believers out of somewhere, they were not sure where, were teaching that salvation only came through circumcision and observance of Jewish food laws.

"Nonsense!" Paulos gesticulated as he spoke. "What was the point of the Jerusalem council?"

"Do you suppose it was the Pharisee faction?"

"It doesn't matter who. The problem is, after all our work there, they are deluded by the lies."

Delicately, Timothy offered what he believed as truth. "My understanding is that these adulterers of the gospel claim that you are not a genuine authority since you were not one of the original Twelve."

The man stopped his pacing. "That is my understanding as well. It's not enough to have faced opposition in the synagogues. It is not sufficient that we are beaten and imprisoned by Gentile authorities for preaching and teaching the good news." He shook his head. "Now we must counter bad teaching from within the body of believers." Paulos resumed his pacing. "I despise having to defend myself. It's the gospel of Christ Jesus that I am called to defend."

"You need to emphasize who's giving you your authority,"

Timothy said. "These are people who were brought to Christ Jesus through you, and if you remind them of that, and of your specific calling, how you were intent on destroying the Gospel until Christ Jesus himself called you, stopped you, and commissioned you."

"But it's not about me!"

"Yes, Paulos. In this case, it very much is."

He once again came to a halt and drew a hand up to his forehead. "All right," he conceded. "I will defend my case. But"—he pointed that hand toward Timothy—"I will do it only in defense of the Gospel I have been taught. Though some oppose me personally, the Gospel I preach is solid and genuine."

Timothy's chest warmed. *There* is the Paulos he had met in Lystra.

As Paulos resumed his pacing, he spoke slowly, allowing Timothy time to write line after line. After every few phrases, he would say, "Read that back to me," and Timothy would do so. Due to the drought in the region, many goods were in short supply, including ink and parchment, so Paulos would be judicious with both. The single copy would be delivered to the easternmost church in the area, and then copies made there, where the lack of rain had spared them.

On the other hand, the church in Jerusalem felt the drought's results. Food was scarce, and the funds to provide for the poor and starving were low. Paulos told Timothy he was conflicted between journeying back to revisit the churches he had helped establish and finding a way to collect money to help feed the saints in the Holy City.

Paulos poured out his heart to the churches of Galatia. His brows furrowed as he dictated, and he punctuated his thoughts with gesticulating hands. Observing the strain on his teacher's face and the tension in his thin shoulders, Timothy urged him to stop and take a break before they concluded.

"No," Paulos answered, "we are so close to being done." He limped to the writing table and brought his face close to the parchment, squinting at the writing. Then, placing a supporting hand on Timothy's back, he sighed and straightened. "Get up."

"Paulos?"

"Please."

Timothy arose, giving up his seat The older man took the pen and dipped it in the ink, then wrote the closing of the letter. Paulos scratched for a while, then chuckled. Pleased at the lightened air around his mentor, Timothy peeked over his shoulder at the scribbles. He read, "See what large letters with which I write in my own hand!" Timothy laughed along with him.

Chapter Twenty-Three

Ephesus, Asia Minor
56 A.D.

An irritating bead of sweat ran down the valley between Priscilla's breasts. She now understood why most of the inhabitants of Ephesus chose the hottest part of the day to nap. There was little else to do at this time of year. She took in Niko, who, despite the size of her swollen belly, seemed not to notice. "How are you not sweating?" she asked the younger woman.

"Oh, I am sweating," Niko answered. "I think it may be disappearing into the air as soon as it comes out of my skin." She raised a hand and swiped a strand of hair off of her face. It clung to her skin as she secured it behind an ear. "Priscilla," Niko said, "the babe is not very active during the day recently." She ran her hand over her distended abdomen. "Is that normal?"

Priscilla grinned. "Yes, it has to sleep sometime too."

"I am glad you and Aquila have returned from Rome. I missed you, and I would not want to face the duration of my time without you."

"There are some marvelous midwives here in Ephesus, Niko. I will be calling one in to assist anyway. You would not want me to be your only attendant."

"I don't care if you had all the priests of Artemis here with me," Niko said, "I would still want you nearby. You have such a calming effect. And not only on me, on almost everybody."

"I don't know about that." Priscilla waved her off, embarrassed. She had become quite fond of the young wife of Titus since the day the couple arrived in Ephesus with Paulos a few years prior. Paulos had not remained in Ephesus as he, Silas, and Timothy traveled back to Antioch in Syria. After only a few months there, Paulos and Timothy returned. Problems in the Galatian churches created urgency for Paulos, and she suspected the cause to raise money for the church in Jerusalem was more of an excuse to come back through to visit the churches. Not that she doubted the genuineness of his concern for the Jerusalem church. She, too, knew of the persecutions and the effects of famine there. But she also knew the heart of Paulos. Each church the childless man helped establish was like his offspring.

She was not surprised that Silas chose to remain in Syria. Paulos needed someone to represent him there. What had astounded her was to learn of the divisions in the group of believers in Antioch, the separation of Gentile and Jewish. This went beyond language barriers. The divisions were over circumcision and diet. Perhaps the city was too close to Jerusalem.

Ephesus was a prime example of the Greek influence in the Roman world. The Greek goddess Artemis had originally been a local deity of the natives of the area until, as occurred in most cities conquered by Alexander the Great, she was re-named, and the attributes of the Greek version transferred to her. After a generation or two, the original name of the local goddess was forgotten. But the cult of Artemis was such an integral part of the culture in Ephesus that even the many Jews who lived here had difficulty ignoring it. The temple of Artemis was huge, said to be the largest temple in the civilized world, was situated on a hill outside the city walls and the citizens believed it watched over the city. What would happen to Ephesus, the people wondered, if the temple were destroyed again, as it was centuries ago? Not to mention what would happen to the commerce of the city? Ephesus was an important seaport reliant upon temple tourism.

"They should be arriving home shortly, yes?" Niko interrupted her thoughts.

Priscilla peered out the window, judging the angle of the sun. "I should say so."

Niko's parents had operated a prosperous business selling

clothing back in Corinth, where they had trained their daughter as a seamstress. Her family still ran the business, as far as anyone knew. They had little to do with their daughter since she chose to marry and run off with the apprentice of a traveling preacher. However, shy as Niko had been in the marketplace, she was outspoken and headstrong. She had readily accepted the faith of the man she adored and, as Paulos had said more than once, they both, Priscilla and Paulos, had had premonitions about the girl. She would become an important helpmate for Titus, and Priscilla spent much time teaching and telling her the stories of Christ Jesus. So, as Niko sewed and Priscilla adorned some of Aquila's leatherwork, they spent their days together.

Aquila entered the room, his arms full. "There are my girls," he said, "heads together and clucking like hens." He placed his handiwork on a table. "I brought you more to do."

Niko grinned at the abundance of the leather pieces. "Titus was reminiscing with me last night about Persis and her saddle, in Corinth. That was quite the masterpiece, sounds as if."

"But was it!" Aquila replied. "And she was an arrogant one, at one time, anyway."

"And now she is a trusted member of the church in Corinth," Priscilla added. "That was no chance meeting. The Spirit surely arranged it all."

"So, you do not believe it was a coincidence?" Niko asked.

Priscilla shook her head. "I do not believe in coincidence, my dear."

Niko stood and stretched. "I shall go greet my husband."

Priscilla also stood, her knees creaking as she did so. When had she become so old, she wondered. "I might as well go with you and check on how many attended Paulos's session today." She stowed away her tools and followed Niko and Aquila out of the room.

Aquila greeted Paulos and Timothy as they removed their sandals at the door, and Niko rushed into her husband's arms.

"Priscilla," Paulos said, "you should have been there today. A couple came in. Guess what they do for a living? Of course, leather work! They, too, have a stand at the agora where they heard of us." Paulos took her by the elbow. "I wasn't sure where to direct them, so they will be coming here on Friday to observe the Sabbath." He paused as he steered her to a corner of the room where they both sat. "I hope that is fine with you."

"Of course, Paulos. You and Timothy will be here?"

"No, I believe Timothy will be at Lycus's home, and I already promised Junia I would break bread with them."

"No issue. I like teaching those new to the faith."

"But your great skill, my sister, is in organizing."

"Like you."

Paulos frowned playfully. "Do you think?"

Priscilla sensed her husband still standing in the doorway as Timothy chatted away at him. Their eyes locked and her heart warmed to see no condemnation there. She was always the one Paulos was eager to speak to about the work with the believers. In the three years he had been here, the group of followers in Ephesus had grown, another reason they had hurried back from their visit to Rome. Once a week, on Shabbat, all of the believers came together at the lecture hall to worship. But they had also started meeting in smaller groups on the first day of the week, to bring together an offering for the church in Jerusalem. Though that practice had brought Paulos trouble with the leaders of the local synagogues, he still collected the offerings.

The Jewish leaders felt it competed with the Temple tax, especially from the wealthy Gentile God worshipers who attended synagogue. The Jewish leaders had created no small disturbance, ending with Paulos once again imprisoned by the Roman authority. Imprisonment did not satisfy the vultures, however, as they actively sought to destroy him. They almost succeeded, but the Spirit had other plans for him. At any rate, gathering in smaller groups to start the week seemed to work well and was less obvious about the intent.

"Timothy expressed concern about our preaching against the Greek gods," Paulos said, "due to the stronghold the cult of Artemis has on the people here."

"It would not be the first time you caused a commotion over such a thing," she reminded him.

"Not so much from the priests," Paulos replied, "not like in the past. Not even with much of the citizenry. The presence of a large number of our Hebrew brothers in this city for so many years has affected idol worship. No, I suspect the opposition Timothy fears of from our preaching will come from those who prosper from the cult.

Can't have us lightening their moneybags."

Priscilla turned away from Paulos's intense face, toward Titus and Niko, who stood over them, overhearing. She acknowledged a frowning Titus, who knew very well how important the cult of the goddess was in the city.

Demetrius had little trouble convincing his fellow silversmiths that they must do something drastic. Complaining to the city authorities was worthless. No crime had been committed, and the city fathers always played the safest of games, enjoying the *Pax Romana* as much as possible. Demetrius knew that if anything was going to change, they would have to do something themselves, something big. Go around the local government, even go around Artemis's priests.

Three things Ephesus had always thrived upon—magic, trade, and tourism—prosperity all brought by Artemis. She watched over the city and protected it. The Romans had not dared to change her name or attempt to change the culture of her great city. Even the Jews, with their strange habits and beliefs, kept to themselves, largely ignoring the non-Jewish citizens, who did likewise. But then along came these Christians, attempting to change everything. An even stranger group of heretics, they somehow convinced a large part of the city's magicians to give up their craft and burn their books. What kind of mind control must that take, to cause people to burn expensive texts? How were the former magicians to make a living?

And now the tourism trade was suffering. Visitors barely disembarked at the docks before being confronted by the heretics. Their non-violent approach was frustrating beyond measure, and worse, many of the visitors went off with them, duped by their leader, that smooth-talking little man who led everyone astray. Those who would normally visit the Temple never actually arrived at their original destination. Meanwhile, the many silver statues at his stand in the agora stood unsold and unwanted. Lately, there had been a dramatic decrease in sales, leading to a problem with cash flow. His fellow artisans had noted the same.

It was Kriton's idea to involve the Jews. "They hate them more than we do," he had explained. If one wanted to create havoc, the Jews were the ones to go to. They'd been making waves in multiple cultures for centuries. "Plus," Kriton had said, "those people are close-knit. If this man is some renegade Jew, they will go after him like sharks."

The plan was to gather, about mid-morning, and start marching down the main road, the one that went through a residential neighborhood, then past the agora and on to the theater. They would enlist others to join them at various places along the way, to encourage the onlookers, especially those in the agora, to join the march and follow them to the theater.

"We must have some kind of easy-to-chant phrase, something that will get everybody worked up."

"Out with the Christians?" someone suggested.

"No, that will not do. Something positive, something that even first-time visitors right off the boat would get behind." Demetrius swept his eyes around at his handiwork. Selecting one of the silver miniatures of the temple of Artemis, he held it aloft. "This is what we are defending."

"Great is Artemis!" someone else shouted.

Demetrius pointed at the man. "Not just Artemis, but *our* Artemis."

Kriton shouted. "Great is Artemis of the Ephesians!"

On the specified day, the Jewish synagogue leaders recruited people to rally others along the planned route. Another group started the same at the docks. By the time they reached the agora, the street was already overflowing, and they had quite the parade behind them. Once at the theater, the chanting masses poured in, leaving the streets with only stragglers. Best of all, the open-air theater was designed not only to hear those on the stage, but the theater projected a loud event throughout most of the city.

The prize, of course, was delivered by the synagogue leaders. While they did not find Paulos the preacher, they brought forward two of his close companions. A man named Gaius, which was an unlikely name. He appeared to be a non-Jew but not at all Roman. This Gaius and another man, a native Ephesian by the name of Aristarchus, both admitted to be followers of the man called Jesus.

While the chanting increased in volume, Demetrius stood in a hallway within the theater, the place where actors gathered between scenes and before and after a performance. He turned to the two prisoners and sneered. "Do you hear that crowd?" Demetrius spat out his words. "Do you know what they want?"

Both held his gaze, unblinking. Demetrius kept his face blank, though he was surprised at the lack of fear he expected in their eyes. "That crowd wants your leader," he said. "They want his head on a pole." He then pushed them closer to the doorway leading to the stage. "Can't you hear it? Don't you feel it?"

The crowd was worked into a frenzy. Still, the two prisoners showed no sign of fear. "Don't you understand?" he hissed at them. "If they cannot have him, they will be satisfied with you."

The one named Gaius replied. "We do not fear death."

Demetrius scoffed. "Every man fears death. Cover their faces," he said to his companions, "and let's take them out to show the crowd."

The prisoners, heads wrapped in dark cloth, were led onto the stage. The crowd cheered at their appearance. Demetrius indicated to the crowd to quiet. "My fellow Ephesians, our great Artemis and her temple are in grave danger, thanks to the false teachings of the preacher, Paulos." At this, boos resonated through the crowd. "This man has stated that gods and goddesses, like our Artemis, are not real gods! I ask you, where else in the world can one find a temple like ours?" He pointed toward it, and the crowd thundered in response. "Shall we condone such dishonor to our patroness, to the one who guards the great city of Ephesus?"

"No!" the crowd answered, as one.

"This man and his followers would have the great goddess Artemis and her temple not only dishonored but toppled and destroyed!"

"No!" the crowd again thundered.

"The whole area of Asia. No, the entire civilized world worship her, but they want that all destroyed! What say you, Ephesus?"

"Great is Artemis of the Ephesians!" The chant resumed throughout the theater. He let them thunder on for several minutes before he held up his hands for silence.

"Friends, we have here two of the followers of the man, Paulos. They refuse to reveal the whereabouts of their leader!" Boos once again filled the theater. "What shall we do with them?"

Demetrius was sure that, by now, wherever the coward might be, Paulos had heard of the protest. Hopefully, he cared enough for his companions to come to their rescue. For what seemed hours, they waited, keeping the crowd pepped up but with no sign of the man. Demetrius grew concerned that the crowd, wanting blood, would either rush the stage or take to the streets. Occasionally, he turned to Gaius and Aristarchus and question them loud enough that the crowd might hear, but the men were silent and composed. This further angered the people. Eventually, a group of men made their way through the crowd. Relieved, Demetrius assumed it was the preacher being brought forward to them. But then, alarmed, Demetrius turned his back to the crowd, his eyes wide. "Kriton," he whispered hoarsely. "See who it is!"

It was not the preacher. It was the city manager, Alector, with his guards. This was not what he wanted. This was not going to be good.

The city manager strode before Demetrius, and, turning to the crowd, he quieted them. "My good people of Ephesus," Alector opened, "all of us know that our city is the guardian of the Temple of our great Artemis and of her image. In return, she keeps guard over us. Never fear! These men here," he indicated the prisoners, "have neither robbed the temple nor slandered our goddess. If Demetrius and his fellow artisans have a charge against anyone, the courts are available to hear their case and they may press charges. Justice will be served. We are a fair and orderly city.

"However, this assemblage and its clamor places us in danger of the charge of rioting. That is a far bigger threat to Artemis than a handful of simple men. Therefore, if you love Artemis, if you love her Temple, and if you love her city, please. Go back to work and to your homes, before the Romans show up."

With that, little by little, the crowd dispersed. Satisfied that he had calmed them, Alector turned to him. "You and I need to have a long talk, Demetrius," he said. "Let these men go and come with me."

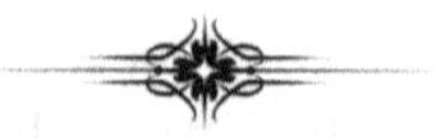

"It was all I could do to keep him here." Acco frowned at Saul as he spoke.

Saul opened his mouth to explain, but Timothy spoke first. "I can only imagine. Thank you for listening to reason, Paulos."

Saul weighed his words. He was experienced at this, knew how to take the blows, was much stronger in spirit, and knew that this was not how his life was to end. He had been given glimpses of that. But once he was convinced that no harm would come to Gaius and Aristarchus, and that the city authorities would be the means to calm that storm, he concluded it may be more dangerous for his friends if he interfered than if he stayed away.

He sulked as Acco and Aquila packed for him and Timothy, that they might leave the city promptly. "Can't this wait until morning?" Saul asked. "Or after Sabbath?"

"Or three moons from now," Priscilla added, her arms crossed. "It is time, Paulos."

"It *is* time," Timothy assured him. "Paulos, for weeks you have spoken of nothing but how badly you want to visit the churches, in Macedonia, in Achaia, to meet up with Lukas, to see Lydia—"

"Yes, but—"

"We can take it from here, Paulos." Priscilla's eyes softened. "I know Ephesus has been your pet project. You have been here longer than, maybe twice as long, as you were in Corinth. You have made tremendous strides here."

"Yes," Aquila added, "surely everyone in the city has at least heard of the name of Jesus."

"Or they live in a cave." Niko did not speak often. But when she did, it was either insightful or amusing.

Saul chuckled. "Niko, my child, leave it to you to know what an old man needs to hear in a situation like this."

"And what kind of situation would that be?" Niko asked, running a hand absentmindedly over her belly.

"His friends kicking him out of their home, of course."

This was answered by a chorus of protest, as Saul and Niko shared his joke.

Once the needs of Saul and Timothy were secured and they were ready for goodbyes, Acco pulled him aside. "It disturbs me that I can't go with you this time. I fear for you and Timothy."

Saul shook his head. "There is no need for fear. You know

that. Until the time appointed for me, something greater than the best bodyguard on earth watches over me."

"I know. But I feel better when I have you in my sights."

"Your son will be born here," Saul answered. "And then the Spirit will need you elsewhere."

"Did you say son?"

"Yes. You are having a boy."

Niko hugged Saul and then whispered in his ear. "I have thought so all along."

"Mothers know," Saul replied. "But, yes. I saw him in a vision as an older boy." He turned to Acco. "You will have a lovely family."

Acco gave a half smile. "Thank you."

"Priscilla," Saul said, turning toward her. The lamps were already dimmed, and as they stood in the entryway of the house, the musky odor of the oil filled the room. She stood in half-shadow, with Aquila behind her. Gently, Saul enfolded her hands. "I leave the leadership of this church of Ephesus in your capable hands. Aquila and Titus will assist you, and there will be others. The Lord will send you some excellent help, from the east."

From the beginning, Priscilla had sensed the importance of Ephesus for the future of Christ's church. She dipped her head and fought the tears that threatened.

"Paulos," Timothy said, "we must go now."

Saul swept his eyes around the room, at the walls, the ceiling, the lamps, as if memorizing their placement, and gazed at the shadows they cast. Anywhere but in the eyes of his good friends. He had never been particularly good at saying farewell. But then his eyes met those of Acco. Would they ever meet again? In a flash of a memory, he was back in a river in Galatia, witnessing the baptism of the young man, their packer, the spray of the cool water falling on him as Acco splashed about. Softly, to his loyal friend and co-worker in the faith, Saul spoke. "I sense that I have lived through this before, escaping in the night, like a thief."

Acco's sad gray eyes clouded. "Once or twice, Paulos," he whispered. "Once or twice."

Chapter Twenty-Four

**Miletus, Asia Minor
57 A.D.**

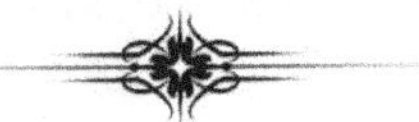

The sun had barely risen above the horizon. Luke tilted his face up to a sky void of clouds. On any other day, it would have held so much promise.

He sighed and lowered his head, eying the ship in dock. His possessions and those of Timothy and Paulos had already been stowed onboard. It left little else to do but to say their goodbyes.

He and Timothy had visited several more cities with Paulos, and several months had passed since they hurried out of Ephesus. Gathering the collection for the Jerusalem church had been successful, and as they ventured now to bring relief to the believers there, Luke knew the heaviness in his soul was nothing compared to that of Paulos.

The man had not slept the previous night. Luke's sleep was fitful, aware of Paulos's awakened state. Luke suspected it was due not to pain but rather the noise in Paulos's busy mind. So many voices providing him with messages, warnings, and directions made it difficult, especially if he had to make an important decision. Luke was glad his gift was for healing and not prophecy. He preferred only his voice in his head.

What concerned Luke most was the conflict he sensed in

Paulos. His drive to get to the Holy City by Pentecost was countered by his love and desire to be with his friends and fellow workers in Ephesus. A sense of home, which had eluded Paulos for many years, was something he experienced there. But the man would eventually get restless. The sense that he was getting too comfortable would cause him to venture on. Recently, Paulos was obsessing about traveling to Rome, of all places. Once word of the fledgling church there had reached him, their plight drew him like a moth to flame. The idea of spreading the good news of Christ Jesus in the imperial city, the very center of emperor worship, was a great temptation for him. How long would it take for the power in Paulos to be noticed in high places? Not very long, Luke ventured.

On the dock, the elders of the church of Ephesus were in a tight circle, Priscilla hanging on Paulos's arm as if he might float away, Aquila poised behind her. Titus and Timothy were among the small group. Luke reached out with a light touch on Titus's sleeve as Paulos addressed them.

"My friends." Paulos cleared his throat of the hitch there. "You know how I lived when I was among you. I have taught you all I know in public, at the agora, at the lecture hall, and privately, in your homes. I have urged both Jews and Greeks to change their hearts and lives, to turn to God, and to have faith in the Lord Jesus.

"Now I must go to Jerusalem, led by the Spirit. I know that prison and troubles await me. When have they not? What more can be done to me that I have not already suffered? Has that stopped me from my mission, the one assigned to me by Christ Jesus himself? No, whatever I shall face in Jerusalem, it will not prevent me from proclaiming the Grace of God through our Lord."

Tears flowed freely down Priscilla's face. Tough as he was, Titus's eyes were red-rimmed, and the man's muscles clenched under Luke's touch.

"I know." Paulos's voice broke. "I know that we shall meet again, my brothers and sisters." He turned to Titus and Priscilla. "Guard yourselves and the entire flock in Ephesus or wherever the Spirit leads you. You have been assigned, not by me, but by God to be leaders, shepherds, if you will, to watch over His people. I know, my friends, that wolves will come among you after I leave you that will not spare the flock. Some of your own people will distort the word to lure others to follow them. Remain alert! Remember that I have continually warned you of this."

It was as if a dark cloud shadowed Titus's face. If ever there was someone who could sniff out these wolves, it would be Titus. Luke knew that Priscilla wanted to think the best of people, and she lacked the suspicious nature that Titus wore like a cloak.

"Friends," Paulos continued, "I now entrust you to God our Father, to the message of his abounding grace, that which is able to sustain you, to build you up, and to give you a great inheritance among all whom God has made holy. Follow my lead, as I lived among you.'"

Paulos halted there. Luke doubted he had run out of words, but once Paulos noted the tears staining Titus's face, he choked on whatever words he had left and sank to his knees. They all joined him as he prayed.

It was the longest and most emotional farewell Luke had ever experienced.

Caesarea, Judea, some weeks later

Although Caesarea was the Roman headquarters for the region, when they entered the city, Saul knew they were definitely in Judea, where the Judean culture would not be smothered. The depth of Jewish history and way of life oozed out around the edges of the Roman influence in the city.

At a small home in the city, Philip and his household greeted them warmly. Saul was eager to meet Philip's four single daughters, all blessed with the gift of prophecy, who lived with and cared for their widowed father. That evening, about the table, Luke and Timothy related their travels, and Saul discussed the state of affairs in the cities where they had established churches. Philip was surprised at the attitude of the Jews of the Dispersion, assuming they would be more open to the arguments of Christ solely due to their cohabitation with the Greeks.

"If anything," Saul stated, "they feel more threatened. They are quite possessive of their faith and are highly incensed once they learn I preach of the Christ. While the most faithful, those who know the prophecies throughout the Law and the Prophets, are able to recognize Christ Jesus in them, those who are more, shall we say, jealous, are hard-hearted."

Timothy leaned in. "And that is when the trouble begins."

"While their hearts are hardened at the time," Saul said, "we must always keep their souls in our prayers. For while they may refuse the offer of salvation through Christ Jesus, they can never unhear what we reveal to them."

Pentecost was fast approaching, but it was with a heavy heart that he contemplated leaving for Jerusalem. In Philip's home, the bed was comfortable, the company pleasing, and he was happy to sleep sounder than he had in years, then rise, wash, say prayers, eat and visit, and then repeat. It was a relief to have a break from the constant responsibility of directing a group of believers.

It was well past midday and warm inside the home, so Saul wandered into the atrium seeking shade, hoping to find a breeze. It was not long before Luke found him. "I have been pleased with your healthy behaviors since we arrived here," the physician said.

Saul indicated space on the bench next to him. "Lukas, I am quite spoiled here. A comfortable bed, fresh water for cleansing, good wine for drinking, and wonderful food. I fear I could get used to this."

"Your color has improved, and I think you are filling out," Luke replied. "I am glad."

"It will not last, you know."

In the pause that followed, the soft tones of someone singing indistinctly within the house fell on his ear. The birds in the garden sang along as he stretched his neck toward the blue sky. He longed to hold on to this moment for as long as possible.

A memory of years ago came to him, kneeling at his mother's feet as she sat on a similar bench in the garden his father had built for her in Saul's hometown of Tarsus. Closing his eyes, he was transported back in time, the flowers' aroma and the streamlet's trickle as if he were there. His mother's perfume hung about him, her beautiful hands folded gracefully in her lap. How different might his life have been if he had followed his mother's desires for him? "There you are, Paulos." Timothy stuck his head out of the door that led into the garden. "A visitor has arrived for you." Saul sighed. "I will be right there." He slapped his hands on his legs. "Well, Lukas," he said resolutely, "that was short-lived. Let's go and see who it is and what he wants of me."

The entire household was gathered in the dining room. An older man stood with two younger men beside him. "You are Paulos," the man said. "I recognize you from my dreams. I am Agabus, and these are my sons. I received a vision about you, and the Holy Spirit urged me to find you, to share what I have seen."

Saul greeted him warmly. "Tell us about your vision."

"Might I have your belt?" Agabus asked.

Saul dipped his head as he fingered the belt at his waist. It was a gift, a farewell gift from Aquila and Priscilla.

"I will give it back," Agabus added. "It is part of my vision."

The afternoon sun cast shadows about them. It was almost time to light the lamps as Saul removed his belt and handed it to Agabus. He sensed tension building in the room. Philip, his daughters, Timothy, and Luke, lined the walls, granting Agabus the floor. One son wrapped the belt around his father's ankles before the other wrapped it around the older man's wrists. A chill crept on the back of Saul's neck.

"This is the vision given to me," Agabus said solemnly. "The Holy Spirit says, 'In Jerusalem, the Jews will bind the owner of this belt in this way and hand him over to the Gentiles.'"

Saul closed his eyes as the entire room erupted with cries of dismay, and his friends surrounded him. They pleaded with him to stay, to not go on to Jerusalem.

"What more warning do you need?" Philip asked. "Paulos, please, stay with us. You may celebrate Pentecost safely here."

"Please," Luke urged, "do not go on to Jerusalem. Give heed to this warning."

"Paulos," Timothy cried. "Someone else can present the collection to Jerusalem. It doesn't have to be you."

"Even you, Timothy!" Saul blurted. He knew Agabus was right. But why? Why did the Spirit urge the man to come here? "Why are you all tormenting me? Weeping and breaking my heart? Do you think I don't already know these things?" He grasped Timothy with both hands. "Don't you know I am ready, not only to be arrested but, if need be, to die in Jerusalem for the sake of the name of Christ Jesus?"

Saul released Timothy and whirled around to those surrounding him. He had no more words for them and no more tears.

The day he came to his senses in that room in Damascus, lying in his filth, he knew that following Yeshua would mean suffering, imprisonment, and, ultimately, his death. Yes, he longed to go to Rome. He would even very much like to take the good news as far as Spain. But if that was not to be, it was not to be. His was not to question the judgment of God.

Saul's belt was withdrawn from Agabus's wrists and ankles before the older man handed it back to him. Saul held the leather in his hands for a moment, understanding only too well the significance of the demonstration, before securing the belt around his waist. Then he met Agabus's sad eyes. "It is well," Saul whispered. "You have done what the Spirit led you to do."

Chapter Twenty-Five

**Jerusalem, Judea
57 A.D.**

Luke entered the cramped, windowless room, followed by Paulos and Timothy. The place wreaked of men's unwashed bodies. A group of men were seated with their backs to the wall on the cushionless floor. Their cloaks and tunics were worn thin, and all of them were barefoot. Luke focused on the older, ragged fellow in the center, whose once-dark hair was mostly grayed, his deep brown eyes cool and direct.

Luke edged to the side of the room, Mnason of Cyprus and Philip close by. The indirect sunlight from the doorway framed Paulos and Timothy, and Luke's eyes darted back and forth from Paulos, who stood before their seated hosts, to whom Luke assumed was James, the brother of the Lord.

"Saul." The older man addressed him in Aramaic. "You have returned."

"James, it is an honor to be here. Have you received the collection from the churches of the West? From Cilicia, Galatia, Asia Minor, Macedonia, and Achaia?"

"Yes." James's words were clipped. "It is appreciated."

"The churches there continue to meet the first day of the week, to collect more to assist the Jerusalem church in its need."

James jerked his chin. "You bring guests."

"This is Timothy." Paulos indicated with an open palm. "While his father was a Greek, his mother and grandmother are of the Dispersion, and he was raised in our ways."

"Circumcised?" someone of the seated group asked.

"Yes," Paulos answered, "by me."

There were some indecipherable murmurs. By their abhorred faces, Luke surmised this was not a favorable answer.

"We could not find a *mohel*," Paulos added, "so the burden fell to me. This is Lukas." Paulos indicated toward him. "A disciple from the region around Philippi, a physician."

Nothing but cool indifference emanated from the seated crowd. Apparently, they did not think much of physicians. Greek physicians, at that. Paulos had expressed to him as they wound their way through the streets of the city how much better he felt about the trip. Despite many dire predictions, including from Paulos himself, he emanated hope. But upon entering this room, Luke had enough doubts for both of them, wondering how this meeting might end.

"Let me update you," Paulos began, "on what God has accomplished among the Gentiles."

As Paulos related one story after another, how the good news of Christ Jesus had been spread from city to city throughout the Roman Empire, how the body of Christ had grown, and how many were baptized and received the Holy Spirit, the atmosphere lifted. Luke stole some glances at the shadowed faces, but mostly he kept his eyes on Paulos, who stood on his crooked legs, sparing no detail. He had not been offered a seat, but Luke doubted Paulos would have taken it. When he eventually concluded, there were a few questions, but his stories were met with praise to God for what had been accomplished. Then, the man sitting on James' right spoke up.

"Brother, there are many believers here among your fellow Jews, thousands of believers, all of them as zealous for the Law as you. There are rumors that you teach the Jews in the Dispersion to forsake the laws of Moses, urging them not to circumcise their sons or observe our customs."

There were murmurs of agreement among the seated. Luke turned to Mnason and Philip, both frowning but silent.

"What then to do?" the man continued. "Those here in the city and those who come for Pentecost now as you have, the news will surely spread that you have returned. So do what we tell you."

Luke noted Paulos's impassive face.

"We have four men here who have taken a vow. Join them, go through the rite of purification with them, and pay for their heads to be shaved."

James lowered his chin toward his chest but eyed Saul, his eyebrows drawn. "When they see you, yourself, observe and guard the Law, the zealous ones will then know that there is nothing to these stories about you, that you would never seek to destroy the Law of Moses."

There was a silence, thick and awkward. Muffled sounds of the city beyond the walls fell on Luke as if he were in a barrel, and he fought the sudden urge to take Paulos by the arm and lead him out of the room, out of the house, out of Jerusalem. He eyed Timothy, who was equally silent, panic filling his eyes.

"We would not ask this, of course, of the Gentiles you have with you." James swept his eyes over Luke and Timothy. "All we ask is that they abstain from eating what is sacrificed to idols and from blood and what is strangled."

"And from fornication," the other man added.

"As per our letter, we sent with you to distribute."

Paulos raised his chin in assent as he shifted his stance. "You are wise. Yes, I believe performing the rite with my brothers here will be appropriate, and of course, I would be happy to pay for the shaving of their heads. Mnason," he said, turning toward their host. "Do we have room to squeeze in four more?"

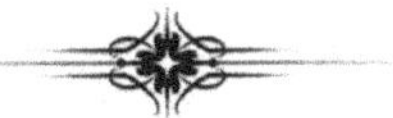

Finally, thought Uzziel. Uzziel and his compatriots had been in the Holy City for a full day and a half, and he was finally going to be in the Temple.

Although nightfall was threatening by the time they entered the gates of Jerusalem, exhausted, dusty, and hungry, he had tracked the brilliance of the Temple from a distance. It stood shining up on its hill, beckoning Uzziel, tugging at his soul. For him, it was like coming home after an arduous journey. Their first night's sleep was difficult, sensing the very presence of God so close, so close. His restless dreams consisted of reaching the Temple grounds, entering the Court of the Gentiles, and nearing the Beautiful Gate, but never quite stepping foot on the stairs.

As the sun neared rising the morning after their arrival, he jumped out of bed and, throwing on a robe, ran into the street to get a glimpse of the source of his obsession, relieved to lay eyes on it. His companions, however, were not ready to go to the Temple. They had their wares to sell off for Temple offerings and wanted to visit a couple of the synagogues beforehand for the latest news and to get a feel for the political landscape. With each new Roman Emperor and each new Roman governor and each new high priest, there were shifts in the atmosphere of the city. Due to the growth of the dangerous Zealot movement in Jerusalem, tensions between the Roman overlords and the citizens of Jerusalem grew proportionally. While the delay frustrated Uzziel, he reluctantly understood.

It had been a few years since any of them had made the trek from Galatia to Jerusalem, and though they received news from travelers back home, it was best to go to the source of information.

At the first synagogue they visited, Uzziel's elation about being in the city came crashing down on him when they learned that the Devil was in town. Hearing the name of Saul was bad enough, but learning that it was *him*, the Cilician, the traitor, the big mouth. Uzziel heated at the mere thought of him. How dare that traitor enter the Holy City? Uzziel knew followers of the Nazarene were in Jerusalem. The brother was the leader of the little group. But James had not betrayed his people and did not eat and drink with Hellenists. James was tolerable as long as he didn't preach. But Saul? Uzziel spat, merely thinking of him.

They learned the Devil was not alone at the second synagogue they visited. He had been seen with a Hellenist in one of the busy streets of Jerusalem. While it was said Saul had made a vow and was paying the way of some other Nazarites, that they were all followers of what they called "The Way" made them all suspect, vow or no vow. If the wretch had made a Nazarite vow, that meant he would be in the Temple. The thought infuriated Uzziel all the more. *Does he really think that he is fooling anyone? He only wants to preach that Jesus in our Temple!*

But his concern that Saul might be in the Temple did not sway his heartfelt desire to be in God's presence. He was not going to let

Saul of Tarsus steal his joy and defile his sacred visit. He had traveled far on dangerous roads. God had provided for him the entire way, and in gratitude, Uzziel was intent to complete the journey and pay his tribute.

At long last, their little group made their way that morning through the maze of the streets of Jerusalem. Even at that hour, the streets were crowded with vendors, early shoppers, servants, and travelers. Uzziel's sense of urgency pressed him forward, his eyes forever locked on the Temple at every twist and turn until they were there. Temple guards stood sentry before the magnificent edifice and its grounds. The closer Uzziel moved, the less he fathomed its vastness.

Uzziel led the way across the court of the Gentiles, headed for the wide steps of the Beautiful Gate. They were close enough to read the inscriptions on the pillars warning away Gentiles or unclean persons from passing the sacred enclosure as they climbed up the first set of stairs. Then they were up the second set and passed through the gate into the Court of the Women.

Uzziel paused and breathed in deeply. His dreams the previous night had not permitted him past that point, and he wanted to relish it. He then removed his money bag and emptied it into the closest collection chest. Replacing the bag on his belt, he stood in the cloister, waiting for his companions to follow suit. Then as one, they passed beyond the second set of pillars into the large open court, already filling with worshipers. There was a preponderance of women there, as this was the farthest they were allowed to proceed. Above the low level of chattering arose the beautiful sound of prayer surrounding them.

A prayer rose from Uzziel's throat, and he closed his eyes, giving in to the moving spirit within him. He prayed the old, ancient, familiar words. His eyes closed, his voice mingled amid the chaos, and he wondered, *Is this what God hears?*

But then, rising above the music of prayers, a man's voice, a certain voice, one he would never forget, fell on Uzziel's ears. Loud, clear, and distinct. His eyes flew open, and he spoke to no one in particular. "He's here."

Uzziel jerked his head about frantically. He grabbed the arm of his closest companion. Still darting his head back and forth, searching, Uzziel said, "He's here. Saul is here."

"How do you know that?"

"I can hear him." Uzziel pushed through the crowd, the others at his heels.

". . .Us this day our daily bread . . ." Clear. Louder. *Closer.* ". . .Our sins as we forgive those who . . . "

There he was. Uzziel reached out a hand, grabbed the man's shoulder, and spun him around. "Here he is!" Uzziel's eyes bore fully into the deep, dark eyes that he hated.

"Brothers!" Uzziel cried aloud. "Do you know who this man is?" People around him quieted, turning, gawking. "This is Saul of Tarsus! This is the man who eats and drinks and lives with Gentiles! Don't let his innocent speech fool you!" He turned to Saul's companions, who had begun to back away. "He preaches evil to our people, strides straight into our synagogues in Galatia and throughout the area, lies to our people, and carries on in the homes of Hellenists. He uses our history, our law, and our prophets to spew his evil, twisting the words of Moses and Isaiah." The crowd murmured. "He has even dared to bring a Hellenist here into the Temple!"

At this, angered men in the crowd took hold of Saul, grasping his arms and his robe at the neck, and they dragged him across the court. His feet scraped across the marble floor, past the pillars, and through the Beautiful Gate. Unceremoniously, they then threw him down the steps. At the back of the crowd, Uzziel shut the Temple doors behind him. He turned toward Saul's body, lying in a heap at the bottom of the stairs. The crowd rushed to Saul, scooped him up, and hauled him across the Court of the Gentiles toward the street, Uzziel hurrying after them.

Once off the Temple grounds, the angry crowd of men cornered him against the wall of a nearby building. "This is the man!" Uzziel thrust a hand toward Saul. "This is the man who said our Law is nothing now that Jesus came into the world!" They stood over him, kicking him repeatedly. The man closest to Saul's head lifted a foot to stomp on him when the pounding of regimented feet marched toward them.

"Romans!" someone shouted, and they turned away from Saul's still body to hide it from view.

Saul had known it was a trap. Everything within him warned him away from the Temple. For six days, he completed the rituals, and the tension within him rose every day. *Beware the seventh day,* it seemed to say. He nearly remained at Mnason's home this morning, intending to send the other four men on. The vow no longer held significance for him that it did for them. But Saul knew this was what he was called to do, what he was meant to do.

So, destiny dictated that Saul accompany the others to the Temple for the seventh and final day of the vow. The five of them concluded with the prayer Yeshua had taught his disciples. Midway through, he was grabbed by the shoulder and found himself face to face with a man whom he had not seen in many years. As he searched for the name, the man screamed in his face, spitting out his words, his eyes burning with hatred.

Uzziel. That was his name. The man who had killed him, once.

Uzziel riled the crowds around them, agitating them with his jealous lies. A deep knowledge filled Saul, and he was unafraid. Unfortunately, the calmer he was, the angrier the crowd became. Saul was numb to the pain as he was dragged through the Temple, thrown down stairs, and carried off the Temple grounds, where he was dumped against a building, and they kicked him. Kicking, like the frenzied animals they had become.

Father, forgive them.

Then, quite suddenly, they stopped. "What is this?" Sternly spoken. Roman, by the manner the Greek was spoken. Feet shuffled and scattered male voices drifted around him. Saul slid open his eyes and blinked.

Roman soldiers peered down at him.

"Can you stand?"

Painstakingly, Saul pulled his feet under himself.

"Help him up."

Two strong hands lifted him to his unsteady feet. Saul staggered before gaining his footing.

"Can you walk?"

"I believe so, sir." Saul's back cracked as he straightened.

"Take him to the barracks. There, we'll discover what happened."

Saul stretched out his hands toward the guards nearing him. They bound him with two chains: one about his wrists, the other about his feet. This emboldened his attackers, who had backed away, and they shouted as they followed Saul and the soldiers to the nearby barracks.

Once reaching the stairs leading to the barracks, Saul turned to the commander, shouting over the murderous din. "May I have a word?" he asked.

"Tell me you are not the Egyptian who caused a revolt recently," the commander replied.

"I am not. I am a Jew from Tarsus, in Cilicia. These—" Saul indicated toward the crowd with his bound hands. "These are my people. Please, allow me to address them."

"*These* are your people?" The commander gave a short laugh. "Go ahead. Good luck."

Saul turned precariously and motioned to the crowd to silence themselves, his chains clanking. The commander and his soldiers stood back but at the ready. Saul swept his gaze at his hushed audience, addressing them in their Aramaic language. "Brothers," he opened. In the back, he spied his panicked friends, Timothy and Luke. He lifted his bushy eyebrows at them in acknowledgment. "Please, give ear to the defense I present to you."

"I am a Jew, born in Tarsus in Cilicia, but I came of age in this, the Holy City, at the feet of the great teacher Gamaliel, educated in our ancestral law, zealous for God, as all of you are today. I persecuted the followers of Yeshua, those proclaiming him as the Messiah, to the point of relentless arrest, under the approval of the high priest and the Great Sanhedrin. Let them testify of me! From them, I received a letter of arrest to take to Damascus, in Syria, where I was to find those in hiding and bring them back in chains." Saul lifted his hands briefly, to illustrate. "In order that they might receive their punishment here in Jerusalem.

"While I was close approaching the city, about midday, bright light from heaven surrounded me and I fell to the ground. Then a voice said to me, 'Saul, Saul, why do you persecute me?' I said, 'Who are you, Lord?' and the voice replied, 'I am Yeshua, of Nazareth, whom you are persecuting.'" There were some murmurs in the crowd. "I asked, 'What do you want of me, Lord?' He answered, 'Get up and go into Damascus. There you will be told what to do.' The light had blinded me so that my companions, the Temple guards who accompanied me, had to lead me by hand into the city.

"A man named Ananias, a devout law-abiding man, well spoken of by the Jews living there, came to me. 'Brother Saul,' he said, 'regain your sight!' With those words, he healed me. Then he said, 'The God of our ancestors has chosen you to know his will, to experience the Righteous One, for you will be his witness to all the world of what you have seen and heard.' I was baptized, my sins washed all away, as I called on the Name."

Saul had them captivated. It was a great story and one he had told over and over. Every time he told it, his soul stirred with emotion.

"After I returned to Jerusalem later, I had a vision of Yeshua, who urged me to leave Jerusalem quickly, as my testimony would not be accepted. I thought that my past actions against the followers would be sufficiently convincing, but Yeshua said, 'Go! I send you far away, to the Gentiles.'"

The mere mention of non-Jews set the mob off again, and they violently threw off their cloaks and tossed dirt in the air. Saul was grasped and hurried into the barracks.

"You know," the commander said, "I didn't understand a word of what you said to them." He lifted his head to soldiers standing along the wall behind Saul. "I believe a flogging will get your story out."

Saul's chains were released, but as a leather strip was gripped to secure him to the post, Saul spoke. "Is it lawful to flog a Roman citizen without a conviction?"

The soldier stopped mid-tie. Noting the truth in Saul's eyes, he turned to his superior. "Sir, this man is a Roman citizen."

The commander's eyes narrowed as he closed in on him. "How can you be a Roman citizen? It cost me a lot of money to buy my citizenship. And you, look at you!"

Saul replied, "I was born a citizen."

The commander straightened and drew back, then ordered all to stand down. Saul knew the consequences the commander would face were he to dole out punishment, even as much as restraining him without a verdict. "Place him in an empty dorm room," the commander ordered. "He's not yet been tried and convicted."

"Sir?" one of his soldiers asked.

"We can't very well release him to that crazed mob out there, they will kill him." The commander took a deep breath. "It is too late today," he explained. "Tomorrow, I shall discover what the Jews accuse him of. Get him food and water. Look like he hasn't eaten for weeks."

"Who do you think they hate more," Timothy asked, "them or us?"

Luke tilted his head. "They?"

"The zealous Jews."

"And 'them?'"

"Sorry. The Romans."

"Hmm, good question," Luke replied. "Now, if you are referring to 'us' as you and me, I would say they categorize us much the same. Though you were raised in Jewish tradition, they still see you as Greek. Me, well, I am a pure, unadulterated Gentile. And while neither of us are Roman nor oppressors of their people, all Gentiles are alike to them. So, to ask who they despise more—"

"Somehow, I don't miss Paulos much right now."

Luke chuckled. He was able to find humor despite the last couple of days hovering near the barracks, alert for any sign of Paulos's release. Philip remained with them until dark both nights, and he and a good number of Paulos's supporters rejoined them in the mornings. Timothy was exhausted but optimistic. The Romans had not shooed them away. Instead, they'd explicitly looked the other way, allowing the friends of the prisoner to remain nearby.

But also, Romans did not routinely keep prisoners. They believed in swift trials, not wasting tax money on housing the accused. Speedy trials and speedy executions were Roman standards.

The examination of the charges against Paulos did not go well for the accusers. Their passion and bloodthirst frustrated the commander. That Paulos was once a trial attorney himself became obvious. When brought before the chief priests and the council, Paulos managed to set them against each other by uttering a single sentence. "I am a Pharisee, a son of a Pharisee," he had declared, "and I am on trial concerning the hope of the resurrection of the dead." A snicker had escaped Philip. He knew what none of the Gentiles present would know: the Pharisees and the Sadducees were in heated disagreement over the issue of what happened after death. That sentence started such a commotion that the commander was forced to remove Paulos back to the barracks for his safety, another reason for Timothy's optimism. After revealing his Roman citizenship, Paulos remained unabused.

"What now?" Timothy asked. "Why aren't they releasing him?"

"Maybe they keep him for his safety," Luke offered.

Philip explained, "They don't dare release him, not while that murderous mob is in the city. What did Paulos do to so enrage that man?"

"He wouldn't stay dead, for one thing," Timothy quipped.

"Paulos was chased out of Iconium," Luke explained, "where that man is from. He then headed up a gang that followed Paulos and Barnabas from town to town. They convinced the crowd in Lystra to stone him."

"Oh." Philip drew out the word. "I see."

"Then, after he woke up," Timothy added, "Paulos got up and walked right back into that city."

"That might do it. Say, who is that?"

They followed Philip's gaze. A young man hurried toward them where they stood near the barracks. "Pardon me," said the young man, "are any of you Timothy, the apprentice of my uncle Saul?"

Philip interpreted his Aramaic words into Greek. "Oh, sorry," the young man said, this time in Greek, "I forgot myself."

"I am he," Timothy answered.

The young man embraced him. "I am Lavi, the son of Saul's sister.

"Is your mother in need?" Timothy asked.

"No," Lavi answered, "but I've learned something I have to talk to my uncle about. It is urgent, life or death. Is he still being held by the Romans?"

"Yes, in the barracks," Timothy replied. "But they are limiting contact with him. We spoke with him once, very briefly, since he was taken captive."

"They will let me in," Lavi said confidently. "I am his nephew. Family is very important to Romans." He started to leave them but then turned back. "Don't let them take him to meet with the Sanhedrin."

Lavi strode to the barracks and spoke to the guards at the door. His wait was not long before the door opened and he was ushered in.

"Of course, Paulos has a nephew who lives in Jerusalem," Timothy said. "Why wouldn't he?"

"He seems to be an earnest young man," Luke added. "I believe him to be sincere."

"What do you think he meant by his warning?" asked Philip.

"Sounds like he has some information that might mean more trouble for Paulos," reasoned Luke.

Some time passed before the door reopened, and Paulos's nephew reemerged. As he strode past them, he made eye contact and gave an imperceptible dip of his chin. The previously quiet barracks exploded with movement, guards coming and going with purpose. The door swung open, and out strode the commander, flanked by several guards.

"You two," the commander said, pointing at Timothy and Luke. "I would speak with you." They approached and the commander lowered his voice.

"I have been made aware of a plot against your friend. A large group of Jews intend to attack and kill him as he is transported. I will not tolerate an attack on a Roman citizen or on my men. We will be moving him." The commander paused. "I cannot reveal the details for security purposes, but I have noted your devotion to our prisoner. Go to Caesarea. Wait for his arrival there."

The commander reentered the barracks. Timothy turned to Luke. "What do we do now?"

Luke took him by the arm, steering him back to their friends. "Philip," Luke asked, "are we welcome to stay in your home again?"

"In Caesarea?"

"In Caesarea," Luke answered.

"Yes, certainly, but why?"

"Because we are going back to Caesarea."
"We can't abandon him here."
"He is going to be transferred," Luke replied.
"To Caesarea?"
Luke gave a dip of his head. "To Caesarea."

Chapter Twenty-Six

Caesarea, Judea
57 A.D.

My brothers!" Paulos embraced both of them in turn.
"We brought food," said Timothy.
"Did you bring parchment and ink?" Paulos asked.
Timothy grinned "Of course."

Luke surveyed the spacious room where Paulos was held by the local Roman government in Caesarea. It contained several tables and a few chairs and boasted plenty of floor space. It even had a window. Paulos sported an obvious lack of chains or leather bindings. "I believe," Luke said slowly, "Silas would be jealous."

Paulos laughed. "It's true. Silas and I were never confined in such grandeur. Come, you two, sit. I have much to tell you."

"We met your nephew," Timothy said. "He's a pleasant young man."

"He is. I hadn't seen him since he was a child," Paulos answered. "He was at the Temple, near a large group of men. When he heard my name mentioned, he eavesdropped. They were plotting to attack me and any accompanying Roman soldiers on my way to stand trial before the Sanhedrin. Lavi slipped away and, having received word that I was being held at the barracks, came directly to let me know."

Luke sat in a chair at one of the tables, his back to the window. He unrolled a piece of the parchment, removed the lid on the ink, and dipped a pen, waiting. Timothy leaned in toward Paulos. As beams of sunlight from the open window highlighted them, Luke wished he had the skill of drawing to capture the moment. This was how he would always think of Paulos: teaching, speaking earnestly, his crooked body bent toward his pupils, sunlight streaming around him. *I cannot draw pictures*, he thought, *but I can draw with words*. So, Luke wrote as Paulos spoke.

"The commander seemed to favor you over your accusers," Timothy said.

"Claudius Lysias is the tribune's name," Paulos offered. "Three times he saved my life. I lift him up in prayer every day."

"Three times?"

"Yes, first when he came upon the group who tossed me off the Temple grounds. They would have killed me then. Not much later, as I spoke to the people from the steps to the barracks. Claudius Lysias has a strong sense of order and justice. You know, once he had me inside their confines, he was prepared to have me flogged, to interrogate me." Paulos grinned. "The man prefers straight answers. So, as they prepared to tie me to their whipping post, I asked him if it was legal to flog a Roman citizen before the sentence was passed."

Luke shook his head. Of course, he did.

"Once he learned I was born a citizen, his respect for me grew tremendously. In fact, I had several chances to speak with him during my confinement there."

Timothy interrupted. "And the third time he saved your life was after he learned of the plot to kill you on your way to stand before the Sanhedrin."

"Yes, of course. The letter he wrote to the governor, Felix, was impressive. He was unable to leave his post, but I sensed he wanted to go with me to Antipatris and then on to here. But instead, he sent a large number of his men."

"Horsemen?" Timothy asked.

"Seventy horsemen, Timothy. And two hundred foot soldiers."

"Two hundred?" Timothy's eyes widened.

"And two hundred spearmen."

Luke paused his writing. "He sent four hundred and seventy of his men for one prisoner."

"He was quite serious about getting me to the governor unscathed."

Luke shook his head. "And you?" he asked. "How were you transported?"

"On horseback. I rode with the horsemen. The foot soldiers and spearsmen traveled as far as Antipatris and then returned to Jerusalem the following morning. It was a beautiful sight, Lukas. I am sorry you missed it."

"We were instructed to go ahead of you to Caesarea," he replied, "by the commander."

"Claudius Lysias."

"Yes, Paulos. I am writing that down."

"Good. When you are done, Timothy must write a letter for me. Well, several letters."

"What happens now?" Timothy asked. "With the governor?"

"Governor Felix has summoned my accusers. They will present their accusations and then he will decide what to do with me."

"So, we should be praying for Governor Felix," Timothy added.

"Pray for the chief priests, too, my son," Paulos answered. "They will most definitely need prayer."

Two Years Later

Saul stood at the window of his quarters overlooking the paved courtyard, toward the governor's palace. The sun was warm on his face, and he closed his eyes, the light warming his eyelids. He was concluding another letter, dictating to Timothy, who sat nearby. "Please, read that last back to me."

The business of the governor of Judea paraded past this window day after day, month after month. Since Felix left his post, however, the compound had been unusually quiet. Save for a few guards who remained to keep the grounds secure, the new governor would bring his men with him. Saul wondered what kind of man Porcius Festus was.

"That is a good place to end," Saul said. "Please give the usual greetings to our friends there in Ephesus." He turned from the window, adjusted his eyes, and addressed Luke. "Get comfortable, Lukas, and tell me all about your journeys."

"After you, Paulos," Luke replied, indicating he should take a seat. Saul sighed as he took the load off his bowed legs, and once they were all seated, Luke regaled them. "There's plenty of time for me to relate my little news. Let's talk about the old and new governors. I feared you would be sent back to Jerusalem upon Felix's departure for Rome."

"His honor, Marcus Antonius Felix is a lost soul, I am afraid." Saul had had several occasions to witness to him, but Felix's fear of hell was greater than his hope of salvation. He had preferred to believe that this world, that this life, was all there was and that if God or 'the gods' were to punish him, it would be while he still drew breath. The concept of the resurrection and eternal torment was more than he dared to fathom. "I believe he kept me here less for my security and more as an incentive against the high priest."

"What do you believe will happen to you now," Luke asked. "Any premonitions or visions regarding that?"

Saul took in a deep breath. How much should he reveal to his friends, who cared so much for him? "I have not seen any immediate circumstances," he offered weakly. "But I have been assured that I will testify to both a king and an emperor."

The door to his quarters opened, and the Roman centurion assigned as Saul's guard entered. "Paulos," he said, "you are summoned by Festus, the new governor."

Saul stood and stretched out his hands. His guard shook his head. "That will not be necessary. Come."

Saul turned to his friends before following the centurion out the door. "Perhaps I can manage to get to Rome." He waggled his eyebrows. "And have Rome pay for it."

Porcius Festus could swear the tribunal seat was still warm from Marcus Antonius Felix's rear. He had not desired this assignment. The entire region stunk of revolt. Although the role of procurator was never considered easy, he now found himself responsible for keeping the peace in the most gods-forsaken corner of the empire. While many men had tried and failed, he was determined to represent Rome's dominant, heavy hand, the conquering race of men he belonged to.

His challenging new appointment, assigned by Emperor Nero, was not his first as procurator far from his boyhood home in Italy. He possessed basic knowledge of the deep-seated problems of the area, but that did not mean he understood them. Jews were scattered all over the cities of the Roman Empire, just as they were here in the capital city of Caesarea. If in the minority, they kept to themselves and did not cause too much trouble. That made it easier to ignore their refusal to accept local city gods and the cult of the emperor. But in this province of Judea, where Jews were in the majority, their governance was an entirely different matter.

No one wanted the task of dealing with the Jews in Jerusalem, the most difficult of them all. Word was they did more infighting with each other than with Roman authority. But his predecessor had had growing issues with uprisings, and Felix's often heavy hand had created more problems than he had eradicated. The most successful of his forerunners had been more political in their dealings with the Jewish leaders.

This is why, while still in Jerusalem the last week or so, acquainting himself with the infrastructure and atmosphere, he judiciously dealt with the Jewish leaders regarding Felix's famous prisoner.

Felix left all his documentation about the man named Paulos. The most important aspect of his case was that the man was a Roman citizen, a fact he believed was not well understood by his accusers. There was little reason to continue to hold him. The man hailed from someplace in Cilicia, after all. The man could simply go home and never bother any of them again. Festus was confused as to why Felix had continued to detain him.

But here they were: the Jews from Jerusalem making their same accusations, even after all these months, and the prisoner himself, whom Festus had summoned for a hearing. The Jews brought the same complaints about him as previous, charges they believed justified the man's death. As they made their accusations, Festus studied his prisoner's expression. He was unmoved by their protests. No wonder Felix had kept him around.

Festus addressed the prisoner. "You understand the accusations made against you, yes? How do you respond?" "I have not committed the crimes of which they accuse me, not against the Jewish law, nor the Temple, nor against Rome," came the answer.

This reply did not please his accusers, who erupted in shouts and curses. Festus raised his hand to silence them. "Do you wish," Festus asked the man, "to go to Jerusalem and be tried there before me on these charges?"

The prisoner turned his entire body toward him. "Honorable Festus, you are Emperor Nero's tribunal. This is where I should be tried."

Truth. This man knows Roman law.

"I have done no wrong to the Jews," he continued, "or I'd have been released to them long ago. Now, if I have committed any crime deserving of death, I would capitulate to them. I am not afraid to die. But, if there is nothing to their charges against me, none may turn me over to them."

Festus raised his eyebrows. Is he daring me to release him to them?

"I appeal to Emperor Nero."

Festus's mouth dropped open as the room stilled. There it is. Once a Roman citizen appealed to the emperor, his case must be presented in Rome no matter where in the empire he might be. His prisoner knew this, had likely known it all these months in captivity, but had hoped that Felix would tire of holding him. Festus, himself, might have released him, though he knew it would anger the Jews. He was willing to do so, as there was no Roman law the man had violated. But now, it was beyond his control. Festus slapped a hand on the table before him and stood, facing his prisoner.

"You have appealed to Rome," he said breaking the silence that Paulos's words had brought. "To the emperor, you shall go."

Several days later, word reached Festus of an impending visit from King Agrippa to welcome him to his new post. Festus found it interesting that Rome allowed the Jewish ruler of the region to still be called king, but the title served to keep the peace. The Judean king's allegiance to the emperor and to Rome was a tradition, and so long as it stood, Rome allowed them to act as figureheads.

He managed to avoid meeting Agrippa while he was in Jerusalem. But he could no longer evade the Jewish leader, as he and his woman were already on their way. Some referred to her as Agrippa's sister, and some as Agrippa's wife. Festus assumed she was both, not curious enough to care either way. What did concern him was whether their reserved quarters in the governor's complex stood ready for them.

They arrived with no small company and, though quite familiar with the grounds, Agrippa had requested a tour with Festus before they shared a meal. The two men crossed the compound, bodyguards both before and behind. As they passed the area where the prisoner Paulos was confined, Festus thought to share about him, to get Agrippa's take on his situation.

"There is a man here who was left imprisoned by Felix. An interesting case. While I was in Jerusalem, the Jewish priests and elders came to me, persisting that I release him to them. Roman law forbids me to hand over a Roman prisoner, and they have a right to face their accusers, so I insisted they must travel here to Caesarea, where he is being held.

"However, they brought forward no charges with any real crime. Instead, it involves differences of opinion of their common religion about a certain man named Jesus, who had died, but the prisoner, Paulos by name, claims he is alive. With no good idea how to address the issue, I asked him if he wanted to go to Jerusalem to be tried there."

"I have heard of this Paulos," Agrippa said. "How did he reply?"

"He appealed to Rome. So, I continue to hold him until I can make arrangements to send him to Emperor Nero."

"They say he is quite the speaker," Agrippa added. "He hails from Tarsus, a city known for oration. He is a former scribe and attorney for the chief priests, so they consider him a traitor. You should have him give a speech."

Festus pondered that information. No wonder the Jewish priests wanted custody of him. This also explains why Paulos preferred to take his chances with Emperor Nero. Custody in the hands of those zealous men meant certain death. "You want an oration?" Festus asked. "I will arrange it. We'll invite some dignitaries to pay you homage."

King Agrippa beamed. "Splendid!"

At the sound of footsteps, Saul lifted his head from his reading, his right forefinger still touching the parchment. Clattering surprised him. Drusus appeared at the open doorway to his quarters, chains in his hands. Saul tilted his head, a question in his eyes.

"Necessary tools of my trade," Drusus said, indicating the shackles. His lips curled at his prisoner's raised eyebrows. "At least they are today."

Saul straightened. "I suppose I am still a prisoner and not merely a guest of our new procurator." He pushed away from his reading and shuffled toward Drusus, raising his folded hands.

As they made their way through a maze of hallways, Saul wore a hint of amusement on his face. He had only just met the new procurator, but he understood him well. The need to remind the people of Rome's occupation of their city was a given. He noted all the soldiers were armed excessively, ready to squelch any rebellious action at a moment's notice.

They crossed the compound, reaching a back entrance to the auditorium. They had not gone far before Saul was ushered into a cramped hallway whose floor slanted gradually downward. The chains echoed eerily in that narrow place, and the weight of them propelled Saul forward. The crowd's noise grew loud enough to deaden the clanking of the chains. There they waited a few feet from a pair of curtains separating them from the floor of the auditorium. Saul stared at the curtains, which muffled the crowd.

"The Judean king Herod Agrippa and his—" Drusus gave a slight pause—"sister, Berenice, have arrived in the city."

"I am aware," Saul replied, his eyes boring a hole through the curtains, picturing the scene the moment he set foot onto the auditorium floor. A familiar warmth surrounded him, and he allowed it to fill him. He closed his eyes, his lips moving in silent prayer.

Give thanks to the Lord our God, for he is good, his steadfast love endures forever.

The crowd hushed, the voice of Festus soaring above them. Saul opened his eyes and lifted his chin, then turned to meet the eyes of his guard, peering into the man's soul.

Drusus did not hold the gaze long. Facing the curtains, the man said, "Your god be with you."

"Yes. He certainly is."

Then Drusus swept back a curtain, and the two of them entered the auditorium. They strode toward the procurator's box, the place filled with stunned silence. A few gasps escaped. Saul scanned the crowd, his face masked. He locked eyes with Luke, sensing his unease. The procurator's box was well below Luke and Timothy, and Saul made eye contact with King Herod Agrippa II, holding his gaze a little longer than what the king found comfortable. Then he turned to Festus, and he waited.

Festus's eyes gleamed with satisfaction. The chains surely gave the impression that this was a dangerous man. The procurator addressed the gathering.

"King Agrippa and distinguished guests, behold the man imprisoned here for some time by the previous procurator, Felix. This is the man about whom the Jewish authorities petitioned me, both in Jerusalem and here, to have him tried by their laws and executed." The crowd stirred.

"After questioning him, however, I do not find any guilt in him worthy of execution, not by any Roman law. At his inquiry, he appealed his case to his Imperial Majesty in Rome. To Rome, I must send him." He paused. "But I have no charges, no crime! What do I write to our Imperial Majesty? Therefore, I have brought him before you, King Agrippa. Your knowledge of Jewish law and custom is indispensable in this case, and your opinion invaluable, so I seek your guidance on this matter after you have examined him." Festus was seated.

Saul noted Agrippa's heavy black eyebrows and dark eyes—small, dull, and set back in his face. The man's mouth was set in a frown. Saul knew about him, about his upbringing in Rome, the death of his father Agrippa I at the tender age of seventeen, and that he acquired the position he now held after the death of his uncle.

Herod Agrippa, the puppet of Rome, was charged to oversee the Temple in Jerusalem and assign the high priest. His recent building projects had caused estrangement with the most devout Jews of Jerusalem. He expressed only infrequent occasions of outward devotion to his religion of Judaism, and Saul knew the gossip surrounding the beautiful sister sitting next to him. Saul stood silent, their eyes locked, waiting.

Finally, Agrippa said to him, "You may speak in your defense."

Saul attempted to lift his right hand out of habit, but the chains yanked his hand back. This caused a few titters of laughter in the crowd. Saul accommodated his typical orator's stance and addressed Agrippa.

"I am honored and fortunate, King Agrippa, that it is in your audience I stand today to defend myself against the accusations of the Jewish authorities. You, sir, are particularly familiar with the Jewish laws, customs, and controversies. Therefore," Saul paused slightly, "I beg your patient audience."

Agrippa sat back, getting comfortable.

"All the Jews in Jerusalem know of my background, from my youth on, of my life with both my people in Tarsus of Cilicia and in Jerusalem. They know that for a long time, I belonged to the strictest sect of our religion, and I lived as a Pharisee. And now, here I stand on trial on account of my hope! My hope is in the promise made by God to our ancestors. The same promise our twelve tribes hope to attain as they worship earnestly, night and day." Agrippa offered a slight dip of his chin. "It is for this hope, your Excellency, that I find myself accused by my fellow Jews themselves."

Saul broke eye contact with Agrippa to dramatically scan the crowd. Most faces were blank. To the audience, he asked distinctly. "Why does it seem incredible to anyone that God raises the dead?"

He turned back to King Agrippa. Indicating himself, Saul said, "Indeed I, a good Pharisee, was convinced of my duty to do many things against the name of Jesus of Nazareth. And that is precisely what I did. In Jerusalem under the authority of the Jewish leaders, the chief priests, I not only rounded up many of the followers of Jesus and locked them in prison, but I also voted to condemn them to death during their trials. So enraged was I, so incensed by their beliefs, I would even hunt after them outside of Jerusalem, pursuing them in foreign cities."

Festus leaned forward with interest.

"It was with this same mission in mind," Saul continued, "that I traveled to Damascus on commission and authority of the chief priests. About midday, along the road, oh King, I saw a brilliant light, brighter than the sun!" Many in the audience also leaned forward expectantly. "The light shone all around me and my companions. It was so bright we fell to the ground! Then a voice fell on my ears. It seemed to be both in me and all around me. And the voice said, in Aramaic, 'Saul, Saul, why are you persecuting me?'" Gasps escaped the audience.

"I asked, 'Who are you, Lord?' The answer came: 'I am Jesus, who you are persecuting.'" This caused murmurs in the crowd, much louder this time. "'But get up!' the voice said, 'Stand up and go into the city. I appoint you to testify to all which you have witnessed. I will rescue you from your people and from the Gentiles, to whom I send you.'" Saul again scanned the crowd and carefully pronounced his next words. "'That you might open their eyes, that they may turn from darkness to light, from the power of evil to God. That they may receive forgiveness and be placed among all the saints.'"

At this, Agrippa's heavy brows pulled, and his mouth turned down. Saul paused and gazed up at Luke, who had physically leaned into the story as well, his face displaying eager anticipation, the fear for his friend overshadowed by the message. Saul shifted his gaze back to the king.

"King Agrippa, I have been loyal to that heavenly vision since that time. In Damascus, I proclaimed Jesus the Christ. I've proclaimed Christ in Jerusalem and all of Judea. And I have indeed proclaimed Christ to Gentiles, that they should turn away from sin and turn to God. For this, the Jews seized me in the Temple and attempted to kill me. They should have succeeded! But here I stand before you. I stand before you, King Agrippa, all because I have proclaimed nothing less but what I learned since I was a youth, nothing but what the prophets and Moses himself proclaimed about the Messiah! That the Messiah must suffer and then, as the first to rise from the dead, he would bring light into the world for both *our* people"—he then indicated the crowd—"and to the Gentiles."

"Insanity!" Festus shouted out, in exasperation. "Too much

education has addled your mind!"

Saul lowered his hands, the chains clinking. "I am not out of my mind, most excellent Festus. I am speaking the absolute truth. Indeed." He gestured to Agrippa. "Indeed, the king knows about these things. He knows of the Law and the Prophets. He knows of Moses. I can speak freely to him because he is aware of these things as they have all occurred in the open."

Saul held Agrippa's gaze, filling himself with the power within, and directed it all toward the king. "King Agrippa." His voice boomed as he emphasized each word. "Do you believe Moses and the Prophets? I *know* you believe!"

The predicament registered on Agrippa's face. He did not dare deny the prophets or Moses, although most of the crowd were Gentiles. Word would reach Jerusalem. The king then chuckled softly. "Are you so quickly persuading me to become a follower of Jesus?" he asked.

Power seeped out of Saul, radiating toward the procurator's box, though it was not Agrippa's faith growing that he sensed. Uncertain of where it was directed, Saul replied, "Whether quickly or not, I pray to God that not only you but all who hear my voice right now might become like me, such as I am." He held his hands out toward Agrippa. "But for these chains."

Berenice, the king's sister, rose abruptly from her seat next to Agrippa, her cheeks flushed, and hurried out of the box. Agrippa rose, quickly following after her. Festus and the remainder of the guests in the procurator's box hurried behind. In stunned silence, the crowd stood in confusion as the spectacle ended abruptly.

Chapter Twenty-Seven

The Island of Malta
59-60 A.D.

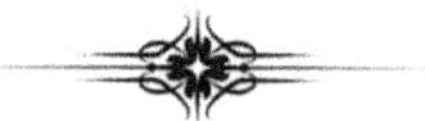

Luke had trouble absorbing their good fortune as he and his friends gathered around a huge dining table. They had so much to be thankful for: the feast before them, the warm bedding awaiting them, and the fact their host was none other than the Roman official of the island.

They had left Caesarea weeks before and, after several stops, landed on the island of Crete. They stayed with some believers there for a full week, Paulos's assigned centurion, Julius, in tow. Paulos had warned both Julius and the ship captain that it would be dangerous to head out at that time, that there would be foul winds and storms, and urged them to wait until spring. But the ship's navigator believed otherwise, and Julius was eager to get home to Rome.

They should have paid heed to Paulos. The experience was so harrowing that Luke never wanted to set foot on a ship again. Storms at sea with no land in sight were bad enough. But the crew threw cargo overboard, and frightened soldiers prepared to kill their prisoners. And stuck in the middle of the sea, they'd run out of food and nearly starved. Their survival was miraculous. Despite ignoring his advice earlier, Paulos assured that the entire ship, crew, and passengers would survive, and here they all were, on the palatial grounds inhabited by Publius.

"Our interpreter tells me," Publius said as they ate at his table, "that the natives claim your prisoner to be a god! Something about surviving a viper bite?"

"I saw it with my own eyes," the guard, Julius, answered. "The natives started a fire for us on the beach because we were all soaked and shivering, having abandoned ship on the reef. Paulos was gathering bramble to throw on the fire, and a hidden snake bit him on the hand."

"Might you show me the bite?" Publius asked.

"It must not have been a viper," Paulos replied as he reached out his hand.

"No, I spied it," one of the other soldiers offered. "It was definitely a viper."

"The hand is not even swollen!" Publius exclaimed. "It healed quickly."

It had been quite a spectacle, as the natives, after promptly killing the snake, waited for Paulos to display signs of the poisoning that never occurred.

"A miracle," Timothy said softly.

"A miracle indeed," Publius agreed. "No less a miracle that your ship found us in these winds. Malta is a narrow island and can be difficult to find for some of the best navigators, much less a storm-damaged ship."

"This man continually assured us," Julius said, indicating Paulos.

"It was a ship carrying grain," Paulos interrupted. "Though other food and cargo was sacrificed—"

"He downplays another miracle, Publius," Julius interrupted. "There was a small amount of bread, and he prayed over it, and it fed the entire ship."

"How many were on board?"

"Two hundred and seventy-six."

"Not counting the rats," Timothy added. Publius chuckled as he eyed Paulos in wonder.

All this was true. The closer Paulos neared Rome, the more like Christ Jesus he resembled. He was even calmer than before, if that was possible. Perhaps it was all those months of captivity in

Caesarea and the many times Governor Felix called for Paulos, off and on, to speak to him about the kingdom of God. Talk of sin and the need for salvation frightened the governor, and he would send Paulos away. Paulos did his best to convince Felix but it was not to be. Nor was he going to make believers out of Festus or Agrippa, not for lack of trying.

And here Paulos was, at a table with another Roman authority, eventually headed for Rome itself.

"You intrigue me," Publius said. "It sounds almost as if you want to go to Rome and have a chance to speak to the emperor in person. You have no fear of nature, of storms, of the sea, or of Romans. Or of me."

"Nor of the Jewish leaders in Jerusalem," Julius interjected. "Drusus, his guard in Caesarea, told me that Paulos argued his defense far better than the attorney for his accusers argued their complaints."

Publius's eyebrows shot up. "Impressive. Bit by a viper and not fallen ill or dead. Fearless," Publius waved a hand toward Paulos. "And indestructible. I can tell by the shape your body is in people have tried in the past and failed."

Paulos ran a hand over his face. "I have been imprisoned numerous times, beaten with rods, flogged by the Jews five times, shipwrecked three times, and stoned. I have faced many dangers and faced death multiple times. What more can be done to me?"

"You have been incredibly lucky," Publius replied.

"Luck has nothing to do with it," Julius replied. "Indeed, I believe his god is with him."

Julius, like Timothy, Luke, and Aristarchus, never left his side, though for a different reason. Julius had taken Saul aside after the embarrassing meal the night prior with Publius.

"You understand why the soldiers wanted to kill the prisoners, don't you?" he had asked him.

"Because the safety of the prisoners was their responsibility," Saul had answered. "If the soldiers were about to die, and a prisoner survived, it would be their fault in the eyes of their superiors, and they would die in shame.”

“Yes,” Julius had replied. “You understand. But you, you saved us. You saved us all.”

“I did not save you. It was the hand of God that did that.”

“But you are why we were saved.”

“You don’t know that, Julius. Perhaps it was for you. I am old and have served the Lord all of my days. I do not fear death because I have met it before, and the glory that awaits me is far better than the pain and suffering of this life. However, I am still here because I have more work to do.”

“What must I do to live like that?” Julius had whispered, the dark shadows creeping about him. Saul had reached out a hand.

“Believe in the Lord Jesus, confess your sins, and be baptized. Then live your life devoted to him and his teachings.”

But Saul knew Julius was not ready to give up his career. He was preparing to seek a wife and had a promising life ahead of him. Julius knew the cost of leaving all that behind. Still, Christ Jesus was pursuing Julius. Someday, the man would stop, turn, and acknowledge his Savior.

Saul opened his eyes at the dimly lit ceiling, the lamps in the room still softly glowing. His companions stirred around him. Saul’s heart soared. The Lord had seen fit that he might serve yet another day.

After their morning prayers, he and his constant companions dressed and were ready to break fast. There was an urgent rapping on the door before it inched open.

“Master Lukas?” A male servant popped his head around the door. “His honor, Publius, calls,” he said in broken Greek.

“We shall all go.” Saul urged them to follow the servant to the doorway of a large bedchamber, where a number of hovering servants and soldiers parted to let them through.

The moment Julius stepped into the suite of Publius’s father, he knew the man was beyond help. Having lost his father a few years prior, he had a fair idea of what Publius was experiencing. The helplessness was the worst part. Hoping desperately that death be delayed, at least for a while longer, helpless as a loved one grew weaker and weaker until his breath left him completely.

Julius stood away from Paulos, Timothy, and Aristarchus as Luke neared the dying man's bedside. The sounds coming from the bed were so reminiscent that Julius wanted to cover his ears. But stoically, he fixed his eyes on a map hanging on the wall, and Julius studied it, ignoring the sounds and smells and the stifling air in the room. The curtains were closed against the rising sunlight, and the lamps were low. The map. Was it a map of the island of Malta? No, wrong shape, he thought. Sicily, perhaps. Maybe Publius and his family hailed from Sicily.

Out of the corner of his eye, Julius noted his prisoner shuffle to Lukas, the physician, who stepped back, allowing Paulos to sit on the bed next to the dying man.

The man would never cease to amaze him. Julius remembered when they'd met, taking his charge from Drusus, who gave a complete briefing. Julius had observed some amazing things and found peace when near Paulos. He watched, mesmerized, as Paulos laid his hands on the dying man, and he knew what was going to happen. Julius had come to expect the unexpected, the extraordinary, from his charge, the man from Tarsus.

Paulos spoke foreign words over the man. But then, all at once, the man on the bed, Publius's father, stopped moaning. Had he died? That would spell trouble for all of them. Julius held his breath. Then the man coughed, and his eyes opened. He sat up, and his son, their host, was immediately at his side.

Julius's mouth hung open. Paulos had brought the man back from the brink of death. Although he knew what was going to happen as soon as Paulos touched the sick man, it was still hard to believe. And then, even less believable, Paulos noted that he had an audience that already considered him a god or at least one very gifted by the gods and charged the servants who hovered about to tell no one what they had seen. Everyone knew, however, that by the way the servants ran off, word of it would quickly filter through the city, maybe the entire island. And they were going to have to wait the winter out here. Paulos would be exhausted by then.

Chapter Twenty-Eight

**Rome
60 A.D.**

The ground floor room Julius found for Saul was small but pleasant, bragging two nice windows. Though surrounded by buildings, for much of the day the sunshine reached him as he sat on cushions beside the windows angled in such a way that a breeze may gently flow between. Timothy sat at a desk nearby, scribbling Saul's dictation.

"We moored in Puteoli because the ship was too large to land at the mouth of the river. Then we traveled over land. Wait."

"Do you want to mention the believers we found in Puteoli?" Timothy asked, his pen raised.

"Yes, yes, of course." Saul waved a hand at him, gazing through the window as all kinds of people streamed past, scurrying in different directions. He wanted nothing more than to study them, to speak with them, to learn their stories. Though he was often disappointed in people, he had learned to appreciate them, nonetheless.

"We stayed over in Puteoli," Timothy offered, "where we happened upon some believers. How does that sound?"

"Mmm, yes. Who sent word ahead to the believers in Rome and the area. When we stopped in . . .What was the name of that town?"

"Terracina."

"Terracina, we were greeted by followers of the Way from Forum of Appia and Three Taverns." Saul turned from the window. "I didn't count. How many taverns were there in Three Taverns?"

"Six or seven, I should think."

"Timothy." Saul laid his hands in his lap. "This is all such a waste of your talent. Christ Jesus did not call you to be a scribe to an old man."

"It is an honor to scribe for you, Paulos."

"Someone of your knowledge and leadership abilities should be in the field. I can't travel to the churches as I am stuck here, waiting on Nero. But you." Saul stopped. He knew Timothy would carry on, taking up the torch from him. Soon enough, he would leave. Soon enough.

"When it is time," Timothy said gently, "I will go. But for now." He pointed to the parchment. "We finish this letter to Titus, Priscilla, and Aquila."

Saul resumed his dictation. "Julius, my guard, has family in Rome and was able to find us affordable and comfortable accommodations as I await scheduling on the emperor's docket." Saul turned back toward the window. "Julius!" he exclaimed. "Wait. Don't write that."

Rising with effort, Saul limped toward the door to greet his guard, his friend. Julius was so close. So close to believing. Saul feared that, while Julius believed in *him*, Saul, the guard was still hesitant to believe in the resurrection. Such belief would come at a great cost.

Saul opened the door to a completely different soldier. From his uniform, this man was a member of the Praetorians, the elite army of the city of Rome. Surprised, Saul pulled back. The Praetorian took it as an invitation and strode into the room. Saul's eyes followed him and thus missed Julius, who came in behind him.

"Paulos," Julius said.

Saul spun and stumbled. "Julius! I didn't—"

"This is Gaius," Julius said. "He will be your new guard. Though I do not believe you need one, as you are certainly no flight risk."

"No, of course not." Saul studied his new guard as he took

inventory of the sparse room.

"You have no weapons," Gaius stated.

Saul pointed to his head. "Only this."

Gaius's face did not crack, not even a twitch of his mouth. His eyes, a strange green-brown color, showed no sign of humor.

"No, of course not," Julius answered. "Gaius, he made his appeal to the emperor, so he is free to go about the city."

After assessing Saul, Gaius took note of Timothy now standing by the desk. He then turned to Julius and gave a sharp dip of his head. As abruptly as he had arrived, Gaius marched from the room.

The Praetorian's footsteps echoed in the hallway as he strode away. "Pleasant fellow," Saul offered.

Julius chuckled. "You are a burden to him. But that's a good thing. He will leave you alone for the most part."

"You've been reassigned," Saul said, understanding.

"Yes. Now that you have arrived safe and await your hearing, you are under the care of the emperor."

"That sounds promising," Timothy offered.

"Not as a guest," Julius continued. "But you truly are free to leave these rooms and wander the city. Some areas, of course, are off-limits to everyone, but those are heavily guarded. You may earn a living or attend a play. You are a Roman citizen, and this is your capital city." Julius handed Saul a bag. "I brought you gifts."

Saul opened the bag and pulled out some black cloth and a leather pouch. Laying aside the cloth, Saul opened the pouch and peered in. His head shot back up to Julius. "I cannot accept this."

"I found some good black tent cloth at a stand in one of the marketplaces," Julius said. "They tell me it came from Tarsus."

The strength went out of his legs, and Saul plopped onto the floor. He stroked the goat hair cloth before bringing it up to his face. He inhaled, the aroma of the cloth filling his senses. *Home.*

"Your friend, Aristarchus. He spread the word that there is a master tent maker here. You will have all the work you want. Or don't want. It is up to you."

Saul continued to caress the cloth. Julius had brought him everything he needed to provide for himself, support the church, and pay his taxes. Though technically under house arrest, Julius had brought him his freedom. "I will pay you back."

Julius folded his long legs and sat on the floor before him. "You have done more for me these few months I have known you than I can ever repay," he said. "This is the least I can do."

"Where is your new assignment?"

"Achaia."

"Athens?"

"Corinth."

Saul tilted his head. "Corinth, you say?" Saul laid Julius's gifts aside and struggled to stand. Julius jumped up, holding out a hand to help. "Timothy."

"Yes, Paulos?"

"Did you hear that? Our friend, Julius, is going to Corinth." To Julius, Saul said, "We have many good friends in Corinth. The churches there need my influence again. But here I am, in Rome, and I cannot go."

"Paulos?" Timothy's mouth was downturned, and his brows gathered together.

"Julius, might I pay Timothy's passage? I would feel better if I knew he was with someone I trust."

"Yes," Julius said. "I believe it can be arranged. I would suggest he bring along one or two others with him."

"I'm sure that will not be an issue," Saul replied. "When do you leave?"

"It will take ten, fourteen days for us to find a ship going to Corinth." Julius turned to Timothy. "That will give you enough time to prepare?"

Timothy sighed. "Yes, I, I believe so."

"Oh, and Paulos," Julius added, "I checked with a connection I have. You are still far down on the list. The emperor may take months to get to your case."

Resigned, Saul replied. "I wanted to get here. There is much work to do in Rome, more than even in Corinth. You know, after my release." Saul tilted his head, and his eyes crinkled. "Perhaps I will stay."

Several months later, in 61 A.D.

As was his habit, Saul sat before his window. Early winter brought with it an odd rainy season with unpredictable, intermittent rain. At times, the same day might carry bright sunshine between torrential rains. But at that moment, the sky was gray, and the lit lamps filled his room with dancing light and the scent of burning oil. Scrunched together and filling the room before him sat twelve men, new believers who yearned to know more.

Saul enjoyed going back to the books of Moses, teaching the Gentile Romans about the faith so that they might better understand the Law and the Prophets, which Yeshua had come to fulfill. It was common among non-Jewish faiths that if good things happened—if one made a sale, had a good harvest, enjoyed good health, or had many sons—it was because the gods were pleased with them. And that if bad things happened, it was because the gods were displeased with them. Yeshua taught God intended for all people to live and live abundantly. And that when good things happened, God rejoiced. When bad things happened, God wept. Come what may, God was always with us, and we, therefore, never had to suffer alone. Indeed, we should never feel alone at all.

In his teaching, Saul thought it best to instruct them how it all started. "In the beginning," he stated, "God created the heavens and the earth."

This group of men before him reminded Saul of those many months he spent in Corinth ten years before. His thoughts drifted to Timothy, still in Corinth, wondering about the believers there. He thought of Julius, too. Saul sighed. He must get another letter to Timothy soon. He would ask Luke to scribe for him this evening after his students left and the two of them had had their evening meal.

"Paulos?"

Saul snapped back to the present. Twelve faces wore expectant expressions. "Sorry. Where was I?"

"You were explaining the concept of the day of rest."

"Ah, yes," he replied. "So, on the seventh day, God surveyed all He had created, and saw that it was good, and then He rested."

"God rests?"

"Maybe He was tired," another man offered.

"In honor of that seventh day, God blessed it, and made it holy," Saul explained. "That is why it is in God's law: Remember the Sabbath day."

"And that is why none of the Jewish merchants or laborers work one day a week?"

"Every Sabbath, to remember how God created the heavens and the earth, and everything in it."

Hurried footsteps echoed in the hall and joined the voice of Gaius. His guard had taken to standing in the hallway at the times Saul had several visitors. The man was still very professional with Saul and his company, but Saul knew he drank in every word, possibly for any seditious discussions, or perhaps out of curiosity. Saul smiled to himself. One or the other.

Aristarchus appeared in the open doorway. Odd, Saul thought. Aristarchus generally was in the marketplace at this time of day.

"Paulos," Aristarchus said, "sorry to interrupt. Someone found me in the marketplace and recognized your handiwork. He asked that I might bring him to you."

Saul's eyes widened in recognition at the man who slid around Aristarchus. It had been years since they faced one another.

"Marcus!" Saul exclaimed and, with some effort, was on his feet, his arms opened wide. The younger man crossed the room and accepted his embrace. "You are in Rome." Saul held John Mark at arms' length. "How did that come to be? Cephas? Cephas is well, is he not? Come in, come in. Luke! See who it is. Aristarchus, you know who this is?"

Saul was surprised at the tears of joy welling up. His last encounter with John Mark and Cephas had not been warm and pleasant. His face heated at the memory of their argument in Antioch. At the time, Saul doubted they would ever meet again.

"Paulos," John Mark greeted him. "Yes, Cephas is well. He was made aware of your arrest and imprisonment in Caesarea. Word of your appeal to the emperor and your subsequent confinement here reached us, even in the churches in Asia. Cephas sent me here, ahead of him, after learning from the church here of all you have been doing in Rome. You have not had your hearing before Nero yet, have you?"

"No," Saul answered. "Not yet. In the meantime," he waved a hand toward his students. "Gentlemen, this is Marcus. He is the right hand of Cephas."

"The Rock!" one of them exclaimed. "One of the original

twelve!"

"Yes," John Mark answered. "The one and the same."

"And he is here now?" another asked.

"No, not yet, but he is on his way. He sent me here to find Paulos and to secure someplace to stay among the believers."

Luke tapped a finger on the desk. "Linus has plenty of room for them."

"There will be more of us than Cephas and I," John Mark added.

"Lukas speaks true," Saul replied. "Linus has many rooms which he now only houses with fellow believers. You are welcome to stay with me this evening, and tomorrow, we can take you to meet the man."

"Linus." John Mark drew out the name. "He is?"

"A disciple of Christ Jesus," Saul interrupted. "And a Gentile Roman. Not to worry, Marcus. You will not be the first Jewish believer Linus has hosted."

62 A.D.

A few months had gone by since Cephas, Markus, and a handful of their students became guests of Linus, who was an excellent host, respectful of his Jewish brothers and sisters and their rituals. Luke knew that Cephas was pleasantly surprised at how they were accommodated.

The home of Linus was surrounded by a high stone wall with thick metal doors. Luke jumped when a small window at eye level slid open. A pair of eyes spied Luke, Aristarchus, and Paulus before it snapped shut. The door cracked, and Luke followed Aristarchus and Paulos through before it was slammed closed behind them. Paulos spoke a blessing on Linus's private guards and Luke thanked them. The courtyard between the walls and the sprawling home was beautiful, the plants blooming with spring flowers. They made their way to a side door, where they knew the believers would be gathered, preparing for the Sabbath.

Paulos halted for a moment, hanging on to Aristarchus, as he shuffled out of the mid-afternoon sun into the relative darkness of the house. In the months Paulos had lived in Rome, he had aged drastically. Luke monitored him carefully, but he suspected years of fasting, lack of sleep, and the abuse his body had taken throughout the years were responsible. Luke had learned long before when to insist Paulos eat and drink, and when to keep his opinion to himself.

They entered a large room that sported windows along one wall, allowing the afternoon sun to light most of the room. They greeted those gathered, and room was made to allow Paulos to be seated next to Cephas. It warmed Luke's heart as the two greeted each other as brothers. Though they might disagree on some things, Paulos always respected Cephas's position as one of the original Twelve.

Paulos cleared his throat. "I received news today."

"From Timothy?" Marcus asked.

"No, from Gaius."

"His guard," Aristarchus explained.

"Ah!" Cephas exclaimed. "You will finally have your hearing with the emperor."

"No," Paulos replied. "I am afraid not. My case was dismissed. The emperor decided there was no basis for the case against me since it was a matter of no concern to him or to Rome."

"Splendid! So you are a free man."

"Yes, though I was looking forward to the opportunity to witness to him."

Cephas laughed. "Only Saul of Tarsus would be disappointed to have his case dismissed!"

Paulos shrugged. "I was assured that I would appear before both emperors and kings, but perhaps I misunderstood. At any rate, I will seek passage out of the area. I am needed in Ephesus."

"You would leave us?" Linus exclaimed. "You are needed here, too."

"Ephesus?" Marcus said. "So soon?"

"The church has grown quickly there," Paulos explained. "And with that growth, leadership is run thin. I want to visit the churches in Asia again, also, as well as Achaia."

"Apollos has appreciated Timothy's assistance," Cephas said. "How are things in Philippi?"

"The Way is oppressed there, as usual," Luke answered. "So, there is growth, but it is painful."

"So, if anyone needs a private room," Paulos said, "mine will be available. I have paid the rent for another year."

"You leave soon, then," Cephas questioned.

"Yes, Cephas, as soon as I am able. You were not intending on leaving for some time, correct?"

"Correct. You were right: the harvest is plentiful here."

"Indeed. The shadows of Babylon are thick and dark." Paulos reached out a hand to Cephus, who took it. "But I leave the Roman church in the best of hands."

Cephas gave a hearty laugh as he squeezed Paulos's hand. Luke sensed Marcus's gaze and turned to meet his eyes.

"Are you taking our local physician?" Marcus asked.

"I certainly hope so," Paulos answered. "Aristarchus can write, but it's quite sloppy and hard to read."

Even Aristarchus laughed.

Linus asked, "You will stay for the meal, yes?"

"We would not miss this for anything," Paulos answered. "If I find passage in the next few days, we will not be sharing Sabbath meal with you again."

Then they sat back and relaxed as Cephas resumed his storytelling.

Chapter Twenty-Nine

Ephesus, Asia Minor
64 A.D.

Saul leaned back on a cushion. He had found one position where the pain was bearable. The afternoon sun, which streamed through a window, warmed his head, and his eyes drooped. Despite plenty of food and drink and a warm bed at night, he had not been sleeping well. Here, in Ephesus, he was content. He might even consider it home, and if he simply did not awaken one morning to go be with Yeshua, that would best he could hope for.

But something was very wrong. If he managed to sleep, his lucid dreams were of horrible suffering and torture. And fire. Big, tall flames with dark, billowing smoke. At times, he awoke short of breath, coughing as if the smoke had filled his lungs.

Unfortunately, the visions did not leave him at sunrise. If he were to fall asleep during the day, the dreams would come upon him. There were times, even while awake, they haunted him. Priscilla might be giving an account of the church's business with flames licking at her feet, robe, and hair. Something was happening, and it was happening to the church, to the Way, and the Spirit wanted him to know about it.

The first news about the great fire in Rome had arrived on the docks weeks ago. The fire destroyed a majority of the city, and many lives were lost. When Saul first received the news, he assumed that it answered the mystery of the dreams and visions, but the news only intensified the violence he experienced. Usually, once he interpreted the dreams, the visions came to a halt. Message received. But no pleas for help had reached them from Rome, nor did they expect it: the Roman church was well supplied financially. The Roman government would raise taxes throughout the empire to finance rebuilding its imperial city.

Aquila, still with good vision, sat nearby. Saul's eyes were too weak to do close work, but he could still cut larger pieces of leather and assist his friend to the best of his ability. He preferred to be self-reliant and hated to live off the hospitality of others. While in Ephesus, he was able to help Aquila to a degree.

Priscilla's staggering footfalls reached Saul before she burst into the room. Aquila was promptly up and at her side, supporting her as she sank into his arms, sobbing. Priscilla never lost her composure. Persis and two other women with her were also distraught.

Aquila brought her to the floor, where he sat, cradling her, patiently waiting for her to recover enough to talk. The women followed his example, and Persis lifted her red-rimmed eyes to Saul, reflecting the horror of his visions. Again, the flames rose, but now they licked at all of them. The hungry growls of beasts filled his ears as if they were in the room. Saul shook his head in disbelief. *No, no, no!* Priscilla had family in Rome, she and Aquila both. Aunts, uncles, cousins, friends.

Once Priscilla managed to speak without his voice breaking, Saul sent everyone else out of the room. They talked into the night until, mid-sentence, she fell asleep. Saul envied her even breathing. He knew that sleep would not come for him that night.

Emperor Nero received a negative backlash over the devastating fire. Although he had opened imperial grounds to help house the homeless, the fact that he claimed a large portion of the destroyed property to create a new garden made him suspect. To deflect attention from himself, guilty or otherwise, he found a perfect scapegoat—the community of Christian believers. To punish them for what he declared treason, Nero rounded them up and made examples of them, seeming to revel in how many ways he might torture them. One of the most heinous was turning them, alive, into human lamps to illuminate his new gardens. Their people were being sacrificed, like lambs at the Temple.

Awkward with a sleeping Priscilla, Saul was stuck between helping her lay flat or awakening her. He was relieved when the door opened, and Aquila padded softly in to check on them. He gently laid a blanket over his bride. "Are you alright, Paulos?" he whispered. "Do you need anything?"

Saul shook his head. The only thing he needed Aquila could not provide for him. Saul arose and entered the room where he slept and kept his few possessions. He stared at the floor, transported back to the days of sharing this space with Barnabas, John Mark, Acco, and Silas. All gone now. Barnabas was dead, and the others were building up the body of Christ. John Mark, in Rome, with Cephas. *Cephas!* Priscilla had not mentioned anything about him. He sensed that Cephas was still alive, certain he would know otherwise.

Saul now understood the visions. He knew what he needed to do. He must fast and pray until he receives full instruction. The Spirit always answered him. He merely needed to clear his mind from earthly things.

After nearly a week of fasting and prayer, Saul received a clear message.

"I am to return to Rome," Saul reported, "to help Cephas and the Roman church however I can."

"Paulos," Priscilla argued, "only death awaits you there!"

"Death, yes." Saul placed a hand on his chest over his beating heart. "But not death alone. This last mission of mine will be the end of this body on earth, but they will not be able to kill the faith."

"Then we shall go with you," Aquila said. "We know the city far better than do you, we know the people."

"We have connections," Priscilla added.

Saul contemplated this. "Yes, I will also need your leadership there when I am taken."

"We should leave soon," Aquila said. "We can make the arrangements."

"Might we leave before winter sets in?" Saul asked. "One winter on Malta was enough."

Chapter Thirty

**Rome
65 A.D.**

Saul tucked his cloak tightly about his neck as the three of them followed their guide through the winding streets. It was dark and cooler than he had expected. Worse, rain had left lingering puddles that soaked their feet. The dimly lit buildings all appeared familiar, and Saul swore they had gone in circles. Few people remained on the streets due to the curfew established after the fire. Their guide, an old family friend of Priscilla's, said little and had impressed upon them the need for secrecy—the imperials regularly paid informants on the street. This was how many of the believers had been found and arrested. Since few were Roman citizens, they were not given the right to trial. It was a matter of guilt by association.

They turned down a dark alley. "Be careful," the man whispered. The stench of waste reached Saul's nose, threatening to smother him. Saul pulled the hood of his cloak over his nose and mouth. His feet soaked from rainwater and who knew what else, Saul crept gingerly before bumping into Aquila, who had halted.

"Grab my sleeve," Aquila whispered. With his free hand, Saul did so, and Aquila led him into a doorway. "Step over the threshold," he warned.

Saul slid a cautious foot forward. Once past the darkened doorway, the door shut behind them. A soft glow glimmered ahead of them, and Saul pulled off the hood of his cloak as they headed toward the light emanating from beneath yet another door. Their guide rapped a rhythm on the wood with his knuckles. A soft sound came from within, and their guide's reply came before the door cracked, then opened fully, and they all entered the room.

Low lamplight illuminated several adults. As Saul and his

companions removed their cloaks, they were met with cries of recognition, and familiar faces embraced him, stroked his arms, and took him by the hand. He introduced Priscilla and Aquila whom the believers warmly welcomed.

"Will you break bread with us, Paulos?" someone asked. Their only food was bread, and there was wine, and he understood why they were gathered. After everyone partook of the communal bread and drank some wine, they talked for a long time. They were eager to know what Saul had been doing since he left Rome and about the work of Priscilla in Ephesus. It was not long, however, before the talk came around to the situation in Rome, before, during, and after the fire. It was how their lives were now defined.

"The stories are true, then?" Priscilla asked.

"Not only men but women and children, too," one of the women replied. "Entire families were clothed with the furs of animals and subjected to starving dogs. Children, racing away, being devoured."

Priscilla attempted to stop her, but there was too much to tell. Though never much of one to show emotion, Saul's tears flowed. He pictured the families, the children. As he mourned them, he was struck with a memory from Jerusalem, many years before, as he and Temple guards pulled crying mothers away from wailing children. A pang burst deep in his chest, and he threw a hand up to press it away. Saul composed himself and said, "I must ask: does Cephas survive?"

"Cephas? Oh yes," came the reply. "We keep him hidden, as he had made himself known to the imperials."

Saul released his breath. No one had yet mentioned him, and he had fretted over it. "I must meet with him. Might that be arranged?"

A few of the men exchanged glances before one of them replied. "He knows you, doesn't he?"

"Yes, we are well acquainted. Tell him Saul of Tarsus is in the city and desires a meeting."

The man inclined his head. "We can let him know you are here. If he agrees, we will fetch you."

Loud noises now made John Mark jumpy. Although they changed locations every two or three days, he found himself anticipating the burst of a door opening and the tread of soldiers echoing in a hallway. The last few months had been hellish for any follower of the Way in the imperial city.

Not that he was concerned for his safety. He would gladly take the place of the innocents if it might spare them. He didn't guard his own life. He guarded the life of his mentor, his teacher, his substitute father, his friend, Cephas. Cephas, who would not leave the city, no matter how many opportunities he was given or how many of them begged him to do so. Cephas, who now snoozed, reclined nearby. The lamps burned low, just bright enough that they might easily reach for their cloaks and disappear once again in the depths of the night if need be. Funny, that. John Mark used to be, not afraid, but suspicious of the dark. Now he found comfort in the protection it gave them.

A door closed softly, alerting him, his ears straining. He fingered the short dagger he had carried after his first visit to Cyprus. He was on his feet as the door cracked open.

"Marcus?"

Recognizing the voice, he sighed with relief. "Yes?"

"A visitor."

Only a handful of them ever knew where they were, and visitors were heavily vetted. "Who?" John Mark stopped as he recognized the stooped figure framing the doorway. "Paulos!" he whispered as he pulled the old man into the room and into his embrace. "He said to expect you!"

"Who is it, Marcus?" Simon Peter asked, sleepily.

"Cephas," Paulos answered, "it is I."

Simon Peter scrambled up. "Saul, my friend! Come." John Mark adjusted the flow of the lamp's oil to increase the light. There were no windows in this inner room and only one way in and out. John Mark guarded that door, his back to it, as the two old men embraced and greeted each other.

"Saul," Simon Peter said, "why would you come back? You

have heard, of course."

"Yes," Paulos answered, "that's why I have come. To offer my assistance to you and to the church of Rome."

"I am sorry I have no refreshment to offer you here. Our accommodations are, of necessity, sparse."

"No apologies needed, my brother. I understand the need for rapid mobility."

"Please, sit. Now, tell me all that you have been doing in the years since we last were together."

"Cephas, my brother," Paulos passed a hand over his face. "I did not leave my warm bed in Ephesus to wander through the dark streets of Rome, risking life and limb, to engage in small talk. I left the church of Rome in your very capable hands, but you are now in unacceptable danger. It is time to return the favor and leave the city for safety."

Cephas shook his head. "I cannot do that."

"Of course, you can. There are as many roads leading out of Rome as there are leading in."

"I cannot leave this place, these people. My destiny is to be here for them, much as the reason why you are here, as well. You understand. I know this."

"Cephas." Paulos reached over and placed his hands on those of Simon Peter. "You are irreplaceable. All the believers, everywhere, need you, need your stories, need your presence, need your wisdom and guidance. Please, let me serve here in your stead. You must endure."

"Saul," Simon Peter replied, "my stories have been recorded, that they may be distributed. Marcus has been of much help in that regard. And the church needs you right now more than me. They need your stamina, your example of strength in tribulation."

Paulos gave a soft laugh. "Listen to us, a couple of old men arguing about who should stay and die."

Simon Peter huffed a short laugh. "That's what it sounds like, does it not? But the truth is, I cannot leave. I had a vision." He pulled his hands away and stood. "I was hurrying away, south out of Rome, the city rising behind me. I was not being chased. I left of my free will. Then, as I scurried along, who should I meet going in the opposite direction, toward the city, but Yeshua, there in front of me! 'Where are you going, Lord,' I asked. He stopped, and his dark eyes burned into me. 'I go to be crucified, once again,' he replied." Simon Peter directed his gaze down at Paulos. "I denied him. Three times. I cannot, I will not deny him again."

There was a moment of silence before Paulos broke it. "You will die here, Cephas."

"So will you, Saul."

Paulos leaned forward, struggling to stand. Simon Peter reached down and gave him a hand. Once standing, he placed his free hand over Simon Peter's, the one that still grasped him.

"We can face that part alone," Paulos replied, "or we can face it together."

"Then, together we go," Simon Peter answered. "Together."

Julius had not slept well, and it irritated him. As one never knew when one might catch the chance, he had learned long ago to sleep quickly, sleep soundly, and awaken ready for action. But the news of Paulos's in Rome had shaken Julius, and each time he closed his eyes, the memory of the man's voice or dark eyes burning with fire flooded him. The arrest of Paulos was one of his greatest fears.

Julius was recalled from Corinth to help quell what the emperor was calling a rebellion in the city. Learning the extent of the punishments, he was shaken to his core. He knew the heart of these non-violent, peace-loving Christians. They were the last group who would do anything to cause massive destruction and loss of life. But the emperor had an understandable issue with anyone who denied his divinity, and the followers of the Way definitely met that criterion. It was the reason Emperor Claudius had pushed out the Jews from the city some twenty years earlier. He could not tolerate their monotheism unless he, Claudius, was the sole god. While their tax money was as good as anyone's and the emperor ignored much of the strange Jewish ways, these Christians were unconcerned or oblivious to the authority of the Roman empire itself. They were far too focused on Jesus.

Which made them ideal scapegoats. Even the Jews did not like them, so it was simple for Nero to blame the Way for any number of things that upset the expected Roman way of life. As a native, Julius understood the emperor's actions. But his experience with Paulos and his companions had given him a soft spot for these people, all very different yet who shared a love for humankind. And while Julius understood the need to deter rebellion and that a heavy hand was necessary to keep the peace, the Roman way had always been to follow the rule of law. The emperor was condemning an entire sect and submitting them to the most heinous punishments solely because he could. That Paulos might be subjected to the same was unthinkable.

Once Julius gave up on sleep, he rose with the sun and dressed in his uniform, assuming his role as peacekeeper with each item, will full knowledge of what he must do. His decision might cost him a promotion to ask for such a thing, but he knew that if he did not at least try, he would never sleep well again. And he valued his sleep. Thus, the irritation.

So it was that Julius presented himself before his superior, hoping to catch him busy enough to approve Julius's odd request without much thought and dismiss him quickly. Not so busy that he might get irked by the request and not bored enough that he might ask probing questions.

"Sir," Julius said, "I request a change of assignment."

His commander smirked. "What's wrong? Missing the Corinthian brothels? Are our Roman whores not skilled enough for you?"

"I request to guard one of the political prisoners. The one named Paulos."

A single eyebrow raised. "One of the Christian rabble-rousers?" Julius's superior referred to one of the papers scattered on his desk. "He is one of the two sect leaders."

Julius gave a curt nod in answer.

"The one named Paulos is a Roman citizen, I understand. Are you a relative?" His superior laughed. "Why would you want to give up your position for such a menial job, guarding a man bound to die?"

"I was his guard for a previous confinement, sir. I know his compatriots."

"You believe you can better serve Rome in this position, though it be a demotion."

"Yes, sir."

The papers were again consulted. "Very good, then. As long as you know that you are being demoted. I reassign you to guard the criminal Paulos. After his trial, sentencing, and execution, return for your next assignment."

Julius waited to be dismissed. Yes, he knew what this request would cost him, career-wise. He still was not sure exactly why he was doing it.

Raising a torch, Julius's face remained impassive as he surveyed the small, filthy cell, shadows oozing along the dank walls. This was a far cry from Paulos's accommodations the last time he awaited trial in Rome. There wasn't even a pot for his waste. Torchlight sputtered in the outer hallway.

This was definitely a demotion.

"Julius?" Paulos's lips were cracked and his voice hoarse. His small frame was curled on the hard, cool floor, his dirty face uplifted as Julius stood over him. "What are you doing here?"

"How long have you been here?"

"I am not quite sure. Sunlight is required to figure that, I believe."

"You have no water."

Paulos raised a hand. "No, Julius. Do not endanger yourself by being here. I am a condemned man. There is no need for you to risk—"

"I will be back." Julius left him and sought water and a bucket for his waste. Upon his return, he told Paulos Julius had been assigned to guard him. "It is too dangerous for any of your people to visit and bring you food or clothing. But it is lawful for me to do so since you are my charge."

"I don't think my previous custodian was so inclined." Paulos fumbled about his waist. "He even left me my belt, in case I were inclined to hurry myself to my sentencing."

Julius sighed and shook his head. "Paulos, tell me. Why are you still in Rome? Your case was dismissed. You had a chance to leave, to go back home."

Paulos gave a short sound from his throat. Julius was uncertain whether it was a laugh or a cough. "Home. Where is your home, Julius?"

"I suppose it would be here, in Rome. I have family here. This is where I was raised and where I return at the end of an assignment."

"I don't have a home, Julius. But I don't consider that a loss. Our Lord Christ Jesus said, 'The birds have nests, but the Son of Man has nowhere to lay his head.' No student is greater than his master, is he?"

"Was he ever held for trial in such a place?"

"I am sure he was. His trial was swift, however. He was arrested at night and was dead before sundown the next day."

"You need to drink. I will bring you something to eat when I return."

"Julius," Paulos shifted his weight awkwardly. "When you return, I will tell you about heaven, what it is like in the presence of the creator of the universe."

Julius cocked his head. He had no doubt that Paulos would do exactly that. "I will return without delay, then," he replied, leaving his prisoner alone in the dark of his cell.

Julius accompanied Saul as a soldier prodded them along. On one hand, Saul was eager for the end of his long walk. On the other, he regretted the loss of time.

Odd that he thought of his mother. She would have had him become a member of the Great Sanhedrin in Jerusalem, married with several children. Yet, it was his father's trade that had kept him clothed and fed all these years. Both Fathers.

His thoughts ran to his sister and her family. Lavi, her son, had saved his life in Jerusalem. She would be crying out to Saul now, "Why did you go back when you were safely away?"

Would he see Barnabas? Who will come to fetch him? He had not recognized the heavenly companion who came for him last time, though there had been a familiarity there. As if he had known him all his life.

The sun above him burned hot. The chains holding his hands

and feet clinked and clunked with each labored step, and they slowed his exhausted body. Julius had urged him not to speak in his defense because he knew Saul was unable to deny his Lord and Savior. But at Saul's accusation, he had been clear. He and his fellow believers had not and would not start a literal fire, as it destroyed innocent lives. But they were certainly starting a spiritual fire that even the gates of hell cannot withstand. "There is no god above the God of Abraham, of Isaac, of Jacob," he had declared, "and it is he, in the form of his Son, who is the true savior of the world!" Those were the words that condemned him, and here they were, shuffling toward his execution.

"I learned that your friend, Cephas, was tried right before you." Julius had been a silent observer through the trial but had remained in Saul's line of vision to provide a friendly face.

Sweat dripped down Saul's back as they wound their way from the judgment hall to the execution grounds. Due to his citizenship status, Saul was spared a public display. But he well knew the fate awaiting his friend, the great rock upon which Christ Jesus was building his earthly church, rebuilding his body, his temple. "Where is he to be executed?"

"He will be crucified as a traitor," Julius answered. "Probably along where the Appian Way enters the city. Somewhere very public, at any rate." They shuffled along, getting closer and closer. "Are you alright?"

"I am right with God. It is you I am most concerned about, Julius. I know your heart. You have freedom waiting for you." Saul knew he should not say much with the other two guards so close. While still dim in his vision, the future held great surprises for the people, not only of Rome but of the entire world. The fire was lit here, lit in Corinth, lit in Ephesus, lit in Antioch.

They entered the execution yard. The flagstones were soaked with dark crimson stains, as were the several posts in the yard. The single executioner stood waiting, his weapon already in his gloved hand. Julius had warned him not to give attention to the man, but Saul did so anyway. The man required absolution due to the nature of his occupation. But their eyes did not meet. His forgiveness would have to come through prayer alone.

The executioner indicated one of the posts, and the other two guards steered Saul toward it. They unlocked the chains about his wrists and affixed them to the post rings. "Father," Saul whispered, "forgive them. They don't know what they are doing." One of the guards forced Saul's head to the post, positioning his gaze away from the executioner. Julius stood as near as he dared, directly in Saul's line of vision. "Look at me, Paulos," Julius said. "Keep your eyes on me."

The wood was sticky against his cheek, and his back ached. Footfalls neared him. At least it would be quick. He would concentrate only on Julius, and then he would be engulfed in the light of Christ. Saul peered into Julius's eyes as the glaring sun blinded him.

Saul.

"I am here," Saul responded.

Out of the light's brilliance, a face hovered before him, obscuring Julius. A face he recognized this time. Saul gasped.

"Stephen?"

Saul had been present at Stephen's execution. He supposed it was fitting.

Are you ready, Saul?

Saul wet his lips before responding. "I was born ready."

Julius sat low on the stool, his head bowed as he studied his hands between his knees.

The afternoon sun streamed through pinpoints in the fabric of the curtains he had drawn closed, dust dancing in the warm beams. His back was to the window, his shadow cast across his comfortable and spacious room in the barracks. His position of importance had afforded him this privilege of solitude.

Earlier, Julius had scrubbed his hands, two, three times, but the dark stains persisted in the cracked leather of his palms and settled under the trimmed nails. The blood stubbornly refused to leave him.

Death was part of his life. Combat required it so. His duty was to keep the peace that Rome had executed throughout their expanding empire, that famous "Pax Romana," kept with sword and dagger. It had never before occurred to him to be concerned about death, nor had he given a moment's thought about what he and his fellow soldiers had to do. He had never considered an execution to be anything but a matter of course. Death *was* a part of life, and while the manner may vary, the end result was always the same.

But today? Today was different. *This* was different. The scene of the order carried out replayed in his head, over and over. The head severed from its body, bouncing, rolling forward before coming to rest facing the heavens. The eyes, once so full of fire, stared, open and dull. The body crumpled lifeless against the post, the body of the man who had intrigued him, rescued him, and taught him. How Julius had stooped, gathered the body in his arms. How he carried the two pieces, wrapped in rough cloth, away from the blood-drenched killing yard.

Julius shook his head and stood. Slowly, he stripped off his uniform, piece by piece, before carefully folding it. In only his tunic, he placed the uniform on the stool. He reached for his headpiece and centered it atop the folded clothing. He laid his leather strapped shoes on the floor next to the stool.

Straightening, Julius contemplated the uniform he had worn for the last ten years. He turned, strode for the door, his bare feet padding on the floor, and then, he was gone.

Author Notes

Somehow, growing up in the church, I had come to believe that the Apostle Paul was a woman hater. I suppose the concept that women should not be heard in church, should not overdress, should be subject to their husbands, and should not be leaders in the church all seemed to be supported by Scripture attributed to him, which caused me to form an opinion. I tried to give him the benefit of the doubt. It was the culture he was from. It was the time period. Maybe something was lost in translation.

It wasn't until I began research for a Sunday School class based on Adam Hamilton's *The Call: The Life and Message of the Apostle Paul* that I had my own Damascus Road experience with the apostle. Paul's words and actions did not align with misogyny at all. Finding no men gathered to worship in Philippi, he preached to the women. There he met the woman Luke refers to as "Lydia." Paul saw the leadership abilities in her and gave her charge of the group of believers in Philippi. Priscilla became so important to the early church that it is believed she may be the author of the book of Hebrews. We know she and Paul worked very closely together. Don't even start me on Junia. There are just far too many references to women Paul appointed leaders to accept the picture of him as one who didn't trust an important role in the church to women.

Saul of Tarsus was born a Roman citizen. Researchers believe this is because his father was a freedman. Either himself or his patronage had been taken as slaves by Rome but had earned their freedom. Saul was quite proud of this fact, and it came in handy several times in his life. Because he was a Roman citizen, he was given a Roman name at birth. That Roman name was Paulus. The Greek version of this name is Paulos. Saul was his Hebrew name, named after the first King of Israel, another fact he was quite proud of. You may have noticed that when the story is told from his point of view, he thinks of himself as Saul for just that purpose. When Saul wrote in Greek, however, especially once he began writing his letters to the churches, he used the Greek version of his Roman name. I have heard many pastors and preachers misspeak and refer to when Saul was "renamed" Paul, and it makes me cringe. Every. Time. I added a story to illustrate the use of his Greek name, and I hope you will understand very well why he did not want anyone using a Greek version of his Hebrew name. I can't say as I blame him.

To really know someone, you must develop a relationship. The only way I've found to have a relationship with those long gone before me is to read their writings. When I learned that Pauline scholars have determined that there are seven genuine letters of Paul (Galatians, Romans, Philippians, 1 and 2 Corinthians, 1 Thessalonians, and Philemon), I studied those letters as well as Luke's Book of the Acts of the Apostles. Where Paul's letters differ from Luke's version, I go with Paul. I figure the first-person version is more correct than second- or third-hand.

There's no good solid understanding of where Paul went after his healing by Ananias once he reached Damascus, but we know there was some time between then and visiting Simon Peter in Jerusalem. Things had to settle down in Jerusalem, and for some reason, Saul could not remain in Damascus. So, I grabbed onto the concept of Nabatea as being the place he probably went more to hide than anything else. I needed a reason for him to leave. Knowing what a brash loudmouth he was, I felt raising the hackles of Jews in Damascus was as good a reason as any. But why did he have to flee from King Aretas's men? Jamelah was a real person, as was her father, Aretas, and her brothers. Her older sister was indeed the first wife of Herod Antipas. I remembered the story of John Wesley having to scootch out of Georgia because of a woman and thought, why not Saul?

So, the story of Jamelah and Saul became a total figment of my overactive imagination. Haven't you wondered why he would have had to get lowered over the city walls, in a basket, of all things? The threat from Aretas had to have been a weighty one, so desperate that lowering him in a basket was the best option. Ananias is the only documented person of all the characters I created in that episode. It was also a theme of Saul's story: helping him could be a dangerous thing to do.

The problem with John Mark presented itself early on. Why would the young man leave his uncle and Saul to go to Jerusalem to be with Simon Peter in the middle of their journey to spread the gospel? I had to have a really good reason and make it a horrifying experience for the young man, one that he would not feel free to discuss with his Uncle Joseph (Barnabas) and Saul.

I also tried to illustrate the cultural clash between Judaism and Greek influence. Monotheism seemed ridiculous to other cultures who worshipped multiple gods and goddesses. Purity of body and mind would have been a topic of contention within that clash and the resurrection of the dead laughable. This is the setting our early church leaders were faced with. I used the made-up characters of Acco and his brother to help demonstrate how odd Saul and Barnabas would have appeared. Then, just for giggles, I turned Acco into Titus because Titus is a nickname, and I figured, why not? There is absolutely no documentation of the association of the two, so please remember, this is a work of fiction.

Saul's first death experience is well documented. Luke has only one sentence about it in Acts, and plays it down as Saul probably did. However, stoning is a form of execution. I tried to clarify that the stone Uzziel threw was the death blow. Uzziel, too, was a figment of my imagination. I needed to personify the group of jealous Jews who tracked Saul and Barnabas, as is referred to in Acts. But I worked backward, knowing how Saul was going to be dragged out of the Temple later and another stoning attempted. Who better than my fictional character to be the ringleader in both situations?

Another question for me was the "thorn" in Saul's side. I read a lot of theories, everything from stigmata to malaria. But there had to be a reason to go to a higher elevation and to get him to Antioch near Pisidia. As a family physician, I have learned a thing or two about migraine headaches from my patients. They can have various symptoms, including something called aura that signals that a migraine is coming. The migraine headaches are miserable and can strike at any time. But often, they can be relieved by a change in elevation. Thus, I reasoned migraine headaches could well have been the "thorn in his side."

You may have noticed I gave Saul's words in Romans to

Stephen as his argument for Jesus as the Messiah. If not, re-read that portion in the first chapter in Jerusalem and then read Romans chapter four. Yes, I used Saul's words against him. It's the kind of thing he would do if he had written this.

One of the most controversial aspects of this story may concern Lazarus. I read Ben Witherington III's argument that the Gospel of John was, if not authored by, at least dictated by Lazarus. The gospel contains stories that took place, not in Galilee as much of the synoptic gospels do, but rather in Jerusalem and that general vicinity, of which Bethany is one. Lazarus and his sisters lived in Bethany. Lazarus is not mentioned in any of the synoptic gospels. We know that Jesus and Lazarus were very close. It is quite possible that Lazarus was a disciple of John the Baptizer who also began to follow Jesus. Jesus had disciples that were not the inner circle twelve.

The son of Zebedee, a fisherman, was a common laborer and not an educated man. Most people did not know how to write. That's why there were scribes. Before the story of the raising of Lazarus in the Gospel of John, the fisherman John is referred to by his name. How did we ever come to just assume that "the disciple that Jesus loved" was John? Scripture tells us there was a price placed on Lazarus's head, but once Jesus was crucified, there was no need to capture Lazarus. Jesus's bestie would be present at his crucifixion. Only one who had died once already would not be afraid in that situation. One who had died and was resurrected would not have to step into an empty tomb to know what had happened. All this to say, I believe Witherington is right: Mary, the mother of Jesus, stayed with Lazarus and his sisters after Jesus's death and resurrection. So that's the angle I took.

We do not know what impact Saul's testimony before Festus and Agrippa may have had, but we do know what kind of impact he had on the world. The determination and passion Saul had to do God's work in his world can be an example for all of us, even if it costs us our lives. The Apostle Paul is speaking to us all when he appeals to Agrippa in chapter twenty-six (also found in Acts 26:29). "Whether quickly or not, I pray to God that not only you but all who hear my voice right now might become like me, such as I am. . . . But for these chains." I hope Saul's story inspires you to commit or recommit your life to Christ.

Acknowledgments

There are so many folks to thank for what you are holding in your hands. It all begins with God the Father, the Son, and the Holy Spirit, who not only created all of us but wants us to know and love Him. To Jesus of Nazareth, God the Son, who left His glory to become one of us, and who paid the ultimate sacrifice that we might have everlasting life. To Saul of Tarsus, whose whispers and visions gave me much inspiration while writing his story.

Thanks to author and agent Barb Roose, whose suggestions helped me narrow the focus of the work. Thanks to ACFW for existing and having conferences that offer chances to speak to and network with other Christian authors, agents, and editors. Without that organization, this work would not have come to print. Thank you to the judges for the Genesis contest. Your feedback was amazing!

Thanks to Janyre Tromp, editor and author extraordinaire. You need to check out her writing; she's great.

Thanks to Cynthia Hickey, editor and author, for meeting with me when she wasn't feeling good, for her prompt responses, and for believing in me and this work. Thanks to Winged Publications for making this a reality.

Great appreciation to Siren Songs Boutique/Gloria Byrd, who created the gorgeous map. They came through for me in a timely manner and with clear, consistent communication. I highly recommend them.

Thank you to my book club, The Bluestockings, in Lebanon/Waynesville/Camdenton, Missouri, especially Brenda, Barb, Kirsten, and Abby. You gals gave me such support and inspired me to keep on trucking. Thank you to my beta readers, Pastor Marsha Vincent in particular, who has been *But For These Chains'* greatest cheerleader, even from the earliest of its days.

Thanks to my staff, past and present. You guys have kept my business and practice, Direct Primary Care Clinics LLC, going as I went to conferences. Thanks, too, for your help when, out of seemingly nowhere, I would shout, "I'm looking for a certain word."

Thanks to my sister, Beth Nansen, for a lot of things. Teaching me to read at such a young age, inspiring me to memorize poems, exposing me to great music, helping me overcome my fear of the dark (*haha!*), not to mention always being up for reading my words. That transcription gig you had sure came in handy.

Thanks to my amazing daughter, Amber, for absolutely everything. I'm super glad your dad and I decided to have kids, and we are so blessed to have you in our lives. Thanks for being a good older sister to your brother, being a wonderful aunt to his kids, letting me catch both of your babies when they were born, being such a great help in the office, always willing to help wherever you can. You are so multi-talented and amazing. Thanks for marrying Peter because he's the best son-in-law we could ever ask for.

And to my husband, Wes. Thanks for trying out for that musical in high school, even though you were a senior and homecoming king and probably had a lot better things to do. Thanks for being a first reader, answering questions, and providing feedback on all kinds of things that have nothing to do with electricity or electronics. Thanks for always carrying a pen in your pocket and supporting my writing as well as my medical practice. You are exactly what God knew I would need.

In memory of our son, Clint Wesley Powell (1986–2021). Thanks for the grandkids, the dogs, the gray hairs, and for always being yourself. Gone far too soon.

References/Further Reading

Barclay, John M.G. *Pauline Churches and Diaspora Jews.* Eerdmans, 2016

Barnabas. *The Epistle of Barnabas.* Beloved Publishing LLC, 2016

Borg, Marcus J. and Crosson, John Dominic. *The First Paul: Reclaiming the Radical*
Visionary Behind the Church's Conservative Icon. HarperOne, 2009

Capes, David B., Reeves, Rodney, Richards, E. Randoph. *Rediscovering Paul: An*
Introduction to His World, Letters and Theology. IVP Academic, 2011.

Cocker, B.F. *Christianity and Greek Philosophy; Or, The Relation Between*
Spontaneous & Reflective Thought in Greece and the Positive Teaching of Christ
and His Apostles. Harper and Brothers, 1870.

Epp, Eldon Jay. *Junia: The First Woman Apostle.* Fortress Press, 2005.

Hagan III MD, John C. *The Science of Near-Death Experiences.* University of
Missouri, 2017.

Hamilton, Adam. *Simon Peter: Flawed but Faithful Disciple.* Abingdon Press, 2018.

Hamilton, Adam. *The Call: The Life and Message of the Apostle Paul.* Abingdon Press, 2015.

Hays, Richard B. *Echoes of Scripture in the Letters of Paul.* Yale University Press, 1989.

Hengel, Martin. *Between Jesus and Paul: Studies in the Earliest History of Christianity.*
Wipf and Stock, 2003.

Hengel, Martin and Schwemer, Anna Maria. *Paul Between Damascus and Antioch: The*
Unknown Years. Westminster John Knox Press, 1997.

Hengel, Martin. *Saint Peter: The Underestimated Apostle.* Wm. B. Eerdmans Publishing

Co, 2010.

Horsley, Richard A., ed. *Paul and Empire: Religion and Power in Roman Imperial Society*. Trinity Press International, 1997.

Josephus, Flavius. Whinston, William, trans.*The Complete Works of Flavius Josephus*.
Thomas Nelson, 2003.

Kübler-Ross, Elisabeth. *On Death and Dying: What the Dying Have to Teach Doctors,*
Nurses, Clergy and Their Own Families. Scribner, 1997.

Kübler-Ross, Elisabeth. *On Life after Death*. Celestial Arts, 1991.

Lumpkin, Joseph. *Paul and Thecla: The Church and the Strong Willed Woman*. Fifth
Estate, 2015.

Neal, Mary C. *To Heaven and Back*. Circle 6 Publishing, 2011.

Neel, Douglas E. and Pugh, Joel A. *The Food and Feasts of Jesus*. Rowman & Littlefield
Publishers, 2012.

Price, Randall. *Rose Guide to the Temple*. Rose Publishing, 2012.

Rankov, Boris. *The Praetorian Guard*. Osprey Publishing, 1999.

Rauche, G.A. *A Student's Key to Ancient Greek Thought*. Watch the Fabulous
Publications, 1966.

Reeves, Rodney. *Spirituality According to Paul: Imitating the Apostle of Christ*.
IVP Academic, 2011.

Sasso, Sandy Eisenberg. *Midrash: Reading the Bible with Question Marks*. Paraclete
Press, 2013.

Suetonius. *The Twelve Caesars*. Penguin Classics, 2003.

Tucker, T.G. *Life in the Roman World of Nero and St. Paul*. Palatine Press, 2016.

Walker, P.W.L.). *In the Steps of Saint Paul: An Illustrated Guide to Paul's Journeys*.

Lion Books, 2012.

Wright, Paul H.). *Rose Then and Now Bible Atlas*. Rose Publishing, 2012.

Witherington III, Ben. *The Paul Quest: The Renewed Search for the Jew of Tarsus.* IVP Academic, 2001.

Witherington III, Ben. *Priscilla: The Life of an Early Christian.* IVP Academic, 2019.

ABOUT THE AUTHOR

Jenny Powell MD is a wife, mother, grandmother, and family physician turned author. She operates an independent family medicine clinic in the Missouri Ozarks. A past president of the Association of American Physicians and Surgeons, she is a former Sunday School teacher and lay speaker, and a long-time church musician. She was a semi-finalist of the ACFW Genesis contest in 2024 and a supporter of Christian writers everywhere. A large unfortunate portion of her brain is dedicated to song lyrics and movie lines.

www.ingramcontent.com/pod-product-compliance
Lightning Source LLC
Chambersburg PA
CBHW070407310726
48977CB00003B/594